# A Rush of Wings

# KRISTEN HEITZMANN

## A Rush of Wings

A NOVEL

BETHANYHOUSE
MINNEAPOLIS, MINNESOTA

A *Rush of Wings*
Copyright © 2003
Kristen Heitzmann

Cover design by Studio Gearbox

Published by Bethany House Publishers
11400 Hampshire Avenue South
Bloomington, Minnesota 55438

Bethany House Publishers is a division of
Baker Publishing Group, Grand Rapids, Michigan.

Printed in the United States of America

ISBN 978-0-7642-0845-4

**The Library of Congress has cataloged the original edition as follows:**

Heitzmann, Kristen.
    A rush of wings / by Kristen Heitzmann.
        p.  m.
    ISBN 0-7642-2606-1
    1. Women artists—Fiction.  2. Rocky Mountains—Fiction.  3. Ranch life—Fiction.
4. Betrayal—Fiction.  I. Title.

PS3558.E468   R87      2003
813'.54—dc21                                                                    2002152592

## Diamond of the Rockies

*The Rose Legacy*
*Sweet Boundless*
*The Tender Vine*

❖❖❖❖❖❖❖

*Twilight*
*A Rush of Wings*
*The Still of Night*
*Halos*
*Freefall*
*The Edge of Recall*

❖❖❖❖❖❖❖

*Secrets*
*Unforgotten*
*Echoes*

*www.kristenheitzmann.com*

KRISTEN HEITZMANN is the bestselling author of seventeen novels, including *Freefall and* the Christy Award winner *Secrets*. Kristen lives in Colorado, with her husband, Jim, and their family.

# CHAPTER

# 1

Noelle pressed her back into the textured wall and tensed, her breathing fast and shallow. Her pulse throbbed in her throat. What was this feeling of prey, of eyes scanning the crowd as a hawk searches a field, circling, circling, until it strikes?

She shrank against the wall, heart pounding at something lurking deep in her subconscious. Fear. Déjà vu. Nightmare. She couldn't move . . . she didn't dare. But she had to. She knew it. Why didn't matter. She'd been propelled this far by something raw, primal. Her mind need not engage beyond the command to run. *Move*, she told her legs. But they wouldn't.

Frantic, she watched the people passing by. The noontime throng surged and stalled and moved with a purpose in the Port Authority Bus Terminal. She alone was still. But she had to go now or it would be too late.

"Did you wash your hands?" Noelle jumped when the woman spoke behind her, tugging a child from the rest room. If only someone could hold her hand, make her move. But there was no one except herself. Her knuckles whitened on the strap of her tote. As the woman and child passed, she stepped into the crowd.

She must not panic. Panic had frozen her before. Now she must move. She hurried toward the exit. *Just board the bus*. Its door opened, beckoned. Before her, an elderly woman mounted the stairs slowly, so slowly.

Noelle glanced over her shoulder, looking for . . . what? Her mind offered no explanation. It had shut down, functioning now on an animal level. Hide. Flee. To someplace deep and dark; no—someplace . . . She couldn't think where, but it didn't matter. Away. Just away. She climbed the bus stairs, pressed down the aisle, and sank into a seat, breath suspended while the bus pulled out from the terminal.

Then she sat silently, alternately dozing and staring out the window as the miles passed, their markers, like the lines on the highway, a pulse soon unnoticed. Day passed into night, light swallowed by darkness. The different terminals were a conglomerate of fluorescent lights, rows of seats bolted to the floor, and everywhere the bodies in motion. Before this, she'd never ridden a bus, never traveled commercially with the masses. Now she was just one more—no different, no one special.

After the first terminal the panic had numbed. She felt invisible, boarding one bus, then another. They were a means only. She cared little where they took her as long as it was away. Her mind had closed down and that was fine. She didn't want to think, to feel. Only to act, and even now that took the smallest effort. Simply sit while the buses carried her away.

But at one station she paused beside a pay phone, biting her lip. Hesitating only briefly, she dug out a handful of change and approached the phone. According to the clock on the wall, it was nearly four o'clock in the morning. If she called the office, she'd get his voice mail, and that seemed better. Though she was twenty-three years old, if she didn't call, he would mobilize a search. Even so, he would wonder why she called from a pay phone in Ohio. But maybe it would be enough.

Holding the receiver close to her mouth, she spoke softly. "Daddy, it's Noelle. I'm fine and I don't want you to worry, but I'll be away awhile." She couldn't tell him why, couldn't tell him where. "I need time to think, to . . . figure things out. I love you." She hung up. *Don't worry?* May as well ask him not to breathe. But perhaps that was part of it. She'd consider that when it was time to think. She rubbed her temples, then boarded a new bus and went on.

———

Inside the spacious office, the noise of the city was muffled by plush carpet, drapes, and heavy mahogany furnishings. Cool air-conditioning replaced the sweltering mugginess of downtown Manhattan. But William St. Claire brooded. Noelle's message, which he'd received upon arrival that morning, had charged his mind and wakened his ulcer. At 4 A.M. she had phoned his voice mail, not wakened him at home, not waited until a normal hour, but nonetheless left a cogent, if perplexing, message.

He jerked his head up when Michael Fallon rapped on the open door. Maybe Michael could make sense of it, but by the look on his face, maybe not. "I'm sorry to interrupt, sir, but I need to speak to you."

"Come in, Michael."

"It's about Noelle."

No surprise there.

"William, she's missing."

William kept his lips in a tight line as he controlled the familiar fear. Just the sound of that word. Missing. He closed the portfolio sharply. "Why do you think she's missing?"

"I've looked everywhere." Michael's blond hair was neatly styled, his suit impeccable. He stood alert, almost mercurial, balanced on the balls of his feet. William held him in his gaze. It was that energy that had first caught his attention, as it so closely resembled his own.

Michael was driven, determined, and one of the few men William genuinely took an interest in. He had nurtured that interest for years. But something in his manner now caused a seed of disquiet and even annoyance to form.

"It's nine o'clock in the morning. She could be having her nails done."

"I don't think so. I searched the bungalow."

Searched it? Noelle's bungalow was near the west gate, across the lake from the main house. Michael had access to the estate, one of the few William allowed that freedom. But why would he search Noelle's home? She couldn't have been gone more than twenty-four hours. They'd dined together the night before last.

"She seems to have packed . . . meagerly."

Of course she had packed. And called. If Michael had approached in any other mode, William would have touched his phone and played Noelle's message. He had heard no terror in her voice, not like—he jerked his mind back to the present. This had nothing to do with that other time. He could put both their minds at ease. But something said wait, some instinct honed by years of vigilance.

"She took the Gucci bag you gave her for Christmas."

He pictured the tote. Not exactly luggage for an extended tour.

What troubled him was the obvious impetuosity; it was unlike Noelle to take off without discussing it first. He would have liked details, an itinerary, a clue as to what she needed to think about—all part of her safekeeping.

Even during college when she had taken an apartment outside the estate, he had kept close watch. Not surveillance, exactly, but near enough. After graduation, when she'd moved back to the estate, he had relaxed, trusted the security system. But that was to keep danger out, not Noelle in. She had a right to come and go and owed him no explanation. Though Michael might make a different argument.

"Michael, what's this all about?"

After an awkward moment, Michael took a small box from his pocket and opened it. "She left this."

Frowning, William eyed the sparkling engagement ring Michael had presented to Noelle, but inside, his relief grew. No thief would have left so valuable an item; no abductor would have removed it from her finger. Michael's alarm was ungrounded. "She said nothing? Left no note?" Why not a message on Michael's voice mail? Even at four o'clock in the morning.

"Nothing."

William leaned back in his chair. Perhaps Michael's unease was natural. It couldn't be easy to tell his prospective father-in-law he'd been jilted. Noelle's irresponsibility surprised and annoyed William, for it was uncharacteristic. But she was not in danger. He had to believe that. "Well, she's an adult. She can make her own choices."

"Yes, sir."

Neither of them sounded convinced. But as much as he would like to deny it, Noelle had grown beyond his ability to control, maybe even to protect. William drew a long breath, felt it clear his head, easing the ache. He could play the message for Michael now, but again he refrained. In the same way he sometimes left a cross-examination at a heightened point, so he'd leave Michael now and watch. He said, "Give her time. It'll work out."

"Yes, sir." Michael's voice sounded tight, but he held his emotion well—another reason he'd brought him up from the ranks of aspiring lawyers to junior partner in the firm. For a young man whose passion ran deep, Michael had amazing control.

As the door closed behind his prospective son-in-law, William sat grimly. What foolish whim of Noelle's was this? Had he not trained her better? She could do worse than Michael Fallon, worse by far. Michael knew what he wanted and had the courage to grab it. He had compensated for his upbringing through sheer determination, unlike the privileged sons and nephews of old money who came to work for the firm on their family's reputations and some flimsy effort at school.

William judged by what he saw here and now. He appreciated Michael's drive to climb up from his wretched beginnings—something Michael never discussed but William had complete knowledge of. Noelle, of course, knew some of it, had even met Michael's mother and sister. Was that it? Had he raised a snob?

No. He shook his head. It must be more than that. Was Noelle afraid to commit? Possibly. There was that element, that unreachable place in her he had sensed more than once. All the more reason for someone like Michael. Noelle needed someone to keep her safe, keep her happy. He leaned back in the leather chair and looked at her picture on his desk. Her hair hung straight to her shoulders, the bangs casually disordered. Her lips smiled, but it was the eyes that held him, her mother's eyes.

It was painful to look into their gray-green and see Adelle. Though the color was his own, the shape of the eyes, the placement in the face, the delicate cheekbones and narrow jaw gave her the same vulnerable beauty. How had she grown into the young woman in the picture? How had time slipped away? Where was his little girl?

The emotion hit him so hard it winded him. *"Where is she? What do you mean she's missing?"* And Adelle almost cowering before him. *"I only looked away for a moment."* Her wretched face pale with terror. William clutched his forehead. This was different. It had to be. But why hadn't Noelle told him she was going? Didn't she know—no, of course she didn't. She couldn't remember. She'd been too young. Too young.

William sighed. This time was different. Wherever Noelle had gone, she would be back. This was not a crisis. A lover's spat, a stretching of the wings, a bid for independence; these were normal. He must allow her the freedom of womanhood. He must not grasp or he would lose her. Wait and trust. She would be back.

He returned his attention to the business Michael had interrupted. This case was tenuous, and the prosecution had wrapped up sooner than he expected. He had ordered his calls held and cancelled all other appointments. He had thought it was about the case that Michael had come to his office, not this business with Noelle. He needed everyone focused. He must focus himself.

He pressed the intercom. "Margaret, see that I'm not interrupted again." He pressed his jaw one way then the other and released the tension in his neck, then looked back at the papers on the desk. *Okay. They want to fight . . . we'll give them a fight.*

He read the details over, piecing them together, searching their relevance. Silently assistants brought him the information he called for and left without acknowledgment. That human hands assisted him was irrelevant. His focus was complete until a tap on the door broke it. He wrenched his head up, scowling.

Margaret stood sheepishly in the doorway, the office lights dimmed behind her. She looked like a small potato dumpling, innocuous and ordinary, but there was nothing she couldn't do, and no one penetrated her web. She was his right arm, and he'd cut off his left before he'd lose her.

He cleared his throat. "That time?"

She nodded. "Is there anything you need before I go?"

"No. Thank you." William leaned back and undid the knot of his tie. He should call it a day, be fresh tomorrow. He was getting too old to work the kind of hours he used to. "I'll just finish up here."

She paused, but she had long since given up remonstrating him. He would finish when he finished, and no well-intentioned words from her could move him one minute sooner. He hid a secret smile as she left quietly. The outer door closed behind her with a solid click. Sighing, he activated his voice mail, replaying Noelle's message. This time he listened for strain, fear, anything that said he should take Michael's cue and panic.

Had he not received her message, Michael's alarm would have been contagious, but he had her own words. *Daddy, I'm fine.* He rubbed his eyes, ashamed at the pulsing joy her voice brought. She was safe! He willed himself to believe it. Eyes closed, he steepled his fingers against his lips.

She had the right to time alone. She hadn't needed to call. She was a grown woman, no longer answerable to him. Still . . . he had traced the call through the office system. What on earth was she doing on a pay phone in Columbus, Ohio?

———

Michael Fallon sat in the darkness of his upper Manhattan apartment, his fingers slowly drumming the edge of the table. He stared at the silver-framed photograph until the light dimmed and he could hardly make out the delicate features. He gripped the frame and held it close, then threw it across the room.

Where would she go? He fingered the three-carat diamond ring, slipped it over the edge of his smallest finger, then flung it too. It struck the glass-covered picture on the wall, glancing off the widespread wings of the hawk that attacked with talons extended, beak open.

He stared into the amber eyes, felt their fierceness. At times he felt like that bird, restless and seeking, undaunted and daring the world to move beneath him. He almost heard the cry from the hawk's throat—not a plaintive cry, but rather one to terrify some small prey into fleeing its hiding place and awaiting his plunge. His plunge.

The hours passed, and he felt immobile, paralyzed. He'd done everything, been everything she wanted, everything she needed. He'd played by her rules. What more could she expect? He slammed his fist on the table. *Where, where, where?*

He had taken Noelle's absence to William St. Claire, hoping the man would mobilize a search. William had means he couldn't dream of. But William hadn't acted as he hoped, and Michael didn't dare tell more than he had. He dropped his head to the table and groaned. Where was she? He never dreamed she would run away.

He woke with the morning light sifting through the shade in horizontal bands. He rose, retrieved the photograph from the floor, and looked again at the face behind the cracked glass. If William wouldn't act, he would find her himself. And if his means were less straightforward than William's, it couldn't be helped. He set the picture on the table and went to the phone. "This is Michael Fallon; give me Sebastian."

Sebastian Thorndike came on the line. "Hey, Mr. Fallon."

"I'm calling in that favor."

Quiet. "What do you want?"

"I'll meet you at six at the Cove Grille."

Michael got into the shower, standing so the water hit the back of his neck and shoulders. Less than an hour later, he walked into the firm of St. Claire, Meyers, and Harrison. One day it would also be Fallon.

"Michael." William motioned him in as he passed his office.

"Yes, sir." Michael approached the mahogany desk.

"I'd like you to hear this."

Michael's throat tightened as he recognized Noelle's voice on the message. Would she say more than—but she didn't. In fact, she said nothing to indicate why she'd gone, where she'd gone. He made a show of relief, but his heart hammered. "When did she call?"

"Earlier." A non-answer.

"From where?"

William shook his head. "A pay phone. I suppose she wants space."

Michael's pulse raced. William knew where; it was impossible he didn't. But he wasn't saying more. He was testing Michael, watching as only William St. Claire could.

William fixed him with an offhand scrutiny Michael had observed in the courtroom. What was he looking for? "At least we know she's all right. We can wait for answers."

Michael forced himself to nod. She could be in the city still, at some hotel or with some friend, though he had already racked his brain and contacted everyone he could think of.

"Now, put that aside. Here's what I have for the court today. As we discussed, you'll do the opening statement . . . since the majority of the jury is female." William gave him a wry smile and stood. He accepted cases only on merit, either precedent setting or high profile, and then only if he believed the client could have acted within the law. But he was not above using every weapon in their arsenal, even, as he had once put it, Michael's good looks and magnetic gaze.

William circled the desk, rested a hand on Michael's shoulder, and spoke instructions he would have thought of himself. The man was savvy, but already their minds worked alike, mentor and student, senior and junior partner, master and protégé.

Two hours later, adrenaline surged as Michael faced the jury, making deliberate eye contact with each member, speaking smoothly, sincerely, and without condescension. Systematically, he refuted each of the prosecution's claims, painting a wash of doubt over the scene depicted by the opposing attorney's allegations.

Their client could be guilty as sin, hiding inside the loopholes, but Michael would so cloud the issue, the jury would stagger. It was a fine line with their sort of clients anyway. The ultra-successful. Not one had risen to the top through hard work and sweat. Not one started with Michael's disadvantage. If they twisted the law in unethical practices, bent the wording or intent, no one screamed. It was only failure or stupidity that landed them in a courtroom—the two things Michael couldn't abide.

But the money was in defense law, not prosecution. Money made every successful defense worth it, and it gave him the personal power he would wield shortly with Sebastian Thorndike. When you successfully defended a guilty man and both of you knew it, that set up a certain *quid pro quo*. He didn't assume his usual clients were guilty of the crime with which they were charged—only the crime of having life too easy.

Thorndike was different. Michael had accepted that case himself, defended it against William's better judgment—and won. It was one of the times Michael had stood up to William, but a man like Thorndike came in handy, something William would not understand.

Mr. St. Claire worked this side of the law for neither money nor power. The Rhodes Scholar Harvard lawyer was anything but needy. No, William practiced defense because he believed in the system. He actually believed in the maxim innocent until proven guilty, and he believed he must make the court prove its claim. His archaic ethics precluded methods employed by other firms, but that just made the challenge greater. William also believed in winning.

Michael returned to the table beside William and received the slightest nod of approval. It was all he needed. He knew he had achieved his goal, to set up a relationship with the jury. Now he and William would subtly work that relationship, ever so subtly.

At a quarter till six, Judge Morril banged the gavel and adjourned the court. Michael wasted no time. He caught a cab at the curb. The Cove Grille was crowded as he made his way between the red-and-white checked tablecloths to the back. The air smelled of charbroiled fish and fries, but he wasn't hungry. Sebastian waited in the corner, taking up most of one side of a booth for four. Michael took his place across from him.

"What is it I can do for you, counselor?" Sebastian's neck was the color and texture of raw chicken.

Michael pulled out a handful of photographs and spread them on the table.

Sebastian whistled. "Looks like a class act."

"She's William St. Claire's daughter."

Sebastian narrowed his eyes. "And?"

"I want to know what she buys—when and where."

"A debutante with a credit card? Give me something challenging."
Sebastian spread hands so smooth he must lotion them by the hour.

Michael crowded the table. "Bank account, airline, traffic violation, manicure, anything. Find her in the system and tell me where
she is."

"What did she do, torque the old man off?"

"No." Something in his tone must have clued Sebastian.

He looked up. "This is personal?"

Tossing a fifty-dollar bill on the table, Michael stood. "Buy yourself
some dinner."

He went next to Noelle's bungalow, paying the taxi and keying in
the code to the west gate of the St. Claire estate. He let himself into
her place, passing silently through each room. How tastefully they were
decorated, colorful and imaginative, so reflective of Noelle.

He had searched it before, looking for her when he realized she had
gone. Now he looked for her essence, for anything that would guide
him to her. He stopped in the bedroom, looked in the closet still filled
with the Donna Karan, Vittadini, and Scassi wardrobe he had provided
piece by piece. She had taken none of it with her.

He pulled open the drawer of the bureau and ran his eyes and
then his hands over the silky negligees. His fingers knotted in the
flimsy fabric. Lifting a rose silk teddy, he brushed it against his cheek,
breathing in the scent of her.

# CHAPTER

# 2

With the bus still humming, Noelle woke in the reclined seat, her palm pressed to her cheekbone. She could feel a bruise, though it didn't show through her skin. She'd noticed nothing when she washed her hands in the terminals, but now she touched her fingers to it, wondering. Other aches intruded, also invisible, and for a moment her mind groped for a reason. But she refused to give it substance, closing it away and locking it tightly in the part of her thoughts and emotions that were thankfully nonfunctional.

Absently, she worked her fingers around the back of her neck. After three days of travel her body protested the inactivity. The same automatic brain waves that had made her move were now saying stop. But not here, not in the city. She wanted someplace obscure. With her tote heavy on her shoulder, she exited the bus.

Inside the Denver terminal, she perused the departures board, noted the Rocky Mountain tour bus listing and its departure time. She grabbed a sandwich from the vending machine, then headed for the counter and purchased a ticket, counting the cash out onto the Formica surface. One more ride and she would stop.

She slid her hand up the smooth metal bus rail, found a window seat, and looked out. The roar of the engine joined the hissing of the brakes as diesel exhaust wafted past. She scrunched her nose. Her senses were awakening, the numbing cloud of panic lifting. She was no longer in shock but was still somehow removed.

Maybe she should have taken her car. It had been her first thought as she'd crammed her tote full. But the need for anonymity had impressed upon her mind, so she had left the BMW at the bungalow and taken a cab to the bank, then to the bus depot. By then her mind had grown hazy. Her first actions had been frantically decisive. After that she'd moved automatically.

But now she took stock of her surroundings. No one shared her seat because her tote strategically barred them. But she slowly became aware of voices and faces around her. What was this disembodiment? She looked at her hand lying on the armrest. The other hand too.

They were her own, but she felt disconnected. She should have paid better attention to psychology. Fight or flight. She chose flight because . . . because . . . She shook her head. That part of her mind wasn't operating, only the animal part that said run. This numb part simply asked, why?

She looked back out the window. Leaving behind the noise and congestion of the city, the bus made its slow, winding ascent. She watched from the rectangular window with the first interest she'd felt since leaving, studying the land as it passed. It seemed at once strange and wonderful.

Pink stone crags towered, unyielding, up both sides of the canyon, sparse, scraggly juniper clinging to their lower edges. Beneath them, lanky pines thrust pointed spires to the sun, marching up the slope amid slender white-barked trees with pale green leaves, tremulous in the breeze. And now she did respond. Something in her was still able to feel, to appreciate.

With a wheeze and hiss, the bus stopped in the small mountain town, and the tourists piled out. Noelle did not follow the crowd up the street to the shops. She stood in the red gravel lot of the sturdy log building and read the sign: Juniper Falls General Store. *General Store?* Was she in a time warp as well?

She looked up the street where her busmates were dispersing into shops. For a moment her courage failed. The land around her was vast, unyielding, more wild and terrifying than Central Park at its worst. Too unknown, too . . . untamed.

But she hoisted her tote and went inside. The wooden floor creaked loudly, and she jumped, her mind overcompensating for its earlier malaise. There was nothing fearsome about this quaint shop.

The burly bearded man behind the counter looked up from his

*American Angler* magazine. "Better than a bell." He grinned, two lower teeth missing.

When she didn't move, his grin widened. "Don't worry; it's the only spot that does it." He hooked a thumb into his suspender just under the grizzled ginger beard. "Did you lose your tour?"

Noelle set the tote down and rubbed her shoulder. "I'm not shopping. I'm looking for rental properties."

He shook his head. "You're about six weeks too late. Everything gets snatched up at the start of the summer." He took a drag on the cigarette that lay in the tray. "Everything but the Walker place, and trust me, you don't want that."

Noelle's heart sank. It hadn't occurred to her that this place might not have what she needed. "Cost doesn't matter."

He sent the smoke out the side of his mouth. "It's not cost, it's condition. Though to hear Ms. Walker talk, it's the Taj Mahal." He shook his head.

"Isn't there anything else?" She was too tired to think of boarding the bus, to drift uncaring again. She would chafe every mile.

The man squinted one eye, considering. "You could try the Spencer ranch. But as far as I know, he's full up."

Hope flickered. That was two possibilities. In spite of this man's lack of encouragement, she'd try them both. "Where is the Walker rental?"

He walked to the door, automatically avoiding the creaky board, and pointed. "Two blocks up on the corner there's an art gallery. The back side on that same block is the Walker place. You'll know it when you see it." He swung his arm the other direction. "Then you'll want that gravel road away up there. Take you to Spencer's."

Noelle saw the zigzagging cut that marked the road climbing the slope behind the town. "Thank you." She shouldered her bag.

"You walking?"

She glanced back. "Yes."

"Air's thin at this altitude."

She nodded, but thin air or not, her legs were all she had. She headed up the street the way the tourists had gone. They were happily milling in and out of the shops. She found the art gallery with a flamboyant window display: an oil of a trumpeting elk with an enormous frame upon a draping of turquoise velour—tacky; a bronze bear with twin young and a wolf carved from driftwood—not bad.

Though a far cry from the galleries she frequented, on a different day she might have gone in just to wander between rows of canvas and absorb style, technique, and theme. But right now her need was to find a place to alight. She had flown as far as she could.

Almost directly behind the gallery around the next corner she found it. There was no question in her mind this was the Walker rental. The sign in the front—*For Rent*—seemed a perpetual fixture. The residence behind the sign looked far less permanent. A good wind could collapse the sagging structure with one final sigh.

Noelle turned and studied the town from there. Several dozen houses dotted the hills in the immediate vicinity. Stores lined the highway, and another cluster of houses bordered the creek side. All the streets off the highway were red gravel. It was certainly not the kind of place anyone would think to look for her.

But she needed a place to live, and Walker's Taj Mahal was not it. She looked up the high gravel road the storekeeper had indicated, shifted her heavy tote, and sighed. The sooner she started, the sooner she'd get there. The mountain air was warm and clean, the sun a fiery untamed ball, burning on her bare shoulders unprotected by her cotton tank.

She breathed in the pine fragrance as she walked, her Italian leather sandals grinding on the gravel. She bent to examine the flowers that grew in the middle of the road, tiny yellow heads with lavender daisy-like petals. A bee hung drunkenly from one tiny bloom, then buzzed to the next. Whatever traffic went up that way must keep to the shallow ruts for them to grow undisturbed like that.

When was the last time she'd seen something wild struggling for existence? Some non-hybrid, wind-scattered seed standing firmly where it landed, just as she did now? The tiny flower gave her courage; strength proved elusive.

As the slope steepened, her breath labored, burning in her chest. Her feet were weights. Thin air? She felt as though she battled some unseen force just taking one step after another. It couldn't help that she'd hardly eaten all the time she traveled and exercised less. At the road's summit, she dropped her head into her hands until the dizziness passed. Her hair slid in silken threads over her fingers, then she tossed it back and looked ahead.

The road ended at the ranch, broadening to a wide gravel apron where a tan pickup and a new red Corvette made an incongruous pair.

On one side of the yard were the stables and barn. Directly across stood the large, golden-hued log house wrapped in a sweeping porch with a swing suspended in the corner.

Beside the house, three small cabins nestled in the tall pines, and two more vehicles were parked there, a nondescript sedan and a white SUV with bicycles on the back. The middle cabin had no car outside, and, with rising hopes, she envisioned it hers. It looked homey in a rugged western way and decidedly sturdier than the Walker rental.

Beyond all this, the meadow climbed to the base of a craggy peak. A rocky stream wound down the center of the meadow and on behind the house. Noelle could imagine it murmuring as she breathed in the wild-flower scent carried on the breeze.

She was too tired to truly appreciate the beauty, but it touched her nonetheless. There was something solid, serene, implacable in the scene before her, and she quickened to it. Though vastly different from anything in her experience, it felt like home. And that was crazy, because home was many miles and a past life away. She walked down the last bit of road, then climbed the porch steps, set down her tote, and knocked.

In his khaki shorts and golf shirt, the man who opened the door looked like a summer cover of GQ, his casual elegance more suited to Daddy's club than a horse ranch in the Rocky Mountains. His too-blue eyes and suave features brought walls up inside her in spite of his easy smile. It didn't matter. Once she'd climbed the steps and felt the porch surround her, she had determined to stay.

She drew herself up. "Excuse me for coming without an appointment, but I was told you might have a cabin to rent?"

He brushed his fingers through his black hair and leaned against the doorjamb. "That would be my brother. I'm just freeloading."

He had none of the shiftless look—in fact the opposite. But there was nothing menacing in his smile, and if she gave in to the irrational anxiety, she may as well go home. There would be no place safe enough. Besides, she'd seen the tour bus heading down while she climbed the gravel road, and it was here or the Taj Mahal. "May I see your brother, then?"

"He's up on the high pasture somewhere, but he'll be down later."

A diminutive elderly woman bustled up behind him. "Hello, can I help you?"

"I'm handling it, Marta." He half turned from the doorway, yet

Noelle felt no diminishment of his attention, and his next statement was for her. "Want to come in and wait?"

Of course he would ask. He wouldn't expect her to stand on the porch. But she shook her head. "I'll just look around."

"I'll show you." He held out his hand. "I'm Morgan Spencer."

It was a natural gesture, an everyday connection, the sort people made on the street or in boardrooms or at a party. It wasn't threatening, but somehow things had blurred, and his outstretched hand brought a tension to her neck like a crane slowly pulling the tendons taut.

Training and common sense won out, and she reluctantly took it. "Noelle."

"Just Noelle?"

"Noelle St. Claire." A thought flashed that she shouldn't have given him her real name. Yet the need for anonymity did not come naturally. Why wouldn't she use her name? It had always opened doors.

"St. Claire. And I can just picture you on the Champs-Élysées. *Enchanté*, mademoiselle." He bowed his head and released her hand.

She smiled in spite of herself. His charm made him less menacing— not that he was truly menacing. That was the worst of it, the way she looked at people now with a shrinking inside she could not account for. She hauled her tote back to her shoulder, but he reached for it.

"You can leave that inside."

She resisted his gentle tug. "I'll hang on to it."

A small sideways smile, then he controlled it and leaned close. "You're right. Marta's dangerous."

Noelle glanced through the open door where Marta had been. That wasn't what she'd meant, and it must seem strange for her to cling to the heavy bag. Wouldn't a bellhop take her luggage at any hotel? Reluctantly, she let him set it inside the door against the wall.

He closed the door. "Now stretch, take a deep breath, and relax."

Did she look so tense? She straightened her shoulders, relieved to be free of the weight, drew a slow breath, and sent her gaze back over the yard.

"Where to first?" He swung his arm.

She didn't hesitate. "The stables." She'd know more about this place by seeing the stables than anything else. Little chance they'd house the sort of horse to which she was accustomed, but her expectations were low.

Morgan motioned for her to precede him down the steps, then

took the lead across the apron to the stables. "You won't see much. The horses are out."

She would see enough, see what kind of place she'd come to. She entered the enclosure and breathed in the smell of leather and manure and hay. She looked over the neat, orderly tack accessories, bridles, saddles, currycombs, and hoof picks. The animals were well kept and cared for. No dark, dingy stalls for droop-necked nags. That spoke well for the rancher and confirmed her desire to stay.

They went back out and Morgan showed her the barn filled with sweet hay and barrels of grain, a tractor blade, and other tools and machinery. It was also a workshop, she concluded. He walked her past the guest cabins, each one a different size and shape, not one plan repeated three times. The builder was either creative or haphazard. She guessed the former.

"That's about it," Morgan said. "Unless you want to tour the main house."

No need for that if the center cabin was hers. She looked up the slope to a white-fenced corral high up the meadow. Several horses were pastured outside it. One, it seemed, was being worked.

Morgan followed her gaze. "Rick raises good quarter-horse stock."

Even at that distance, Noelle recognized the shape. From an artistic viewpoint the quarter horse was less symmetrical, less elegant than other breeds but splendid in its own right. As a girl she had loved horses, had drawing pads full of them. She'd spent as many hours drawing thoroughbreds as riding them.

And here she was on a horse ranch. What irony. Or was it? She was making her own decisions now, consulting no one. Maybe she had willed this place for herself, created this reality. And why not? It made as much sense as anything else.

She took in the wide, steep meadow as though she'd brushed it there on a giant sheet of stiff rag paper, then breathed life into it and stood back to watch. As she did, a horse and rider charged down the meadow and came to a sliding halt before them in a scatter of gravel. The man leapt from the roan's back as the horse reared, then stood nervously, tossing its head and chafing the reins, its raw power barely contained. The animal was magnificent.

The man spoke low, gentling the stallion with his hands until it stopped fighting, though the sheen on its hide rippled still with barely suppressed energy. He led the horse to the holding pen between the barn and stable, then returned. This was the owner of the ranch. It must be. His was a Rocky Mountain face, angles and shadows, eyes the color of earth.

"Hi there." He pulled off his work gloves and smiled. "Rick Spencer."

Morgan spoke for her. "This is Noelle St. Claire. She wants a place to stay."

"When?"

She answered for herself. "Now . . . today."

Rick swatted a darting fly away from his face. "I'm afraid all the cabins are taken. Booked solid through the middle of August."

Morgan said, "There's room in the house, Rick."

Rick glanced at his brother, then back to her. "That's against my policy. I'm sorry."

"Professor's got a room. So has Marta." Morgan's tone was congenial, but Noelle felt an undercurrent between them. If Rick rented rooms in the house, why wouldn't he rent her one?

"Marta's on staff."

"And the professor?" Noelle smoothed a strand of hair back behind her ear and used the information Morgan had provided.

Rick hooked his thumbs into his belt. "How long did you want to stay?"

How long? She hadn't thought that far. "Indefinitely, I guess."

"Did you try in town?"

She looked back down the road toward the town. "The only place was—"

"The Walker rental."

She turned back, sensing by his tone he would not suggest it. "That's right."

He squinted past her. "Ms. St. Claire, I don't rent rooms in the main house to women."

Had she heard him correctly? What sort of Neanderthal was he? A quick glance toward his brother revealed a cloaked amusement. "Doesn't that violate fair-housing standards?"

He never flinched. "It's for your protection."

A shadow crossed her spine, but she ignored it. "Morgan's already told me Marta's dangerous. Who else should I fear?" She couldn't believe she'd said that after running like a rabbit these last days. Her words actually sounded combative, and yes, there was something inside her that wanted to fight, something that battled against her normal restraint and compliance. The blind fear that had driven her here fell away in its wake. She would not be afraid!

Rick brushed his jaw with the back of one hand, a subtle change in his eyes. Submission? Compassion? "I guess there's room in the house. Nothing fancy."

She searched his face. Did she look like she needed fancy? Did she telegraph who she was, what she came from? "That'll be fine." She had won. She had taken a stand and beaten him down. Terror and exhilaration vied. She turned to the corral. "Your horse is wonderful."

He followed her gaze. "That's the first time he's made it down without throwing me."

"What's his name?"

"Destiny."

A thrill passed through her. *Destiny.* "Why?"

He shrugged. "It just came to me when he was born." He glanced at the horse circling his confinement, his roan hide still quivering and nostrils flaring.

Noelle followed the stallion's stride with her eyes. "He's spirited, but not mean tempered, I'd say. He wants to obey but can't get rid of the wild."

Rick appraised her. "Sounds like you know horses."

"Some." She smiled.

Morgan groaned. "Don't get him going, Noelle. He'll have you standing out here in the sun all day."

Rick slapped the dust from his pants and gave Morgan a raised eyebrow. "Come on, then."

She followed him to the house with Morgan behind, a sudden misgiving tugging her insides. Though she'd fought for the right to stay, she knew nothing about either of them. Could she walk inside the house with two men, on a ranch she knew nothing about, where no one would think to look?

But that was exactly why she was there. Maybe she hadn't created this place, but she'd found it, homed to it with some instinct that had to be truer than following where others directed. She was no longer blind and mute. Something else had awakened within her: resolve.

She stepped inside and lifted her tote once again to her shoulder, looking up at the lofted ceiling of the main room. It was more like a lodge than a house, she thought. But it welcomed her as few places did. She sensed . . . what? Haven. Yes, haven.

"Give me just a minute." Rick strode into the kitchen off to the right of the main room.

Morgan motioned for her to go in as well, though she would have considered the kitchen off limits. Shouldn't there be a sign that said *Employees Only*? Or was this a place where people came and went from the kitchen without disdainful looks from the staff? Green plaid curtains hung at the window above the sink where Rick washed up, providing the only color beyond the golden hue of the logs.

She tugged the strap of her tote higher onto her shoulder and cleared her throat. "You haven't given me a rate."

Rick looked back over his shoulder. "If I don't know how long you're staying, I'm not sure how to charge you."

"What are my options?"

He washed the dust and sweat from his face. "For a single room, twenty-five a night, one fifty a week, or let's say . . . four hundred a month."

She hid her amazement. "I'll take it for a month at a time." Nowhere on Long Island would she find a closet for that. But while he was in the mood to be generous . . . "Meals are included?"

Morgan smiled, obviously enjoying her tactic. He was certainly easier to read than his brother

Rick turned the faucet off and shook his hands. "The cabins have kitchens, but not the rooms. Unless you want to take your meals in town, you can join us in the dining room. I'll let Marta know."

"Are there others on staff?"

Rick wiped his hands dry. "Just Marta."

"She's all you need," Morgan added. "Housekeeper, cook, and drill sergeant." He winked.

"And don't you forget it." Marta bustled into the kitchen from what must be the dining room. Spare in stature with mousy hair streaked with gray, she moved deliberately, wasting no motion. For her small size she seemed to fill the room with energy.

Her skin crinkled over pointy bones, but her smile was warm, touching Noelle with a motherly affection foreign to her. In her experience, there were two types of domestics. The lazy ones who served because they had no drive to do better, and the ones like Marta who thrived on their work and generally ran things accordingly.

Noelle noted the lighthearted affection in both men's faces. There were also two kinds of employers, those who made their help family and those who made them feel servile. She saw by his demeanor which kind Rick was and lowered her guard.

He hung the towel in its place. "Marta, this is Noelle. She's taking the first room upstairs."

Marta gave her hand a brief, tight squeeze. "Glad to have you, dear."

"We all are," Morgan added.

Rick reached for her tote. "I'll show you your room."

She surrendered the bag and followed him up the stairs to a wide hallway that crossed the main area as a balcony, then led to rooms on either side. She stopped behind him at the first door.

"This room has a three-quarter bath, shower only. There's a tub in the full bath at the end of the hall, but it's common use. I'll have Marta bring up linens." He opened the door and set her tote inside. "The meal schedule's on the door. My office is directly downstairs. You can bring your payment there when you're settled and pick up your key."

That was it? No contract, no questions? Noelle glanced in, then turned back on a sudden impulse. "Are the horses for use?"

"Can be. You'll need to sign a waiver." He seemed on the verge of saying something more, then merely appraised her. His was not an expression she knew, not containing the interest she'd recognized at once in Morgan's. "Well, if you need anything, Marta and I are usually around somewhere."

"Thank you." When he left her, she surveyed the room: the bed made of cleanly hewn pine logs the same color as the walls; a bureau, also pine; a writing table and chair. It was as though the room was made out of the mountain.

Crisp, white curtains hung at the window. From there, she viewed the woods that grew behind the house. Fat mountain chickadees flitted from branch to branch on the tall, scraggly pines, and a magpie hollered raucously from the rail.

Noelle closed the door behind her. She hoisted the tote onto the bed and dumped the contents—some clothing, toiletries, and a makeup bag that held the cash she'd taken out of her account. She opened it, took out four crisp bills, and folded them into her shorts pocket, then searched the room for someplace to stash the rest.

The absurd simplicity of her space left her few options. From what she'd gleaned of Rick, there would be no loose floorboard, and Marta's obvious efficiency ruled out the mattress. Noelle looked again at her makeup bag. Maybe obvious was best. She brought it into the bathroom and set it on the wooden shelf under the mirror.

Then she crossed to the bed, gathered up her personal items, and added them to the shelf as well. Until she thought of something better, it would do. Marta didn't strike her as the snoopy sort, whatever Morgan said in jest, and if Rick was uncomfortable with her even being in the house, he would hardly raid her room. She closed her eyes and allowed the tentative peace to grow. Inside the solid walls she felt small and enclosed. She felt safe.

D ownstairs, Rick went into the office, moved the mail from the chair to the desk, and sat. He booted up the aging Pentium tower and glanced up as Morgan leaned on the doorjamb.

"Not your typical mountain mama," Morgan said.

Rick opened his bookkeeping program. "Nope."

"Don't pretend you're impervious. I heard the rates you stammered."

"I didn't stammer."

"Well, you gave her the deal of the century. You even threw in meals."

"I always include meals for the rooms without kitchens." Though he did usually charge them separately. Rick brought up the ranch accounts. Finances were good at the moment. Last week's sale had put him ahead, the cabins were solidly booked, and what he took in from Miss St. Claire, he could sock away toward feed. Besides, she had the look of a sparrow needing to light.

And that was the only reason she now had a room in the main house against the policy he'd established from the start—fair housing notwithstanding. He didn't rent rooms to single women because the house was also his home. He didn't advertise the ranch. Word of mouth brought people who knew it was a Christian operation, and he ran it accordingly. Reputations were hard to salvage, and he guarded both his and his guests'.

Morgan looked pensive. "What do you suppose her story is?"

"I don't know." Rick brought up the column *Long-term Guests*. He hadn't had many stay monthly before. Though he could rent the cabins as residences, he preferred vacationers and had no trouble keeping them rented by days or weeks. And as the cabins were only minimally heated, they were summer lodgings only.

"She comes from money."

Rick typed in Noelle's name. "You don't know that."

"Oh, come on. You haven't lived your whole life on this mountain."

He keyed in her room and the fee he'd named. "It's her business."

"I suppose. Well, I saw her first, so I'm trumping you."

"You don't have to trump. I don't date my guests."

Morgan clicked his fingers. "Good thing I don't have your reservations." He pushed off the doorjamb. "This R and R might turn out more interesting than I thought."

Rick paused his typing and gave his brother a glance. Morgan always saw possibilities, but Rick sensed something brittle in Noelle St. Claire. She wasn't looking for excitement.

---

After folding her meager wardrobe into the bureau, Noelle eyed the small but clean shower. The thought of running water was ambrosia after traveling, especially in the sooty tour bus. She'd inhaled enough secondhand diesel to taste it still. Rick hadn't seemed impatient for payment, so she stripped and showered, holding her face to the stinging spray. Her skin tingled.

She was coming back, awakening from the daze. She rubbed herself dry with the coarse, white towel and hung it on the wooden rod on the log wall. Everything was hard, rustic. No pampering heat lamp, no lush towels, no elegant wall coverings, only bare wood. No amenity she would have previously expected as a matter of course. The lack invigorated her.

She dressed in shorts and a sleeveless cream knit shirt. Now that she had a place to stay she would see the town, get to know her surroundings. She'd never done anything like this, and she had to get it right. She bit her lip, wondering at that thought. At some point she would have to face reality, but since it presently eluded her, she would take each thought as it came. She locked the door from the inside and crossed the landing that overlooked the main room downstairs.

The heavy log walls angled up two stories to the vaulted ceiling. A stone fireplace dominated one wall with bookcases flanking either side. Across the fireplace was a massive log mantel, and above that hung a plain wooden cross, pine like the rest. It was the only ornament in the room.

No feminine touch softened the space. No color accented the pale wood, lichen-covered stone, and saddle-tone leather couches. No curtains blocked the view from the wide front window. It was a man's place, untouched by a decorator's hands, almost primitive in its simplicity.

She went down and found the office underneath her own room. No one was inside, but a metal key lay on the desk with her name on a yellow Post-it. The note said, "Please leave your rent on the desk." He probably didn't realize she had cash. She took out the four hundred-dollar bills but couldn't leave them lying there. She would give them to him later but took the key now. She put both money and key in her pocket and walked out.

Morgan sat in the corner chair in the main room, one leg crossed over his knee. As she passed, he looked up from his newspaper. "All settled in?"

"Yes." No need to tell him she hadn't yet paid. She started for the door.

"Where are you going?"

A quiver of fear licked up like a flame. It wasn't him. It was inside her, like a frayed nerve reacting and not knowing when to stop. What was dangerous, what wasn't? And when would it stop? It was a perfectly ordinary question, and she answered, "To look at the town."

"Want a ride?" He folded the paper down over his knee.

"No thanks."

He stood anyway and met her at the door with an easy stride. "The walk down's not so bad, but up's a bear. Much worse than my bite."

Had he sensed her fear? Her mind whirring over endless possibilities of danger? She could drive herself crazy with *what-ifs*. And the walk up the gravel road was daunting. "All right." An instant trembling chased up her spine, but she resisted it.

He fished his keys from his pocket. "How'd you get up here?"

"I walked." She passed through the door he held.

"I mean up to Juniper Falls."

"The tour bus."

"Aha." He closed the door behind them. "So what brings you here?"

"I liked the look of it." The questions were inevitable, but she hoped her terse answers would discourage him soon. She slid into the fawn leather seat of his car. Of course, his was the Corvette. "What does FSTLN mean?"

"Hmm?"

"Your license plate."

"Oh. Just add vowels."

Noelle solved it in her head, and as the gravel flew behind his tires, she fastened her seat belt. Though the grasses brushed the underbelly of his car, he drove with just enough velocity to keep her attention without putting her over the edge, literally. Then he parked in the central lot outside the general store. *Fast lane* indeed. She surveyed the street before her as he walked around to let her out.

"To the right, tourist row, down that way, the real town. Which will it be for starters?"

She followed the sweep of his arm with her gaze. "The real town."

"It is something of a relic. The theater, for instance, was converted from an opera house in the forties and still shows a whopping one movie at a time, at least six months later than anywhere else."

Noelle smiled. "Quaint."

"Here's the bank. It was robbed fourteen times in its first year, 1884. So they called in the Congregational minister, had him bless the place, and it's never been hit since."

Noelle stared at the stone structure. It looked like a toy compared to the skyscraping bank buildings of New York City. Finches fluttered around its eaves, ducking in and out of the tiny apertures, and a mud-and-daub nest in one corner showed where a pair of rock swallows had raised a spring brood. "That's interesting."

"Coincidence, really. The silver shipments stopped changing hands here and went to Golden instead."

She smiled again. "Sounds like you know your history."

"I got all that from the professor."

"Professor . . ."

"Jenkins, your fellow guest at the ranch."

"Who else is there?" Since she had a guide, she may as well use him to learn what she could.

"A family from Michigan, three members of a Pathfinder Club, and a couple on their honeymoon. Won't see much of them. But the professor likes to gab." They passed a hardware store, a drugstore, and an ice-cream parlor.

Noelle paused at the French patisserie. "Is it any good?"

"Want to try it?"

"No, just wondering." She started on before he could encourage her to share one of the pleasant umbrella tables on the patio. It was one thing to catch a ride and let him show her around, another altogether to linger and chat over pastries.

The general store she'd already seen, and there was a modern, though tiny, grocery mart. Across from that a square stone building housed the library, post office, and city hall. Next to that was the Roaring Boar Grill and Saloon, made of red granite with huge rough beams supporting a peaked roof.

Morgan stopped. "That's it, except for private residences, the church there, and behind it the new community center for civic activities."

"Such as?" She looked at the low-peaked warehouse-type building that looked completely out of place behind the old stone church.

"Oh, you know, Elks Club, ladies guild . . . a quilt show now and then. Pure excitement."

Noelle smiled. He was irreverent but amusing, and her intimidation lessened. But her head throbbed and she was uncommonly tired.

"You okay?" Morgan eyed her.

She nodded. "My head aches."

"That's the altitude. Drink lots of water. You'll acclimate in a few days. You want to see the tourist strip?"

"Not really."

"There just might be a curio you can't live without—ceramic hind end of a horse with the clever quip 'Rocky Mountain quarter horse.' Even has a slot for quarters. I won't tell you where."

Noelle groaned.

"I bought one for Rick in honor of his profession, but I haven't seen it displayed."

"I can't imagine why." She stepped over a missing chunk of sidewalk.

"All sorts of treasures. Bottle of fool's gold that people buy to prove they really are."

"No thanks."

"Don't want you to miss out on the priceless finds that bring the bus people every day."

"I'll bear responsibility."

He shrugged with an emphasized sigh and led her back to the car. He held her door open and she climbed in, steeling herself for the drive. In truth, though he rode the edge, he was an accomplished driver, far safer behind the wheel than she'd be on those curves. As Morgan's Corvette hugged the road up to the ranch, she looked down at the town nestled below.

He glanced over. "Sleepy little afterthought, isn't it."

She nodded. But it was perfect. No one would expect to find her in a little place like Juniper Falls. She could just disappear. When they reached the ranch, she went up to her room, tucked her legs beneath her, and sat on the bed. She'd landed. And now her life was her own. She breathed deeply.

———

After a short nap and several glasses of water, Noelle's head had stopped aching. But she was hungry. She checked the schedule on the door and thankfully started down for dinner. A thin, stoop-shouldered man was already seated at the table; the professor, no doubt. She noted his Roman patrician nose and deep-set umber eyes beneath graying brows. His short-cropped beard had a dark brown V between two gray patches on his chin. She wondered if it was cleft underneath.

Rick spoke from behind her. "Noelle, this is Professor Jenkins, here for a couple of weeks on sabbatical. Professor, Noelle St. Claire."

"I'm pleased to meet you, Professor."

He nodded formally with a smile. "Likewise, Ms. St. Claire."

Rick took the chair at the head of the long pine table, and Noelle sat on his left across from the professor. Two middle-aged men and a slightly older woman were introduced, and Noelle guessed them the Pathfinders Morgan had mentioned. The family from Michigan must be using their own kitchen, and, as Morgan had suggested, the honeymoon couple did not join them.

Morgan followed Marta in from the kitchen as she carried the first steaming platter to the table. "You can't say that, Marta. I dated a girl so nice her worst nightmare was not getting to heaven. No joke. She dreamed she was in line behind Mother Teresa, and St. Peter told the bent old woman, 'You could have done more.' She dragged me through more good deeds—"

"There's nothing wrong with wanting to better the world." Marta turned back for the kitchen.

"Don't I know. Just gotta have fun doing it." Morgan took his place and winked at Noelle.

It could have been a family argument, a naughty nephew and a favorite aunt. She wondered if Marta was related, but the physical characteristics were too disparate. Though, to be sure, Rick and Morgan were different enough. Marta laid out the meal: pork chops, potatoes, buttered peas, and rolls still steaming—exactly the kind of fare Noelle had expected there. Marta's swift, concise motions were like the darting of a ground squirrel, but at last she stopped and stood at the foot of the table.

Noelle laid her napkin in her lap and reached for the rolls, then stopped, fingers extended, as Rick bowed his head and said, " 'I will extol the Lord with all my heart in the council of the upright and in the assembly.' "

She stared. She couldn't help it. Never would she have taken him for a praying man, though now the cross over the mantel made sense.

"For this food we are deeply grateful. Bless it for our use in your service, O Lord. Amen."

*Amens* surrounded her. Catching Morgan's amusement, she dropped her gaze. She hadn't meant to be so transparent, especially with Morgan more attentive than she wanted.

The professor turned to her. "Visiting from New York?"

She looked at him in surprise and with more than a little concern. "How did you . . ."

"I detect an accent."

"My tutor would be disappointed to hear that." Noelle sliced open the steaming potato, noticing the glance Rick and Morgan shared. She shouldn't have said that either. She wasn't used to guile.

"I'm a bit of a linguist, you see—a trained ear." The professor leaned forward. "While you lack the obvious accent, your diction does betray you. Long Island?"

She gave him a slight smile, but her heart thumped. Since she'd given her name, it would be a simple matter for them to trace her back to . . . But why would they? She'd done nothing wrong. She could go where she pleased, do what she pleased. What she'd lived before was the farce. This was real.

Morgan passed the rolls. "How's the book coming, Professor?"

"Oh." He shrugged. "I'm ruminating. That's the most important part." He nodded to Noelle. "I'm writing a history of western expansion through the anecdotes of small towns such as Juniper Falls." The timbre of his voice belied his spare, lanky frame, the long, almost delicate fingers with which he precisely cut his meat. He had the hands of an academic.

She responded politely, thankful when Morgan engaged him and the professor's attention shifted from her. As he and Morgan conversed, with interjections from the hikers, the talk washed over her, just as it had so many times with her father and his associates. She felt invisible and was content to remain so.

Morgan seemed undaunted when Professor Jenkins corrected him. He shrugged carelessly and offered his rebuttal. Even she could tell he was fudging, but the professor took pains to correct him again. Rick said little but had the look of a man who attended every detail.

She was glad to be left to her thoughts. The food was like heaven. Marta was a good chef. Or maybe it was simply the first meal not from a machine that she had eaten in days. Whichever, its simple comfort and satisfaction was a healing balm. She cleaned her plate without shame.

Morgan engaged her eyes. "There's a band at the Roaring Boar tonight. Want to go?"

"No thanks."

"It's a good band," he coaxed.

She shook her head. "Not tonight." Or any night. She handed over her plate to Marta's waiting hands, excused herself, and left the table.

She went to the bookshelves that flanked the fireplace and searched the titles. There were classics from Homer to Mark Twain with a few by Michener and Clavell. Quite a few by C. S. Lewis and T. S. Elliot, whom she hadn't read. Tom Clancy was the only current New York Times bestseller among them.

The other shelf held travel guides, historical, wildlife, and nature books. She found a Rocky Mountain botanical guide not unlike the one she'd studied for the Northeastern states. She slipped it from the shelf as Morgan approached.

"You can't possibly think that would be more entertaining than a night on the town with the best band the Boar sports."

She turned to him. "I'd like to recognize the plants I encounter here." To own and absorb this strange place, to make it hers.

"That's what the daytime's for. The night was made for fun."

She had him pegged now, but merely opened the cover of the botanical and said, "No thanks."

"We'd have a good time."

She expected he would. But she was not there for a good time. "No thank you, Morgan."

This time he shrugged and left without her. And that was telling as well. He might coax, but he didn't force the issue. She released a slow breath. She was learning, reading them, apprehending her situation and those others within it. She glanced up from the book as Rick crossed to the door after Morgan. "Excuse me. Are these for anyone's use?"

He took a jacket from the hooks and reached for the doorknob. "Help yourself."

Through the front window she watched him cross to the stable. It seemed he wasn't joining Morgan in town. He was going back to work. For brothers, they could hardly have been more different. If she'd had a brother or sister, would they be her opposite? Staring at the darkening window, she imagined a sister, brave, brash, and outspoken.

With a sigh, Noelle carried the botanical guide to her room. No doubt many of the plants, trees, and flowers pictured would be ones she already knew. But mountain flora had to differ from that of sea level, and she was genuinely interested in what she might find in her new environment. Before she settled in, though, she checked the money in the makeup pouch from the shelf, counted each bill. She should have taken more than two thousand dollars, but she had only been thinking of travel money, hadn't thought past her escape.

Paying bills had never occupied much of her thoughts. It was automatic; she either signed for her expenses or used a credit card. She never carried cash. To walk around with four hundred dollars in her pocket—She realized with a jolt that she hadn't given Rick her payment. It was still in that pocket.

But he hadn't asked for it. Was he a careless businessman? It seemed contrary to what she'd noted as his methodical and diligent nature.

Well, she could hardly chase him down as the evening drew toward dusk. She left the rent in her pocket and replaced the makeup bag on the shelf. The money ought to be in a bank, even the little one in town, but an account could be traced. She would have to figure that out, but tonight she was too tired.

After changing for bed, she read until her eyes would not stay open, then turned out the lamp and curled under the coverlet. She had never slept in a place so unfamiliar, except on the numerous buses from the past days, and already that seemed like a strange interlude, a pinch in time that may not be real. Lying in the pine bed, she drifted into a warm, nebulous calm. The sleep that had been fitful as she traveled now came heavily, and she gladly succumbed.

Without warning, she sensed the shadow above her, heard the beating of the wings. All her flesh trembled, and she crouched, pulling the grass down around her. But the blades were too thin and brittle to conceal her. Helpless, she grasped at them, frantic to cover herself, then, despairing, turned her face up to the cruel beak and talons.

# 4

William St. Claire sat in his office. He stared at the plaques on his wall—certificates, awards, and mementos of achievements that did nothing to lighten his mood. Not after a miscarriage of justice, a guilty man set free. He was not fool enough to believe every client innocent of the charges against him, though the Constitution presumed so. But this time the realization of his client's probable guilt came after he had accepted the case. It didn't change his job; the man was entitled to defense, the best his money could buy, and William had billed accordingly. But where was the strength of the system? Why was it so easy to win? And why was his heart still in prosecution after all these years?

The prosecutors should do their job as effectively as he and Michael did theirs. He sighed. He was getting old—he would turn fifty-nine this year. He sat down in the smooth leather chair and massaged the back of his neck. Where were the answers he'd thought he knew? How brash and arrogant he'd been as a young man. But no more. Now he understood too much and believed too little.

Ordinarily when he felt this gloomy he would call Noelle, have her come for supper. Simply seeing her restored his spirits. But that wasn't possible just now, was it? Ohio. Was she there, or had it been only a stop along the way? And why had he withheld her location from Michael?

Maybe Michael could have suggested some reason his daughter would be calling from a pay booth in Columbus, Ohio. But then, maybe not. And something had kept William from telling. Did he trust Michael? As much as he trusted anyone besides Noelle. He sighed. It would sort itself out. He had to believe that and not let irrational fears make a bogeyman in every shadow.

Noelle was safe. She had sounded calm. And if she'd never done anything like this before, it wasn't as though she couldn't do it now. She was twenty-three years old. Hardly a child, certainly not the vulnerable child she'd been when . . . His stomach seized. Would it ever cease, the physical reaction to the memory, to the awful, awful memory?

Or was it another instinct? One he should heed? It wouldn't hurt to learn where she was. He wouldn't interfere, just . . . He pinched the bridge of his nose. Where was the balance? His daughter was grown and intelligent, and she has assured him she was fine. His need to know should not violate her right to privacy. He would wait . . . for now.

———

Noelle awoke to the scolding of a magpie outside her window. The early morning sunshine poured into the room, and she stared at the log walls and ceiling, then made sense of it as full consciousness returned. Hardly a vestige of the dream remained, and she felt surprisingly refreshed. She slipped out of bed.

When she had showered, she pulled her hair into a loose French braid. She dressed in jeans and a V-neck T-shirt. She could hear Marta humming in the kitchen as she started down the stairs, a homey sound that cut straight to her heart. The staff at home would never draw attention to themselves that way.

She replaced the botanical guide, then wandered into the dining room and noted the long table set with plates, white stoneware on wood. An extra table leaned against the wall, and shelves held stacks of dishes, glasses, and mugs to accommodate many more guests than were currently at the ranch. This room also was unadorned, everything serviceable, bare. This morning it seemed bleak. It cried out for some artistic touch, even a simple centerpiece.

Glancing around the room, she saw what she needed. Taking with her a glass water pitcher and knife from the shelves, she went outside. The air was chilled, raising the flesh on her arms and legs, in spite of yesterday's heat. How could it be so cold in July? But that was something else to file in her memory about her new environment at that elevation.

Shivering, Noelle filled the bottom fourth of the pitcher with small stones and water from the creek. The smell of the juniper grew pungent as she sliced the tender branches and stood them in the pitcher. She carefully added thorny stalks of wild roses, then went in and set the pitcher in the center of the table, turning it one way, then edging it back just a little.

"That's nice," Rick said behind her.

She spun, her heart leaping like a rabbit to her throat.

"Sorry I startled you."

She drew a sharp breath. "It's okay." But it took some time for the jolt to pass.

Marta bustled past with the coffee cake. She stopped and eyed the floral arrangement. "What's all this?"

"Flowers." Rick took the cake from her with a soothing glance.

Marta raised her eyebrows, then went back to the kitchen.

Noelle knew that look. Her cheeks heated. What was she thinking? She was a guest, not a resident. "I should have asked."

Rick set the coffee cake on the table. "Marta's . . . practical. She thinks a water pitcher is for water." He slid out her chair, but before she sat, Noelle took the four hundred dollars from her pocket and held it out to him. "I meant to give you this yesterday. I didn't want to leave it on the desk."

He took the bills with just a hint of surprise, then tucked them into his shirt pocket. "Thanks."

"I'm sorry I forgot. But you didn't ask."

He shrugged. "I knew where to find you." He eased the chair in as she sat.

Marta returned with coffee and fruit wedges, then made a third trip, returning with sizzling sausages and hard-boiled eggs. The family from Michigan, two stout adults and three preadolescent kids, followed the steaming platter to the table. They'd used their kitchen last night, but they must have preferred Marta's breakfast to their own—with good reason.

Rick seated the mother beside Noelle and greeted the kids by name. For all his reserved temperament, he was a warm host.

"I'm Shelby." The woman held out her hand, soft and short-fingered.

Noelle squeezed and released it. "Noelle."

"Up here alone, are you?"

Noelle nodded. Would her business be discussed at every meal?

"I *dream* of slipping away alone." Two deep dimples appeared in

Shelby's cheeks when she smiled. "But this crew wouldn't survive if I did."

Marta came to stand at the end of the table, and Noelle guessed they wouldn't be waiting for the Pathfinders or honeymoon couple. The food was hot and ready. She flicked her eyes up to Marta, who seemed to have put the flower arrangement from her mind. Her face was serene as she stood, head bowed, while Rick prayed.

" 'Happy the man who fears the Lord, who finds great delight in his commands.' Lord, you are the source of all joy. Bless this day and this food for our nourishment. Amen."

Noelle kept her hands in her lap and did not stare. This was obviously a ritual he would repeat each time they ate. When he finished, the kids grabbed for the coffee cake, scolded by their mother but not dissuaded from grabbing the pieces with their hands and plopping them on their plates. Noelle took the platter from Shelby and helped herself with the server from the other side. The cake was still warm and she smelled its lemony sweetness.

"Coffee?" Marta held the pot above Noelle's cup.

"Thank you." Noelle took a bite of cake. It was moist and light and the tiny gray poppy seeds crunched in its softness. She savored it silently. Why did everything taste better here—even with the children shoving whole sausages into their mouths and mashing their boiled eggs? Everything seemed more vibrant, more real. She added cream to her coffee and glanced at Rick.

His features were regular, not the sort to turn heads wherever he went, not like Morgan's, not like . . . She shuddered away from another image, forced her mind back to Rick. He moved with controlled mastery, and his forearms, bared beneath the loosely rolled denim sleeves, were lean-sinewed like the horse he had ridden yesterday, his hands calloused but clean. He dug his fork into the cake with a determined stroke.

"Room all right?" He met her glance for a moment.

"Yes, it's fine." She had slept well enough.

"Too bad you didn't get a cabin." Shelby patted her hand. "They're so cozy. We had a fire last night."

"We popped popcorn in a weird black box on a handle." The oldest boy looked exactly like his mother, though more thickly freckled.

"And Sean dropped it in the fire." His younger brother was a smaller copy with thick freckles across his nose.

"Did not."

"Did too."

"Boys." Shelby's husband had a high, thin voice.

"Well, he did."

"Did not."

Shelby rolled her eyes as though Noelle knew how it was. In truth, she knew no such thing. She thanked Marta for warming her coffee, then sliced into her boiled egg and lightly salted the slice. She had wondered if Marta would join them, but except to replenish the coffee, she stayed in the kitchen. Noelle had never given thought to it at home. That's where the servants belonged. Why, here, did it seem strange?

Everything seemed strange. She felt drunk with possibilities. She was free, independent, alone. It was deliciously heady. The reasons that made such a step impossible for Shelby might be different, but it was no less a step for Noelle. Never again would she be trapped. Never would she allow anyone power over her. She was not invincible, but now she would be shrewd.

Shelby's family filled the room with noise: questions, bickering, laughter, and excuses from Shelby. Noelle was glad they were there. It would be uncomfortable to sit at the table alone with Rick. He responded pleasantly enough to anything directed his way but didn't seem to generate conversation. She thought of her father, though there was very little to connect them. William St. Claire was the epitome of class and culture, and Rick seemed . . . unconcerned with either. Two different worlds, though maybe the same type of man packaged differently. With the exception of religion.

Noelle looked at Shelby's husband. His head was round as a bowling ball, the dark hair thinning on top to reveal a sheen. Even shaved he bore a five o'clock shadow, and his nose was a small round bulb. He was shaped like an inverted spark plug, but Noelle guessed when he took to the mountain on his bicycle he was tougher than he looked.

When they were nearly finished eating, Morgan came in, collapsed into a chair with a groan, and reached for the coffee carafe Marta had left on the table her last trip through.

Rick slid it closer. "Morning."

Morgan nodded. His eyes were heavy, one cheek still creased from whatever he had lain on, no doubt without moving. His night at the Roaring Boar must have been quite entertaining.

"Well . . ." Shelby seemed to take that as her cue. "I guess we'll be off for the day. Taking the bike trail, you know." She nudged Noelle's arm.

Why did the woman assume Noelle knew and understood all her thoughts and duties? Noelle smiled politely as Shelby gathered her chicks and herded them from the room. Then she turned to Rick. "I'd like to ride this morning. Is there a procedure?"

The corners of his mouth deepened, though she wasn't sure what amused him. "Greenhorn or equestrian?"

She wasn't altogether sure what he meant by greenhorn, but equestrian certainly fit, and she answered accordingly.

"Then the procedure is you sign my waiver and I get you saddled and show you the boundaries. The ranch borders the national forest, and it's easy to get lost up in there. If you ride well enough to go on your own, you'll still have to stay within the area I show you." He tossed down his napkin and stood.

Noelle followed him out of the room with a last glance back. If Morgan realized he was alone, it didn't matter. His forehead rested on his palm, supported by his elbow to the table. His other hand clutched the cup of coffee he had yet to drink, and his eyes were closed.

They went first to the office, where Rick put her rent payment into his cashbox, then took a clipboard from the wall. It was a standard liability waiver, which Noelle knew meant very little in case of accident. Anything could be challenged, and personal injury suits were almost always settled out of court. But she would not be getting injured. She signed her name.

In the barn, Rick saddled a bay mare and a buckskin gelding. The buckskin appeared to be the only non-quarter horse he owned. "You've ridden a lot?"

"I'm competition trained." She didn't tell him her equestrian training had ended at age fourteen and she'd ridden only sporadically since. It wasn't something one forgot.

He gave no indication her declaration had impressed him anyway as he held the head of the mare for her to mount. She took up the reins, prepared to extinguish his doubts.

Again that sideways smile. "She won't respond that way. She's trained Western."

"Oh."

"Hold both reins together." He adjusted them in her hands. "That's why they're tied like that."

"I see."

Rick looked her over, adjusted the stirrup, then mounted the buckskin. Swinging the horse's head around, he clicked his tongue. Noelle experimented with the reins until she felt the mare's ready response. It was different but not difficult to adjust. Her training in all other aspects was complete. He'd see that for himself.

The pale gold grass of the meadow rasped under the hooves. On either side, the slopes up to the rocky crags were wooded and carpeted with spongy kinnikinnick and wild roses, both plants she recognized from the mountain botanical guide. The quiet seemed to swallow her as they passed under the trees.

Her senses heightened. The hooves softly crunched the rusty pine needles, releasing their scent. She could almost feel the pristine secrets of the wood opening to her. Wisdom and knowledge. If she stayed to listen, what would she learn?

Rick turned in the saddle. "There's no fence dividing the national forest and the ranch, so keep to this side of the stream." He indicated the larger stream to her left, and she nodded. They came out of the trees and skirted the fenced pasture, which held an inner corral. She guessed that was a training corral, and no animals were inside it.

But in the pasture itself were the roan stallion, Destiny, and two others, one red like the colt and one black. They tossed their heads and ran, manes and tails like banners. Their wild abandon touched an ache inside her. What would it be like to ride the roan, to feel his strength and spirit?

"Do you think that colt would carry me?"

"Not a chance."

"I'm a capable rider. I've had extensive training."

"I doubt you've ridden an unbroken colt with a will of his own."

"There's always a first time." She smiled, but it had as much effect on Rick as on the crags above him.

"Sorry." He turned away from the pasture. Across the meadow they climbed back into the trees more steeply than before. "I want you to stay away from that high ground up there. The shale on the slope is unstable."

Noelle eyed the ridge he indicated with disappointment. It would afford the perfect view of the whole valley below. He was certainly full of rules and restrictions, but she merely nodded and followed him back out to the meadow.

She surveyed the long draw down to the ranch. It was shaped like a shallow U with the creek down the center and the grasses rich on either side. The house at its base faced squarely up to them, and she wondered who had placed it so capably.

"Come on." Rick urged his horse and they cantered down.

She resisted the urge to kick in her heels and challenge him. Now that she'd had a look, she wouldn't jeopardize her chances to ride the ranch alone. She reined in at the yard. "Do I pass?"

"As long as you follow directions."

She held herself straight in the saddle. *Follow directions. Oh yes, sir. If there's one thing I know, it's how to follow directions.* She brought the horse around and headed back into the trees. The white-barked ones were aspen, she now knew, and their notched leaf stems were what made the vibrant green leaves tremble in the breeze. Quaking aspen, they were called, and they were beautiful.

She wished she had brought her art supplies, then Noelle recalled seeing a section in the general store that might have something she could use. With a sketchpad and pencil—or even better, paints—she could capture the beauty of this place. She looked down toward the ranch house. Rick was no longer in sight.

If she skirted the house along the creek, she could ride down the gravel road to town. Rick had said not to cross into the national park property. She was neither crossing that stream he'd pointed out nor climbing the high ground he'd forbidden. She was only riding to town.

First, she tied the horse behind the house, snuck up to her room, and took another bill from her pouch. Then she rode down and reached Juniper Falls without incident, crossing the highway the greatest challenge. But the horse was even-tempered and steady. She tied it outside the general store and went inside. The same man was behind the counter.

He smiled. "Guess you found a place to stay."

"Yes. Thank you for your help."

"Rick know you've got that mare down here?"

She hesitated before shaking her head. She had hoped no one would notice.

"Can I get you something?"

"I'll just look." She turned for the shelves that held sketchbooks and other art supplies. It was actually a good selection in several media. She knelt and opened a wooden case that held a portable easel, watercolors, brushes, and heavy-weight stiff rag paper. Not the quality she was used to, but sufficient. She could add to the set as needed. She also chose a sketchpad and pencils and brought it all to the counter.

"Find what you need?"

"A good start, anyway."

"We get quite a few artists up here. That's why I stock that stuff."

So she wasn't alone in her reactions. Such natural beauty cried out to be captured.

"I can order things from my supplier as well. Let me know if you want something specific."

"I'd look at a catalogue, certainly." This was better than she'd hoped. "But this'll do for now." She paid for the items and thanked him. At the door, she turned. "If I walk next time, could the mare be our secret?"

He picked up the cigarette from the tray and drew in the smoke, then smiled. "He won't hear it from me. But he might from the rest of the town."

She could only hope not. With the wooden case under one arm, she walked the horse across the highway, then mounted and rode up to the ranch. She left the animal in the holding pen beside the stable and went inside. Up in her room, she set the art supplies on the table and rubbed her inner thighs, surprised to feel sore. But then, it had been a long while since she'd been on horseback. Keeping her legs straight, she bent and lowered her palms to the floor, then sank her chest to her knees.

The stretch of hamstrings and calves felt good as she reached behind her legs and worked that final pull. She let her upper body hang, then slowly drew her arms up over her head. She reached high, then swung down to the side and around. She bent her knees to plié, then did a series of jazz moves and spun.

She smiled grimly at the small oval mirror above the bureau, quite a change from the glass wall in the studio. She tucked her toes between the logs of the wall at about the height of a bar and stretched both legs again. She should establish a routine, yet the thought vied with her current rebellion. No routine, then, but she would exercise—when she felt like it.

The next morning, Noelle stood on the porch and gazed at the serene beauty of the rosy crags against the cerulean sky. Birdsong floated on the breeze. On the meadow a horse whinnied, and the air was pungent with pine and sage. In that moment, she experienced morning anew, as though everywhere else time passed, but here it was created. She'd been right to come. She hadn't planned it—reacted only—but she'd done exactly what she needed to.

"Enjoying the quiet?" Morgan joined her at the porch rail.

"Yes."

He looked better than he had the previous morning, but she'd seen nothing of him the rest of that day. Maybe he'd slept it through. He said, "You don't mind solitude."

"I like it."

"I prefer people." He leaned his forearms on the rail.

"Any people?"

He shrugged. "I have a broad tolerance."

She laughed softly. "I see." And she had seen it in the way he interacted either with her or the group. Age and gender were no barriers for someone like Morgan.

He eyed her. "You have a nice laugh, Noelle."

And that was her signal. She reached for the wooden case she had set on the porch.

He was quicker and lifted it himself. "Heading off again?"

She nodded.

"Want some company?"

"I work better alone."

"Work?"

"Paint." She indicated the box he held. "Watercolors, paper, and easel."

"Aha. So you're an artist."

"I'm schooled in art." She shrugged.

"And here I thought you were a spy."

She laughed again, but concern flickered. Why would he think that, even jokingly? Did he wonder about her? Did they all?

He held her case to his chest. "Why don't we search out some fun instead?"

"No thanks."

He sighed. "You're certainly stuck in the 'no' mode."

She reached for her case. "Will you excuse me?"

He handed it over reluctantly. She headed down the stairs, then frowned as Rick led out the mare again. She was a nice horse but stolid and mild-mannered. Noelle craved an animal with spirit. Hadn't she shown what she could do?

He obviously caught her look. "Aldebaran's a good horse. She knows her way home if you get into trouble."

Noelle stroked the dark muzzle. "I won't get into trouble."

"Or stray from the ranch."

She glanced up quickly. Was he referring to her episode in town?

"You do understand the boundaries stop here at the stable?"

She nodded, chagrinned. If he'd hollered or scolded or revoked her privilege she would have insisted he hadn't mentioned that boundary before. But he did none of that.

He tied the wooden box to the back of the saddle. "Then this mare's a good choice."

"Have I another?"

"String horses." He tightened the cinch. "They work pretty well for riders who don't know a stirrup from a rein."

That was a compliment at least, an acknowledgment of her ability. "I could take the buckskin. . . . What's his name?"

"Orion."

That gelding at least had size and power. "Well?"

"Nope."

She sighed. Better not push her luck just yet. She recalled Rick's blessing that morning, thanking God for all he'd been given. No point arguing with someone who thought God gave him dominion over everything that crawled the earth.

She mounted. All she wanted to think about was the sunshine on the meadow above her, the willing horse beneath her, and the scene awaiting her brush. She brought the mare around and started up the slope.

The morning chill lingered, though the sun was sharp in the sky. The creek in its stony bed called to her with the voices of naiads. She almost expected to see the water spirits take their maidenly shapes and dance along the banks. She dismounted and dipped her fingers into the flow, stunned by the icy touch. Even the summer sun did little to warm the water, fresh from some spring or glacier melt.

The professor said all the rivers in Colorado sprang from the mountains and flowed outward. No other rivers flowed in. Touching the water now, she felt the newness. This was a beginning for her too. She remounted and continued on, turning into the woods. Light and shadow played over her as she rode.

Aldebaran stepped nimbly through the woods, and Noelle patted her neck. She was a sweet-tempered horse, if lacking in spunk. Unfortunately they were too well suited. But Noelle was changing that. It wasn't spunk that had driven her here, but now that she depended only on herself, something stirred inside. She emerged into the bright sunshine of the meadow, the high pasture and the fenced corral ahead. Rick had driven up in his truck and was there running the colt around and around on the long rope.

She stopped to watch. Slowly he pulled in the rope, talking low. The roan's hide rippled with the sleek muscles beneath, quivering as Rick reached out and stroked him, then ran his hand down the neck and wither. Rick's own muscles bunched as he gripped the saddle horn. With a smooth motion he was up.

The horse reared and kicked, bucked stiff legged, then jackknifed. Rick landed in the dirt and the colt stopped kicking, wasting no effort once his goal was met. Rick got up, shook himself off, and caught the colt's rope, then led him to where Noelle stood at the fence. "He thinks he has to do that."

The horse tugged against his hold, and she reached a hand to his muzzle. "I'm sure I could ride him."

"Yeah, he's just itching to carry you."

"Maybe it's only you he fights."

"I kind of doubt it."

"You won't know until you let me try." She gave him her full, most winning smile.

Rick returned it with his lips only. "Sorry."

She cloaked her annoyance. "Why doesn't Morgan work the horses with you?"

"He doesn't like pain."

She laughed. "And you do?"

"I don't exactly like it, but I accept it as part of the process."

"Why is he here at the ranch?"

Rick rubbed his forehead with his sleeve. "He's between things."

"Oh." Unemployed, downsized, canned. All the situations that "between things" euphemized. Noelle tickled the horse's chin, and he nodded. "I think he likes me."

"Morgan?"

She frowned. "Destiny. I think he'd carry me."

"Forget it."

She added stubborn to her listing of Rick's nature and left him to find a suitable scene to paint. She hadn't gone far enough though, as Shelby's boys swarmed her from the woods with a hundred questions, killing both the wisdom of the trees and the naiad voices.

"Where'd you get the paints?"

"Can I try it?"

"How come you get a horse by yourself?"

"Can we ride it?"

*Yes, take her and leave!* But then the morning light was gone on her subject, and the creative flow strangled. She packed up her materials and folded the easel back into the case. Then she looked at the three boys, noting their eager freckled faces.

"Where's your mother?"

"She told us to scram."

Why hadn't she thought of that? "Did your parents sign a waiver for you to ride?"

The oldest shrugged. "I don't know. They didn't want to pay extra for horse riding."

*Pay extra?* Rick had said nothing about that.

"They don't like horses." The oldest boy ran his forearm under his nose.

"I do." That one was Sean, who had dropped the popcorn into the fire.

She nodded to the oldest. "What's your name?"

"Sam."

"Climb into the saddle, Sam." She held Aldebaran's head while he mounted clumsily. "Have you ever ridden?"

The boys shook their heads. She was probably on shaky ground, but refusing them now seemed cruel. Every child should experience a horse at least once. Her first ride had been magical.

She helped Sean up behind the saddle, and he wrapped his arms around Sam. She lifted the youngest into the saddle with Sam. A tight fit but manageable. "What's your name?"

"He's Scotty," Sam said.

She placed the redhead's hands on the saddle horn. "Hold on tight right there, Scotty."

She took the reins and walked Aldebaran carefully from the trees into the meadow. The boys' grins bunched their freckles, but they held still and stayed quiet, a feat she hadn't thought possible. They were probably terrified. She walked the mare all the way to Rick's corral, where he once again circled the stallion on the long rope.

Seeing them approach, he slowed the horse and drew it in. As she stopped Aldebaran, he caught hold of the rope at Destiny's halter. Without speaking, she wrapped the mare's reins and removed the boys one by one from Aldebaran's back. They clambered onto the fence, peppering him with questions. With a smile she mounted, turned the mare's head, and went back for her wooden case, satisfaction fairly oozing from her pores.

———

Just before dinnertime that evening, Rick approached her on the porch. "I don't suppose the boys told you their family didn't sign a waiver."

"They thought probably not." She smiled. "Sure enjoyed the ride, though, didn't they?"

He hung his thumbs from his belt and eyed her. "The reason I have the waiver is so all parties understand the possible dangers."

"Is Aldebaran dangerous?"

"Noelle . . ." He seemed at a loss. "Do you have a problem with rules?"

Yes. More so than she'd ever realized. "I thought they'd enjoy watching you work."

He held her gaze straight on. "Was that what you thought." His tone made it an untruth, not a question. "Their noise and monkeying on the fence put Destiny so far over the edge, I had to quit." He lifted one foot to the middle step. "But that's not the point. I run a careful operation. I can't have people crossing highways on my animals and giving rides to kids without permission."

She winced inwardly but had no answer.

"I pay plenty in liability insurance, but I'd prefer not to place a claim. This ranch has a reputation, and so do I."

He did have a point. She said, "I understand."

He drew himself up. "Good." Then he took the steps purposefully and went inside.

Noelle took a slow breath. What was she doing, antagonizing the man who'd given her a place to stay? What if he asked her to leave? The thought was sobering. She didn't want to leave.

Checking her watch, she went inside for dinner. Morgan must have found his excitement elsewhere, because he didn't join them. A new family had taken the Pathfinders' cabin, and the professor turned his welcome on the lanky couple and two preteen daughters. The honeymooners also appeared, and the talk turned spiritual—the professor probing and the others responding enthusiastically.

Professor Jenkins's esoteric input contrasted with the newly married couple, who talked as though faith in God was a relationship as real as their own, not one mythology among many. Noelle tried not to stare. The husband was probably her own age, but the wife spoke like a child with embarrassing naïveté. Could she actually believe the things she said?

Noelle stayed quiet but studied them all with interest. Rick said little as well, though what he offered seemed pithy in a way she wasn't sure she understood. As soon as she could, she went upstairs with a history of Western women. She slept deeply that night without dreams—at least none that made her shake and whimper. Maybe the ghost that chased her there would stay away for good.

Only birdsong and crickets broke the silence the next morning as she slipped out into the predawn glow. She had wakened early, eager for the day in a way she'd never been before. She glanced at Professor Jenkins, who leaned on the porch rail, pipe in hand. His piquant tobacco mingled with the ranch smells and the mountain flora.

She raised her face to the coolness. "Good morning."

"Good morning to you." He lifted his pipe to her.

"Ruminating?"

His smile formed crescent creases around his eyes and deepened the lines beside his mouth. "Have to. You see, my treatise is on expansion itself, the drive behind it and the human spirit that longs for it." He cradled the bowl of his pipe with his palm. "To capture the essence of the human spirit . . . now, that's a challenge."

"Quite an undertaking. Why does it matter?"

He turned. "You are an artist. Why?"

"Well, I've had—"

"Please don't tell me because you were instructed in art. I passed you in the woods yesterday as you worked, and I saw no trained animal."

"What did you see?"

"Someone in love with the beautiful, transcending the natural." He puffed on his pipe. "I think, like me, you seek that same human spirit and perhaps a part of the divine as well."

She regarded him closely. "How did you come to that just from seeing me work?"

Professor Jenkins smiled. "Not just from that. I'm also a student of human nature."

Noelle looked out at the paling sky. "I don't think my work is as lofty as that."

"Do you paint for money?"

Now there was a thought. "If I could."

He motioned with his pipe. "A touch of the practical perhaps, but it's not at the heart of what you do."

"I guess you're right. I've never made a cent on it." Nor even tried. She laughed. "Well, I'll miss the sun if I don't hurry."

"It'll rise again tomorrow."

"But it won't be the same as today's."

"Ah. You prove my point."

She found Rick in the stable and waited while he picked Orion's hoof, then applied a thrush-prevention product to the sole and frog. He looked up as he released the left hind hoof and raised the right. "Out early today?"

"I want to catch the sunrise."

"Your mount is ready." He nodded toward the mare.

Noelle took Aldebaran's reins and led her out. There was no point arguing. Rick was as implacable as the crag that rose up from his land. But he'd made his position clear. It was his ranch and he ran it with integrity, a value she could respect. Last night's conversation had clarified exactly what sort of place she'd come to. She wondered for a moment what direction the table talk would have taken with Morgan there. Was he the dark horse he appeared, or did he espouse the same beliefs?

Noelle shook her head. It didn't matter. As she rode, she matched her motion to the steady rhythm of the horse. She crossed the stream and climbed the slope, until she saw what she wanted. Then she dismounted, tethered the mare, and unstrapped the wooden box.

The birth of sunlight sent shafts through the trees that illuminated them with gold and glanced off the dew-dropped aspen leaves. Clumps of mountain mahogany and sumac huddled beneath the trunks, while a wild rose rambled above the kinnikinnick. Wild strawberries bloomed with tiny white petals surrounding a raised yellow button.

Noelle assembled her easel and laid the stiff rag paper onto it. She squeezed dabs of paint onto her pallette and unscrewed the lid from the distilled water. She closed her eyes and drew the crisp mountain air into her lungs. *Someone in love with the beautiful.* Perhaps, Professor. Perhaps. She dipped her brush and drew it across the white with a swath of beige that would become the crag.

When she returned to the house, Professor Jenkins was once again, or still, at the table on the verandah, papers scattered around him, pipe puffing. "And were we successful?"

"I'm not sure." Noelle dropped down beside him. "Tell me what you think." She pulled the watercolor from the case and set it before him. Waiting, she caught her lip between her teeth.

Tipping his glasses down, he gazed at the work, silence stretching. Then, "I'm no artist by any stretch. But it seems to me you could seek a practical avenue for this caliber of work. Have you talked to the gallery?"

Noelle shook her head.

"I would."

She could tell by his frank expression he didn't flatter. He believed she had potential. Her spirits soared, but she masked it as she returned the picture to its case. "And you? Is your work progressing?"

"I'm moving on tomorrow."

"You mean leaving?"

He nodded.

She felt an unexpected disappointment but said, "In the true spirit of expansion."

He chuckled. "Exactly."

# CHAPTER

# 6

Michael woke in a sweat. The dream had been too real, a reenactment of the one thing in his life he'd undo if he could. No, not the one thing. He would undo most of his life if he could. He passed a hand over his eyes, groaning. The dream had drained him, and he couldn't afford that. William needed him sharp.

To the man's credit, nothing had changed between them professionally these last weeks. William compartmentalized his life, and Michael aspired to that deep a focus. Now was a good time to perfect it. They scarcely mentioned Noelle; an unstated understanding that the other would be informed the moment there was any news. But Michael wondered. If he learned from Sebastian where she was, would he tell William?

He looked at the red numbers on the clock. He always woke before the alarm, though not usually so rudely. He shook the dream from his mind. Of course he would tell William. But not until he'd made her see, made her understand. What had happened was not what he'd intended.

He showered, dressed, and took a cab to work. He reported smartly to William's office. The man looked gray. "William?"

William motioned him to a chair without looking up, then set aside the paper he was studying, folded his hands, and at last met his eyes.

"Are you ill, sir?"

William smiled grimly. "That bad, is it?"

"I only meant . . ."

William held up a hand. "Nothing but the truth."

An attempt at humor. Michael smiled obligingly. What was wrong with the man? His chest seized. "Is it Noelle?" Had they spoken? Had she . . .

"Did you know that she was kidnapped?"

"What!" Michael exploded from his seat.

William shook his head. "Sit down." He motioned with his hand. "I don't mean now. Obviously. I wouldn't be sitting here if she were in danger."

Flushing at his foolishness, Michael took his seat, tried to get inside William's head. What was he doing? Did he suspect . . .

"It was years ago. But I spent a terrible night remembering. As you noticed."

So they'd both been wrung out. Michael felt a surge of pride that he'd overcome it better than William.

"She was five years old, about to turn six." William pinched the bridge of his nose. "You think you've covered the possibilities, but you never think of some things until they happen. And it did. A parent's worst fear."

"Who took her? Why?"

William stood up and walked to the window behind the desk. "I was prosecuting a federal case, a defendant with deep connections."

Michael knew William had started out in prosecution, then switched to defense law. Was this the reason?

"My case against him was tenuous, but I had the reputation, the tenacity to pull it off. So they took Noelle." He made a sweeping gesture. "Just took her."

Michael frowned. He hadn't known any of that.

William shook his head. "They found the place I was weak."

The place he was weak. What would he do if he knew the truth now? "What did you do?"

William leaned slowly back in his chair. "Resigned my position as district attorney."

"Why not just lose the case?"

"And be vulnerable the next time?" William raised his eyes. "Defense law was safer. The feds don't kidnap children."

"What happened to Noelle?"

"The police found her tucked up next to the lions outside the public library."

"And the defendant?"

"Not guilty."

Michael dropped his gaze. If the case was weak, even William might have lost it, but the fact remained he'd capitulated for Noelle, had broken what Michael had up to now considered an unbreakable code. It didn't diminish William. If anything Michael admired his mentor more than ever and felt a keen kinship. They would both do anything to have Noelle back.

"I took precautions after that, thought of every possibility. She was never vulnerable again. I made sure."

"Did she . . . was she damaged by it?"

William's pause was a moment too long. "Frightened. She was terribly frightened. But the psychiatrist said severe traumas are often forgotten completely. I'm sure she has."

Michael's head spun. Severe trauma. Was that why she had over-reacted, panicked, all but turned catatonic? Could he use that to explain—if it came to it?

William pressed his palms to the desk. "Then, of course, there was Adelle. Her death created a whole new problem."

Michael switched tracks, glancing at the photograph of William's late wife.

"I could guard my daughter from danger, but . . . What control had I over sickness and disease?" William pushed back from the desk and stood. He walked to the window and looked out. "I screened everyone. Provided tutors instead of schools where illness propagated. But . . ." He dropped his head, shaking it slowly. "Did I push her away? In keeping her safe, did I smother her?" William turned around, as bleak as Michael had ever seen him. It was a measure of their relationship that he showed it now.

Michael frowned. Hadn't those been her words, or very nearly? But it wasn't William she meant. Michael swallowed. The tendons in his neck drew taut. He wanted to tell him it wasn't his fault, but whom did that leave? He said, "You did your best."

William walked to his desk and perused the folders but seemed unable to make sense of them. "Where are we today?"

Michael slipped naturally into the role being offered. With precision, he delineated the day's work on the two primary cases. William remained pensive as they talked, but Michael sensed his focus returning. A remarkable man, William St. Claire. He would put the night behind him, the past behind him, even Noelle's absence behind him. When they entered the court, William would be honed and ready. Sometimes Michael imagined himself William's son. One day he would be, if only in law.

———

The side streets were growing familiar as Noelle walked, eyeing light and shadow, a quaint house with a rose rambling up its terraced porch, a deserted mine tunnel with juniper across its mouth. Stopping in front of a yellow wood-frame house with a sagging porch and a bicycle against the rail, she studied the scene.

The clump of aspen in the front caught the breeze and scattered tremulous shadows across the window. From the side a dog yapped, dodging as a boy lunged for the leash and skidded across the ground, then gained his feet and continued the chase. She smiled. *The human spirit, Professor.* She missed him.

Shelby's family had been replaced in the cabin by a hard-muscled pair of mountain climbers, the woman as long-limbed and focused as her husband. Today they were tackling the crags on the mountain above the meadow. Noelle could not fathom dangling by a rope attached to a belt, held only by a thin metal hook over a thousand feet of empty space. But those two seemed to thrive on it.

The honeymooners' cabin was now occupied by three potential eagle scouts and their leader, working on some mountaineering badge or award of some sort. The third housed a couple from Denver on a getaway for their tenth anniversary. Rick had spoken truly that his place was booked through the summer, though without the professor, she and Morgan were the only guests in the house.

It was an odd arrangement and different from any living situation she'd had before. But she wouldn't change it. Not even for the spacious and well-appointed bungalow she'd occupied on her father's estate. Looking at the small yellow house before her, Noelle realized just how far from home she was.

She shifted her case to the other hand and walked on. The shadows had lengthened, and she made her way down the rutted dirt road to the paved highway that cut through town, then crossed the gravel lot to the general store. After searching the shelf, she laid a pack of gum with a dollar from her pocket on the counter. Rudy ground out his cigarette and gave her change.

"Thanks." She scooped it up and turned, smack into Morgan. Her dime and nickel went flying.

He steadied her around the waist, laughing. "Where's the fire?"

She didn't share his amusement. "Excuse me." She backed out of his grip and retrieved her change from the floor.

"Let's have dinner." Morgan reached for her case. "I'll take you to the Roaring Boar. A little dinner, a little dancing . . ."

She shook her head.

"Come on, break loose a little." His smile was contagious; white teeth and eye crinkles made her think once again of a GQ model. Morgan would fit into Daddy's circle on looks alone. "They have barbecue brisket that's to die for."

She glanced at Rudy behind the counter.

Rudy nodded. "Good stuff."

With the two of them coaxing, how could she decline? "We'd have to let Marta know."

"Absolutely." He motioned her out, then sent Rudy the raised eyebrows. Had they plotted it? Impossible. Neither knew she'd be there buying gum. Morgan simply found accomplices everywhere he went. And she'd fallen for it.

He put her art case into the Corvette's trunk, drove her back to the ranch, but caught her as she reached for the door handle. "Sit tight. I'll tell Marta I've got you."

*I've got you.* A chill passed through her as he got out and went inside. What was she doing? She bit her lip and clenched her fists. He'd asked her to dinner, nothing sinister. So why were her palms sweating and her heart racing? Thoughts threatened to surface, but she forced them back, staring up into a thin, sappy pine, catching her breaths sharply.

She was answerable to no one but herself. She could go with Morgan or not. Even now she could change her mind—go inside the house, her haven. She could . . . and call herself a coward. Sooner or later she had to stop avoiding life. She raised her chin. Sooner. A rush of confidence filled her.

She released her clenched fists and managed to smile when Morgan returned, strutting like the handsome peacock he was. Let him strut. He might think he'd won, but the victory was hers. She had chosen. Her mind, her decisions, her life was hers.

The Roaring Boar, true to its name, was boisterously noisy as they walked in. The high ceiling was heavily timbered with colorful heat ducts throughout. Above the long polished bar hung a boar's head, looking as though it had charged through the wall.

She grimaced. "I wouldn't want to meet that in a dark alley."

Morgan held her chair. "Looks like the nun who taught me third grade."

She laughed, recalling a quote by Gelett Burgess: *"To appreciate nonsense requires a serious interest in life."* Was Morgan ever serious? Or did he specialize in nonsense?

He eased her chair in. "What are you drinking?"

"Club soda . . . with lime."

He hung his head to the side. "Don't tell me you're underage."

"I'm not."

"On the wagon?"

"I prefer club soda." Nothing to dull her senses and leave her vulnerable. Nothing to weaken her control. Never again.

Morgan sighed. "At least it's not a sanctimonious reason. I'm past my Boy Scout days."

"Did you have any?"

"Very briefly in the hazy past."

Morgan ordered drinks and a Texas brisket on a bun for each of them. "It's the house specialty. They'll serve it in less than a minute with fries to boot."

"Less than a minute?"

"No one orders anything else. If they did, the cooks would personally come out and flog them."

Again she smiled. She wasn't sure how to take Morgan Spencer, but he did amuse her, and his words proved nearly true. She eyed the monstrous sandwich dubiously when it came.

Morgan made a show of spreading his napkin on his lap. "Two hands; dive in. And no raising your pinkie."

Her glare only made him laugh. He was in rare spirits, though she didn't take all the credit. He seemed to feed on the gathering crowd and rowdy atmosphere and the many people who came by their table to chat. He introduced her to more of her neighbors than she had yet met. Was there anyone in the room he didn't know by name?

As they finished eating, the band assembled and tuned, tested the microphones, and practiced riffs on their instruments. Noelle watched them, keenly aware of Morgan watching her. When the band began to play, the room erupted with hoots and cheers. They did a classic bluegrass tune, "Wabash Cannonball," and she felt its fervor grow just like the powerful train it bespoke.

Morgan rubbed his hands. "It's warming up now."

"They're good."

"Come on." Morgan stood and held out his hand. "I'm guessing you dance like an angel."

"Why?"

"The truth?" He led her to the dance floor. "You have the legs for it." He took her hands and broke into a country swing. He was smooth and swift and sure, with an almost liquid motion.

Noelle laughed when he spun her out and back. "I don't know this step."

"You follow like a dream."

"I'm trained in ballroom, ballet, and jazz. But I've never learned country swing."

He spun away and clapped, then grabbed her two hands and pulled them wide, coming chest to chest with her, then back out. "You may not know the moves, but you sure have a natural rhythm."

"Tell my jazz instructor that. She gave up on me. But then, she worked with Broadway hopefuls, and I was not in that league."

"I'd put you in a league all your own, Noelle. At the top of the class."

"I could swear that's a line."

He laughed. "It's true. I have an eye for quality, and you're . . . prime." He caught her down into a dip, and she noted the sharp cut of his Adam's apple and the five o'clock shadow beneath his chin and along his throat. He held her there as the song ended; then the crowd applauded the band and he raised her gently.

She shrugged out of the crook of his arm. "They don't need much warming up."

"Oh, it gets warmer than this." Morgan stood her to his right for the line dance. "Just follow me on this one. It's total insanity."

"Oh no. No, I don't do this. . . . I haven't learned . . ."

He tugged her back. "Forget learning. Just experience." He stepped, kicked and turned, then lifted his foot and "slapped leather" as the song instructed by hitting the side of his shoe. They turned a quarter turn and started over. "You're supposed to wear boots," he called over his shoulder, "but I draw the line there." Still, he was a chameleon, blending into the scene, taking on the mannerisms, the mood around him.

Noelle faked her way through the dance as the line swept her forward and back, three steps to the right and kick, then again to the left. Spin, slap leather, quarter turn, repeat. It wasn't that different from chorus line, but she'd hated that. She blew out her breath, relieved, when it stopped.

The lead singer stepped up to the microphone. "Hey, I want to welcome everybody here tonight. We are gonna have a hand-clappin', boot-stompin' good time, so grab on to your partner and get ready, 'cause we're gonna shake the walls."

The small crowd roared, and more couples filled the floor. Noelle was pressed closer to Morgan than she intended to be, but he kept her on the dance floor the entire first set, teaching her new steps and moves, then stood up to the bar for a shot and a beer. She drank a fresh club soda, then went to the ladies' room, which was relatively clean but cramped and lacking any continuity of color and design. The lavender stalls and crimson tiles made her cringe.

As she washed her hands at the gold-flecked double sink, she glanced at her reflection. Her cheeks were flushed, and strands of hair escaped the reverse French braid. She tucked them in with her fingers, cooled her cheeks with damp palms, shook her hands, and looked for a dryer. She settled for the paper-towel dispenser and went out.

Morgan had his back to the counter, elbows behind him. He watched her cross the room, even while he chatted with the tall brunette beside him. He drained the last half-inch of his beer and set the mug down. "Ready?"

"For what?"

"More hand-clappin', boot-stompin' good times."

"I don't know that I'll survive another set like the last one." Though she had enjoyed the dancing more than she'd expected.

"Well, you're in luck. The second set is different."

"In what way?"

"They open the mic."

"Like karaoke?"

"Live accompaniment." He led her by the elbow back to the table. "They'll play oldies, classic rock, and country. What's your preference?"

"I'd say rock, but I don't want to do it."

She sat down as the lead guitar announced the open mic, but before Morgan took his seat, the crowd started chanting, "Morgan, Morgan, Morgan . . ."

Noelle looked at him in surprise.

"I guess they want me to lead off tonight." He leapt onto the stage and took the microphone. "Good evening, all you gorgeous ladies and *sorry*-lookin' gents."

Boos and hisses and laughter followed.

"You might have noticed I have someone special with me tonight. Give a hello to Noelle St. Claire if you haven't already."

Hoots and whistles. Noelle kept her eyes on Morgan. He turned and spoke to the drummer who raised his sticks and counted out the beat. Then the bass guitar came in. The lead threw back his head and howled, then played backup as Morgan began to sing "Little Red Riding Hood."

His imitation was better than his voice, which wasn't bad. Noelle bit her lip, then laughed behind her hand. Morgan lit the place up. He had real talent, even if he wasn't undiscovered star quality. She glanced around at the laughing, catcalling crowd. How could they help but respond to his antics? And, yes, he made a very believable big, bad wolf. At last he threw his hands into the air to absorb the applause, then jumped off the stage.

Joining her at the table again, he took her hand in his. "What do you think? Carnegie Hall?"

Noelle freed her hand. "Worse have made it. Where did you learn?"

"Learn? As in musical instruction?" He looked amused.

"Yes."

"No instruction. It's kind of a family thing."

"Family? I can't imagine Rick getting up and doing that."

"Oh, you'd be surprised. He can have fun when he wants to." He downed the complimentary shot and raised his glass to the sender, a woman with flaxen braids. "I just do it better."

"Your hubris astounds me."

"No, it doesn't. Anyone who can say 'hubris' with a straight face has a good share of it herself."

She had intended it jokingly, but he hadn't missed a step. As a chunky blonde in tight jeans and a ponytail claimed the mic and began to sing "Austin," Morgan accepted another complimentary shot and beer chaser.

"You're going to look and feel the way you did the other morning."

"Ah, but I've learned the secret to having a good time." He put his lips to her ear. "Never consider the consequences in advance." His eyes were reckless bolts of blue. "Break free of the shackles of restraint and bow to Bacchus and Diana. The possibilities are endless. Let me get you something."

"No thanks." Some possibilities were not worth it.

"Why not?"

She merely shook her head. He sighed and downed the second shot, then led her back to the dance floor. She followed less eagerly. The lights had dimmed, and he drew her close as the band played and the blonde sang, not too poorly, the heartbreak strains of the Western love song.

He rubbed his cheek against her hair. "You smell nice."

She turned her face away.

"You're not easily romanced, are you?"

"I'm not interested."

He laughed. "Don't break it to me gently, Noelle. Just say it as it is." He stroked her cheek with his fingertips. "Oh, lady, you feel good."

She stiffened. "It's getting late."

"*Au contraire*, mademoiselle, the night is as young as you are beautiful."

She fought the panic as she pulled free of his arms. "Why don't you ask someone else to dance?"

Rejection flickered in his eyes, but he shrugged. "Okay." He seated her, ran his hand along her shoulders, and left. Her tension eased as he found a willing partner. More than willing. The woman with the flaxen braids. Morgan talked, and the woman laughed. He whispered, and she leaned close. He held her heart in his hands in those few moments alone. He might not be dangerous in the typical sense, but there were many kinds of peril.

Noelle traced her finger around the edge of the cocktail napkin. An ice cube popped in her glass, and she studied the pale green cells of the lime. When she looked up, another woman hung on Morgan's arm, even before he released the first.

Rudy, from the general store, leaned over her table with a smile. "Want to dance?"

She shook her head. "Thanks, but I'm leaving now." She got up and went out into the night. After a week of traipsing up and down from the town to the ranch, she knew the way, but once past the glow of the old-fashioned street lamps, she was amazed by the density of the darkness.

She looked up. No moon. A shiver ran down her back. She glanced over her shoulder at the Roaring Boar, still roaring, then sighed and started up the gravel road. By the crunch of gravel and the ridge of tufted grass, she knew the edge and kept inside it.

The darkness was almost tangible, giving the illusion of substance, and she stopped suddenly, reaching out to touch what appeared to be there. All her senses probed the darkness, but her hand slid through empty air. Nothing, only her mind playing tricks. She licked the dryness from her lips.

Suddenly from her left, a huge beast leapt onto the road before her, and she had just time to make out the shape of an elk before it bounded down the other side. Her heart pounded in her ears as she stood frozen. "Just an elk!" she gasped. "Just an elk. Morgan, I could shoot you!"

She thrust forward, anger replacing the fear. She climbed until she felt the grade cease, then, cresting the rise, saw the lights of the ranch below. Relief washed over her. She had made it back alone, once again proving her independence, and Morgan Spencer could roar all night at the Boar for all she cared.

She opened the door softly and stepped inside. The mellow golden light of a single lamp warmed her. Beside it, Rick sat on the hearth in the great room, head bent as he softly picked an acoustic guitar. He played, unaware of her presence, with a tender yet compelling mien, his fingers deft on the strings, urging the melody from wood and steel and singing softly.

So he *was* musical. She had only half believed Morgan. Rick's voice was deeper, and she was strangely moved, though she couldn't catch the words that sounded like *Selah, Selah* . . . It was more the mood of it. She tried to imagine Rick on the stage like Morgan and failed. There was something too . . . intimate, too private, in what he did. She felt like an intruder.

Looking up, he stopped, but there was no embarrassment. "Where's Morgan?"

"He wasn't ready to leave." Rather than stand there looking as awkward as she felt, Noelle sat down on the couch across from him. "I thought you'd be sleeping." He was definitely the early to bed, early to rise sort, and she'd hoped to sneak in with no one aware of her predicament.

"I wasn't sure you'd make it home in one piece."

He'd waited up for her? She wasn't sure what to make of that.

"Did you walk back?"

"Yes."

He frowned. "Morgan should know better than that."

"He was occupied when I left." She hooded her eyes to hide the annoyance. He probably would have seen her home, but she hadn't wanted to break up his fan club. "I didn't know you played."

"I don't get it out much until winter." He slipped the strap from his neck.

"It was beautiful—what you were playing."

"Thanks."

She wanted to ask him to play more but couldn't gather the courage. He shut the case and tucked the instrument into the closet. "Guess I'll call it a night."

"What about Morgan?"

"He'll find his way. Do you need anything?"

"No, thank you." Looking after him, she mused that he'd handled the guitar with the same strong gentleness as he did Destiny. He was an anomaly; on the one hand hard and immovable, on the other almost vulnerable.

She didn't wonder about his musical training. She recalled the professor's words to her. Rick was no trained animal. He tapped something deeper than notes on a page. He brought music from inside himself.

Why, then, did he do it all alone with no one to appreciate it? Or was that really such a mystery? Didn't she also perform her best when no human eyes were there to judge, no other ear to approve or disapprove? Wasn't there joy in the act itself?

A longing awakened in her, one she'd ignored these last weeks. It throbbed in her chest with each beat of her heart. Music was one thing she'd left behind with regret, one thing she missed. Looking around with a feeling of displacement, she sighed.

It didn't matter. All she needed was shelter and anonymity. The rest was trappings. She left the lamp on and went upstairs, closed and locked her door. Tension still knotted the tendons in the back of her neck, and she reached back and rubbed it out.

It wasn't just the trek through the dark and the fright from the elk. It was Morgan's arms around her as they danced and the brush of his fingers on her cheek. She pressed her eyes shut and clenched her hands. She had handled it. She was in control. But the shakes came anyway.

# 7

N oelle entered the stable late the next morning. She had slept in
for the first time since arriving at the ranch and felt a little groggy
because of that. Rick had the string horses stabled and was grooming
them. She leaned on the stall. "Is something happening?"

"I have a group coming up to ride." He drew the rubber-toothed
currycomb across the horse's hide with swift, gentle strokes, working
the loose hair out and leaving its sides shining and sleek. "If you're
wondering, Morgan made it in last night. Late."

"At least my leaving didn't spoil his party."

"Nothing spoils Morgan's party."

She stepped into the stall and laced her fingers in the horse's mane.
"You're not very much alike."

He ran the brush down the wither and foreleg. "Nope."

She stroked the mare's head as he curried. "There are similarities,
though. Features, mannerisms, though you're more . . . purposeful."

"Is that right." Rick leaned an arm on the horse's back and eyed
her.

"And you both have a certain sideways grin—see, there it is now."
She enjoyed his discomfiture as he dropped his head and worked a
tangle from the mane.

"You're observant."

"My art instructor had me sit for hours doing nothing but scruti-
nizing details. If I was painting a still life, he'd have me observe each

flower's center, feel the texture of the petals, note the rigidity in each stem. Then he'd seat me at a distance where none of those things could be seen. But I had internalized my subject, and he believed I could then capture it more fully on paper."

"Could you?"

"With varying proficiency."

He nodded. "You still learned something valuable."

"What?"

"To see what's around you."

It surprised her that he would consider that valuable. He seemed too practical to value observation for its own sake.

"I kept Aldebaran for you." He hung the comb on the wall. "Should I saddle you up?"

"No thanks. I'm going to town this morning. Unless, of course—" she gave him her most entreating smile—"you want to saddle Destiny for me."

"Nice try." He smiled back, flashing white teeth, even except for one lower tooth that crowded forward. There was nothing smug in the smile, only unrelenting stubbornness—and a dose of amusement.

She shook her head and went out. Pausing at the stable door, she glanced back over her shoulder and found him still watching. He wasn't ogling, just watching with that look she didn't understand.

In the house, she lifted the stack of watercolors she had selected as her best. The case was still in Morgan's trunk, so she carried them loose to town. The tourist section displayed T-shirts, bumper stickers, and ceramic curios; some, as Morgan had aptly described, so crass or tacky they made her cringe. The best sported mountains, pine trees, aspen leaves, and the fragile purple columbines with gold-lettered COLORADO to differentiate them from other states' knickknacks.

Then she approached the fine arts gallery she had seen when searching out rental possibilities. The door stood open. Paintings displayed on walls and easels surrounded sculptures and pottery that showed some promise and imagination. Would her watercolors join their ranks? Noelle drew a deep breath and went in. "Ms. Walker?"

The woman stood up from behind the counter and tugged her fuchsia blouse down over her ample belly. It was probably a rayon blend, but she'd produced enough static to make it cling. Her sandals squeaked as she walked around.

Ms. Walker was a far cry from the stately gallery owners to which she was accustomed, but Noelle hid her thoughts. Too much rested on this contact. "I'm Noelle St. Claire. I've brought the paintings we discussed."

"Let's have a look." Ms. Walker tongued her gum between her side teeth and cheek.

Noelle set her work on the counter. She'd had her talent acclaimed by friends, fellow students, and instructors, and she had the professor's opinion. But she'd never had it appraised for sale, never needed a commercial value assigned to her art. Now so much hung on this . . . eccentric woman's opinion.

Ms. Walker raised the bifocals that hung by a tropical-print cord around her neck. One by one, she scrutinized the paintings. "Hmm. I like your use of color and light. You do catch the mood."

Noelle's hope piqued. She knew what original watercolors cost. She'd purchased some that inspired experimentation and improvement of her own style. But that was before she'd ever considered making a living by it. And those were New York galleries.

"I'll tell you what, I'll frame these six, and we'll see how they do. It's a fifty-fifty split minus the cost of the frame."

Fifty-fifty seemed low, but she nodded. It was a starting point, to see if she actually could support herself with her art. The town population would not be a sufficient customer base, but the continuous influx of shoppers—bus people, as Morgan called them—were her hope.

She signed the consignment agreement, then walked out of the shop and looked down the quaint main street with a sense of partnership. She was represented now among the ranks of residents and businesses. One more step toward independence. With her steps lightened, she fairly ran up the road.

When she reached the top of the rise over the ranch, Noelle threw her arms up and laughed. If these paintings sold, it would be the first independently profitable thing she had ever done—monetarily, at least. And the cash she still kept secreted in her makeup bag no longer limited her.

For the first time, she thought past that day, past tomorrow. She felt certain the paintings would sell, certain her efforts would be rewarded. She scanned the mountains around her. Could she make a life for herself away from what she'd known before? She had been thinking in temporary terms; now she could make it permanent. The ranch as her home? Why not?

She strode swiftly toward the ranch. There were things she needed if this was to be home, more clothing certainly. It was laughable how she'd managed with what she'd brought. And there must be better art stores in Denver. She had the skill, and now she had the outlet. If she meant to take it seriously, pursue art as a profession, better brushes, paint, and paper would make a difference.

She stopped outside the house and looked up at its solid log walls, the porch like arms crossed around its heart. Yes. As her paintings sold, she would renew her cash and make a life for herself. When one of the cabins became available, it could be her own place. She walked inside, heady with anticipated success. All she needed now was transportation. She started upstairs, then heard Marta scolding in the kitchen and went that way instead.

Hunched over his coffee at the kitchen table, Morgan groaned. "Leave off, Marta. I feel bad enough as it is."

It seemed Bacchus and Diana were having their revenge. Recalling her fright last night, Noelle tried not to gloat. She needed a favor, and Morgan was her best bet, though she wasn't sure yet whether guilt or charm would serve her better.

As she stood undecided, he reached up and took her hand. "A thousand apologies for not seeing you home."

Guilt, then. "It'll take a thousand after the fright that elk gave me in the dark."

He winced. "Sorry."

"However, I'm feeling magnanimous."

"You are?" He glanced up.

"Celebratory, actually. Ms. Walker accepted my work on consignment." She removed her hand from his grip.

Rick walked in behind her. "What work is that?"

Noelle turned. "Paintings."

Rick headed for the sink, ran his hands under the water. "Marta, where's that lemonade you promised?"

"In the refrigerator."

He toweled his hands. "Ms. Walker doesn't have the best reputation, Noelle. You sure you want to do business with her?"

"It's the only fine arts gallery in town."

"So what if she's a charlatan." Morgan rubbed his temple. "More unholy alliances have proved fruitful."

"Exactly." Noelle smiled and watched it penetrate his fog. She had him right where she needed him. "And I have a favor to ask."

"Anything." He again captured her hand.

"I want to borrow your car."

"Anything but that."

She sat down on the bench beside him. "Morgan, I need to shop. Some real stores."

"Real stores."

"In Denver, I assume. I need clothes and art supplies." She glanced at Rick. Maybe she should have tried for his truck.

Morgan toyed with her hand. "Well, I owe you one. I'll drive you down."

That wasn't what she'd planned. "If I could just borrow—"

"I love you, baby, but you can't take my car." Morgan released his grip and pressed a palm to his forehead. "Just give me a chance to kill this headache."

Noelle wasn't at all sure she wanted to get back into the car with Morgan—certainly not spend the day with him. The helplessness of her situation crashed in again. She was no freer than she'd been. But that would change. She would change it. Somehow.

Rick leaned against the counter with his glass of lemonade. "Don't make her walk home this time."

Morgan scowled. "I don't need a lecture from you."

"You might do well to listen to your *younger* brother." Marta snatched his mug and swiped a cloth over the table. "If you had half his sense and twice your conscience—"

Morgan suddenly stood and took Noelle by the arm. "Let's get out of here."

But she stopped at the stairs. "Just a minute." Though she had credit cards in her wallet, she would not use them. She ran up, took money from the floral bag, and went back down. He ushered her out the door, and she resolutely climbed into the Corvette, understanding his reluctance to lend the vehicle. She never had driven winding mountain roads, had actually driven her own car very infrequently. The limo had been more convenient.

"*John, I'll need the car brought around at two. Sheila, see that my dress is pressed by four. Daddy, I'll have dinner in the library.*" She cringed. That wasn't life. It was some sort of fairy tale. Daddy had built a tower and put her in it. Only he'd given the key to . . . Noelle pressed her eyes shut and drew a long breath.

"You okay?" Morgan reached across and fastened her seat belt.

"Yes." Whatever she encountered in this world could hardly be worse than the nightmare flashes of whatever happened before. But that was over now. She had both the means and the will to adapt and make this life her own. No more fear, though Morgan's driving kept her on the edge. She didn't know whether his head had stopped throbbing, but it was certainly clear enough to drive with intensity. He seemed relaxed and confident, but she was used to their chauffer. Morgan downshifted for the grade but slowed very little. Well, she had asked for it.

He said, "Let's see a little of the city."

Classic Morgan. But it wouldn't hurt to expand her knowledge. If Denver was the nearest major city, she ought to know it a little at least. "All right."

They drove an hour and a half down, toured the city, walked through downtown, shopped some stores and boutiques, and had lunch. Though nice enough, Denver was hardly awe-inspiring.

As though he'd read her mind, Morgan said, "It's not the Big Apple."

She didn't want it to be. That was the old life. This was new, different. She was too. "It has its own character."

"Every city does, I guess."

They located an art store, and though they were not cheap, she bought a substantial supply of quality materials, unsure when she would get down there again. Then he drove her to a mall and parked in a far space of the covered lot, where he no doubt hoped to avoid dings on his doors. She had rarely shopped in malls, preferring boutiques and catalogues and even more exclusive shops that created one-of-a-kind designs.

But she wasn't buying that sort of clothes, and it was heady to think of shopping from a rack, ordinary clothes for ordinary people. It took some getting used to. But four hours later, she handed Morgan another bag and started for the next store.

He caught her arm. "Noelle, you look gorgeous in everything you've bought"—which wasn't so much considering everything she'd tried— "but I've paid my debt."

She had hardly thought about him, except when she'd pirouetted in the triple mirrors and caught his appreciative looks. She hadn't intended to torture him, but he was obviously exasperated, something one of her chaperones would never have shown. But then, Morgan wasn't in Daddy's employ.

He spread his hands. "What is it with women and shopping? How can changing clothes three thousand times in four hours put such a shine in your eyes?"

She smiled. Maybe now they were even. "I just want to look—"

"No." He took her hand. "Why don't we have dinner and catch a movie."

She tensed at the earnest look in his eyes, the touch of his hand. A shard of panic shot through her and must have shown.

Morgan tucked his chin. "Look, I'm sorry I came on to you last night. You are a little piece of perfect, but it won't happen again. Let's just make a night of it and enjoy ourselves."

She'd gotten what she needed; now he was exacting payment. But she owed him nothing. She pulled her hand away. "I think we parked on the west side. We should get up the mountain before dark." Especially if his night driving was as intense as the rest.

"Before dark? You turn into a pumpkin?" He cocked his head.

She started walking.

He caught up and hooked an arm over her shoulders. "Come on, Noelle. I deserve something for all this."

She shrugged him off.

"Dinner and a show."

"No thanks." She quickened her step.

"We'll miss Marta's meal anyway."

She slowed. He was right, and she'd hardly touched her lunch, an overcooked chicken breast sandwich with a nasty sauce they passed off as southwestern ranch.

"We'll compromise. There's a place up the canyon toward Juniper Falls."

"Let me guess, barbecue brisket that's to die for."

"Authentic Bavarian cuisine."

She looked away, tempted against her better judgment. But now that he'd mentioned it, her mouth watered. "It's on the way back?"

"It is."

"Is it far?"

"Nowhere near what we've walked."

She eyed him dubiously. Last night had shown her all she needed to know.

"My best behavior. Scout's honor." He held up the Boy Scout fingers, but his eyes were mischievous.

"You said you'd put that behind you."

"I can resurrect it."

She looked into his persuasive face. He was used to succeeding, she could tell. But he had been a patient and amusing companion, had given up his day for her. "Okay, we'll make an *evening* of it."

He clasped both hands over his heart. "Have I ever exulted so?"

"Probably." She started to walk, but he caught her arm.

"Duck into a dressing room and put on that wine-colored dress."

The only dress she had purchased, and as she recalled, Morgan had pulled it off the rack. Intending for her to wear it with him? "What about you?"

"I've got slacks and a jacket in the car."

She frowned. He carried a change of clothes in his car?

He raised scout fingers again. "Be prepared."

Nothing surprised her anymore.

Morgan checked his watch. "I'll take what you don't need to the car and meet you back here in fifteen minutes. That leaves no time for browsing."

She sighed. "Fine." The nearest dressing room was probably the one she had just left, so she went back there and put on the sleeveless burgundy dress. The scoop neck revealed her collarbones and sternum, and the soft fabric molded to her shape, before falling just above the knee. It was more than flattering; it was inviting. Exactly what Morgan didn't need, but she should have thought of that before she bought it. She removed the tags and dropped them into the bag, then found the nylons and heels she'd bought to match.

Where had she thought she would use it all? She hadn't. She'd just shopped. But Morgan had probably planned it. She had a sudden inspiration. He'd said fifteen minutes, but she'd go fast. Putting her other clothes into the bag, she went out and quickly searched the racks. Just something to—There, the rose blouse with soft ruffled sleeves. Not perfect, but it would do. She snatched a size small from the rack and carried it to the checkout counter.

He must be waiting by now. She paid for the blouse, had the clerk remove the tags, then stood in the three-way mirror and put it on over the dress, tying it at the waist. No *Vogue* statement, but less revealing by far.

She went to meet Morgan. He waited in khaki slacks and the golf shirt he'd worn down, a navy sports coat and garment bag over his arm. He really did keep a dressy casual change in the car. Obviously prepared for his opportunities. What was she doing? He raised his brows and said, "What's with the blouse?"

"You like it? Good."

He took her bags without further comment. After stuffing the rest of her packages into the trunk, they left Denver behind. The Edelweiss Chalet was not far up the canyon. It perched on the edge of a shallow, stony creek, a portion of which pooled into a circular pond. Spotlights sent rays from the footbridge across the water, and at the edge, Canada geese and ducks squatted with their heads under their wings for the night.

With the pine tree shutters, gingerbread trim, and stony mountain canyon surroundings, the restaurant did look Bavarian. "You weren't kidding about authentic."

"Nope." Morgan climbed out and slipped his suit coat on.

"Maybe they'll have an accordion playing 'oompah.' " She giggled.

He went around and opened her door. "I'll have him serenade you."

"You mean you won't do it yourself? How disappointing. No kara-oke accordion."

He gave her a hand out. "I have my limits."

"*Really.*"

"Really." He caught her elbow and led her in.

The room was packed with tables, red-and-white chintz curtains on the windows, giant beer steins along the walls—and a stocky accordion player at the far end rocking the flexible side of his instrument as his fingers played.

Morgan leaned close and whispered, " 'Beer Barrel Polka.' Wanna dance?" He pinched her elbow with a wry grin as a wide-hipped woman showed them past the old couple cheek-to-cheek on the tiny dance floor to a table near the window overlooking the pond.

The hostess's ample bosom was tightly confined by her stiff white blouse, perhaps accounting for her pained expression. "Enjoy your dinners." She stood their menus on the table but her face never changed. Noelle refused the bait in Morgan's expression as he seated her.

"Now, *fraulein*, we'll pretend this is a *biergarten* in the Tyrol, guzzle a stein or two, and enjoy the oompah."

"All but the stein or two."

Morgan took his seat. "*Weiner schnitzel* without beer is like cake without icing, cream without sugar, day without—"

"Then have beer with your schnitzel, but remember we have to make it up the canyon. I'm not walking."

"I tell you what. I'll be responsible and you . . ."

Noelle opened the menu. "What would you recommend?"

"I have no clue, but we'd better be ready when *Frau* Sauerkraut returns, or else."

Noelle hid her laughter with the menu. "She's not a server, only the maître d'."

"Look around you."

She did. The two buxom waitresses in German costume were very similar in shape, if less daunting in demeanor.

Morgan's mouth pulled sideways. "It's a family operation."

Rolling her lips inward against the smile, Noelle set down her menu. "I won't be able to face any of them now. You order for us, and I'm going to the ladies' room."

He sat back. "Lose the blouse while you're in there."

She walked into the bright, twin-stalled ladies' room. After washing up, she stood at the counter and untied the knot of the blouse. It was really about trust. Her pulse throbbed. She held the ends apart and stared into the mirror, then tied them up again. Morgan would be disappointed.

She squared her shoulders and wound her way back to the table. His indulgent smile showed he had expected her refusal. So why did he push her? She looked down and saw the menus were gone from the table. "What did you order me?"

"Tripe and brains."

She shook her head as he stood and held her chair.

He ran his hand up her back and briefly squeezed the nape of her neck. "I took the fraulein's suggestion for the night's special, *Jaeger Schnitzel* with *spaetzle* and red cabbage." He raised one eyebrow. "I thought it prudent."

She laughed again and something hard softened inside. She didn't need to know what, just allow it.

Riding up the canyon after dinner, she relaxed in the soft leather seat, warm and drowsy. In all, she had enjoyed the day very much, certainly more than the one before. Morgan was indeed a chameleon. He'd been true to his word, no remnant of the raucous cowboy, and he hadn't come on to her at all.

"Penny for your thoughts," he said.

She turned his way and smiled. "I was thinking I had a nice time with you."

"I had a nice time with you too, Noelle."

It was dark when they reached the ranch, the sky pierced with stars. He let her out and went around to the trunk. She had actually made a haul, she noticed as he unloaded the bags, handing her the first few so he could carry the rest. She went ahead of him to the porch and climbed the stairs.

He stopped her at the door, setting his load down. "What's the hurry?"

Recognizing the routine, she kept hold of her bags. "Thank you for driving me down, Morgan. And for dinner."

"You're welcome. Did you notice the stars?"

"I watched them all the way up." She couldn't help glancing again, then caught herself. "Would you mind opening the door?"

He gave a quick laugh. "Sure. I'll even carry up your bags. No tip required."

CHAPTER

"You're not concentrating, Michael. It's not like you to let a detail slip that can cost us so badly." William frowned.

"I'm sorry, sir. I don't know how I could have overlooked that exhibit."

William sat back in his chair. They were both wearing thin. Their client, the celebrated target of a defense department investigation, was furious they'd slipped up. William cared little for that. *He* was furious himself they'd slipped up. If he had to lose a case, it should be on the merit of the prosecution, not his own failure.

"I have no excuse, William. I missed it."

William nodded. He far preferred such an admission to any number of plausible excuses, the top one being Noelle's continued absence and the pain that was causing Michael Fallon. Though they hadn't discussed her disappearance in the last week, he saw the strain, knew it was on both their minds. And it shouldn't be. Not with a case going bad as this one was. "What do we have left?"

"Ilse Blandon."

William scowled. "They'll tear her to shreds."

"She's Smythe's only alibi."

"And you and I both know it's full of holes. I don't like holes."

"I don't either." Michael's face was earnest. "But since I missed the receipt, I have no choice. Let me examine her. I can make her sympathetic to the jury, William."

"I've no doubt. The problem is the cross-examination will anni-hilate whatever you do."

"Not if she's prepared."

William pressed his palms to the desk. "I'm sure you don't mean to tamper with the witness."

"Of course not." His eyes, however, said that was exactly what he meant.

"Michael." William eased back in his chair. "Sit down."

"Sir." Michael took the chair.

"There are two hard and fast rules in this firm. The first is we don't lose. The second is we don't cross lines. Do you understand me?"

"Yes, sir. We win."

His brazen misinterpretation amused William. "We win within the parameters." He stood and walked around the desk. "We can cut a deal."

"No." Michael paced. "Smythe is my responsibility."

William pursed his lips. "Our constitution says he's innocent. Make Farrar prove otherwise, Michael."

"Then let me make Ilse sing." Michael's eyes took on a sharp ferocity.

"Make her sing without tampering. Parameters, Michael, let us sleep at night."

Michael released a sharp breath. "You're right, William. It's only that . . . I blame myself."

"We all might have missed it. It happens."

Michael sat without answering, still made no excuses. Then he stood up, nodded, and went out.

Michael was intense. That was a great advantage, but William wondered sometimes if the fire inside might one day consume the young man. He hoped his words had found their mark. Knowing that they did everything according to the law was the only means to peace in this business.

Michael hated facing William St. Claire with his failure. Anyone might have missed it? Not William St. Claire. No detail escaped the senior partner—not a travel account receipt that put the defendant at a place he shouldn't have been at a time that matched the testimony of the prosecution's main witness.

William would not have missed it. Never. Yet he had not blamed, and for that Michael was supremely grateful. His failure with Noelle had been hard enough to bring to William, but if he failed professionally too . . . Not after he'd worked so hard! *Parameters*.

He pressed his eyes shut. He prided himself on knowing William's mind, matching his will to the older man's, reaping his wisdom and cunning. But this time, losing would be his fault alone. And lose they would, unless he could make the jury believe . . .

Winning was not an end; it was a means. And Michael did not really care whether he slept at night. He couldn't fail William, not now, not after Noelle. Even more than he craved Noelle, he needed William's acclaim. If he were careful, so very careful that not even William suspected . . . Michael headed for his office. He needed to think, to think hard.

———

"Three paintings sold, Morgan." Noelle could not keep the news to herself as she strode into the patisserie and found him at the counter.

"Bravo." He turned, clapping without sound, then motioned her ahead of him in line.

"In just two weeks, I've found success."

He leaned his hip to the counter. "Were you lacking it before?"

"You don't understand—you couldn't." She'd been afraid to check with Ms. Walker at the two-week mark. But she'd girded herself and gone in. And three of the paintings were gone, the sales verified by Ms. Walker and the percentage paid in cash at her request. Ms. Walker had hemmed, but Noelle convinced her to pay cash with as little explanation as she could manage.

She pointed to two flaky croissants in the glass case, then held a hand up to Morgan. "Don't take out your wallet. I'm buying."

He chuckled. "By all means. Now tell me what I don't understand."

Noelle handed one croissant on waxed paper to Morgan, paid the girl, then took the other and turned. "This is totally new." She headed for the patio. "This is the first time, the first thing I've done that . . . well, that earned money."

Laughing, Morgan held her chair. "And you're just full of it, aren't you? I see dollar signs in your eyes."

"It's not that, it's . . . it's not even the money; it's that I did it myself." Noelle took a long breath. She couldn't make Morgan understand what this meant to her. He would have to know how things had been, how she'd been, how different and alien she was from all of this—to be sitting with him now in this Rocky Mountain place with cash she'd earned in her pocket.

The sunlight warmed the butcher-block table where they sat, but the mountain breeze was cool. Where else did the air feel so fresh? She bit into the croissant, savored its buttery richness, and enjoyed having Morgan there to share the moment.

He pulled the end from his roll, leaving fluffy tatters dangling from his fingers. "Supposing I know nothing about the headiness of success, what is it you feel most?"

Noelle sent her gaze across the street to the small church perched above an ancient stone wall. "I feel safe."

"Safe?" He hunched forward. "Now, that's not what I expected."

"What did you expect?" She dabbed the corner of her mouth with the scalloped edge of the paper napkin.

"Proud. Hungry. Invincible." He squinted one eye. "Safe?"

Noelle lingered over her bite, unsure herself why she'd chosen that word. "I wasn't sure I could do this, make it on my own, with no one's help. But I can." She met his eyes. "I can find myself."

"And that's safe? Trust me, you might not like what you find."

She studied the handsome lines of his face, softened by fewer late nights and more fresh air. Did he dislike what he saw in himself? She supposed that was true of everyone to some degree. She might disappoint herself as well. But it didn't matter. "For the first time I can be whatever I want."

He matched her gaze and held it. "Is it that easy?"

"Now that I'm free."

"Free?" He snorted. "Now, that's naïve."

She sat back and toyed with the edge of the napkin. "Not if every moment of my life has been scheduled with tutors and charity events and one function after another. Imagine being guarded at parties and chauffeured everywhere and told with whom to speak and whom to avoid. Every breath you take and every step monitored and controlled."

His expression told her she'd said more than she intended. "Go on."

Dropping her eyes to her croissant, she kicked herself. "That's all."

"Come on, now. You've been here almost a month and that's the most I've had from you." His smile was coaxing, but his eyes probed deeper.

She should have known better than to put Morgan on the scent. Unlike Rick, who respected her privacy, Morgan kept nosing, prodding, cajoling. *So tell us, Ms. St. Claire, about your celebrated father and all the high profile cases he's won. Tell about the bodyguards, the bevy of servants, the privileges you've had to replace a normal life. Share what it's like to grow up with your friends handpicked and scrutinized, your dates . . .* Her heart slammed her ribs. She started to shake.

Morgan leaned back in his chair. "That makes me crazy, you know. Here I've been the picture of responsibility. And I'm not getting anywhere with you."

Her throat tightened. It was her own fault. She had let the surprise of her success take her off guard, and Morgan was too savvy to miss the chance. Why did he have to ruin the moment? She pushed her chair back from the table. "There's nowhere to get."

"There might be if you'd give it half a chance."

She stood and walked off the patio. His chair scraped as he scrambled to follow.

"Hey." He caught her arm as she started up the street.

She shook him off. "I don't want a relationship."

He caught her elbow again. "Fine. There's nothing like a relationship to ruin a good time."

Always glib. A line for everything. Suddenly he seemed as flimsy as the men who pandered to her father. He was nothing more than a shell, an actor playing a part. He was nothing. She kept walking.

"Okay." His voice softened. "I'm sorry I asked. It's just . . . you've gotten to me."

She didn't like the change in his tone. It was honest, free of bravado. She didn't want to hear the real Morgan. She didn't want to think of him as anything but the half-crazy ne'er-do-well he seemed. She turned up the gravel road.

"Ah, come on." He slung his arm over her shoulder. "You don't have to play hard to get. I'm easy. I'll marry you, diamonds and all."

An image hit her hard, a diamond ring, slipped from her finger into a velvet box. Her stomach knotted, and she yanked herself free. "Don't ever say that again, Morgan. Not even in jest. Just leave me alone."

She spun and left him standing in the street. Every part of her shook, and the depth of the emotion terrified her. Where had it come from, this fury, this . . . engulfing panic? She didn't care how hurt Morgan was. She didn't want him to want her. She never asked him to. Marry her? Diamonds and all? She pictured her finger again with a stone the size of a marble, then closed her eyes against the memory.

She couldn't look. She had reveled in confidence just moments ago, felt new, changed. And Morgan had swept it away. No, not Morgan. She'd done it herself, opened a past she couldn't look at yet, couldn't consider. Noelle clenched her fists and kept walking. Her breath came quick and short, as it had her first trip up that road.

Panic accented it. Her hamstrings burned, but she kept walking past the house and on up the meadow. She wished she could walk to the edge of the world and step off. She wished she could walk right out of herself. Every time she found safety, freedom, happiness, something brought her back.

She gripped her arms around herself to stop the trembling and kept walking. Endorphins released by the exertion slowly eased the panic as she approached the corral in the high pasture, huffing.

It appeared the colt was in a temper today. She winced as Rick landed hard in the dirt. Destiny hadn't done that for a while, but part of her didn't blame him. Why should he be forced to follow Rick's commands? Though she herself had wanted to ride the horse, she saw it differently now.

Rick stood up slowly and slapped the dust from his jeans. With a hand to his lower back, he limped forward. He obviously meant to get back on. She had to hand it to him. He was determined. Destiny reared, then circled. Rick waited.

She came up to the fence. "Maybe you should leave him alone."

He didn't turn, kept his eyes on the horse. "Can't. Especially now. If I leave it at this, he'll figure throwing me's the way to win." He walked slowly toward the horse. Destiny back-stepped and snorted.

"Come on, boy. Come on."

The colt tossed his head. Noelle wanted him to buck, to kick, to run for his freedom. She wanted him to break through and fly to the mountains. His sides quivered. He whinnied, then put his nose into Rick's outstretched hand.

*No. Don't give up. Don't surrender. Stay free.*

"That-a-boy." Rick ran his hands over the stallion's neck and got hold of the reins. He slowly pulled them tight until he had control. Then he swung back up and the stallion sidestepped but didn't rear.

Noelle's heart sank. Maybe there was no escape.

"I'm going to ride him down, let him run it out. Can you get the gate?"

She worked the loop loose and pulled open the gate. Rick thundered down the meadow, giving Destiny his head. She couldn't tell which of them was more determined and guessed it was a toss-up. But they couldn't keep it that way; one's determination would destroy the other's.

She plodded back down, spent and cross. Rick was rubbing the horse down by the time she got to the stable. Destiny's coat shone over his smooth musculature, and he held his neck arched. It seemed Rick had dominated but left him his dignity. Maybe that's all there was.

She let Destiny snuffle her hand, feeling a desperate kinship. "He's amazing."

"That's why I've babied him so long. I don't usually put up with so much, but this one . . . he's special. One in a million." His love for the horse was in his voice. But if he loved Destiny, how could he bear to break his will?

"You're not going to sell him, are you?"

Rick shook his head. "I have too much pain invested."

What about Destiny's pain? If she rode him she'd give him his head, let him have his way, let him fly with her wherever he wished. Maybe she'd even let him go. She stroked the horse's nose. "I know I could—"

"Forget it. You saw what he did today."

Rick spoke calmly, but she snapped back, "You're awfully stubborn."

He looked up from the horse with his serious brown eyes trained on her. "And you're awfully persistent. But you're not going to ride this horse."

Turning, she stalked out, anger again surging inside. She shook her head, battling the irrational emotion, and crossed to the house. She quickly mounted the stairs and slammed her door behind her before dropping to the bed. Hands pressed to her face, she breathed deeply but found no relief.

Rick was impossible! And Morgan was too. He didn't show up for dinner, which was a strained affair, and if he came in at all that night it was after she slept—though it was a long while before she was able to.

Rick sat quietly before the Lord. It was one of those mornings he felt truly close; no questioning, no doubt about the sovereign presence of God. The awesome glory, the saving grace—as always he was humbled by it. Those moments were a gift he didn't take lightly. But it surprised him to have it come now.

He'd been distracted, busy. His thoughts were scattered, most of them landing on Noelle. She'd been irrationally testy the day before. Again he'd viewed her brittle edge. What was she doing in Juniper Falls? Why did she seem so . . . needy?

What did she need? And what was it to him? Why he felt responsible, he couldn't say. But he did. Morgan would laugh to hear that. Rick frowned.

Morgan had not come in last night. He guessed his brother and Noelle had fallen out, though if there was much of a relationship to fall out from he hadn't seen it. For Morgan to go so long with such little result was a novelty. Rick repented the thought. In the presence of God he had no right to think badly of his brother. He looked up to the rafters of the small wooden chapel and admitted he had no right any time. Morgan was who he was, and it would take an act of God to change that—as was necessary to change his own wayward ways.

They were all flawed. Rick pressed his back to the wooden pew and closed his eyes. He liked these moments before anyone else arrived. He had considered the priesthood for a time. But he'd never been sure, not sure enough to pursue it. Now he worshiped God in this small chapel with an assorted body of believers.

A traveling priest made the rounds once a month, and the other weeks Pastor Tom held services. They were a small enough congregation to come together in spite of their differences. For each one, the relationship was personal. Christ was real; serving Him, joy. Even his everyday work, raising horses and tending his land, Rick dedicated to God's service. It was a good life in spite of its worries.

His thoughts strayed again. And this time he let them go. Who was Noelle St. Claire? What did she need, what did she want? Why was she there—to provide Morgan a distraction? If Morgan wasn't careful, he'd get in deeper than he wanted to. Or was this time different?

Rick drew a slow breath. It wasn't his business. But it felt like it was. *What do you want from me, Lord? Show me your will.* The strongest longing in him was to serve God with the heart of David. His Savior was so real at times it made everything else dim. So why did Noelle continue to shine? He closed his eyes and prayed, *Keep me from impure thoughts. Whatever is true, whatever is noble, whatever is right, whatever is pure, whatever is lovely* . . . But that was part of the problem. His thoughts sprang right back where they'd been.

" 'I can do everything through him who gives me strength,' " he murmured. He just needed to believe it.

———

Noelle woke up late, as cross and tired as when she'd lain down. Her sense of belonging had deserted her. As she dressed in jean shorts and a collared tee, she looked around the Spartan room with distaste. It made her Manhattan apartment look like a penthouse. The whole thing would have fit into her walk-through closet in Daddy's guest bungalow, not to mention the estate house itself. She sank to the bed and dropped her face to her hands. What was she doing anyway?

She took up her brush and ran it through her hair until it shone, then walked to the small mirror, tipped up her jaw, and examined her profile. She smiled bleakly. She had her mother's beauty. Nothing would change that, though gift or curse she wasn't sure. What if she could walk into a room without heads turning? If men didn't want to own her, control her—her throat tightened—destroy her? She shook her head. That was paranoid. Who was trying to destroy her?

She quickly braided her hair and went out. The house was quiet. No humming, no bustle. She realized it was Sunday, Marta's day off. She went into the kitchen and stopped short.

Morgan sat at the table, seemingly calm and alert, no sign of a hangover. He didn't say anything but poured a second cup of coffee and handed it to her. Had she misread him yesterday? Maybe his comments had been nothing, her reaction ridiculous, an emotional extreme.

She took the cup silently, avoiding his gaze as she sat down across from him. What was there to say? She certainly did not want to discuss yesterday, but sitting silently with Morgan was not an option. "Rick's at church?"

"His little catchall for sincere souls."

That meant the other families at the ranch were too. She'd realized quickly enough that Rick's guests were almost all Christians. She didn't know whether he advertised it that way, but word obviously passed within the ranks. She felt more than ever an outsider, and it rankled. "I've never known a praying man before," she said, more sharply than she intended.

Morgan chuckled. "I always figured Rick would be the family priest."

She sipped the coffee, then doused it with cream and tried to picture Rick in flowing robes and Roman collar. But contrasted with the last sight of him eating dust at Destiny's hooves, she failed.

At least Morgan resisted the Sunday morning call. "Why don't you go to church, Morgan?"

"I grew out of it." He smiled sideways. "Why don't you?"

"I've never been, though I've studied the various world religions." Morgan glanced up. "So what do you believe?"

"I don't know. Nothing, I guess. I mean, not like faith. Maybe what I see and what I sense. I believe what I know." She met his eyes, surprised by their penetrating gaze. "Do you believe in God?"

"There's a difference between believing and belonging." He finished his coffee, stood, and poured another cup.

"I thought in Christianity you couldn't do one without the other." Or was there an intellectual middle ground? Knowing without succumbing?

Morgan breathed the steam. "Believing in a higher power, even a Judeo-Christian God, makes more sense than any manmade explanation for the realities of life." He motioned out the window. "Do you really think all that happened by accident?"

Incredible beauty had always stirred doubts of accidental design. But if it didn't happen from some cosmic explosion and myriad transformations of matter . . . "If there was some intelligent design—designer— wouldn't that being have some control over its work?"

He sipped and nodded. "Exactly. Only in this case, the extreme being gave each little creature his own choices—that freedom you find so intoxicating."

"So you don't have to belong?"

He met her eyes, maybe reading more into her tone than she intended. "You have to follow the rules if you sign on. I have a hard time thinking inside that box."

"So you believe in God but choose not to follow?"

He shrugged. "I understand my nature. Therefore, I know my eternal destiny, regardless of what I believe."

"That's macabre."

He laughed. "Maybe."

Truck tires ground on the gravel outside. Through the window she watched Rick climb out. He didn't look like a puppet who belonged to a higher being or to anyone else for that matter. He looked confident, complete, almost as he had looked the night he'd played and sung to someone unseen. A finger of fear stroked her spine. What kind of being so overtook one that no physical presence was required?

He came inside. "Morning." His brusque, candid manner dispelled her thoughts. Rick poured the coffee and drank, then sputtered, "Whew, Morgan."

"I like it strong."

"Strong is one thing. This is tar."

Morgan turned to her. "Why don't we take a hike?" He acted as though nothing had happened between them the day before. Maybe nothing had. She had overreacted. Again. When would it stop, this triggering of fears that made no sense? She looked out the window. It was a brilliant day, and getting outside would ease her disquiet. But she didn't want to be with Morgan, not alone. "What about Rick?"

"It's his day of rest," Morgan said.

Rick added water to his cup and gave her an enigmatic smile but didn't argue with Morgan. What would he do all day? Pray?

"No thanks." She drained her coffee, then stood and rinsed the cup.

Morgan didn't stop her when she walked out, but he was at the base of the stairs when she came back down with her paints. "There's some beautiful scenery up in the national park."

She paused two steps above him. "There's beautiful scenery right here."

"We could drive to the foot of the trail and walk up."

She leaned her hip to the banister. "I'm sure some of the other guests would be glad to go." She went down past him.

He followed her out the door. "You'll need fresh inspiration to remain successful."

She glanced over her shoulder. "Spoken from the success guru?"

"You might be surprised."

Resigned, she huffed out her breath. "All right, Morgan. Show me a scene I can't resist."

The wind blew her hair as they drove up into Rocky Mountain

National Park and parked at the foot of the trail. It was hotter than she expected, in spite of the white, bulbous clouds building to the west. Morgan pulled a navy blue nylon pack from the trunk.

"What's that?"

"Water and snacks."

"How responsible."

"I told you so." He took her art box and worked it into the pack, then shrugged it onto his back over the olive green shirt that accented his tan.

She could do worse for a tour guide. When he didn't push, he was good company. She followed him to the base of the trail and started up the winding path. It rose gently, then more steeply up the mountain until it rounded a curve and zigzagged up. He reached out and helped her over a rocky stretch, then led the way on up. As they came out above the trees, the full heat of the sun hit them, and Noelle sagged against the stony outcropping. Flushed and perspiring, she took the water bottle Morgan handed her.

"You okay?" He eyed her dubiously.

"I'm not used to this." She bent at the waist, pressing her diaphragm until all the used air in her lungs was expressed, then straightened and drank from the bottle.

"You should be acclimated."

She held the back of her palm to her forehead. "Guess I'm a lightweight. You look like you just strolled Park Avenue."

"I run."

"I dance." Though she hadn't maintained her routine.

He smiled. "Maybe you should pirouette the trail."

"Very funny." She drank again, gazing out across the pine slopes with rocky crags like balding pates. In the distance she could see lower lands, golden pale, stretching away to hazy distances.

"See anything you can use?"

She shook her head slowly. "It's too broad. A watercolor wouldn't catch it." It called for oils on a sweeping canvas. "It's amazing though."

Morgan pointed. "There's the town, and there to the left is Rick's ranch. Pretty little piece."

"It's beautiful." The sight brought a quiver to her heart. "How did he get it?"

Morgan leaned against the rock wall beside her. "He and Dad purchased the land. Rick built the place."

"Literally?"

Morgan nodded. "Log by log, with his own trees and a little help from his friends. He even built most of the furniture." Pushing off from the wall, Morgan slipped the pack from his back and set it down. "He's a real mountain man. Should've lived in the old days."

The breeze caught her hair, and she brushed it out of her eyes. "And you?"

"Strictly twenty-first century. I live in the moment." He reached out and turned her face to him. "Like this moment. Right now."

"Morgan." Why did he have to make her uncomfortable when he could be so charming?

His gaze intensified. "What fate brought you here, Noelle?"

She moved out of his hand, unwilling to think again of some higher being directing her universe. "I brought myself."

"What are you doing in my life?"

"I'm not." Her heart started pounding, and she turned away. Had he fooled her in the kitchen? Hidden his feelings to get her alone on the mountain? Her back stiffened.

"You can deny it all you want. But you're here for a reason."

She shook her head.

"It's because you need me."

Blood pulsed in her ears. "I don't need anyone."

"I'm not saying you love me. I might be nothing to you. But you need me." He looked supremely confident of that.

Did she? Was there some cosmic accident that brought them together for . . . "For what?" She scarcely spoke it.

"To break through." He took her hands in his. "Somewhere in there is the real Noelle. But something won't let you out."

His touch sent shards of panic through her. She pulled against his hands. He resisted. Part of her knew he was trying to help. Part of her sensed the absurdity of her reaction. But she started to shake, fear crawling her spine. Her throat cleaved. "Please, Morgan." Her voice broke.

In her mind a hawk cried. The sunlight shone red through its tail. She could imagine the talons pressed up into its creamy breast. Its shadow ran across her face and her breath would never come again. Fear would paralyze her chest until—"Please!"

Morgan released her.

The expulsion of her breath hurt, and she sucked the new air into her lungs. "I want to go."

"Where?"

*Someplace safe, safe from the shadow of the hawk.* "Back. I want to go back to the ranch."

He stood a long minute, trying to reach her, trying to find what he thought he saw. The real Noelle? Then he sighed and shook his head. He waved his arm down the trail. "After you."

She didn't care that she hadn't painted a stroke, that she'd climbed all that way with nothing to show for it. She started down the steep trail. The panic attacks were worsening, and she didn't know what caused them or how to stop them. Her foot slipped on loose gravel and she slid.

Morgan gripped her elbow. "It won't help to break your neck. I promise not to eat you, even if I am the big bad wolf."

It wasn't Morgan. She knew that. But things he did, things he said, caused her panic. Why? Because he was trying to break through? She shuddered, slipped again, and reached out instinctively for his arm. It was crazy to reach for and run from him at once.

"Wait a minute." He helped her down the steep bend, then seated her on a tumble of huge, smooth boulders. "Calm down. Relax. Breathe."

He was right. It was ridiculous. But she couldn't control her emotions. Thoughts pulsed in her mind. Images. Wings. He waited silently, no doubt thinking her insane. She pressed her fingertips to her forehead and closed her eyes.

"Here." He handed her a chocolate chip granola bar. "It'll get your blood sugar up."

"Thanks." She took it, trying for normalcy, and ate it in silence. It seemed to help, but maybe it was just the panic passing. She should explain, but how could she when she didn't understand it herself?

"You want to talk about it?"

"No." She steadied her breath, stilling the inner trembling. She wanted to be strong. Had to be. She knew that much, in the same way she'd known to run. Instinct.

Morgan handed her a fresh Evian. She drank without speaking, then handed the empty bottle back.

"Turn." He nudged her shoulders until she faced away from him, then with slow strokes rubbed the stress from her neck. The muscles relaxed in spite of her. "You okay?"

"Yes." But she wasn't. And they both knew it. She stood up and walked at a normal pace, forcing herself not to hurry. At the car, he paused before letting her in, his hand resting on the small of her back, but his touch was no longer menacing. Morgan wouldn't hurt her. Would he?

The drive was silent. Maybe now he would believe she was not in his life for any reason at all. But his words troubled her as she went up to her room and sat alone. Who was the real Noelle? What did Morgan hope to see? The person she had been? The helpless, pleasing, dutiful person others ruled? She had left her behind as a snake sheds its skin, leaves it lying useless in the sand. But who was she now? Maybe she was nothing, a speck of insignificance in a universe whirling out of control.

Morgan thought there was more inside her. And there was: hurt and fear and a rage that would wash him away—and underneath all that, the reason. One she couldn't face. Fine. She didn't have to. She had run once, she could do it again. But she felt a painful reluctance. Why? She had no roots here. Her roots had been sheared, and maybe they'd never grow again.

As she sat on the bed, her abdomen cramped. She hurried to the bathroom and saw the evidence of her monthly flow. With a hard expelled breath, she dug a tampon from her toiletries. No wonder she'd been so weak and fatigued; hormones, most likely, had caused her emotional overload, though she'd never had such an extreme shift.

Sudden volatile trembling assailed her as she staggered from the bathroom and collapsed onto the bed. She wrapped herself in her arms and drew up her knees to her chest. She made no sound but the quick rasping of her breath. Why did she feel such tremendous relief?

# 9

Michael put on his hand-tailored gray suit coat over the crisp, white shirt and strode out of his office. The lights still showed under William St. Claire's door, but he didn't head that way. He'd accomplished all he could on that front. He'd been brilliant, made Ilse Blandon so sympathetic a witness the jury had fairly cheered. And he'd done it without compromise, William's way.

Not that he would have lost sleep over a less ethical tactic, but the challenge was greater, the success sweeter. And the court had adjourned before cross-examination. The jury would sleep on his presentation. All good. He went out of the office and took the elevator down. Even at six o'clock it was damp and sweltering.

Leaving the air-conditioning was like entering a sauna, but the smell of the city was no cedar steam. He hailed a cab and snapped directions to the driver, his elation rapidly dissipating. They inched along, but Michael was in no hurry to arrive. He forced this trip on himself at disgustingly regular intervals, but he would just as soon never reach his destination.

He flipped open his laptop, inserted a disk, and paid no further attention to the traffic until the driver hung his head back. "Here we are."

Michael peered up at the decent, brown brick apartment building. He paid the driver and went inside. The elevator was sluggish as usual, rising up to the thirteenth floor. Of course, it didn't say thirteen on the elevator. The buttons discreetly jumped from twelve to fourteen, but he had pointed out how ludicrous that was when everyone knew the next floor up from twelve was thirteen. He smugly remembered his mother's consternation at that. One more superstition, one more excuse.

The poodle-shaped sign on the door read *Frieda* in tiny black paw prints. He let himself in. His mother sat in the center of a white, circular sectional. One hand cradled a mixed drink, the other the latest *Enquirer*. She glanced up and spread her lips into a wide, wet smile. "Michael . . ." She patted the couch beside her.

"Hello, Mother." He eyed the dog hair matting its surface and remained standing. But he kissed her when she craned her neck up. "Where is the yapping mongrel?"

Her face pinched. "I called you seventeen times last week. Ruby had a seizure, a series of them." Her eyes teared up. "A brain tumor. I had to put her down. The doctor said it wasn't treatable." Her hand trembled when she drank.

"Good riddance." Michael pulled one side of his mouth up.

"You're a dreadful son! I know you got my messages. I sent every one through your highfalutin voice mail, and you never called."

"But I'm here now."

"Pour me another drink."

He took the glass and filled it with bourbon, then added a splash of coke to feed her delusion. He handed it back. "Have you heard from Jan lately?"

Her lips shriveled. "Of course not. You only ask to torment me. You know she never calls, never. Never comes to see me, never writes. She pretends she has no mother, that I'm dead or worse. I might even be dead, and she'd never know, never care."

Michael waited until she finished. "Well, then, have you heard from Noelle?"

She sagged into the couch. "No."

"Are you sure?"

Her eyes shot up to his. "Of course I'm sure. Do you think I'm senile?"

At the rate she was killing brain cells, it was a distinct possibility. His non-answer annoyed her most of all.

"Why do you come? Do you enjoy causing me pain?"

"I want to know if you hear from her."

Her gaze became piercingly clear. "Why?"

"She's gone."

"What do you mean gone?"

"Vanished."

She fluttered a hand to her chest. "Abducted?"

"No. She left."

"She left you?"

"Yes." His voice was brittle. "Hard to believe, isn't it, Mother?"

"You drove her away," she whimpered. "The one person who would have loved me, who would have been a daughter—"

"Don't fool yourself. She pitied you, nothing more."

"Beast. Bas—"

"Go ahead and say it. Who did sire me, anyway?"

She turned away, drowning her upper lip in bourbon. She was well on her way tonight. One more, maybe two, before she passed out.

Michael's lip raised in disgust. "I never can remember which affair it was that resulted in Janet, either. Poor Dad. But then, you never had much use for him. At least he had the sense to die. I shudder to think, though, what would become of you if I didn't foot the bills."

She reached for his hand. "Oh, Michael, don't torment me. Sit down here beside me."

With a grimace, he lowered himself to the couch.

She stroked his hand. "What would I do without you? You're the only one who cares, the only one who ever did."

"I hate to disillusion you, Mother, but I don't care. Caring went by the wayside long ago, thrown into a heap with love and trust . . . the nice intangibles that people think they can't live without. But I assure you it is quite possible. Other things take their place: power, greed, avarice . . ."

"Don't talk that way. You only do it to frighten me."

He laughed bitterly. "It's the truth. A good dose of your blood runs in my veins, Mother, drowning out whoever's genes formed the rest of my DNA. Except for the pathetic crutch of alcohol, I'm quite similar to you."

She wrapped her arms around his neck and hung. "Don't do this to me." Her mascara ran down one cheek in a blackish streak.

"Have I upset you? There, now." He reached for a tissue. "Blow your nose and have a swipe at your face. You should know not to listen to me. I stopped listening to you years ago." He waited while she blew her nose, then stood and refilled her glass. "Better?"

She nodded.

"Then I'll be on my way."

"I'm going to buy a new dog." The ice cracked in her glass.

He draped his suit coat over his arm. "How nice."

"Don't you want to know what kind?"

"No."

She waved her glass. "I may want you to help me choose."

He reached for the door. "Leave me a message."

Another cab took Michael home. He went directly to the bedroom and hung his coat. He removed his tie and looped it over the rack, then eyed his posterior for dog hair. It appeared most had remained on the couch. He opened his top shirt button as he went to the kitchen and checked his phone messages.

"Michael, it's Janet; please call."

He frowned, listened through the next ones, skipped several after a word or two, then called her. "Hello, Jan. What's up?"

"Oh, Michael. Did you work late?"

"I went to see Mom." His eyes traveled the edge of the black ceramic counter to the black-and-silver wash guard behind the kitchen sink. He wiped a fingerprint from the edge with the cloth that hung on the chrome bar.

"How is she?" Jan's voice was small.

"It's all right, Jan. You don't have to pretend with me. What did you need?"

She cleared her throat. "I hate to ask again, but . . ."

"Just say it."

"My dump of a car. Now it's the carburetor. They said it could be over a thousand dollars before they're done."

He sighed. "Dump it, Jan. You can't afford to park it anyway."

"I have to have my wheels. Michael, I . . ."

"All right. Send me the bill." He'd resurrect the decayed machine yet again. At least she didn't have to worry about it being plundered and stripped, which was the main reason he didn't replace it. The worst she faced was having it towed as abandoned scrap. A new car would make Jan a target in the neighborhood she called home.

"Thanks a bunch."

Her gratitude was automatic and expected, as were his services. He smiled grimly. But after all, it was Jan, and whom else did she have?

Who else had there ever been for her? He lowered the phone, but she spoke again.

"Michael . . ."

"What's that?" He returned the receiver to his ear.

"I heard Noelle is missing."

*Where? How did she hear?* "I don't know that missing is correct. She knows where she is."

"What happened?"

He leaned against the chrome barstool and stared across the room at the silver-framed oil painting. The hawk stared back. "I'm not really sure." He shook his head. "No, that's not right. I know why she left but not why things happened as they did."

"You must feel awful."

He laughed dryly. "It rivals anything we knew before."

"I'm sorry."

"Yeah."

She sniffed. "What are you going to do?"

"I don't know."

"Michael?" Her voice was plaintive and he knew what was coming. "Should I go to see Mother?"

"No." He twisted on the stool to look at the small photograph of his sister that sat on the corner of his kitchen counter: elfin features, a scrawny frame draped in a black miniskirt and knee-high vinyl boots. "She'd swallow you whole."

"Thanks." She sounded like a child running off to the candy store. He'd absolved her once again.

Michael hung up the phone and pinched the flesh between his eyebrows. He'd pay Jan's bill when it came. He didn't send her money; never sent her money. Just paid the bills when she requested. He rubbed the back of his neck. Except for their blond hair, he bore little physical resemblance to Jan. More so to his mother, unfortunately.

His hand started to shake. He cursed his mother aloud. She had tainted him. Somehow she had tainted him. Why else would he have failed so badly with Noelle? The aching seized him. Where was she?

He dialed Sebastian. "Anything?"

"And whom do I have the pleasure of addressing?" The creak of Sebastian's chair was audible over the phone.

"Don't play games with me. Have you found Noelle?"

"Well, I would have, but the most I can tell you is she withdrew two thousand dollars from her bank account. She's using cash, man. That makes my job a little harder."

"Why would she use cash?"

"Hello. So guys like me can't tell guys like you where she is."

Michael frowned. Noelle had thought that out? He knew she wasn't stupid, but her education hadn't exactly included eluding people. What instinct was she operating on?

"Keep trying. Cash runs out." Even if she earned a paycheck— which he couldn't imagine her doing—she'd need a bank account to cash it. No way would Noelle think to use a pawnshop or anything of that sort. Sooner or later she'd revert to what she knew. Then he'd have her.

———

Noelle sat with her portfolio open across her knees. Outside, the night was deep, but the main room was warmly lit. In the golden glow, she studied her paintings, one by one, deciding which to bring Ms. Walker next. She eyed them critically, preferring to reject them herself rather than see them passed over by Ms. Walker's demanding eye.

Perched on the edge of the hearth, Rick rubbed his saddle with soap. She breathed the nostalgic smell and remembered days spent in stables when she was as gangly as the thoroughbreds she rode—her most carefree days.

Morgan hadn't mentioned her attack on the mountain. Instead he'd been purposely non-confrontational, spending the last couple of days with the other guests, especially two young women from Dallas whose *Thy-ank yous* expressed how grateful they were for his attention. Both nights he'd stayed out late in the town and dragged painfully out of bed the next morning—but not this evening.

Marta had retired to her room, and Noelle was alone with the two brothers she was beginning to trust. It wasn't so unusual, considering her male-dominated life. Most of her life she'd been surrounded by Daddy's friends. The turbulence inside her just days ago had eased. She felt almost peaceful, even though she was still miles away from all she'd known and whatever she'd fled.

She didn't want to think back or forward. For now it was enough to take each day as it came. As Morgan said, live in the moment. Maybe he had it right after all. She glanced at him, recalling her first impression. He no longer looked out of place. He belonged, and, in spite of the strain between them, so did she. Yes, she belonged in this place, with these two dissimilar men, with Marta, with the ever-changing flux of families and individuals who came to stay, then moved on.

Rick turned the saddle across his knee. "So when are you leaving?"

Noelle startled, but he wasn't asking her.

Morgan rested his arms along the back of the beige couch. "I fly out in the morning."

Morgan was leaving? She stared from one to the other. "Fly out where?"

He uncrossed his ankles and sat forward. "Chicago. I have an interesting prospect."

A prospect? Is that what he'd been doing all day closed inside Rick's office? "You mean you're getting a job?" From the edge of her eye, she caught Rick's smirk and realized how she'd sounded.

Morgan frowned. "Work isn't a foreign concept to me, Noelle."

"I didn't mean that. It's just . . . sudden." She closed the portfolio. She hadn't spoken to Morgan alone since their hike. Even if she had, what could she tell him? And what would it change?

"Sudden? This is the longest I've ever stayed." He stood up and stretched. "But I seem to have exhausted my possibilities here."

"So you're just leaving?"

His smile twisted. "I'm touched, Noelle. I'll imagine you missing me." He blew her a kiss and started up the stairs.

Imagine her missing him? Why should she? But as she watched him climb, she wondered. Like the professor, he'd made his mark—even more so. But now she realized she didn't know Morgan at all. What kind of job was he trying for?

Rick laid the saddle on the hearth to dry. "Morgan's no slacker. More of a prodigy."

She didn't hide her surprise. "Prodigy? What does he do?"

"Turnaround management. Saves businesses. Major corporations. His name is known in very high-powered circles."

"Morgan?" The ne'er-do-well cad and cutup she'd spent weeks with and never glimpsed with more than a capricious nonchalance?

"With his Wharton MBA he went into corporate finance, and from there he began saving the world. Found some smaller companies floundering with great ideas and no clue what to do with them. One merger with IBM set him up pretty well."

Morgan Spencer a Wharton graduate? A financial prodigy? No wonder he could take a month off if he felt like it. And she'd been so uptight about her own background she'd never asked. Other things now came clear: his choice of clothing, his car. No wonder she'd pictured him at Daddy's club. But he'd put her off with his very first statement, *"I'm just freeloading."*

"So this is a consulting job?"

"If he takes it. He's pretty particular."

She looked up the stairs again where Morgan had disappeared. She'd flaunted her few sold paintings and mockingly called him the success guru, when that was exactly what he was? And his job was to fix things, find solutions no one else saw. No wonder he'd seen through her.

She closed her portfolio with an exhaled breath. "He never said a word. I mean, all those stories he told and—well, most men would have dropped a hint, bragged on that kind of success."

Rick shrugged. "He comes up here to get away. Relax. He hasn't said so, but it must be draining to have everyone expecting you to solve their problems. It takes a toll."

Yet he'd tried to do just that for her. Maybe she should have let him. She gathered her portfolio to her chest and stood up. "Well, good night, Rick."

"Good night."

# 10

Noelle slept fitfully and awakened to a dim, dreary day. She lay in bed and watched the drizzle run down the windowpanes. Things were changing, and it unsettled her. She forced herself to rise, wash, and dress, then dragged downstairs. Morgan had his suitcase by the door, and he stood beside it, buttoning his raincoat, ready to leave. Would he have gone without saying good-bye?

He turned. Already he looked different, or maybe her perception had changed. Now that she knew his potential, she saw it in him. Yet before . . . How flimsy impressions could be. Or had he purposely hidden himself? A prodigy escaping the pressure. What if he had told her his profession at the start? Would their time together have been different?

She had thought him a chameleon the night at the Roaring Boar. Now he was changing colors again. Her throat tightened. "Not a very nice day to fly." It was a stupid, useless thing to say.

He took her hand and pulled her close. "Give me a reason to stay?"

New color, same lizard. "Good-bye, Morgan."

For a moment she thought he'd say more, but he only squeezed her hand and disengaged. He must no longer believe she needed him. Good. Because she didn't.

"Ready?" Rick joined him at the door.

Morgan gave her one last wink and followed Rick outside. As the door closed behind them, she went into the dining room. Marta had set out bran muffins and fruit compote, but no one sat at the table. Well, she was in no mood for morning banter anyway. She took a muffin and wandered back to the front room. Drizzle obscured the outbuildings. It was too wet to ride out and paint, so she returned to her room.

Downstairs the vacuum hummed, one of Marta's endless jobs. She didn't know what Marta did in her room at night, but all day the woman worked, seemingly content with menial tasks, as though they defined her. Noelle looked into the oval mirror. How would she define herself?

Artist? Perhaps. It was the means she'd found to support her stay, though it barely covered her current minimal expenses. It was a start, but was that all she was, who she was? *The real Noelle.* She'd never had the chance to be real—until now.

Voices floated up from downstairs, guest families congregating in the lodge, held inside by the rain yet seeking companionship, distraction. They must be playing a game, a team game by all the hollered guessing, adult and children's voices alike. She could go down and join them, but her natural reticence held her back. She didn't like crowds, had never learned the herd mentality, having never been herded into school but privately tutored instead.

There had been group activities, her dance and riding lessons, her college courses, though much of that had been individual study as well. But as she'd told Morgan, her preference was solitude or at least limited numbers. Was it preference or habit?

She looked around the room. The overcast weather gave the golden walls a sickly pallor. Everything smelled damp, and the dripping of the gutters was a constant drum. She walked to the window. Misty trees like ghostly shadows faded up the slope. Her gaze deepened. How well the scene matched her mood, yet it was beautiful in its own haunting way. She absorbed it, or it her, until it was there, inside. Then she took out her paints and created it.

Maybe she wasn't only an artist, but it was a part of her. The professor had seen it. He saw her as someone in love with the beautiful, in search of the divine. Maybe not the latter, but then . . . maybe . . . She looked at the painting before her. It was different from her others. Usually she did so much with light, with shade and hue. This one was subtle, almost monochromatic.

Would Ms. Walker like it? It didn't matter. This one was powerful.

It came from some shadowy place inside her that had responded to the weeping skies, the questions, the void. She wouldn't care if it didn't sell. It was a personal communication.

But of what? Gloom? Loneliness? The need to be known? She felt a flickering loss that surprised her: homesickness. She and Daddy had been close, even with him away so much, for so many long hours. She could admit she missed her father, even some of her friends. Her throat tightened as wings once again flashed above her, then dissolved as soon as the image came. These wings were different, though. Stylized. How strange.

Noelle scrunched her brow, trying to bring the image back, but couldn't. Other wings threatened to fill her mind, but she forced them away. *Not the hawk.* Not now. She wasn't ready. Shaking her head, she dispelled the memories.

She left the painting on the easel to dry and sat on the bed with the vignettes of Western women she'd brought up from Rick's shelf. Reading about such women as Augusta Tabor and Helen Hunt Jackson underscored her own trek westward and the expansionist spirit Professor Jenkins had sought to explain. Though Juniper Falls was scarcely the frontier those women had helped settle, it was foreign enough to what she knew.

As she read, the room grew chilly. Long pants and a sweat shirt were more in order. But when she took off her shorts the button fell and rolled on the floor. She scooped it up and laid it with the shorts as she finished changing. The voices had ceased downstairs, and only Rick sat in the corner chair beside the fireplace when she went down. It was likely too damp for him to work outside, but she couldn't recall seeing him just sit. Didn't he, like Marta, thrive on diligence? Yet there he was. So much for impressions.

"Excuse me."

He glanced up, and she realized he'd been reading, the book in his lap hidden by the angle of his leg. "Did you need something?"

"I've lost a button. Could Marta—"

"She's doing housekeeping in the cabins. But there's a needle and thread in that cupboard behind you." He pointed to the top right door in the wall unit.

*A needle and thread. Uh-huh. Well, how hard could it be?* In the cupboard she found a lidded basket that held a pincushion and spools. As luck would have it, there was a needle already threaded with white to match her shorts. She took it and sat on the couch where Morgan had lounged the evening before.

"Where did everyone go?"

"Movie theater." His attention was back on the book.

She studied the task at hand. Holding the button in place, she poked the needle through and caught her finger underneath. She gasped and jerked it out. No blood, but how could that tiny pink spot hurt so much?

"There's a thimble in the basket." Rick spoke without looking up.

How would he know what she needed? she thought, then snorted. She probably could have asked him to do it. She pictured his long deft fingers attaching the button, his placating smile as he returned the shorts, mission accomplished. The very thought annoyed her.

And she could do without a thimble, thank you. She yanked the thread and it went all the way through, leaving the button still completely unattached. It must need a knot of some sort. She tied the end of the thread and went through the button again. The knot stuck, but she realized she should have come up from the bottom for it not to show. Never mind. If she made the button stay that was good enough.

She pushed the needle through and back, then checked the stitches underneath and realized the finger had bled after all, on the shorts. Great. And how did she secure the thread? Another knot, of course. She pulled the needle out and tied one like she had at the start, then bit it off with her teeth. Rick glanced up. No doubt there were scissors in the cabinet as well.

She laid the shorts in her lap. "You're engrossed. Some bestseller?"

"You might say." He held the book up, and she saw the gold lettering. *Holy Bible.*

"Is it any good?"

He smiled. "It's great."

Sucking her finger, she carried the needle and remaining snippet of thread back to the cabinet and stuck it into the pincushion the way she'd found it. "I've studied Buddhist, Greek, and Hindu myths and Native American folk tales."

"I don't consider this mythology."

"What, then?" She sat back down on the couch.

"The Word of God." He said it simply, as though he really believed it.

"So God wrote the book?"

"His Spirit inspired those who did."

She lifted the shorts and wiggled the button. Maybe it would hold. "Like automatic writing?"

"That's a demonic counterfeit."

She laughed. She couldn't help it. How could he say something so ludicrous? "You mean little men with horns and tails poking people to make them write?"

"I mean real forces of evil that ensnare people's minds and lead them away from the truth."

His straight, earnest face caused in her an obtuse desire to provoke him. "Truth is subjective."

"Is it?" He fingered the tabs and flipped the pages, scanned, then read, " 'For this I was born, and for this I came into the world, to testify to the truth.' " He looked up. "Do you know who said that?"

She shook her head.

"The Son of God. The Messiah."

"You mean Jesus. How was he any different from Buddha or Mohammed or even Plato? They all taught truth."

"Only one of them *was* truth." His eyes seemed to deepen, to hold her, tell her . . . what? And how could she possibly answer? How could someone be truth? Truth was logic, proof, thought, and decision. He was speaking symbolically.

"You don't really . . ." She heard tires on the gravel outside and turned. "New guests?"

Rick leaned to look out the window. "My dad with the foals." He took his hat from the hook by the door and went out into the misty yard.

Noelle followed, even though he hadn't invited her. Standing just outside the door, she took in the worn brown truck and horse trailer, which had pulled up between the house and stable. Rick's father climbed out and came around. He was a thicker version of Rick, same angular bone structure, though he was gray haired and had Morgan's blue eyes. The two men clasped hands, then hugged.

Rick said, "You just missed Morgan. He left this morning."

"Figures." Rick's father stood back with one hand still on his son's shoulder. "How're things?"

"They're good. How's Mom?"

"Ah." Hank patted Rick's back. "Missing you boys."

Their easy affection stirred envy in her, and surprise. Rick looked genial and warm. Not that he'd been cold with her, only this was different. This was . . . family.

Wrapped in her own arms against the chill, she watched from the porch while they opened up the trailer. The drizzle had stopped and the mist lifted, though the skies were still gray. She was learning that even in the middle of summer the temperature swings at this elevation were broad. Working together, the two men backed the horses down from the trailer. One was a sorrel with a white face and socks, the other a bay, both quarter-horse stock with the short front-legged, workhorse power.

She could tell they were quality bred. Their hides shone and their eyes were bright and spirited. Their backs were straight, higher in the withers than the croup and longer in the belly than the spine, the perfect proportion for saddle horses. She couldn't resist any longer and went down.

Stepping back, Rick almost trampled her, then caught himself awkwardly. He turned to his father. "Dad, this is Noelle St. Claire."

"Hank Spencer." Rick's dad shook her hand. "Are you vacationing up here?"

"On a kind of permanent basis."

"She's boarding with us." Rick reached for the sorrel's harness.

"Aha. Do any riding?"

"She's a capable horsewoman." Rick stroked the foal's muzzle, checking one eye, then the other.

Noelle stared at him, surprised. He'd kept that opinion to himself.

"Good." Hank patted the horse's withers. "Put her to work with these fillies. There's nothing like a woman's touch to take the wild out of a horse."

Noelle's heart leapt. "That's what I've been trying to tell him about Destiny."

"Thanks, Dad." Rick smiled grimly.

She cooed to the bay that stood nervously. "But you're the pretty one, you sweet thing." From the corner of her eye, she caught Hank's gaze moving from her to his son and back again. And she saw her chance. "Why don't you come in for some coffee, Mr. Spencer?"

"Call me Hank. And coffee sounds great. Rick, you can manage?"

"I can manage."

She didn't miss Rick's frown as he started for the stable. Hopefully, she'd have time to make her case. She led Hank inside. Why it mattered so much, she couldn't say. Because it was denied her?

No, it was something she needed to do. A quest. And this was her chance, a better chance than she'd ever have with Rick alone. She brought Hank to the kitchen and found Marta preparing lunch. She must have finished in the cabins, and before Noelle could start her argument, Hank said, "Hello, Marta."

"How was your trip, Hank?"

"Longer than ever."

"At our age, nothing's as easy as it used to be." She took a large can of corn from the pantry.

"That's true. But I'm not complaining. As they say, it beats the alternative."

Marta laughed. They seemed to know each other well and just might keep talking until Rick came in.

Noelle went to the corner and poured Hank a mug of steaming coffee. "Cream?"

"No, thank you." Hank took the mug gratefully, sipped, then sighed with satisfaction. "Now, that hits the spot."

Marta's face flushed with pleasure, but before they got going again, Noelle started her bid. "Those are beautiful animals you've brought."

He smiled like Rick at the mention of his stock. "You know horses?"

"Mainly thoroughbreds. The stable where I trained specialized in jumpers."

"Ah." He drank again.

"But Rick's quarter horses are fine too. That roan, Destiny, in particular."

Hank nodded. "Oh yes. Not many like that one."

"I know I could tame him down—if I ever got the chance to try."

Hank had betrayed his soft heart the minute he hugged his son. This had to work. He shrugged. "Well, Rick seems to appreciate your ability."

"Riding maybe. But not with Destiny. He's convinced I can't help him there."

Hank eyed her. "But you'd like to."

"I'd love to. Destiny already responds to me, though Rick won't admit it."

Hank grinned. "Well, we'll see what we can do."

"Thanks." She flashed him a radiant smile, not at all feigned, and ignored the twinge of conscience. Rick could have been reasonable on his own.

When he came in, Noelle intentionally avoided the subject. She'd used the same magic with Hank as she had with her own daddy, and he would work on Rick better than she'd been able to. If it needed tweaking, she'd take what opportunities came.

But when she went down for dinner the cabin families had already filled the table where Rick and Hank sat, and Marta had even set the second long table in the dining room. She heard little of Rick's conversation, as she and two mothers shared their table with seven talkative children. Not even Morgan could have gotten a word in.

As one family, then another, retired to their cabins for the night, Noelle, too, slipped away upstairs, leaving Rick and his father alone. Maybe now Hank would speak for her. Maybe tomorrow she'd ride Destiny.

———

Under the afternoon sun the next day, Rick led Destiny over to his father, reading the satisfaction in his eyes. Dad was too good a horseman to miss the roan's quality. The horse still breathed hard from the run he had given him. But though he was tired and currently obedient, he was anything but docile. No, this was one horse that would follow its heart. Rick would have to earn its mastery.

"You've done well with him, son."

Rick stroked Destiny's muzzle. "He's something, isn't he?"

"He's something. Good blood will show. And every now and then it all comes together."

"Yeah." Rick patted the horse's neck.

"He's responding well." His dad leaned on the fence.

"Better these last few days. Seems to have given up throwing me." Rick tethered the horse.

"Once they make that decision it's pretty clear sailing. I think Noelle could give him a try if she's as capable as you say."

Rick frowned. There it was, and he'd expected it. "She's capable enough on a well-trained horse. I've practically given over Aldebaran to her."

"She'd sure like to help with Destiny." Yep, Dad was wax in her hands.

Rick knew well enough how hard she pressed. "She used her green eyes on you, Dad. You know as well as I do—"

"I'm not saying turn her loose on him. Keep him on the tether."

"Even on the tether . . ."

"Oh, come on, Rick. What can it hurt? She's a delightful young woman. Knows jumpers." Dad raised a hand in a reasoning gesture Rick knew so well. "She's competition-trained with thoroughbreds. They're flightier than Destiny by far."

"He's not flighty." Rick held the horse's nose, conceding in his mind that Destiny had come a long way since the first time Noelle asked to ride him.

"There, then. Give her a try." Dad's voice had that genial coaxing Rick remembered too well.

Rick shook his head. "I see how it is. Fine. You can tell her she's won."

"I'll leave that for you." His father winked.

Rick lifted Destiny's fore hoof and checked the frog. "You have it wrong, Dad. It's Morgan she's been seeing."

"Morgan?"

"That's right." The horse had seemed tender, but Rick didn't see anything to irritate the hoof. He dropped it.

"I see."

Rick was sure his dad did see. Probably more than Rick wanted him to.

"Well, she's an enchanting creature."

"And conniving."

His father laughed. "That's the best kind. Just like your mother. Puts the spice into life."

"Yeah." Rick palmed a baby carrot for Destiny. "Cayenne pepper." And she wasn't a believer, was hostile to the gospel, and . . . well, not at all the sort of woman he assumed God would choose for him.

But he did respect his father's opinion, especially when it came to horses. He'd learned everything at Dad's hands, most of all the touch that won an animal's allegiance. No brute force could accomplish that. A browbeaten horse would turn at the first chance. And a stubborn one would resist a weak hand until it was long in the tooth. It was the right blend of constancy and gentleness that made submission possible.

Just as it was with God. No deity that ruled with fear and torment could win the hearts of its followers. They became animals themselves, thinking of baser and baser modes of worship until they threw their very infants to the flames. Only in Jesus was submission perfected, God made man. And through Jesus, man committed his heart to the only entity worthy of service—something else he'd learned from Dad, whose heart was always humble before God and whose example Rick strove to follow.

But humble or not, when they gathered around the tables for the evening meal, Rick avoided Noelle's hopeful glances. If Dad wanted to tell her he'd acted on her charm, taken her part against the better judgment of his son, let him. But the other families kept the discussion on kids and religion, which didn't become contentious since they were all like-minded. Except Noelle, though he noted she didn't press her arguments on Dad or the others. That must be his singular privilege.

After dinner, his father followed him outside and assisted with the evening chores. Rick was glad for the time alone with him, especially since the visit would be a short one.

"So how is Morgan?" Dad's tone was neutral, but Rick knew what he asked.

He just didn't know how to answer. He heaved a hay bale to the manger at the side of the stable and snipped the wire. "New Corvette, new contract, all the time and pleasure money can buy." He pulled apart the bale as the horses clomped over and dipped their heads, tearing at the aromatic hay with ivory teeth and flapping lips.

"Drinking?"

"I've seen him worse."

Dad was not averse to a beer on a hot day, but they both knew that wasn't what he meant. He rubbed the back of his neck. "I promised Mother I'd ask."

Rick nodded.

Dad reached to help with the second bale. "Maybe he'll find a reason to straighten out."

Noelle flashed to Rick's mind, but he didn't say anything. He could be way off base, but if she were strong enough to straighten Morgan out . . . well, he couldn't see that happening. Of course, she had outmaneuvered him on the Destiny matter. He turned the faucet on over the trough, guessing he'd have one peaceful night before she was on him like a horsefly on sweat. Dad had armed her, and there was no getting out of it.

His father left early the next morning, and sure enough, Noelle was ready the moment her hand dropped from waving Dad off in his truck. "Rick, did Hank—"

"You know he did." And there came the full force of her eager eyes and way too confident smile. "All right, come on." He hoisted the saddle into the bed of his pickup.

Noelle climbed into the truck. "It's a shame your father couldn't stay longer."

"Lord knows what I'd be doing if he had."

She didn't bother to hide her satisfaction as they drove up. He looked at the stallions running in the high pasture and Destiny trying to reach them from the training corral. His muscles gleamed in the sunlight as he strained and circled. This was crazy.

Rick stopped Noelle at the gate. "Wait out here." He whistled through his teeth. The colt stood still for the bridle, but that was the easy part. He'd been halter-trained almost from birth, had taken to the bridle without concern. Rick fastened the reins to the fence, then tossed the blanket over the horse's back. Destiny stomped one back hoof but still made no move.

Noelle leaned on the fence. "You've tamed him already."

"Don't let him fool you. He wants to obey, but he also wants his way. It's a battle inside him."

Destiny snorted and jerked up his head as though to prove him right. Rick hauled the saddle from the truck and put it on over the pad. He could feel Destiny quiver and spoke to him softly. "You know this part, boy." He fastened and tightened the cinch, gently kneed the air from the horse's belly, and gave the cinch another tug.

He unfastened the rope. "I'm going to take him first and see what kind of mood he's in." He swung up into the saddle. Destiny wheeled, and Rick pulled him back. "Whoa there." He nudged him with his knees and Destiny started forward, then broke into a trot, followed by a lope and canter as Rick urged him.

They circled the enclosure. Destiny seemed eager to please. Round and round they paced, his hooves chunking yesterday's drying mud. Noelle leaned on the fence, waiting. Each time he passed, Rick saw her look up expectantly. Well, he may as well get it done. He dismounted before her. "You sure about this?"

There was no mistaking the look she gave him.

"All right, then." He attached the tether rope to the bridle, and Noelle climbed up. This was new for the horse, and he could sense Destiny's confusion. No one else had ridden him, no one but Rick, and even that was a tenuous arrangement at best. "Steady."

Slowly, he played out the rope as the horse backed. He tried not to convey his concern but watched for a widening of the eyes, bunching muscles, flaring nostrils. More rope. Destiny twitched. Suddenly he reared, and Rick tugged him sharply down.

Noelle clung. "Let him run!"

His heart jumped. "Not on your life." He held Destiny's head immobile until he sensed submission, in both rider and horse. Again he let the rope out. This time the horse stayed calm. He led him to the center of the corral. Destiny began to circle, built speed, but kept steady. Noelle moved in sync with him. At least there was that. Destiny could do worse than a well-seated horsewoman.

Rick trained the horse's control, now urging him to a canter, now slowing to a walk. He made him stand, then circle, then stand again. Destiny didn't want to stand. He fought the rope but obeyed until Rick urged him again. Noelle did nothing more than ride, but she seemed as intent on learning Destiny as the horse did her. When Destiny had done enough, Rick brought them to a stop. The horse stood calm as Noelle swung down. Another good sign.

"Satisfied?" Rick asked.

"Not even close." Her eyes shone. Her faraway look was gone, and she seemed achingly present, her vibrancy unveiled.

He couldn't help but respond. "Want to help me train him?" The words were out before he considered.

"Do you mean it?"

Did he? One look and he wondered what he'd done. Give her an inch, she'd take the whole ranch. "Now that you've got a taste of him, you won't let it go."

"You're right."

" 'Course I'm right. When you want something, you don't quit until you get it." He undid the cinch and pulled the saddle off. "You have a real subtle way, but it doesn't hide that mulish streak." He hung the saddle over the fence.

"I'm not mulish," she said.

"Yes, you are."

"I am not."

"You are." He removed the halter, and Destiny bolted for the pasture.

"And you're argumentative."

"Only when I'm right." He hauled the saddle to the truck.

"That's smug." She followed him over.

He closed the tailgate. "You've been pushing for this since the day you came. Then you had Dad weigh in. If that's not mulish . . ."

"What's mulish is the way you refused every request."

"You rode him, didn't you?" He pulled open her door.

"Only because I had your—"

Leaning over her, Rick raised his brows. "Yes?"

"Because Hank saw my point."

He grinned. "Is that what he saw?"

Noelle raised her chin. "What, then?"

"Oh, the way you peer up through those eyelashes and flash your smile." His eyes went over her face. "Dad's a pushover, but I'm not."

"Then why did you ask me to train with you?"

Rick looked out to where Destiny grazed. "Because he responded." That was half true. The other half he wouldn't admit. The way he'd felt when her eyes filled with whatever it was he'd seen there.

Her smile was pure satisfaction. "I told you he would."

Shaking his head, he waved her into the truck and closed the door. "Thanks, Dad," he muttered as he crossed to his side. But maybe she was right too. Maybe he'd been mulish, unwilling to believe that she might succeed where he was struggling. And then there was the rest of it, the time they would spend together, the companionship of a shared goal.

He pulled onto the apron and parked. "You did a nice job. Thanks for the help."

"Maybe I could help with the new foals too."

Yep, the whole ranch. He had to grin. "Maybe."

# 11

D riving through the traffic, Michael seethed. Ilse Blandon had broken under cross-examination, no other witness could outweigh
that defect, and there was the matter of the receipt, tangible evidence
of their client's opportunity. The judge had withered both William and
himself with his comments before the jury went out to deliberate, and
Michael still stung from William's cool displeasure.

He almost resented the man for not chastising him. If it weren't for
his relationship to Noelle, would he be so lenient? Michael pulled his
sister's junker to the curb and got out. He'd already phoned for a cab
to meet him there, but it hadn't arrived. He went down the curbside
stairs and rapped on the door with one knuckle.

Jan opened, and Michael held out the keys. "It's running again."
He'd picked up the car and paid the bill, but returning it was always
the hardest part, seeing how she lived.

She took the keys and waved him in. "I feel bad . . ."

"Don't."

At nineteen, she looked washed out and tired. Her blond hair
hung limp. There were circles under her eyes, and her skin had that
translucent quality that made her look fragile, more fragile than she
was. She had faced the truth, cut strings he couldn't cut. She was free
of the past, on her own.

Not that she did very well at it. He looked around the studio apartment, slightly larger than an elevator, with stained floors and walls.

The bed was folded up to the wall, but the bedclothes hung out the side. There was scarcely space to walk around the dishes and clothing that cluttered the floor.

He walked to the counter, picked up the bottle of Jack Daniel's lying on its side. His blood ran cold at the thought of Jan being a lush like Mother. "What's this?"

"Bud left it." She shrugged and tossed it to the trash. It hit the edge and knocked the can over. "Oops." She giggled and bent to stuff everything back in.

"Does he stay here with you?"

"What's it to you?" She tossed her hair and reached for a pack of cigarettes.

What was it to him? The men she saw made his skin crawl. Why couldn't she see what they were? He'd worked himself ragged to escape this ugliness, had won a full academic scholarship to Harvard Law School, graduating in the top two percent.

And not only that. He'd learned the mores of the upper crust until he could assimilate without effort, while Jan wallowed lower and lower. She'd be diseased before twenty and it wasn't her fault. A fresh surge of hatred for his mother seized him.

Oblivious to his darkening mood, Jan giggled again, an unnatural sound.

With a swift motion, he gripped her chin and bent her head back. She shrieked and struggled, but he held firm. It was there in her eyes. "What are you on?"

"Nothing. Just a little upper."

"From Bud?"

"It was, like, free. Given to me."

Sure. That's how it started. You only paid once you were hooked. "Where'd you get it?"

"I don't . . ."

He tightened his grip. "Where!"

"Okay. Bud." She pried his fingers from her chin.

He swallowed his fury. "Listen to me, Jan. . . ."

"Like, get off my case, all right?"

He forced his voice to calm. "This is no place for you. Let me set you up."

She tapped a cigarette free with a smirk. "Like Mom? Can I be a bird in a cage too?"

He didn't show the hurt. Jan was high or she'd never have said it. She knew what it cost him, not in money but in his soul, to hate the woman so much and still see that she had a life, even a comfortable one.

She put the cigarette between her lips and flicked the lighter. "I'm not doing anything hard." She inhaled and blew the smoke slowly. "I just, like, want to make it on my own."

As though she could make it without his help. Her memory was awfully short. "Cut loose of Bud. He's a scumbag."

She shrugged. "So he's not hoity-toity like Noelle. Have you two even—"

"Stop it, Jan!" He gripped her shoulders and tossed her to the beanbags along the wall. What was the use? He could wring the truth from a witness, spin the truth for a jury, but he couldn't tell the truth to the ones who mattered.

He couldn't tell Jan she was ruining her life. And he hadn't told Noelle she made every day worth living. That with her, he almost felt . . . human. Instead he'd proved he wasn't.

Jan rolled to her side, frightened but sullen. And suddenly it wasn't Jan he saw crumpled, it was Noelle. His heart pounded; his eyes burned with unshed tears. He reached down to help his sister up. He could tell her. Jan was probably the only one who would understand. But he didn't.

———

Noelle flounced down on the couch and glared out the front window. She'd earned the chance to train Destiny, had one glorious time on his back, then awakened ready for more. The clouds that had moved in overnight hung misty and cold, but that wouldn't stop her or Rick, either, she was sure. Not that he was anywhere in sight to ask. And she knew because she'd gone out and looked extensively and had damp stringy hair to prove it.

She crossed her arms and dropped them across her ribs. He had to know she'd be aching to continue. Yet even though his truck was in the yard, he was nowhere to be found, except perhaps the places she hadn't looked, like his bedroom and bath. But if Rick were still in bed, it was time to call 9-1-1. No, he was up and out somewhere, intentionally frustrating her.

The door opened and Rick stuck his head in. "Ready?"

She jumped up. "Where have you been?"

He drew his brows together and rested his palm on the doorjamb. "Working."

"I tramped all over the ranch."

"I know."

She clipped her hands to her hips. "You know?"

"I saw you."

"From where?"

"The stable roof."

She looked out the window at the stable's roof that slanted low on the backside. She could have missed him there, but if he'd seen her . . . "Why didn't you say something?"

"Like what?"

"Like 'here I am.' "

He stood a long minute without answering.

"You must have guessed I was looking for you."

He hung his thumb in his belt. "No, actually . . ."

"Oh, never mind. I just wanted to get an early start before it rained."

"And I just thought I'd patch a spot on the roof before it rained."

She held his slightly mystified gaze and realized how high-handed she'd sounded. "Oh." Yes, patching the stable roof before a rain was a good, worthy use of his time.

"So . . ." His mouth pulled to one side. "Are you ready?"

She expelled a quick breath. "Yes."

He looked her over. "Where's your coat?"

"I don't have one." In the summer heat of her shopping trip in Denver, a coat had not been on her mind to purchase.

"Come with me."

She followed him to the stable where he pulled from the hook on the wall a poncho like the one he wore and slipped it over her head. It fit like a tent, but he didn't snicker. Rick knew when not to tease. Together they climbed into his truck, and he drove up the storm-hushed slope. Destiny came to meet them, seemingly eager.

Maybe because of the impending storm, Rick let her take him fresh, though he kept a secure hold of the rope. The air was pungent with wet hide, the reins slick in her hands, the air brisk. It was invigorating—for Destiny as well. He paced with energetic steps, and she exulted in the horse's motion, his ready response.

She neither wanted, nor tried to, control him, and she was certain he knew it. Theirs was the mutual understanding she had wished between the animal and Rick. They were one, linked by some connection of mind and soul. Rick might be training him, but she was winning his heart.

The sky rumbled and without further warning spilled large heavy raindrops. She had been damp already, but it was pelting by the time Rick gripped her waist and swung her down.

"Get into the truck."

She ran even as lightning flashed and thunder punctuated his words, rain slashing down cold and hard. She dove into the truck's shelter as Rick unsaddled and released Destiny to the pasture. With water streaming off the brim of his gray Stetson, he dumped the saddle into the back and yanked open his door. He pulled off the hat to climb into the cab. His breath steamed the windows as he filled the space beside her and shut the door. Then he turned and grinned, so unexpected and boyishly she had to laugh.

He rested his forearm on the wheel. "Sorry. I thought it'd hold off a bit."

She looked through the streaming windshield. "No holding that off."

"It's about time. It's been too dry." He started the truck, and the wipers swished away the watery curtain.

The days had been for the most part clear and sunny. There certainly hadn't been any rains like this one. And there were the horses standing in it. "Are they all right? You don't need to bring them in?"

"They don't want to come in."

It seemed true. They stood, necks arched and heads high. "What do you call the black stallion?"

"Hercules." He put the truck in gear and started down the sloshy meadow.

"And Destiny's sire?"

"Red Skelton."

She turned to see if he was joking.

He read her look. "He was named and papered when I bought him."

"Poor thing."

Rick swung the truck around a rushing rivulet. "I call him Red. He doesn't seem to mind."

She rubbed the rain from the back of her neck. "And you named his foal Destiny. I thought he needed the sire's name incorporated."

"On paper he's Red Destiny."

"Sounds Marxist."

The corners of Rick's mouth quirked. "I hadn't thought of that."

"Who's his dam?"

"Aldebaran." He eased the truck over a dip. "I told you she was a good horse." He parked in the yard and turned off the engine.

Sheets of rain obscured the house and turned the yard into thin strips of gravel between pools. Its force thrummed in her ears. "Guess you're glad you patched that roof."

He glanced sidelong. "I'll check with you first next time."

She raised her chin. "I just think you might have said something."

"Uh-huh."

"I mean, given your outspoken and gregarious nature."

He cocked his head and stared out at the rain.

She watched it, too, for a minute. "This should take care of the dryness."

"Depends. When it comes too hard and fast it mostly washes away. Ground this steep and dry can't take it in."

"But there's so much of it."

He nodded. "It's the kind of rain that flash floods. If you're ever caught out in it, head for high ground away from any streambeds or gullies."

The storm was daunting. "Should we make a run for it?"

He leaned close to the windshield. "Doesn't look like it'll stop any time soon."

With her neck already wet and the cab getting steamy, running from the truck to the porch wouldn't be so bad. "I say we do it."

From opposite sides of the truck, they ran to the porch, water splashing up their legs. Gripping her hand, he pulled her up the steps to the door where they stopped, breathless and soaked. Noelle caught her streaming hair back with both hands as Rick opened the door and waved her in, but Marta stood in the entry—mop in hand. Noelle felt as though she'd been caught jumping in puddles. She shrugged out of the poncho and dutifully handed it over, then followed Rick's example and shed her boots.

"I think a fire's in order." He went to the fireplace in his socks, crumpled paper under the grate, and arranged logs and kindling on top. She joined him as he lit the edges. A fire on the first of August. Only in the mountains.

"It'll be warm in a minute." His voice alone warmed her. That and his sock feet.

She looked down at her own and suppressed a laugh. "Destiny responded well to me."

Rick poked the fire. "Well enough."

"Admit it. He was eager to perform."

Rick leaned on the mantel. "I wouldn't say eager."

Noelle turned her back to the fire and let the heat rise up her legs and spine. "I can take him by myself."

"No."

She huffed. "Then why did you tell your father I was capable?"

Rick shrugged. "Just being polite."

She shook her head. "You meant it."

"Oh yeah?"

She turned and held her hands to the fire. "Why don't you save yourself the argument and just say yes?"

"Because the minute I do you'll start pushing for the next thing."

"Which is?"

"God only knows."

She met his gaze, and they smiled with their eyes, warmth reaching deep inside her.

---

Noelle basked in the coolness the following evening, lulled by the rhythmic creaking of the porch swing, one leg folded up beneath her. The crag was stained with rubescent rays of westering sun. In the grasses below, crickets sang, but beyond that, silence. It was Marta's day off, Rick had gone to Denver, and the cabins were actually empty until tomorrow. Noelle had the ranch to herself. Luxury.

She had painted a scene of eroded ground, cut into veins and cracks by yesterday's rain on either side of a white-faced aspen scrubbed clean behind the ears, with mushrooms that had sprung up overnight in the bright springy moss at its base. It was a study in contrasts and the tenacity of mountain life. She was learning.

An engine and tires in the gravel ended her solitary reverie. Rick's truck pulled in and came to a stop, but he wasn't alone. Morgan climbed out looking rakishly handsome, sleeves rolled, tie loose. He must not have taken the job. As Rick headed for the stable, Morgan strode up the steps and raised her to her feet. "More beautiful than before." His eyes roved the length of her. "Did you miss me?"

"You were only gone five days." But his piece was back in her puzzle and it did fit.

"Well, I missed you."

"Why didn't you take the job?"

He cocked his head. "I presented my proposal; they accepted. I'll be facilitating a sticky merger, so the Windy City is going to be home for a while. Want to come?"

"I don't think so, Morgan."

"I'd show you a good time."

"I have a good time here." She pulled her hands free.

He shook his head. "Some things never change. But that's okay. No rejection fazes me. I have a heart of steel." He gave her a suave smile. "Let's go somewhere. I only have tonight."

Her heart thumped. "You came back for one night with me?" Did he expect she'd make it worth the trip?

"I came back for my car." He brushed her arm with his fingertips. "But I'm accepting offers."

"Your car?"

He nodded. "I left it in the barn. I just flew out to negotiate. Now that I know I'll be there awhile, I'll drive out." He took her hand. "Come on."

She let him lead her off the porch to the Corvette in the barn. He uncovered it and opened her door, expecting as usual to whisk her off on whatever adventure he envisioned this time. As she hesitated he cocked his head and hummed "Little Red Riding Hood." She flashed him a glance. He was not the big bad wolf; she knew that. He was only Morgan. She slid into the seat and he closed the door.

Dusk was deepening as he backed out into the yard. Rick crossed behind them and went into the house. Morgan shifted into drive. "Have you eaten?"

She shrugged. "Marta's day off."

"Good." He pulled to a stop beside Rick's truck, climbed out and took an insulated container from the bed, then got back in and set it on her lap.

"What's this?"

"Picnic."

She looked out at the deepening sky. Picnic?

He took the gravel road slowly since the rain had deepened the ruts and the Corvette rode low on the grasses rubbing beneath. In town, he turned right, heading up toward the national park. If he thought she was going to hike in the dark with elk and fox and bears and mountain lions . . .

He drove to a half-circular lookout and parked. She stared out at the early stars pricking the clear sky. Morgan got out and opened his trunk. What was he planning this time?

Near the edge of the lookout, beside the boulders that marked its drop, he spread a woolen blanket. On that, he placed a three-wick candle that he lit with a lighter. She climbed out and watched, goose-flesh rising on her arms in the evening chill. She was glad for the jeans she was wearing.

He came and took the insulated cooler from her, then noticed her shivers and handed it back. He reached into the car, took out his suit coat, and wrapped it over her shoulders. Then he took the cooler and placed it on the blanket. "Voilà. Picnic." He motioned her to sit.

His jacket smelled of his cologne as she held it close around her. He unzipped the cooler and removed several packages. "French bread medallions, goose liver pâté, smoked gouda, and grapes."

He took out a bottle of club soda and two plastic flutes. "Not my beverage of choice, but in consideration of your preference . . ." He poured her flute and passed it.

She sipped. "When did you plan all this?"

"In the airport. One of those gourmet shops."

She smiled. "It's nice."

"I would have chosen more, but Rick was antsy."

Noelle imagined him waiting while Morgan compiled their picnic. She hadn't known he'd gone to the airport; he'd only said Denver. "We should have invited him."

Morgan gave her just the look she expected.

She spread a medallion with pâté. "I'm sure he's hungry."

"He's got a whole kitchen."

That was true. But they had the starlit mountain vista and an orange moon creeping up the horizon. Rick would have blessed their food. She took a bite. "Delicious."

Morgan pulled a grape from the stem. "So are you bored yet, holed up on the mountain with Rick and Marta and assorted guests?"

"Not very. And we had company."

"A flatlander from Kansas with a fat wife and twelve kids."

She cocked her head. "Wrong."

"Who, then?"

"Your father." She straightened the napkin across her knee.

"Dad was up?"

She nodded. "He brought Rick a pair of fillies to start. He was sorry to miss you."

"I'm sorry too."

"The best part is, he convinced Rick to let me ride Destiny. *And* train him."

Morgan sat back with a grin. "Good for Dad. Bet it gave Rick fits."

"He only convulsed once or twice." She laughed.

"So how is it?"

"Destiny? It's . . ." She recalled the feeling of being on his back, sensing his mood and matching hers to it. "Beyond words."

Morgan reached across and grasped her hands. His eyes were deep as the night shot with moonglow. "Promise me one thing when I'm gone."

Her throat tightened. "What?"

"You'll stay just the way you are right now. You won't climb back into your shell."

She searched his face, saw there something real and painful. He cared. He truly cared. "I promise." But she was far from sure she could keep it.

# 12

The next morning's sun beat hot on Noelle's head as she perched on Destiny's back. Morgan had left an hour before in his Corvette, top down, music playing. He had asked her again to join him in Chicago. He wouldn't be Morgan if he hadn't, but it was out of the question, especially after the terrible night she'd had, wrenching awake from a dream more real than any of the others. She'd actually felt the plunge of the hawk, the assault of its talons. Her head beat now with the glow of amber eyes. Ridiculous. She'd never been attacked by a hawk.

Something had happened, obviously, to trigger such horrific dreams. One didn't leave everything and run halfway across the country without cause. And something kept her from returning or even communicating with that portion of her self. What fragments broke through her resistance triggered panic and nightmares. So, yes, something had happened. But it was now about moving on.

Noelle was safe at the ranch. She had her painting, and now she had Destiny. She had purpose and identity. Morgan wanted to find the real Noelle, but she wasn't trapped inside. She didn't exist—yet. The person who cowered in her dreams was not the real thing. She had nothing but scorn for that compliant being. She could stay buried forever.

Rick brought Destiny to a stop. "Are you ready?"

She tugged herself into the present. "More than ready."

He unclipped the tether rope. She had the stallion to herself.

He was hers to control, or she was his. She absorbed his energy, the power of smooth muscles in his back and shoulders and loin. He was magnificent.

Rick stood close. "Easy now. Take him around. Let his energy control the pace."

Noelle did as he said, thrilled by the horse's nervous power. She circled him, round and round, feeling him relax until he pranced obediently, willing and eager. She let out the rein, and he quickened his step, choosing his pace, working out his nerves.

She understood. She didn't need Rick's admonition to give Destiny his head. This was his time as much as hers. *You're free, Destiny.* A sudden urge seized her to let him run, to feel the rush of his speed, his wild blood. She stopped him before Rick. "Let me take him down the meadow."

"No way." He deflated her dream with two words. Who did he think he was?

"I can do it, Rick."

He shook his head. "You can't handle him if he bolts."

"I can; I know it."

"He's getting restless. Take him around the corral."

Around the corral, around the corral. The story of her life! Anger flaring, she kicked in her heels and immediately realized her mistake. Destiny bucked and twisted, his power unleashed. Her arms wrenched and strained. She lost her hold and slammed to the ground, her breath stopped by the impact.

She rolled, gasping, and saw Rick lunge. He stood over her, guarding her from Destiny's hooves as the horse reared and charged, then veered away, tossing his head. Air flooded her lungs, and she staggered up behind him.

He kept his eyes on the horse but clipped, "Are you all right?"

She drew a sharp, choppy breath. "Yes."

He turned briefly, and she caught the full force of his expression. "That sets us back. Now he doesn't know what to expect from you. Or me."

He was right. She swallowed her damaged pride. "I'm sorry."

He looked at Destiny, standing nervously, pawing one hoof. "You'll have to get up again. He's enjoying what he did."

Her heart jumped, but it wasn't fear. He was letting her try again, letting her undo her wrong. A rush of gratitude filled her.

He walked toward the stallion, confident and steady. If the horse read his body language as well as she did, he would not run. Rick caught the reins and patted Destiny's neck. "Now come slowly." He kept his attention on the horse but spoke to her.

She obeyed.

"Get on up." He held Destiny's head while she mounted, then said, "And don't vent your temper on the horse again." Though his voice was low, there was no mistaking his anger. He was a fine one to talk about temper.

If he had just let her take Destiny down! The moment had been right for both of them; she knew it. But Rick had to control, protect. She was sick to death of that kind of protection, as though she were some invalid or idiot with no will of her own. But she bit back her retort. She had mishandled it and wanted this opportunity too much. He had also put himself between her and Destiny's hooves.

"Talk to him now."

She bent and stroked the stallion's neck, felt his hide quiver, then still. "I'm sorry, Destiny. I should never have kicked, no matter how provoking your master is." She kept her voice soothing as she nudged the horse with her knees and avoided Rick's eyes.

The pain in her hip proved him right. She couldn't control the horse. Not yet. Maybe not ever if the animal pitted its strength to hers. Not even Rick had strength for that. It was in the mind, in the training, that they were able to manipulate Destiny at all. In the horse's own willingness. And it had been there. She had sensed it, matched it, then spoiled it. She tried to find the rhythm they'd had before but couldn't. Their connection had severed. She brought the horse to a stop and dismounted.

Rick took the reins without speaking. She had betrayed his trust, jeopardized his progress. She shied when he reached toward her, but he only touched a finger to her jaw, a scrape she only now became aware of. "Ask Marta for something to treat that."

She nodded, knowing well enough the infection she could get from a scrape in a horse corral. Daddy had been manic about cleanliness, especially after contact with the horses. He'd been manic about anything threatening her health. Again the shadow, and a rush of wings in her ears. Was it Daddy?

Rick opened the gate to let her out. "Do you mind walking down? I want to finish here." He meant remedy the damage she'd done. He wanted time with the horse alone. She had failed him and Destiny both.

"Rick . . ." She looked into his face. "I'm sorry."

"Next time you'll know." He gave her a brief smile.

Next time. There'd be a next time. And she wouldn't spoil it. She nodded, then slipped out of the corral and started down the meadow.

———

With Rick gone to an auction the following day, Noelle's hopes of proving herself with Destiny faded. She didn't dare take him alone after learning what the animal could do to her. She was sore all over from her fall. How did Rick do it, day after day, getting tossed and climbing back up again?

She sighed. She could saddle Aldebaran, ride out and paint, though riding the mare after Destiny wouldn't be the same, even if it was his dam. And her creative energy was at low ebb. The muse had fled. Morgan was right; it could be dull at the ranch. She wished he had stayed longer.

What would she do if she were home and feeling glum? Have a manicure, a facial? She looked down at her plain, clipped nails, thought of the women she might have called to have lunch at the club. She didn't miss one of them, not one. But then, neither she nor Daddy had let anyone come too close. She had taken his cue there, picked up his suspicious nature.

Instead, she'd poured herself into the arts, as he had the law. She'd graced Daddy's table and philanthropic events, his prize, his model daughter. Compliant child; the phrase could have been coined for her. Whatever Daddy had valued, she'd aspired to.

But now she was a woman. Did she even know what she wanted? She wanted to train Destiny. Why? Was that just another feather in her cap? No. There was something in his struggle, something to which she connected, though it did seem contradictory to fight for the chance to ride him yet want to see him free. How could she want two such opposite things? Freedom and control. They vied in her.

She tossed back her hair, stood, and paced in her room. The walls seemed close. Her breath quickened. Panic built inside. She pulled open the door and stepped onto the landing. She was not trapped. She was not in danger. As her breast stilled, she pulled the door closed and went downstairs.

Marta hummed in the kitchen. Noelle wandered to the doorway and watched her wiping down the counters. Again that sense of purpose. Like Rick. They seemed to know their place in life, while she floundered.

Marta looked up. "Come on in."

Noelle walked to the butcher-block table.

"Can I get you something?"

"No, thank you." What could Marta possibly provide that would make any difference at all?

Marta smiled. "You're stir crazy."

Noelle sighed. "It shows?"

"You need to keep busy. Next to faith, work is the surest road to happiness and well-being."

Both Rick and Marta certainly ascribed to that. Work and faith. Were they happy? "I'm not sure what to do."

"Not painting today?"

Noelle shook her head. "I wanted to continue with Destiny, but with Rick gone . . ."

Marta rinsed the cloth in the sink, then squeezed it dry and hung it on the rack. "I'm just preparing to make bread. Want to help?"

Noelle ran her fingers along the edge of the table. "I don't cook."

Marta actually stopped. "Not at all?"

Noelle licked her lips. "I'm sure Daddy would have provided a chef to train me, but, to be honest, I never saw the need." Nor had she been welcome in the kitchen at home.

Marta turned from the sink, appraising her. "That bad, hmm?"

"Poor little rich girl." Noelle gave her a brief smile.

Marta chuckled. "Privilege can stifle ingenuity. We have so much we take for granted. Some of us more than others." She didn't say it unkindly, but Noelle felt rebuked.

Had she taken her good fortune for granted? Expected all the service and benefits as her due? It was life, her life. Now she was trying to fit within a new reality. She could no longer expect things to be handed to her. Learning to cook might be just the next step to filling out the self she'd started defining as artist and horse trainer. "Do you think you could teach me?"

"Do you want to learn?"

Noelle looked about the tidy kitchen, tried to picture herself with arms up to the elbows in dishwater, or cutting and mashing and beating a batter with a wooden spoon like Martha Stewart. Well, why not? She nodded.

Marta opened the pantry door and pulled down a cream-colored apron. She handed it to Noelle. "Baking bread isn't the easiest to begin with, but we can do it together."

"Thank you."

Marta took out the large mixer and bowl. "Get some hot water in the measuring cup there. Six cups steaming from the faucet."

Noelle read the lines on the measuring cup and filled it as Marta directed. By the time Marta measured out the yeast and honey, the water had cooled enough to add them. The mixture foamed up.

"Now measure the flour and salt." Marta showed her the amounts on the worn recipe card, though Marta didn't seem to look at it much. "And the oil."

Noelle did as she was directed. Then Marta poured the yeast mixture into the bowl and lowered the heavy beaters. Noelle held the bowl steady as the beaters pulled and twisted the dough.

At last Marta said, "Turn it out onto the floured board."

Noelle dumped the soft mass, and Marta demonstrated the kneading. Noelle buttered her hands as Marta had done and pressed them into the soft mass.

"It'll take more than that."

Noelle pressed the heels of her hands through to the board. She turned the dough and tried it herself. It took a while to master the rolling, wedging movement, but she enjoyed the light and springy feel of the dough and its warm, yeasty aroma. A simple pleasure.

"That should do. Now we cover it and let it rise."

Noelle nodded. She had studied the concept of leavening; she'd just never seen it in the making, certainly never done it herself.

Marta rummaged in the pantry, pushing and stacking items, then shook her head. "I'm clean out of vinegar. I'll have to run to the market." She turned and untied her apron. "There's a stack of potatoes by the sink. Peel them and set them to boil in the pot there. When the bread doubles, punch it down and let it rise again."

Noelle hadn't planned on doing more than the bread. But that had worked out rather well. "Okay." When Marta left, she took up the paring utensil. Her first swipe slid over the potato skin with no result. She pressed the peeler hard and swiped again, gasping when it nicked her knuckle. She held her finger under the running water, then tried again. The potato skin came off in small chunks.

Annoyed, she wondered why she had volunteered. For that matter, she'd said nothing about peeling potatoes. But preparation was part of the cooking process. Did she want to learn, or didn't she? Where was that satisfaction Marta exhibited? Next to faith, work brought the most happiness? She'd hate to see what faith was like.

Noelle gouged the potato and caught her fingertip. With an unsavory word, she tossed the potato into the sink and sucked her finger, then turned to see Rick in the doorway, his expression singularly annoying. "Did you want something?"

He leaned on the doorjamb. "Is Marta around?"

"She went to the market. For vinegar."

"Oh. And you're . . ." He raised a questioning hand.

"I'm helping; what does it look like?" She should not have given him that ammunition, but he didn't take it, just nodded slowly, raised his eyebrows, and left.

She'd been rude, but he had caught her at her worst. Taking up the utensil, she hacked at the potato. She wished now she'd never walked into the kitchen. Marta made it look easy, bustling around as though there were nothing to turning out her wonderful meals.

Noelle tasted blood on her fingertip but had no idea where to find a Band-Aid. Another cold-water rinse seemed to do the trick, but as with sewing the button, her gains of practical skills might leave her quite literally all thumbs. But she'd been given a task, so she kept on. Potato after potato. She blew the strand of hair that fell over her eye and kept peeling until the stack was done. Then she rinsed the brown-speckled film and traces of blood from the spuds and put them in the pot. She clamped on the lid and turned the burner on high.

Peeking at the bread in the bowl, she saw that it had indeed doubled in size. What had Marta said? Punch it down. She gave it a good punch and the dough collapsed, but when she raised her hand, it clung like alien tentacles. She had not buttered her hands. She pulled at the sticky dough, but then it clung to her fingers. She yanked free and washed off the excess dough.

Well, that was taken care of. Noelle put the cloth back over the bowl. Now that it had to rise again, she could leave it. So she wandered out to the main room, peeked into Rick's office. If he was through at the auction, maybe they could work Destiny, and she would prove herself capable and trustworthy in spite of his expression as he left the kitchen. She never claimed to be a farmwife.

But the office was empty. She went down the hall to the back door, then stepped outside near the cabins. The first was still vacant, the next two rented by older couples enjoying the quiet mountain ranch. Wandering past, she squinted up the meadow. Was Rick working Destiny without her? She didn't see him and the truck was in the yard, but he could have taken Orion up.

She walked far enough to see that he wasn't in the high training corral, then went back down. She glanced into the truck bed. There were a few items on the tack blanket against the cab but not much. The auction must not have been too exciting. So where was he now? The stable roof again? She walked around and checked, but he wasn't there. With a sigh, she turned back and went inside.

Her nostrils quivered at a terrible smell coming from the kitchen—and smoke. With a cry, she rushed down the hall. Smoke billowed from the pot on the stove. She grabbed the lid, then flung it to the floor as her palm seared. A hand gripped her shoulder, and Rick shoved her toward the sink and turned the faucet on.

She held her hand under the cold rushing water that made her arm ache but took the sting from the burn. She held it there as long as she could stand it while Rick turned off the burner, grabbed a pair of hot pads, and moved the pot across the stove. It was charred black; what she'd seen of the potatoes when she pulled off the lid were shriveled and brown. All her work!

He crossed to the sink and turned up her palm. "Let's see."

The red welt throbbed. He pulled a knife from his pocket and at first she thought he meant to lance the burn. But he sliced off a pointed succulent spear from the plant on the windowsill. He slit it open and laid it on her palm. The gel inside felt cool and sticky and, amazingly, eased the pain.

She eyed the leaf darkening slightly on her palm. "What is it?"

"Aloe." He took down a first aid kit from the cabinet over the refrigerator, applied an anesthetic ointment, and wrapped her hand with a thin layer of gauze.

Though he was gentle, she winced. "What happened to the potatoes?"

"The water must have boiled out."

Water. She hadn't added any, but now she realized potatoes couldn't boil without water. Her cheeks flamed, but before Rick could notice, Marta rushed in, waving at the smoke.

"What on earth?"

Noelle turned. "I—"

"Sorry, Marta. We weren't watching it." Rick nudged Noelle toward the door. As Marta caught sight of the charred pot and started to exclaim, he pushed Noelle outside. "We'll be down for lunch." He herded her into the truck.

She dropped her face to her fingertips. Couldn't she do anything right? "I should have stayed and cleaned up."

Rick started the engine. "You don't want to be in there just now."

Noelle dropped her hands to her lap, wincing at the pain in her palm. She was twenty-three years old and failed at even the simplest tasks. No, she'd never cooked a meal. Her apartment kitchen had been only decorative, thanks to take-out and delivery. In the bungalow she had used a toaster and microwave and coffeemaker, none of which required anything more than touching buttons. She closed her eyes and tried to ignore the painful burn as Rick drove up the slope.

What was he thinking? Why had he stepped in that way? Did she telegraph helplessness?

He parked and turned. "You won't want to hold the reins."

"I can do it."

He pushed open his door. "I want to try something different anyway."

Destiny waited at the gate. It gave her a pang to see him so still and willing. Where was the fight he'd shown yesterday? Rick had stayed out with him long into the evening after she left.

Destiny nickered, obeisant as Rick approached. She felt cold inside. What had Rick done? His stroking hands and soothing tones, his uncompromising will had subdued the stronger animal. Without her to disrupt it, his gentle determination had won the horse's heart. She reached a tremulous hand to Destiny's mane, suddenly uncomfortable beside the man who could accomplish that.

"Ready?" No preamble, no remonstrations about yesterday's misconduct, as though he'd forgotten it completely.

She glanced up briefly. "I'm ready."

He saddled but did not bridle Destiny. "Can you balance without the reins?"

"Of course." She mounted. "How do I direct him?"

"You don't."

She sagged. Was he reverting to the tether? It hung by the fence, but he made no move that way. "What are we doing?"

"Have you heard of a horse hooking on? It's when the animal chooses to work as one with its master. I think Destiny came to that last night, but I want to try it out."

Her curiosity piqued. Rick stroked Destiny's head and muzzle. He gently chucked the horse's chin, and the stallion bumped his nose into Rick's chin. She stared. Destiny had returned the gesture! She watched, fascinated, as they playfully butted each other.

Rick glanced up. "I've never done this with a rider. I don't know if it will confuse him, but I thought you should be part of it. You might be so much baggage, or you might distract him. We'll see."

*So much baggage. Thank you very much.*

With nothing but his will connecting them, Rick faced east, his shoulder even with Destiny's nose. He took a step forward and stopped. The horse likewise took a step. Rick strode five steps and the horse followed. He turned to his left, then to his right. The horse kept beside him, mirroring his movement.

What force of character did Rick possess to so enchant the horse? And where did that leave her? She, too, moved with Destiny as Rick directed. Fear stirred. No. She wasn't baggage.

Rick turned, but the horse didn't turn with him. Destiny seemed confused, or was it her own striving emotions the animal sensed? Rick reached a hand to the stallion's head and turned him. She was disappointed by Destiny's immediate obedience. She almost willed him to revolt. *Don't do it. Don't acquiesce like a dumb, docile beast.* Now she knew which she wanted—freedom for Destiny more than control.

"Noelle."

She startled. "What?"

"I'm trying to do something here. Are you with me or not?"

Had he read her thoughts? Had her rebellion shown? She swung her leg over and jumped down. "I've had enough." She ducked through the rails and walked away. She wanted to be alone, away from Rick, from Destiny, away from herself. She passed into the trees, breathing the scent of living pine sap. The forest was wild, untamed. But Rick had even taken the trees to form the walls and floor and roof of his house, his furniture. He'd shaped and fashioned them to his will, as he had Destiny.

She reached out and touched the rough, sticky bark, put her face close and breathed the sweet, almost butterscotch scent. She ran her finger over the bubbly crystallized sap and felt the strength of the tree. The breeze rustled its needles. She dropped her forehead to the bark and closed her eyes.

She couldn't blame Rick. He had been true to himself, never wavering. She was the one who'd betrayed what she wanted for the horse. Freedom and control could not coexist. Yet Destiny had seemed eager to please Rick, playful and peaceful. He'd lost the wild fear, the quivering hide, the rebellious arch of his neck. He marched proudly in step with the man who had claimed his affection. Was there peace in submission?

A screech sounded in her mind, the sound from an open beak. Amber eyes. She cowered, searching the sky above the pines. What insanity was that? She was not a mouse or a rabbit to fear the sky. Not the sky. The hawk. Her chest constricted, and she wrapped herself in her arms. Why did that image persist?

Rick had watched, surprised, as Noelle headed into the trees. Why had she quit? This was the most rewarding part of training, when the animal at last hooked on, when he joined you in his spirit and will. He had expected her to appreciate it, had anticipated her pleasure. Yet he'd felt her striving against him. Destiny had felt it, too, hadn't known which way to go. But why?

He opened his heart to the Lord's wisdom. Had he done something wrong, hurt or offended her? He had employed extreme control of his temper the day before, had not lashed out, and today he'd given her a fresh chance. He thought over their encounters from the time Morgan left, at breakfast where he'd said he was going to the auction. Nothing offensive in that, though she'd obviously been disappointed.

Then the scene in the kitchen . . . What on earth was she doing all that for anyway? But he hadn't laughed or teased, as he'd been tempted. He'd resisted and left her to the task until he saw smoke coming from the kitchen window, after which he'd ministered to her burn and delivered her from Marta's disapproval.

He shook his head, unable to equate any of that with Noelle's response. Walking away, she'd had that brittle look he'd first seen in her, at once broken and bewildered. Maybe he should talk to her. What would he say? He had questions, but he didn't think she'd answer. He had answers, but she had to want to hear them.

Lord? A strange, harsh verse from Zephaniah came to mind. "She obeys no one, she accepts no correction. She does not trust in the Lord, she does not draw near to her God." He sensed a thread of truth. By all indication she didn't know or reverence the Lord, but how would that apply to her behavior just now?

She had intentionally vied with him. But he wasn't her master. She owed him no obedience, beyond basic cooperation. She was the one who'd forced the issue, enlisted Dad, and won the chance to work together for the goal. Had their success disappointed her?

Maybe she only wanted the challenge. By all indications she was exactly what Morgan thought her—a wealthy ingénue trying out the world for size. Was she just bored and spoiled enough to only want what she couldn't have? Then why did his heart sense brokenness? Or was he so out of his league that discernment failed him?

He pushed away from the rail, turned back to the horse, and noticed Destiny's gaze had also followed her. Rick grinned. "You don't have to hook on to everything, horse."

Destiny butted him with his nose, and Rick returned the affection. With a last glance over his shoulder, he returned to the center of the corral, Destiny on his heels.

CHAPTER

# 13

The smell of burnt potatoes lingered when Noelle went inside. Marta's humming did not entice her in that direction; instead she gave the kitchen a wide berth. She wouldn't make that mistake again. Standing in the main room, she missed Morgan. They could have hiked or spent time in town. She would have known what to expect, how to be with him.

On the table lay Rick's Bible, the words that connected him to some invisible being who claimed to be truth, who wanted absolute submission. She imagined all the movies she'd seen where some black-coated fanatic wielded the Bible like a weapon. Was it magic, like a staff or wand? Was Rick under its spell and therefore empowered to subdue helpless creatures?

"Is that you, Noelle?"

She cringed. "Yes, Marta." And reluctantly she stepped into the kitchen doorway. She may as well make her apologies and be done with it.

Marta waved toward four golden loaves of bread steaming on the table. "I thought you'd like to see how it turned out."

Noelle stared. "That's the bread?"

"As pretty as any I've made myself."

The loaves had a wholesome, rich aroma that filled the kitchen, in spite of the potatoes. The bread had worked. They were beautiful. A flickering satisfaction eased her wounded pride.

"Now." Marta rested her knuckles on her hips. "We've got work to do."

"You . . . want me to help?" Noelle asked.

"Hungry guests expect dinner. You want to learn, don't you?"

Noelle tipped her head. "I'm not sure I do anymore." But she couldn't stop looking at the beautiful bread. Four plain loaves, yet she felt as proud of them as her paintings. She glanced at the pot, half filled with some soapy white liquid. "What were the potatoes for?"

"German potato salad. That's why I needed the vinegar." The whole reason she had gone to the market, but Marta shrugged. "No matter. We'll make do without."

Like Rick, Marta was giving her another chance. She thought of Rick in the corral with Destiny. She'd been unfair in her judgment. He had done something wonderful and she'd scorned it. Maybe now she could make it up to him. "Let me wash up."

Marta's smile sent warmth that buoyed Noelle as Marta showed her how to flour and fry the chicken, slice and steam the carrots. It didn't bother her to have Marta scrutinize and correct, since it was done gently and she sensed a true concern in the older woman. There had been few enough women in her life, and Noelle had been close to none. Not even a good female friend.

She looked at Marta. Thirty years separated them, maybe more. They were opposite in personality, polar in beliefs. Marta was measured and faithful; Noelle was fed up with restrictions. But there was no judgment just now in the older woman.

"It's kind of you to help me," Noelle said.

Marta poured the oil and vinegar into a cruet. "I'm a Titus-two woman."

"I beg your pardon?"

"In the Bible, book of Titus, chapter two, the older women train the younger ones. Don't find many interested in what I know, though. Seems they're more into computers or the stock market or . . . well, just about anything." Even while she talked, Marta's hands were busy adding herbs and seasonings to the cruet. "Not much respect for keeping a home these days, cooking and cleaning."

Noelle pointed out the obvious. "It's not really necessary, is it? With fast food and—"

"See any golden arches from that window?" Marta jutted her chin.

Noelle smiled. "Not here. Or I might never have thought of learning, and I am glad to be, in spite of being culinarily challenged."

Marta laughed. "You're not challenged, just disadvantaged."

*Disadvantaged?*

"Don't hang your mouth open. Plenty a rich person has been neglected where it counts."

"But, Marta . . ."

"I don't doubt you've had privileges enough; you're obviously well educated in some areas. But if you don't mind me saying so, there's something missing, isn't there?" Marta's voice softened.

Noelle looked down at her hands. "Why do you think that?"

Marta held the knife above a sprig of fresh parsley. "Am I wrong?"

Noelle sighed. "I don't know." She hoped the woman wouldn't probe further. Something missing? How about whole chunks of her memory?

Marta minced the parsley. "The heart of everything is faith. Without it, life has no meaning. With it, everything is ennobled. Even scrubbing that pot." She jutted her chin toward the burned potato pot.

"Do you want me to—"

"No." Marta shook the dressing, then poured it from the cruet. "You can toss this with the salad tongs. Lightly, so you don't crush the tomatoes."

Noelle did as Marta directed, blending the herbs and oil and vinegar into the cucumber and tomato salad. It smelled delightfully pungent. At Marta's direction she placed the bowl into the refrigerator. Preparing the meal was easy with Marta there telling her each step. Marta's knowledge and confidence gave her courage to try.

Maybe that was it for Destiny too; he felt secure in Rick's guidance. He succumbed because he wanted to, not because he couldn't help himself. Was she the one who had misunderstood?

Noelle heard Rick come inside and climb the stairs. He must be washing in his room, but he would be down to eat. As Marta heaped the chicken onto the platter, Noelle tore a small square of foil. With deft fingers she folded and twisted the foil into a tiny origami swan. She grabbed a sprig of fresh parsley and laid it atop the mound of chicken, then tucked in the swan.

Marta raised her eyebrows. "What's that?"

"Garnish." Noelle heard Rick in the dining room. Did he smart from her earlier lack of enthusiasm? She had behaved poorly. She drew a deep breath, then carried the platter to the table, a peace offering.

He didn't look angry. When she set the chicken before him, he breathed the aroma. "Mmm. Nothing like fried chicken to cover the smell of burnt potatoes." There was teasing amusement in his eyes, certainly not the mood she'd expected. He bent and touched the tiny wing of the swan, the only thing on the table totally hers. He raised his eyebrows. "Nice touch."

"Thank you." She gathered her breath. "Speaking of touch, you did an amazing job with Destiny."

"It's not over. He's just turned a corner."

"A big corner."

"It's all about trust."

But unlike Destiny, she'd had her trust betrayed. Something had made her run away, something gave her a jaded eye, caused the panic attacks, the fractured images. Even if she couldn't remember what, she recognized the effects. Broken trust was not easily fixed, and the only way she knew to be safe was to trust only herself.

———

Michael shooed the fluffy white-and-gray Shih Tzu from his leg. When it persisted, he kicked its ribs with the toe of his loafer.

"Michael!" His mother's face pinched.

The dog must be even more brainless than her last, as it still yapped at his ankle. He reached down and snatched it up by the scruff.

"Oh, Darling, Darling. Don't hurt Darling, Michael."

He tossed the dog into the coat closet and closed the door.

"Now, what kind of place is that for a dog?" His mother pouted.

"I won't be here long. Then you can save Darling from the dungeon."

She stepped close and stroked his suit lapel. "You look very handsome today. Were you in court?"

"Yes."

"How did it go?"

He pushed her hand aside and strode into her living room. "How do you think it went, Mother?"

"I bet you were superb."

"Well, you're wrong." He turned to face her. "I was ineffective. I failed to connect with the jury, to convince them of anything I said. I fumbled and forgot my point and acted like an imbecile. William St. Claire took over for me." His mentor's action wrenched his insides and played over and over in his mind. A second failure.

"But why?" His mother pulled her boa-trimmed robe tighter at the waist and headed for the wet bar. She couldn't stand his failure and took it personally. That was the one good thing to come from today's humiliation, seeing it upset his mother. Michael seethed. To be replaced by William, in court, in progress. He flinched.

William's decision had been right. He had seen the need and acted on it. The truth was, Michael couldn't keep the facts straight, could hardly concentrate. He'd dreamed of Noelle and wakened weeping. Actually weeping. It was getting worse. Time was not healing the wound; it was festering it. It ate at him like a cancer.

If he could just find Noelle and make her understand. How could she stay away so long? Had she contacted William again? Had she told him? No. William St. Claire would have him prosecuted, imprisoned, and disgraced if he knew. Michael rubbed a hand over his face. Didn't she know losing her was worse than any of that?

The ice clinked in his mother's glass as she approached. "Have a drink, dear. It will soothe you."

"Soothe me, Mother? It makes me an animal."

She smiled. "Don't be silly."

"No? Ask Noelle if you don't believe me."

His mother stopped, paused her glass halfway to her mouth. "She's back? Have you spoken to her? Is everything all right?"

"No. No. And no." He smiled wickedly. "I have no idea where she is, and I'd be the last to know."

Mother sank into the couch, her robe parting to reveal more than Michael ever wanted to see. She was oblivious. "But why? What happened?"

"I told you; I'm an animal."

"You're a god. Adonis." She raised her glass in toast, then gulped her drink.

Michael sneered. "Adonis was not a god. Only a lowly youth loved by a goddess."

"Noelle is no goddess. How could she be and reject you?" Another gulp.

By the glaze in her eyes, she'd had a few before he came, the mint on her breath when she greeted him a shabby clue. Though why she bothered, he didn't know. "And how is your liver today?"

She glared. "I'm as fit as you."

Michael laughed. "Oh, Mother, that's rich. As I'm not fit at all."

"You've never had a sick day. We have pure genes."

Michael walked to the couch and hovered over the pathetic woman who'd birthed him. "So did the Caesars. And as you know, they were all quite mad."

He left her with her mouth hanging open in fear and dismay. At least that parting shot was effective. If mother had been on the jury . . . But that thought was too ludicrous to pursue. He went to meet Sebastian in Central Park. Sebastian could track anything in cyberspace, but Noelle had done nothing, it seemed, that could be caught in his web. She had left her car with its global tracking system right on the estate, had used no phone or credit card, opened no account, not even checked e-mail or surfed the Web. Had she climbed into a cave? How long would two thousand dollars last? Or did she have help? Was she with someone else?

His gut knotted. Oh, she had denied it, but . . . He swiped a handkerchief over his suddenly perspiring brow as he stalked to the taxi at the curb. He *was* going mad. There was no other explanation. As hard as he tried, he couldn't think, couldn't focus, couldn't function.

---

William had made up his mind. He had to consider everything. And the truth was, his shining star was falling. It was common enough in the profession, with the hours, the mental acuity required, the stress. But William knew it was more than that. Noelle had crushed Michael's spirit when she left. And as there had been no word from her since that solitary phone call, he could not even discuss it, persuade her to consider the pain she caused. Time to think was one thing. Total abandonment, another.

Yes, she had the right to time alone, time to think, to do whatever she was doing. William paced across his plush carpet, making no sound at all. Wherever she was after nearly two months, did she consider Michael at all? William understood heartache. He read the signs in Michael, but he couldn't let it affect their work. He had the firm to think of, their clients and their reputation. The other partners were rightly concerned. He stopped before the picture of Noelle.

She had never been so reckless, certainly not with another's hopes and feelings. He'd taught her to be charitable. Even if Michael had upset her, hurt or angered her, surely this was excessive! She was ruining him, and there was no way to communicate, to remedy that.

Or was he misreading it all? His first reaction had been to doubt Michael, but dealing with Noelle's absence together these last two months had cemented a kinship with Michael and affected an irritation toward Noelle. Maybe that was unfair, unnatural after all the years centered around her. But then her disappearing for two months was equally unnatural.

Margaret's voice came over the intercom. "Michael Fallon for you, sir."

William drew a slow breath. "Send him in."

Michael looked like a man reaching meltdown. At any moment, the explosion would blow him apart. He tried hard to mask it, but William saw the strain as clearly as he might in a witness ready to break.

Michael cleared his throat. "I know what you have to say, William."

"Do you?" William motioned him to a chair.

"Do you mind if I stand?" He was brittle enough to break.

"Sit down, Michael. This isn't a sentencing."

Michael sat. William took another side chair instead of the one behind his desk. They were friends, colleagues, mentor and pupil. They were almost father and son, except for Noelle's apparent change of heart.

Michael took a pen from the desktop and studied it, clicking the end in and out. A vein pulsed in his temple. "You're justified in your decision, sir."

"Am I?" William folded his hands.

Michael looked as though he meant to go on, but he glanced up. William's chest ached. The fire inside the young man needed to be directed outward. It was burning him alive.

"I want you to take a leave."

Michael seemed surprised. He'd obviously prepared himself for the worst. He didn't have an answer ready, and William was glad. He wanted to be heard.

"I know the strain Noelle's disappearance is causing."

Michael stiffened. "I don't blame her for my mistakes, William."

"Whether you blame her or not is irrelevant. The results are not healthy for the firm, nor for you." William reached out and took the pen from Michael's hand and set it on the desk. "There's no letter of resignation for you to sign. I expect you to unwind, refocus, and come back. I'm not putting a timeline on this. Your position with the firm is secure. But I want you back altogether." He dampened his lips. "Regardless of Noelle."

Michael dropped his chin. He might have looked grateful for the clout William carried as senior partner, the weight he'd thrown to keep Michael from being dismissed. Instead, he looked devastated.

William softened his tone. "This happens. You're not the first supernova. Just see that your meltdown isn't complete." He paused. "I've put a lot of energy into your development. Prove me right."

Michael jerked his head up. "I don't deserve this."

William smiled. "Just get through it."

Michael seemed to consider that with a clearer head. He nodded. "A few days might be good."

"I think longer. I want you one hundred percent." William put force behind the words.

The muscles tightened at the joint of Michael's jaw. "May I ask you something, sir?"

William nodded.

"How many days did you take when Adelle died?"

William sat a long time, holding Michael's gaze. Then he swallowed and said, "Four."

Michael stood. "I'll take four days."

William watched him walk out, his heart surging with pride and worry—exactly what he would feel for his own son, what he'd felt for Noelle so many times. Four days would not be enough, but there was no way he'd tell Michael that.

––––––––

The sun blazed on her shoulders as Noelle stood just outside the stable. The late August heat was sharp and dry. The breeze rasped across the brittle grass, chaff floating in gusts. She'd taken for granted the dazzling sunny days until rust-colored pine needles intermixed with green and everything had a drawn, crisp look.

With her paints, Noelle hoped to capture just that look. More and more she wanted an emotion in her landscapes. Not just the fertile beauty, but the need as well. Nature was fragile. Life was fragile.

Last night's dream had reinforced that thought. She was glass, a glass picture lying flat where anyone could step, and all around her, bright yellow light as through a window. But the light was not comforting. It revealed her, lying helpless, waiting to break.

Rick led the mare out, checked the cinch, and handed her the reins. He gazed up the meadow and frowned. "Don't go too far." He'd been like that these last weeks, tense and curt.

"I just need something to appease Ms. Walker."

"How's that going?" He tied her paint box behind the saddle.

"Fine. She wants all the paintings I can do."

He held the stirrup for her to mount. "And she's dealing fairly with you?"

Noelle swung into the saddle. "She's compiling an exclusive collection of my work. She has great expectations."

Under his breath Rick muttered, "I'll bet."

Noelle started to argue, then stopped. It was nice for him to be concerned. Destiny had developed a sore tendon, so they hadn't trained him in days, and she missed their interaction. Destiny's progress was remarkable, though it now felt as though Rick's training was directed more at her. *"Try to think like a horse,"* he'd said the last time they were out. His was a gift, a true empathy toward the animal, and though she tried, she couldn't break through as he'd done.

Not that she wouldn't keep trying. It gave her a new focus. Not quite "anything you can do I can do better," but certainly if Rick could accomplish it, she could too. He had been busy with the new influx of guests, basic equestrian instruction, and long days of horseback tours for non-staying guests as well. Those could be the most frustrating for him because such riders didn't have time at the ranch to understand the flow or Rick's style.

"You were kind to that boy this morning."

"Peter? He just needed direction."

Noelle tipped her head. "You're patient with ignorance."

He shrugged. "Ignorance can be cured. It's willfulness that's hard. He's a good kid."

"I don't know that his mare thought so."

Rick rested his hand on Aldebaran's rump. "Well, that's why I help them improve. Saves the horses discomfort. I don't think I'll let him take off on his own, though."

She didn't expect he would. Very few of the guests were given the privilege of taking the horse's alone. She was grateful for that right, and now she knew and appreciated Aldebaran's value. The other mares and geldings were so docile as to serve well in a trail line but not much fun to direct on her own. The stallions he didn't rent out, and Orion was Rick's workhorse.

He mounted him now, gave her a brief touch of his hat, then turned Orion's head and clicked his tongue. Where was he going? She could have asked to ride with him but didn't. Except when they worked Destiny, Rick gave no indication he craved her company. So she watched him go, then started off herself. She wanted to paint something small, not grand and sweeping.

The ground crunched beneath the horse's hooves. She spit the fine chaff that caught in her lips from a gust of wind and searched the landscape for a small vignette to paint quickly. She was determined to paint every day if she couldn't train Destiny. She noticed a dip filled with rose brambles and columbine. It was unremarkable except for the dry, crumbly cut in the bank above, where hung a shaggy veil of hair-like roots, desperate for moisture. She liked the contrast between that and the shaded columbine and roses, almost a subclimate beneath the parched pine trunks. That would do.

Because of the wind, Noelle held the paper clipped to the easel board in her lap and sat cross-legged on the ground, where she was somewhat sheltered by a boulder and three large pines. The sun was high overhead, shrinking the shadows to nearly nothing. She studied the scene: pale pink petaled flowers, deeper rosebuds with curled emerald sepals. She listened to the drone of the bees and the rustle of birds in the tops of the pines.

Noelle caught her breath as a fat-chested mountain chickadee flitted to the springy patch of dusty roots, its black-and-white feathers pristine against the dull brown veil. Even though the bird took wing a moment later, she would include it. She sketched quickly, then used the paints.

The scene proved a good study, and Noelle appraised her effort. This one might have a place in the exclusive collection. And that would make it worth more. She laid the painting across her knees, looked up through the narrowing boughs above her to the sea blue sky, and felt deeply satisfied.

Mr. Vogel, her old art instructor, would be disappointed to have her thinking so prosaically. *"Beauty for the sake of beauty."* How many times had he said so? Well, that was fine until you needed to eat and pay the rent—which she managed now with the sales of her work, the rest of her cash dwindling. She packed up her supplies and returned to the house.

Orion was in the yard, still saddled, but she didn't see Rick. She unsaddled Aldebaran and put her into the corral beside the barn. Then she went into the house and placed the painting in tissue to take to the gallery tomorrow. Her room was stifling; at least the gusting wind outside moved the air. She went back out and settled into the porch swing.

Marta's humming came through the upstairs window like a cat's constant purr. A honeybee buzzed the asters at the steps. She looked up the long meadow to the base of the mountain, then up the wooded slope and over to the next crag. Something caught her eye, something different, something . . .

Leaning forward, she stared, squinting in the bright sunlight. "Rick?" she called. He must be close, with Orion standing ready that way.

"In here."

She hurried to the barn and found him rummaging through a toolbox. "Rick, I think I see smoke."

He spun. "Where?"

"High on the next mountain over from your crag."

He strode out, his expression grim. "It's high, but the wind could drive it down." He took out a cell phone she hadn't realized he owned, placed the emergency call, then tucked the phone back into his vest. "I've got to get the stallions."

She pushed the hair out of her face. "Can I help?"

He glanced at Aldebaran in the corral, but she was no longer saddled. "I can manage." He mounted Orion and galloped off.

As Noelle watched, the puff of white on the mountainside spread up into the flawless blue sky, the orange glow beneath leaving no doubt to its source. She imagined the dry, rust-colored needles bursting into flame. It was far from the pasture, farther still from the ranch—not on Rick's land, but with a shift in the wind it could be.

Rick returned with Destiny and the stallions in tow. Noelle helped him corral them. The horses nickered and shied as Rick confined them, back-stepping uncertainly. All the animals were agitated, smelling smoke and sensing danger.

Rick led Orion over to where Noelle stood. "I was afraid of this."

"Is it bad?"

He slapped the dust from his thighs. "After two dry years, the trees are basically tinder."

"But we've had rain."

"Not enough to raise the sap content in the trunks."

"Can Juniper Falls fight it? I didn't see a fire station."

"It's a volunteer outfit. But smokejumpers and others'll come to fight it together." He turned to remount Orion.

"Where are you going?"

He looked up the mountain. "To check it out. We need to know what we're up against."

"But Rick, you can't—"

"I can at least get close and scout the terrain and conditions. Fire will follow the easiest path in the direction it's blown."

A truck with six forest service workers pulled into the yard. A volunteer fire vehicle came directly behind. Noelle backed off as they got out and spoke with Rick. Of course, his ranch would be the most accessible place to mount an attack, from what she'd seen on her jaunts. Above and surrounding the meadows of the ranch were mostly forested slopes, crags, and gullies. The base of the burning peak had a meadow of its own, but getting there would be difficult.

Rick nodded and rejoined Noelle and Marta, who had come out from the house. "They've put Juniper Falls on standby to evacuate. If the word comes, you'll want to pack up your things and be ready to leave within an hour's time."

Noelle's mind staggered. Leave? For where? And how? She had no transportation and nowhere to run. She couldn't do it again. She couldn't. Rick put a hand on her shoulder, no doubt reading her concern as he did his animals'.

"It's just a first alert. That fire needs to cover a lot of territory for that, and if we catch it now . . ." His gaze returned to the graying column of smoke.

"Will you leave?"

He shook his head.

A wash of relief. "Then I'm not either. They can't make me, can they?"

"No, but I can."

She looked up into his face. Would he? For her safety, she was sure. How could he know she was only safe there at the ranch? Well, she'd find a way to stay. Unless the fire burned down the meadow and headed directly for the house, she was not going anywhere.

"Marta, alert the guests—the Andersalls first, with all those kids. They should pack up right now, just in case." He turned to Noelle. "If you get the word to move, you and Marta can take her car and head for town. They'll direct you from there."

Noelle had no intention of going to town or anywhere else in Marta's Ford compact, but now was not the time to argue with Rick. "What about the horses?"

"Once I scout out the fire, I'll worry about that."

Noelle nodded. As though he could do everything by himself. "Should we soak down the house or something?"

Rick looked at the house, then up the valley. "We'll play that by ear. I've got to go." He mounted and brought Orion around.

It was true Orion would get up into the area more easily than any motorized vehicle on the ground. How long did it take to organize something like this? The two trucks followed Rick to the uppermost edge of his meadow; then she lost sight of him in the trees but whispered, "Be careful."

The thought of the flames devouring the brittle grasses and parched bracken, growing and bursting with destructive power, frightened her. The thought of Rick riding into the midst of it frightened her more. But the thought of leaving was the worst fear of all. She just wouldn't do it.

Marta drew a single breath. "We need to pray."

Noelle snapped, "You think prayer can stop a forest fire?"

Marta's sharp eyes darted from the mountain to her. "God created both the forest and the fire."

*Then why allow one to destroy the other?* Noelle watched the fire grow and spread with terrifying speed. Marta headed for the cabins to warn the guests to prepare for evacuation. Noelle refused to believe they would have to leave. If God was such good friends with Rick and Marta, surely . . .

But what was she thinking? This was nature, not some superstitious hocus-pocus. The training and knowledge of the teams amassing at the top of the meadow would stop the fire, not whispered words to a mythological God.

Another team arrived, and another. They would need a base to support them with food and water at least. Couldn't she and Marta do that much? That was a reason to stay. A surge of gratitude filled her. Gratitude toward whom?

CHAPTER

# 14

Under the direction of the smokejumpers, Rick trenched the base of the mountain, creating a dirt line as wide as the tallest trees that might fall. Some with chain saws cut and dragged trees from the natural break they'd chosen. No sense trying to clear the forested land farther up. Those trees would burn. Aspen would regenerate from underground roots. Conifers would have to start over from seed, unless the initial tree survived the burn. Some would if the bark was not burned through.

Until they got air support, they couldn't fight the worst of the flames, could only hope to contain the spread. Their goal—to trench a line too broad for the fire to jump. The volunteers without gear worked at a greater distance than the smokejumpers, who had parachuted in to begin the containment. Thanks to Noelle's quick eye, they had gotten to it sooner than many fires of its kind, but already the mountainside crackled and groaned. Inside, Rick groaned as well.

*Fire.* In the dry years the danger was always high. For the last weeks he'd looked out for it, praying for rain as the state banned campfires and even propane stoves. But this one, it seemed, nature started on its own. The sun's heat beat down on his back; ash and smoke billowed around him with the acrid smell only a wildfire made. Sweat stung his eyes, rolled down the back of his neck, and moistened his hands in his gloves.

High on the mountain, pines blazed like beacons, towers of flame that leapt from treetop to treetop as whole trunks exploded, sending fireballs hundreds of feet. The carpet of pine needles kindled, and fire roared along the ground. Everywhere smoke rolled like a choking fog, and he gasped for clean air even at the fringe. But he dug tenaciously, breaking the ground, clearing it.

One thing in their favor was the wind direction. It took the flames up and away from Juniper Falls. If the direction changed, the valley would form a tunnel the flames would rush through like a blowtorch. His throat constricted at the thought. His land, his home . . . all gifts. He had to remember that. And the Lord's will be done. But it was hard to relinquish control, to accept even as he fought.

*Lord, all this is yours. I won't resist if you need to take it. But until then, I'll fight with all I have. You command the wind and the flame. Help us now.* He jammed the shovel into the earth and dug.

————

Taking a break from their efforts inside, Noelle paced the yard, straining to see progress on the mountain. A slurry bomber passed over, dropping red clouds of water, fertilizer, and fire repellant just ahead of the blaze. Earlier a helicopter with a bucket on a long rope had begun dipping in nearby reservoirs and dropping water into the heart of the flames. But the fire engulfed more and more.

She jumped at the blast that jolted the ground, slapped the crags, and echoed back. Another followed, and fresh clouds of smoke and dust blurred the base of the mountain. The fire fighters must have set those charges themselves. A bulldozer chugged up from the meadow, cutting its own access as it went, making way for water tankers to follow. Would any of it be enough? The sky was a sickening brown, the sun a red orb as it sank behind the peaks.

Where was Rick? What was he doing up there in the smoke and fury? Was he afraid, or did he just trust his invisible God? She went to the porch and watched from the corner. Smoke stung her eyes and nostrils. Ash floated like snow. She tasted it in her teeth. But she stayed outside, waiting to hear, waiting for Rick, and hoping she would not need to leave the ranch. The very thought drained her.

The Andersalls had gone, rather than risk an emergency departure. Both the other families were ready to do the same, though they hadn't decided to actually check out yet. The Elams from the second cabin stood outside now and watched with her.

A medical team had set up a first aid station in the main room of Rick's house, as his was the nearest shelter. The smokejumpers had their own camp, but they came down to the house for food and supplies. With help from Red Cross volunteers and people from the town, Marta made sandwiches and kept a steady supply of coffee brewing, along with pitchers of water and bottles of Gatorade for the fire fighters to quench their thirst. Other supplies like sunscreen, lip balm, gloves, and bandanas arrived, and Noelle helped distribute them to fresh teams of fire fighters.

As a pickup truck brought a team down to rest, she went inside to help Marta and the others. This was the smokejumper team, who had been brought in to plan the attack because of the fire's proximity to developed land and communities. Noelle handed a plate to a woman with a thin blond ponytail clipped up in the back and asked, "How's it going out there?"

"I've seen worse."

That was encouraging, wasn't it? "So we won't be asked to evacuate."

"If the fire reaches the first trigger point, this whole area will be put on voluntary evacuation. By the second trigger point, it won't be voluntary."

"But it's not moving this way." Noelle prodded for the assurance she knew the woman could give.

"The conditions could change in a moment. If you're worried, you should go ahead and find a safer place."

Noelle's throat tightened. Did she look so ineffective? This was a woman who flew around the country stabbing the throat of dragons. And Noelle was afraid of leaving the ranch? Why? How had she been programmed, disabled? She knew how—Daddy's overprotective sphere and her own nightmares.

The man next to her took the plate Noelle handed him. "Thanks."

"You're welcome. Um, have you seen Rick Spencer up there?"

"Is he on one of the teams?"

"This is his ranch. But he's working on a containment line, I think."

"He'd be with the volunteers, then." He glanced at his smokejumper colleague.

She shook her head. "Sorry." They went to the main room to join their team members, who sprawled and ate and talked through a much-needed, though probably too-short, break. Noelle caught bits of their conversation, reminiscences of worst moments they'd faced, fires so massive they created their own weather, even snow—though how that worked she couldn't imagine. Maybe this one would make it rain.

Noelle went back outside. Rick hadn't come in to eat or rest. The sun set, smoke-dulled stars appeared, the night grew dark. Emergency teams used the third cabin and the extra rooms to sleep in shifts while others continued their vigilance. Noelle couldn't sleep, so she dozed on the swing, then woke at the sound of hooves on the gravel. She sat up. Rick slid from the horse and led Orion to the stable. He had to be exhausted and hungry, but it was a while before he emerged. He had taken care of the horse first.

He climbed the stairs, and she jumped to open the door. "Are you all right? What can I get you?"

He just shook his head, went in, and collapsed on the couch. The main room was empty. The Elams and Johnsons had gone to bed, confident they'd be notified of any danger. Though a volunteer waited in the kitchen, Noelle got Rick a roast beef sandwich herself. She poured him a glass of cold water and carried them into the other room.

He took the water and drank. "Thanks." His voice rasped.

"You went all day without eating." She held out the sandwich.

"No thanks." He rubbed his face with grimy hands.

"Marta would scold you into eating something."

He lay down on the couch, indifferent to the soot that covered him. His face grew slack in the lamplight. He was asleep already.

She took a blanket from the linen closet beside his office door and covered him. She'd wanted to know how bad it was, if they were beating the fire or if they would have to leave in the night. Could he sleep so deeply if that were the case? Well, she wouldn't get any answers now. She wrapped his sandwich and put it back into the refrigerator, then went up to bed.

Several times through the night she woke, smelled the smoke, and went to the window. The glow on the mountain remained. They'd be evacuated if it worsened. She went into the bathroom and counted the remaining hundred-dollar bills in her makeup bag. How far would the money take her, and where would she go? She closed her eyes and hoped she wouldn't have to find out.

When she woke, Noelle looked out at the thick, red sky. The mountainside was lost behind the veil. Her heart jumped. Maybe the fire had burned itself out. She rushed to wash and brush her teeth, ignored her hair, and threw on jeans and T-shirt. She went down, but the couch was empty. She found Marta in the kitchen with an older couple from town, baking muffins and scrambling eggs.

"Where's Rick?"

"Gone back up." Marta emptied a skillet of eggs into a larger pan from which the few people milling about helped themselves.

Noelle sank into the chair. "Then it's still burning."

"The winds picked up last night. We've been put on voluntary evacuation."

No! The fire must have reached the first trigger point, whatever that meant. "Are you going?"

"I have a job to do." Marta took out a large pan of muffins and set them out on the counter.

"Did Rick say what we should do?"

"They're directing people from town to shelters. I'm sure you could shuttle down with someone."

Noelle shook her head. "I mean, how we can help. What can I do?"

"Just what you've been doing." Marta set a muffin before her.

But it didn't seem like enough. How could handing out Chap Stick make a difference?

"According to the fire fighters, this is not the worst of the fires in the state. They've moved some of the Hotshots to Evergreen."

Noelle pushed up from the table, knowing she had to stay hopeful. "That's good, isn't it? If they don't need them here, it must mean—"

"It's a matter of degree. Each fire gets a rating, and Evergreen has more valuable real estate in closer proximity to the fire."

Noelle turned her attention to the smoke-engulfed mountainside. "Did Rick eat? I couldn't get him to eat last night. He went all day with nothing."

Marta emptied a third jug, then paused. "He was fasting."

"I beg your pardon?"

"Fasting and prayer avail much."

Marta might as well be speaking a foreign language. How could going without food help Rick? "That's absurd. How will he keep up his strength?"

Marta smiled. " 'Those who hope in the Lord will renew their strength. They will soar on wings like eagles; they will run and not grow weary, they will walk and not be faint.' "

"Well, he was weary last night, practically fell asleep sitting up."

Marta didn't answer, just poured out Styrofoam cups of coffee for the half-dozen volunteer fire fighters who prepared to start their shift. Noelle sighed. She didn't understand Rick and Marta's hocus-pocus, but it didn't matter. If Rick thought sacrifice could save his ranch, more power to him. If only it worked.

She went outside. It was hard to distinguish anything through the smoke fog. Shielding her eyes, she paced the porch before going back inside for another day of handing out supplies and making sandwiches. She wanted to keep watch from the porch, to know that evacuation would not be necessary. But helping was better, and outside her eyes streamed tears.

She kept thinking of the blonde and other women she'd served sandwiches or given bandanas or sunscreen. They were up there equipped with shovels and axes and hoses and training that Noelle had never even considered. The most she wielded was a paintbrush. So no one would consider her heroic. How did that fit her developing image of herself?

She coughed smoke and ash from her lungs. One couldn't be everything. She just needed to know who she wanted to be. Two men drove up in a maroon extended-cab truck, but they stopped in the yard, not proceeding up the meadow as so many other vehicles had. They climbed out and one sent her a wave. "We're taking Rick's horses down."

She looked from them to the stable and corral that held the animals. Had Rick asked for them to be removed? She started down the stairs. "Does he know?"

"He called for help. We'll just hitch up his trailer and take them four at a time."

If Rick was moving the horses, did that mean he thought evacuation imminent? Or was he just being cautious? If it came to mandatory evacuation, the fire fighters had said they'd have to leave within one hour. They could never move out all the horses in that time. Surely he was just being his normal methodical self. But he did have a firsthand view of the situation. Maybe it was worse than the smokejumper had led her to believe.

Her heart thumped. No. She would not panic. Maybe she couldn't face down that dragon. But she could face her own. What was the worst that could happen, a few nights in a shelter? No one would know her, recognize her, report her whereabouts. It was paranoid to think so. This was Colorado, not New York. If her picture had ever made a paper out here, it was news to her.

Noelle strained to see up the meadow. She didn't expect to see Rick any time soon. Maybe not until the fire was out or he was too tired to keep on. How long would it take? The light hardly changed as the sun climbed the sky. The heat was heavy.

"Excuse me."

Noelle turned to Mrs. Elam, the guest in cabin two. "Yes?"

"May we check out?"

Noelle looked from her to the mountain where Rick was. Had the woman assumed she was staff? She could get Marta, but a new influx of fire fighters needing breakfast had her passing muffins and coffee and eggs. Noelle nodded. "Sure." She brought the woman into Rick's office. A computer sat on the desk, but it was not booted up and she doubted she could access his files. So she'd do it the old-fashioned way. She found a memo pad. "Three days, right?"

"That's right. We'd reserved for five, but . . ."

"And how much per night?" Noelle searched for a pen to record the transaction.

"Sixty-five."

Noelle glanced up. Not even the difference between cabin and room could account for that discrepancy. Sixty-five dollars a night for a mountain cabin was both reasonable and expected. What surprised her was the difference between that and what she paid. She hid her confusion, though, as she tallied on the calculator, then took Mrs. Elam's check and cabin key. "I'm sorry you couldn't stay."

"No controlling Mother Nature. At the least we'll have a story to tell."

A story. Rick was up fighting to save his land, and they'd have a story to tell. But of course that's all it was, not her home. Noelle smiled. "Good-bye."

Before she'd left the room, the Johnsons came in. "Guess it's us next." Mr. Johnson held out his credit card.

"I'm sorry. I don't know how Rick runs that."

"Oh." He glanced at his wife. "I suppose we can write a check." Mrs. Johnson shrugged.

"Sixty-five a night? Two nights?" Noelle asked.

He nodded as he flipped to the checkbook in his billfold. And she paid roughly thirteen dollars a night for a month at a time. A quiver passed through her. What did Rick mean by charging her so little? She had assumed it was commensurate with the cabins. Not the same, surely, but a fifty-dollar per night discrepancy?

She left both payments and keys on the desk and went back outside. The two family vehicles drove down while a tanker truck cut through the yard and up the meadow, leaving dusty tracks in the ground. All the crushed and torched vegetation, the serene beauty decimated. As was her peace. Noelle shook her head, depressed.

But then a sudden gust of wind blew down from the mountain and fear jumped inside her. *No. Not down.* She hurried to the stable and saddled Aldebaran, one of the horses Rick's friends had not yet evacuated. By the time they came back for the next four, she'd at least know her fate.

The wind picked up as she rode, and gray sky roiled above her. As she neared the stallions' corral, still far from the actual fire, she choked, wishing she'd tied on a bandana. She could make out the sound of a helicopter, but she didn't see it through the smoke.

There was a gash at the mountain's base, separating the slope from the meadow that led to the ranch and another farther along beneath the actual burn. Those must be the containment lines cut with bull-dozer, chain saw, and shovel. The teams had talked about the line last evening. Giving the fire a continuous line of nothing to burn was not easy since it could burn up to two feet underground.

But trenching was the best hope for containment. Rain the best hope for extinguishment, and wind the worst condition for spreading the fire, especially when directed toward the ranch. And it was steady now, blowing into her face, blowing toward Juniper Falls. Rick's pickup was parked on the near side of the gash, but she didn't see him. The wind strengthened, and she drew close enough to see the flames flare up with each gust.

Something wet struck her cheek, and she raised her face to the sky. Had clouds moved in above the smoke? A thunderstorm? Another drop touched her forehead, then more. Had the wind brought rain? *Rain!* More drops fell. *Oh, let it be enough!*

Fervently she wished for the clouds to burst open as they had that day with Rick at the corral, to drown the flames as it had drowned the yard. Rick had warned her of flash floods, but now she hoped for nothing less. No fire could withstand that, could it?

The rain came in earnest as she turned the horse about. She pounded down the slope, the horse's hooves splashing water, the wind blowing cold spray. Before she reached the ranch it was a downpour as powerful as the other. She stopped the mare in the yard and held her face to the sky.

Circling on the horse, she let the water run down her throat, stream from her hair. She spread her arms wide and caught the pelting drops in her cupped palms. *Oh, come, come; keep coming.*

The heavy drops became pellets that stung, then tiny balls of ice. She hurried Aldebaran into the stable, then opened the gates and shooed the other horses into shelter. When she had them in their stalls, she gave them fodder. If this storm was enough, no more animals would need to be moved.

The hail struck the roof with the staccato raps of a million tiny drums. She looked out to see the stones bouncing like grasshoppers in the yard. The gravel was covered in white, piling up like snow. She didn't know if hail was effective against fire, but any precipitation had to be better than none. Then she thought of all the firefighters without shelter from the beating pellets. At least the stones were not large.

She snatched Rick's poncho, held it over her head, and ran for the house, bursting in upon Marta. "It's raining! It's hailing!"

"I know. Thanks be to God." Marta was kneeling beside the couch, scrubbing the soot from where Rick had slept. How could she clean now? Noelle wanted to snatch her up from her knees and drag her into the yard, to show her, to soak her, to make her see. Then she noticed Marta's lips moving as she worked. She was not on her knees to scrub only. She was thanking God.

Noelle looked down at the puddle she had made on the floor. Silently she grabbed a cloth from the kitchen and swabbed it up. She glanced at the clock. Two-thirty. Then the hail turned again to rain. There was hope. Surely there was hope. Would Rick think his prayers and fasting had brought the rain? Was it possible they had?

She climbed the stairs to her room and stripped off her soaked clothes. Rubbing herself dry, she imagined Rick with rain pouring off his hat brim, soaking him to the bone. Had he, too, thrown wide his arms and exulted? She put on a dry blouse and denim shorts.

Marta tapped her door and called, "Noelle, you have a phone call."

Noelle froze, heart pounding, euphoria seeping from her in a rush. A phone call? Who would call? Who knew where she was? A thought paralyzed her. Could he find her?

"Noelle?"

She couldn't answer. Fear snaked around her throat and squeezed. Marta knocked again.

"Yes . . . I'll be there in a moment." Noelle forced the words. If it was, she would race back upstairs and—She imagined herself throwing things into her tote and leaving. No. She would not leave! Not now, when they'd beaten the fire.

She finished zipping her shorts, then forced herself to open the door and went down. Her fingers were cold on the receiver. "Hello?"

"What's with having all the excitement without me?"

She almost cried with relief. *Morgan.* "You mean the fire?"

"I saw it on the news. Juniper Falls is on the tube, if you can believe it, though you didn't get top billing—hardly more than a blurb and a single helicopter shot—not when major real estate is burning up near Evergreen."

"I guess not." Noelle cleared the strain from her throat.

"How bad is it?"

"Bad enough. Rick's up fighting it. But it's raining now. Oh, Morgan, it's pouring like you wouldn't believe." She saw through the window that the rain continued.

"Well, that's good. Are you all right?"

"I'm fine." Now that her heart had resumed a normal beat.

His voice softened. "I wish I was there."

"You'd have been pressed into service."

He laughed. "Yeah, better Rick than me."

Was there anything Morgan cared enough about to fight for, as Rick had fought for his land?

"Hey, I'm getting a call. Ciao."

As she hung up, the shaking started. Of all the stupid times to panic. She held herself in her arms. It was nothing more than Morgan's curiosity. But the call could have meant too much. She closed her eyes.

"Are you all right?" It was the smokejumper she'd spoken with the day before. Others of her team came into the kitchen behind her.

Noelle nodded. "Is it out?"

"Only cleanup now." She brushed dripping hair back with her forearm. "Then we're out of here."

The woman took a bottle of water from the counter and drained it. "If the rain keeps on, it'll do our job for us. Oh, how we pray for rain."

There it was again. Prayer. Had it brought the rain? Why would God start the fire, then send the rain? Just to prove He could? What was she thinking? Imagining some white-robed, hoary man on a throne tossing fire bolts, then pouring buckets to quench what he started.

"Oh," the woman said, "I met your husband."

"I beg your pardon?" Her shaking increased.

"Rick." The smokejumper refilled her bottle and took a swallow. "Right before I came down."

Noelle expelled her breath. "He's not my husband." She pushed the platter of sandwiches toward the woman, trying to sound normal. She could stanch this attack if she tried. There was no need for panic, not now. "I'm boarding here at the ranch."

"Oh. Well, thanks for the sandwich." The woman paused. "Are you sure you're all right?"

"I'm fine." But she wasn't fine. The shaking intensified, and she had to get outside, even if she only went as far as the porch. Rain gushed from the downspouts at either end of the porch, and she stood breathing deeply until the shaking stopped. Water soaked the yard where nearly all the hail had dissolved. A truck sloshed down and stopped to let the fire fighters take a pit stop.

"Is it over?" she asked them.

A tall man swiped water from his walrus mustache. "Not over, but a heck of a lot closer than before."

Noelle bit her lip with another rush of gratitude inside. Yes. It was going to be all right. Juniper Falls might be on the news, but she was safe, hidden away on this ranch that had been threatened but hadn't succumbed. She stayed out in the storm for the next several hours; then the rain slackened and ceased, leaving ragged strips of cloud. The yard was a rutted mess, but she praised the rain anyway. The smoke had been washed from the air, though the rain scent was tainted with soaked charcoal. Yet even that much was a relief. She closed her eyes and let the quiet settle over her.

Then she heard a pickup and looked up the meadow. Her heart jumped. She gripped the rail as Rick parked his truck and climbed out, soaked and grimy. His gaze caught hers with an expression she'd not seen before, a look of pure triumph. Her heart raced. Yes, they had triumphed, had beaten the forces of nature.

He climbed up the stairs with more spring in his step than she could imagine. Two days of grueling labor and little sleep. But it was as Marta said. He had renewed his strength. Somehow.

Noelle hurried to him, almost reached for him. Her heart danced at what he'd done. His muscled body was outlined by the soaked T-shirt, victory in his face. If anyone had power over the mountain, over the fire, it was this man.

She gripped her hands together. "Is it out?"

"There are still hot spots, but the rain was a godsend." His smile was totally without guile.

*Godsend.* He truly believed his God had sent the rain. Rick's strength and tenacity, and that of the others, had been unfailing. Yet that wasn't what he credited. They couldn't bring the rain. And if it hadn't rained, would their strength and effort have been enough?

He wiped his forehead with his sleeve and looked up at the house. He was quiet a long time. "Sure makes you appreciate what you have."

She sighed. His ranch was safe, and so was he. But now she saw through the triumph to his exhaustion. "You must be worn out."

He rubbed the back of his neck. "I'll be a lot better after a shower." The rain had turned the soot to grime, black circles of it beneath his eyes and lines between his fingers. "I'll just see to the horses first. Are they still here?"

"Except for the stallions, one gelding, and four mares that your friends moved out. But I've already stabled and foddered the others."

He raised his brows. "You did?"

She nodded. "They'll be fine until morning."

"Thanks." He reached for the door.

"Marta has food." Would he tell her he was fasting still? Or even that he had been? Would he say his fasting had stopped the fire?

He turned with a smile. "Good." Then he went inside.

———

Rick scrubbed the grime and weariness from his body. Even accustomed to work as he was, his muscles ached. But inside, his spirit soared. He had stood at the top and looked down at his place, solid and secure.

When the winds picked up, they'd come awfully close to losing the fight, until the rain came.

God's mercy. *Thank you, Lord.* He'd already said it again and again, but his whole being swelled with gratitude toward the One who held all things in His hand. God had heard his prayer and answered.

Rick lathered the soap over his face. He didn't want to think how he had looked to Noelle, all bushed and blackened. She didn't seem to mind though. Seeing her standing on the porch was almost like coming home to her. For one crazy moment he nearly shared the thrill of victory by crushing her in a grip he might not have released for way too long.

He turned his face to the spray. No good thinking like that. It was relief in her eyes, relief that he'd saved her the trouble of moving on. The waiting must have been tough on her, worse than being in the thick of it. He wouldn't have wanted to stand back, watching.

He rubbed his hands over his face. She'd gotten the horses out of the storm and made sure they were fed. Marta wouldn't have thought of that, but Noelle had. All things considered, she was becoming a help. All things considered, he was getting used to having her around. He frowned, gave his face a final rinse, and climbed out.

He toweled his head, shaved, and dressed in clean clothes. *Ah.* A new man. He went downstairs to the beef tips and rice Marta had waiting. Broccoli steamed in the bowls, fresh rolls huddled in the baskets, and there was not a paper folding or embellishment to be seen. This meal was pure Marta. He would never discourage Noelle's culinary attempts, but the results were sometimes challenging to appreciate, especially on Marta's days off.

Just now, however, Noelle hovered between him and the fire fighters still on the scene, all enjoying Marta's cooking with a deeper than culinary satisfaction. If Rick's contentment included Noelle's attention along with the relief of saving his and others' property, he could hardly be blamed. Her eyes shone as they had when she'd first ridden Destiny, and she didn't turn away from his answering glance. He could get used to that, too, but it was not at all what he intended.

She was his guest and deserved to stay without overtures from him, no matter how unintentional. It was all part of his code, and something he hadn't struggled with before. Two things made it difficult now; she was lodged in the house, not her own cabin, and she'd been there long enough to feel like family.

# 15

William St. Claire shoved aside the papers on his desk. What was Noelle doing? Two months away, no word, no use of credit or calling cards, no activity on the checking account she had accessed before leaving. Why?

He shook his head. She would have told him if she was in trouble. She had always kept him informed, though in the months before her departure, she had become increasingly non-communicative. He leaned back in his chair and considered that. He had attributed it to a natural breaking away or perhaps her absorption with Michael Fallon. They'd been together so much, maybe too much.

Michael. After returning from his four-day rest he'd been consumed with perfection. Not one detail did he leave unscrutinized. He was putting in as much time as William. He'd driven off one legal assistant and had another on the brink. His focus was dangerous, like sunlight through a magnifying glass, scorching anything beneath it.

Michael was burning himself out, and William could do nothing to stop it. If only he knew how to find Noelle, to tell her what she was doing to Michael. The thought confused him. His first allegience was to his daughter, of course. If she were there to explain . . . but maybe that was part of it. She had excluded him, denied him the chance to champion her, to counsel her. She didn't want his counsel, maybe resented it. How long had she felt that way?

William frowned. Michael's trouble was present and immediate, and Michael did look to him and respected his opinion. Why had Noelle terminated their engagement? Why disappear so abruptly and stay away so long?

A fresh unease stirred. Had he misunderstood her call? Was she saying more than it seemed? Well, it had been long enough. He pressed the intercom. "Margaret, contact Myron Robertson."

In a moment, he lifted the receiver. "Myron. William St. Claire. I have a situation. Any chance we can get together?" Myron Robertson was the best P. I. he knew. He hung up and called Michael in. "I'm putting Myron Robertson on Noelle."

Michael looked surprised, and something else flickered there momentarily.

William continued. "I'm confident that once we locate her things can be worked out."

Michael's throat worked, the tendons at each side drawing tight. "William, if Noelle wants to end our engagement, it's her decision." His eyes darted to the side. Unease, or something else?

"Michael?"

He fingered the coins in his pocket. "She . . . hadn't been herself. I didn't say anything because I thought it might be stress or something. Prenuptial nerves. I never imagined she'd take off like this even though . . ."

"Even though?" William's own concern amplified.

Michael strode to the window and looked down at the city a long moment. "I should have spoken sooner. If I'd known about that earlier event in her life—"

"The kidnapping? What does that have to do with it?" Had he missed something critical? Denied what he didn't want to see?

Michael didn't turn from the window. Avoiding eye contact? "Maybe nothing. I don't know how any of that works. But, William, I think Noelle imagines things."

William noted the nervous timbre of his voice. Natural when making that sort of accusation about a man's daughter. But he was wrong. Noelle was not delusional. He would have known, the psychiatrist would have picked it up, surely.

As Michael finally turned, William caught the shift in his eyes, slight enough that another might have missed it. But then, Michael was a master at concealment. That's why he worked a jury so well, making them see only what he wished. What was his purpose now? Manipulation?

William swallowed the tightening in his throat. "What did she imagine?"

Michael drew his brows together in a look of pain. "I don't want to speak out of turn."

"Tell me what you know."

"Absolutely nothing." Michael's hands closed at his sides. "It's just . . . is it possible she's paranoid?"

William narrowed his eyes. "Paranoid? Clinically?"

Michael moistened his lips, checked his pager, and slipped it back into his pocket. "I have an appointment, and . . . I don't want to say anything equivocal. I would never say anything against Noelle." True pain washed over his face. "I love her."

"I know that. But if you have information I need . . ."

"Please believe me. If I had thought her condition dangerous—"

"What condition, Michael?" It was the first time he'd ever raised his voice with the man.

Michael jolted. "She thinks people want to hurt her. She feels controlled by normal interaction, imagines danger and threat. I think she has a paranoid-delusional condition."

Blood siphoned from his veins as William stood mute. Not possible he could have missed something like that. Yes, Noelle was timid . . . understandably. Even if she'd forgotten the incident, it had affected and subdued her.

"I have to go. Ms. Henley is waiting." Michael raised a hand and dropped it. "Don't take anything I've said as . . . I only know what I saw. And maybe I misinterpreted it."

"Michael." William's tone stopped him at the door. "Was it you or Noelle who ended things between you?"

Michael shook his head. "I love her." He went out.

William released a slow breath from his stunned diaphragm. Had he missed something crucial? Did Noelle imagine some delusion she fled? He squeezed the bridge of his nose. Did some fear, some terror, lurk in her subconscious and cause a disorder he'd never realized? Or had it only surfaced in her relationship with Michael?

"*She thinks people want to hurt her.*" Had she been damaged in those days she had been held? His mind was swift to deny it. But it was possible, wasn't it? It had always been possible, though he'd almost bullied the doctors into denying it. Now he forced himself to ask, had she been abused?

He dug his fingertips into points across his forehead. That was the question he'd refused to face. They had no reason to. She was a pawn, not a plaything for some pervert. They had taken her to force his response and released her as soon as he did, though it took days to recuse himself and have it accepted when he could not say why. But didn't abuse explain the possible paranoid behavior Michael referenced?

He was fairly sure they hadn't slept together. At any rate Michael had never spent the night at the bungalow, and to his knowledge Noelle had not stayed at Michael's place.

Or was this another smoke screen? Michael was hardly sound himself these days. Was there more behind his self-destruction than a broken relationship with the woman he loved? William released his breath slowly through his teeth. It was time to find Noelle.

———

Michael walked back to his office and took a drink from the artesian-water cooler. Ms. Henley could wait. Did William doubt him? Did he suspect? He dumped the water down his throat and crushed the cone-shaped cup. Everything he had said was true. Noelle had taken the simplest things out of context, resisted and accused.

He sat down and stared at the wall. Did he want her found? Of course he did. But not by William's man. He must see her first. He must make sure that . . . He dropped his forehead to his fingertips. Couldn't she see? Hadn't she known it was all because he needed her? It didn't matter if she was afraid or delusional. He would take care of her.

The first time he'd seen Noelle, he had determined she was his, the daughter of the senior partner of the firm. His position was ensured in both the firm and New York's society. But that wasn't it. She was exquisite. Sheltered and untouched, with an air of mystery, a purity, a perfection he could hardly bear.

She was everything he dreamed of, everything Jan should have been, could have been if life had played fairly. He had lost the fight with his baby sister. But Noelle was new, fresh, beautiful, uncorrupted. William St. Claire had created a masterpiece, and Michael longed to possess it.

It had seemed an impossibility. Her life was so thoroughly controlled; he had no way in. Until William himself opened the door. It was as though his desire had willed it. Suddenly William invited him in, and Noelle . . . oh, Noelle.

Where had she found the courage to leave? It was the last thing he would have expected, and he did not often miscalculate. Where was she? Sebastian Thorndike still had nothing. After all this time, she'd done nothing traceable. She must have help. She must be with someone. There was no way she could do this herself.

He slid a legal pad closer and began a methodical list of everyone he knew she was acquainted with. He had already called, asking if they knew her whereabouts. Now he would have Sebastian track them as well. If someone was hiding her, there would be a pattern, a hotel, a property, something. And when he found the nest to which his bird had flown . . .

The carbon tip of his pencil snapped. He tossed it aside and grabbed another. Once she understood how sorry he was . . . yet she'd driven him to it. He would never willingly hurt her. Never. His phone buzzed, informing him again that Ms. Henley waited. He laid the pencil straight across the pad and asked for her to be admitted.

———

Noelle looked out the window of her room at a foreign land. Fog clung to the ground, even thicker than the smoke had been—was it only last week? The dark pines stood stark against the white until they paled, then vanished. Tiny droplets of water clung to the tips of the needles and dropped when they swelled beyond bearing.

What mystery did the woods hold this day? What secrets would the still air whisper through the mist? What magic lay shrouded and mute? She longed to know, to seek the heart of the mountain that called, that embraced her. She pressed her palms to the smooth log walls. Why did they not melt and let her pass through as a dream walker unsubstantiates and crosses the barriers of the mind?

She stood a long while, until her breath became a matching fog on the glass. Then she went down the stairs to the great room. She found Rick at the fireplace, kneeling on a broad canvas, his head and shoulders thrust up into the cavity. Black dust sworled around him.

"Cleaning the flue?"

His sound of assent was muffled by stone and steel. He thrust with his arms holding the long pole of some tool that caused billows of dust to descend. Marta would be attacking the room with her duster with equal fervor the minute he was done.

Though it was morning, the room was dim as dusk. "It's so foggy out."

"It'll burn off soon. The crags are probably clear now."

Noelle looked out, pictured the valley filled with fog, tips of trees piercing the veil, and above that the rocky peaks shining in the sunlight. Just imagining the scene quickened her excitement. "I think I'll ride."

He pulled his head out and tugged the bandana from his mouth. "I can't get you saddled up just now." He was nearly as sooty as he'd been from the fire. And with the bandana he looked like an outlaw.

She smiled at the thought. Father Rick, the outlaw. "I can do it myself."

He smudged his face with his shoulder. "Well, Aldebaran's in the stable."

Aldebaran. Did he think she'd take another? Maybe Destiny?

He took hold of the pole again. "Don't go far. It's easy to lose your bearings in a fog like this."

"I think I know my way around by now."

"You think you know a lot of things." He pulled the bandana over his mouth and tucked his head back into the fireplace.

He'd been saying all kinds of cheery things like that this last week, testier and more bullheaded than ever since the fire. Some days he scarcely spoke at all, and not once did he demonstrate the warmth he'd shown when he came off the mountain soot-stained but victorious. Maybe crisis brought out his best. Unfortunately, that left all the normal time.

Noelle sighed as she went out. She saddled Aldebaran, then rode up, her face raised to the chill mist, but the woods were silent. Where were the secrets she sought? She had traveled this land too many times. She needed something new, some place that would sing a fresh song in her heart. She told herself she had no specific destination, but when she came to the shale slope below the high ridge, she knew she had intended it from the moment Rick spoke of the sun shining above the fog.

She looked up there, to the forbidden ridge. From her perspective it was as solidly fog-bound as the rest. But geographically it would be the place to test Rick's assumption. Yes, he had told her to stay off, but he'd also thought she couldn't ride Destiny. She had learned a lot since then. She had proven herself, whether he chose to acknowledge it or not.

She could see the wet shale peeling from the mountainside, a few scraggly pines erupting at the edges of its cracked and brittle surface. But there was a narrow, grassy trail through most of it. Room enough for a single horse if she was careful. Besides, she no longer acted of her own accord. She must appease the restless spirit that drove her.

What was it? Morgan would say fate. Rick might call it God. Whatever it was, she had to go, had to see. Just as she'd had to come to the ranch. She no longer pretended it was an accident. She was meant to be there, as she was meant now to climb this slope. She started up. The mare was surefooted, though, in fact, the grass was slick and the path uncertain.

She encouraged the horse gently as they wove up the slope. When they broke through the fog, the mare leapt the last few paces to the shelf. Noelle's breath suspended. Here was the heart that beckoned, the soul of the mountain unveiled. The crag ablaze with light, the woods below engulfed by cloud. Pure beauty.

A painful yearning pierced her breast for the power that had drawn her, the force that had snatched her from the talons and hidden her here in the crook of its stony arms. What was it? What presence did she sense? *Who are you?*

She left Aldebaran loose while she set up her easel. Fresh storm clouds would soon challenge the sun, but right now its radiance held sway. She must capture it before it was lost, not only for her collection but somehow for her soul. She painted the scene even as it changed around her, one painting and then another, heedless of time, hunger, or thirst.

It was awesomely beautiful, and she remembered Professor Jenkins. *Yes, Professor, I am in love with the beautiful.* Or had she found part of the divine as well? Her breath came in quick, tremulous bursts. Even Morgan attributed the beauty to God.

And suddenly, there was more than root and stone, more than mist and light. Something live, something more real than life quickened and surrounded her. She felt it. She wanted it. *Tell me. Show yourself.* She closed her eyes against the tears that stung behind her lids.

How long she stood that way she couldn't say, only that time seemed suspended. Was this the being Rick worshipped and obeyed? The one in whom Morgan believed but to whom he could not belong? Was it even real, or did she imagine it—a fantastic journey of the mind?

A raindrop touched her finger, and she looked up. The darkened clouds had moved in like a giant rolling wave, and with them something else, something sinister that strove against her, denying the other presence. "No . . ." Fear crawled her spine, and with it a memory dark and uncertain, her voice small and afraid, "Are you God?" And the answer gruff and sarcastic, "Yeah, kid. I'm God." Panic raced in. What was that thought? She couldn't connect it to anything she knew, yet suddenly she felt exposed.

Swiftly, she gathered her things and tucked them into the wooden case. In her haste, she pinched her finger in the easel and drew her breath sharply at the sting. Thunder rumbled. Aldebaran stamped, restive in the damp, then threw up her head and whinnied. Noelle's heart jumped at the answering neigh from below. Rick called out and she sagged. She was in for it now.

Where was the one who had drawn her? Where the voice she had followed? It had deserted her. She was alone, stripped of the glory and bare in her disobedience. Swiftly she strapped the case onto the saddle and mounted as Rick came up through the fog.

His face was dark as the gray, roiling clouds above. "I told you not to come up here." His anger hit her squarely.

"I didn't go over the shale, I—"

"You think you're above the rules, don't you? You won't listen to sense; you just keep pushing the limits!" He'd never yelled before, had never shown her this side. She saw him now as a man, strong and capable of anything.

Her trembling grew so violent she knew it must show. Inside her surged an animal need to flee. With a cry, she kicked in her heels and the mare jumped forward, plunging down over the shale.

"Noelle!"

She kicked Aldebaran, frantic for escape. The shale shattered. The horse slid, twisted, and crashed down hard. Noelle screamed as pain shot through her, the mare's weight suffocating as the animal thrashed, then stumbled up. Noelle gasped, pain slicing her head, shooting through her leg. Once again time suspended, but this time the void was cruel.

Above her the pine spires danced a dizzy spiral. Around her, bits of shale tumbled and rolled. Rick was coming. No, he passed her by, leading Orion down on foot. He would leave her to the mountain. Her heart raced, then stilled, so still she was uncertain it beat.

She moaned, fighting the blackness. She had feared the sky, but it was the ground that broke her. The glory she had imagined was gone. It was too sublime. She had no right to grasp it. She had trespassed on the gods and even now slipped into the darkness.

Then Rick was beside her, touching, probing, willing her back into her flesh, back to the pain. His probing hands hurt, and with a jolt she remembered his rage. She pushed up and fought him.

"Lie still." He eased her back to the ground, took off his jacket, and laid it over her. "Where does it hurt?"

"My leg." Straining, she caught a glimpse of her leg bent at a sickening angle.

"Where else?"

"My head." She gasped as he fingered the spot turning spongy at the back of her skull.

His hand ran down her neck and along her spine. "Here? Anywhere on your back? Your neck?"

Could she be paralyzed? It had been Daddy's fear that a fall from a horse could cripple her. He'd almost forbidden the riding lessons, until she had wept and begged. Noelle closed her eyes as Rick's hands studied her spine. She had already moved her head, raised up to fight him. "No. My leg. My leg." That pain seized her consciousness.

Slowly he slipped his arm beneath her shoulders and then her knees. "I'm going to lift you onto Orion."

Her leg shifted, and she screamed. "Don't, Rick!" Her breath caught raggedly.

"If I don't, I'll have to leave you here and get help. I don't have my cell phone, and by the time search and rescue could get up here you'd be soaked through and in shock." His tone was calm and soothing, explaining her reality.

She hadn't noticed the rain coming down. It sifted through the needles of the trees. She could feel it on her cheeks, cold and terrible. She braced herself for the pain, but even so cried out when her leg moved again. Her stomach heaved.

Rick splinted the break with one large calloused hand while he wrapped his arm around her upper body. Then he let go the leg and lifted her swiftly. She screamed again. She couldn't stop it. Her thighs shook uncontrollably as he swung her onto Orion's back.

"Hold on."

She made her hands clench the saddle horn, though her head throbbed and everything whirled. Had she mentioned her head? Now that she was upright, it pounded with relentless force.

Rick climbed up behind. "Rest your leg on mine so it doesn't swing." When she didn't respond, he maneuvered his leg snugly against hers.

Her head reeled. Were they moving, or was it everything else? Fresh pain surged until she no longer identified the damaged parts. Every part of her shook now, though she was wrapped in Rick's jacket. It was oversized and reminded her—a flash of something. She was crying in the back of a car, and a man's stiff woolen coat was wrapped around her. Another disconnected fragment. Like the voice, "Yeah, kid. I'm God." In that strange accent.

She couldn't remember more. But she needed to. Why? She fought the dark confusion. Everything was swirling out of focus. What was real? She leaned against Rick's chest and groaned when the horse started down the steep slope. Every stride jarred her. The throbbing in her head dulled as stupor set in.

Arms were around her, and she felt their pressure, holding her firmly, trapping her. She fought the restraint, sudden terror rising up. "No," she moaned. "Michael, no!"

———

Rick swallowed his dread. Her loss of consciousness was bad. He kept talking, calling her name, but she didn't respond. She had drifted into some fearful place and fought against his arm before collapsing. Now she lay limp, and he could only hope to get her to the ranch and call for an ambulance. Why hadn't he grabbed the cell phone? He'd carried it every day looking for fire. But now when he needed it most . . .

He held Noelle's inert weight with one arm and directed Orion with the other. He stopped trying to make her respond and focused on reaching the ranch. He should have known, but he hadn't anticipated—

His anger surged again. What was she thinking, going over the edge like that? She could have killed herself and the horse. Aldebaran. He hated to leave her up there on the slope, but lamed up as she was, he couldn't take the time to lead her. His first responsibility was to Noelle.

She felt fragile in his arms, as he'd known she would from the first. It was as though the brittleness he'd seen had transferred from her spirit to her body. She was a wounded bird, but he couldn't splint her up. She needed a hospital.

He kicked himself. Why had he scared her like that? What caused the anger that replaced his concern? He had sensed danger and gone looking, not to holler or blame. But seeing her up there, precarious at the edge, in the storm on the shale . . .

And then he knew. He'd been broadsided by the enemy. His concern had left him open, and Satan had twisted it to anger. He had focused on her disobedience when he should have seen her fear. He should have spoken gently, eased her down. But he hadn't. Rick looked up to heaven and the rain ran down his face. He'd been chastised, and he nodded. He deserved it.

CHAPTER

# 16

Something pressed on her eyelids like weights, and then she realized it was her eyelids. A throbbing awareness kindled and strove through the mire that slogged her mind. Her eyes flickered open, but light and substance swam in the murky depths. White, pocked tiles, lights, metallic bars . . .

Her leg was stiff and elevated, her chest tightly constricted, her head throbbing a rhythm with no tune. Her mouth was filled with down, a thick, cloying dryness. She breathed the cool, sweet air from the tube taped to her lip. Another tube ran from her arm to the bottle overhead.

A face leaned over. "How're you doing?"

She couldn't place the face. She didn't know the voice. She tried to answer, swallowed the dryness in her throat, then closed her eyes again.

Darkness. A cold shadow taking form. In the back of her mind, she knew it, somewhere deep . . . Suddenly the shadow moved with great sweeping wings, and in a rush came recognition and terror. Her eyes flew open and the shadow fled.

The light was different than before, warmer, softer. She located the source, a lamp by the chair in the corner, the chair where Rick sat, composed, as she'd seen him a hundred times. Why did she imagine him angry? Was it another warped dream? Maybe she was crazy.

A quick glance confirmed different walls and ceiling. How long had she lain in limbo, caught between fear and pain by the gauzy mists of oblivion? And had Rick been there with her all along? She stilled her breath and watched him a moment before he felt her scrutiny and looked up. No spark of ire touched his eyes. They were warm brown orbs, velvety soft, not angry as she remembered. Had she imagined it?

He stood and came to the bedside. "Are you awake?"

Was she? She moistened her lips and felt the oxygen tube beneath her nostrils. She took only tiny, shallow breaths, but the air smelled sweeter. One hand was wrapped in tape, which held a needle in her vein, the clear tube spiraling up to the bottle hanging above her.

Rick leaned on the bed rail, the muscles of his forearms rippling. He was potently present, like the cleansed earth after the rain. Or was it the calm before the storm? Would he lash out now when she was helpless? A flash of memory: "*I told you not to come up here.*"

She expected panic, but it didn't come. Maybe she was too weak.

He clasped his hands together. "I'm sorry, Noelle."

Her mind stumbled. She had missed a turn, skipped a link. Maybe the mists still held her.

"I shouldn't have spoken to you that way."

What way? What had he said?

"Can you forgive me?" He said it simply, but she didn't understand. What was he asking? What did he want?

She nodded, but her neck was so stiff, she wasn't sure he noticed.

"The doctor says you're improving. The surgery went well."

"Surgery?" Her voice was a ghost of its normal self. She didn't remember any surgery. How could they do surgery without her consent?

"Yeah. They removed that stubborn streak." He cracked a surly smile.

She frowned. He was teasing. Poking fun. Making light of . . . "What's really wrong with me?"

He expelled a slow breath. "Compound fracture in the leg, ligament damage repaired by the surgery, bruised ribs, and a concussion."

Her head felt like mush. There had been a man in a coat, talking, explaining and explaining though she hadn't understood him, then a clipboard. She supposed he'd explained her injuries and she had agreed to the surgery. How strange not to remember.

"What happened?"

"You took a fall. On the shale."

Shale. The shale slope? The ledge? Bits of images came to her.

Sunlight and fog. Rick's face in the rain. A horse's back tipping up, the hooves flailing to the side. . . . "Aldebaran?"

"She'll mend." But his voice had thickened.

Noelle closed her eyes. She could almost sleep again. But the door swung opened and someone bustled to her bedside. She thought of Marta, but the voice was high and throaty.

"Checking your vitals, honey. You're looking better today."

"Am I?" Noelle opened her eyes. And what did she mean by today? Was it a different day?

"Sweetie, if I looked so good after what you've been through, I would think I'd died and gone to heaven."

*Died and gone to heaven.* How close had she come? Was there a heaven, a hell? Some mass delusion for weak-minded people, or maybe her mind had lost touch with reality and looked for any alternative.

The nurse checked the intravenous bag. "Before you know it they'll have you in rehab. We have a real wiz down there—Kelly will fix you up like new. Or better." The nurse marked the chart. "Anything you need, honey? Some juice?"

Noelle shook her head even though her throat still felt like cotton. As the door closed behind the nurse, all she could think was, *Rehab. Surgery.* She fought the panic. How would she pay? The money she had left wouldn't cover this expense, nor could she hope to earn it through the gallery. She could not file through her insurance without revealing where she was. She was trapped.

Her thoughts flashed to her father, and her chest tightened painfully. No. She closed her eyes against the tears, and again sleep beckoned. She couldn't sleep. How could she rest with worry gnawing her mind? She shuddered, then felt the warmth of Rick's voice.

"Don't worry, Noelle. You'll heal."

He didn't understand. He didn't know. She forced herself to meet his gaze. "I need to get out of here, Rick. I can't pay for this. I . . . don't have insurance." She didn't know what to expect, but she expected more than his bland expression.

"We'll figure it out."

How? How did people do things when they had no money with which to do them? How did people deal with expenses beyond their means? She had never known want, never faced need. She had never even wondered before.

She must make him understand. "I can't—"

"Don't worry." Now he leaned close, the rail pressing into his arms. His look compelled her trust, her belief.

She sank back. "I should never have gone up there. I should have listened to you."

"Yeah." He arched his eyebrows and nodded. There was neither condemnation nor anger in his tone. He merely acknowledged the truth. She didn't understand him. Why was he no longer angry? He had every right to be.

He took her hand between his palms. "It's going to be all right."

How could it be? She felt drained, empty, afraid. All she had gained, all her safety and freedom were gone.

Rick released her hand, but she wanted to grasp his again. *Don't leave. Don't abandon me* . . . He stepped back, and that one step seemed a chasm. "Get some rest now."

Noelle watched mutely as he pulled open the door and with one last glance, left her. A tear slid down her cheek. Her throat ached, and the dull throbbing in her head intensified, as did the fear. What would she do? She was immobile, in debt, helpless, and the dark dreams seemed more real than the waking. She felt utterly terrified.

---

Rick didn't miss the fear in Noelle's eyes as he left the room. Sure, it was natural to be apprehensive after an accident and injury like hers. But there was something more, something raw in her. What did she fear? It couldn't be him. He hadn't been that angry. And even if he had raised his voice, was that enough to risk her life?

Now this new thing. Why was she without funds or insurance if what Morgan believed was true? Did she come from money? And if so, why couldn't she access it? What about the people she had talked about in her delirium? What about her father?

He needed answers. He wasn't one to pry. But in Noelle's case, something told him he had to. If she was in danger—the kind of danger he saw in her face, felt in her trembling, heard in her whimpering—he needed to know.

He shook his head. "Lord, guide me here. Don't let my emotions get in the way of your plan." *Sure.* Outwardly he might have control of his emotions, but inside, holding her injured and helpless . . .

He remembered the time the rock swallow had flown into the picture window at home. He must have been eight or nine. He had heard the thump and run outside. The soft downy feathers of the bird's breast ruffled as he scooped it into his hands. The flutter of its heart had been so quick and shallow.

He had held it, warm, and waited. He remembered the sudden frail grip of its feet on his finger when he thought it would open its eyes and fly. But it hadn't. Its heart had stilled, and it had grown cold in his hands. He remembered his tears as he carried it across the field, scraped out a grave, and covered it with earth and leaves.

Noelle reminded him of that bird, flying blindly, unaware of the glass. Why? It was time he found out. At least enough to know what to do next. Rick went first to her room and searched through her things. He found her identification, credit cards, phone card—insurance card. Why did she say she had none? Concussion?

There was a picture of an older man, sharply dressed and poised. Her father? Rick checked the back side, but there was only the year. 1999. He turned it over and studied the man's features again. She'd spoken of her father, or rather to him, in her delirium, in rushing streams Rick couldn't follow. Mr. St. Claire was the responsible party on her insurance card even though her driver's license put her age at twenty-three.

Did she live at home? Was she Daddy's girl? Then why did she run away? He looked at the photo again, trying to see something in the features that would indicate a monster. Would she carry his picture if he was as bad as that? *Lord?* But his spirit didn't quicken. For now, he'd believe William St. Claire to be what he seemed. Still, it wouldn't hurt to find out what he could.

Rick went downstairs and logged on to the Internet. His search brought him to a Web page that he studied at length. Actually, William St. Claire was more influential than he had seemed. A flourishing legal practice and a philanthropic foundation for underprivileged youth. Morgan's impressions had been right on. Were his own completely crazy? How could Noelle St. Claire possibly need his help? Then he pictured her brittle fear. Was that real? Or was he still trying to save the bird?

----

Michael hurried through the rain to the taxi. William's man Myron had uncovered nothing more than Sebastian, which at least proved Sebastian wasn't lying. So that left Michael's own list. He gave the driver an address. Seeing the friends face-to-face gave him the opportunity to read body language, a skill he'd developed almost as acutely as William St. Claire.

So far, no one had betrayed any hidden agenda, and their ignorance had been sincere. But there were men on the list Michael had wondered about before, men he knew would do anything for their chance at Noelle. And guys from her art school, flakes and freaks, he'd thought, but maybe not. Maybe not.

He told the taxi to wait and hurried out to the next door. Thankfully it was covered by a small peaked roof. His questions evoked the same response there as they had at the last address. "Noelle? No, I haven't seen her. Is everything okay?"

"When was the last time you saw her? Did she seem nervous, afraid?" Michael made sure to plant that thought.

"I don't think so. Has something happened?"

A guilty person would not lead the conversation that direction, but Michael probed anyway, until he was sure, then disengaged. Another dead end. "If you hear anything, call me."

Back to the taxi. After seven more stops, Michael gave the driver a different sort of address. They arrived at an elite boutique that specialized in one-of-a-kind designs. Michael paid him and got out. The place closed in three minutes, but they wouldn't flash the lights on him. They knew him too well.

The elegant proprietress approached, her gray hair in a chignon at the nape of her neck, her classic skirt and jacket impeccable, her nails flawless. Diamonds glittered in her ears. "Good evening, Mr. Fallon."

"Good evening, Jacqueline."

"Something for Noelle?"

It was ludicrous; he didn't pretend otherwise. But he sent his gaze over the tasteful displays. "Yes. Something special for her homecoming."

———

As Rick carried her into the house, a rush of relief flooded Noelle. She was home. She was safe. Maybe it wasn't rational to feel that, but she couldn't help it as once again the log walls embraced her. Her heart rushed with their comfort, and she drank in the room as she might the face of a loved one.

But one thing was different: a daybed near the fireplace mounded with pillows. Rick headed that way. The unstained frame was smooth as satin and smelled of freshly hewn pine. He must have just built it. He'd built it for her.

"Oh, Rick . . ."

He settled her in across its length, elevating her leg on soft, tweedy pillows at the end. "I don't suppose you'll be doing stairs for a while, and this way you won't be stuck in your room."

His kindness humbled her. That he would think how confined she would feel in her room . . . She wished she had words to thank him. They were there, just jumbled up in her throat behind the tears.

She stroked the soft pine of the bed's back. "You built it."

"It's just logs."

It wasn't just logs. It started as logs, then became a bed, beautiful in its simplicity. His hands had transformed the rough logs into a couch for her.

He said, "There's so much wood felled from the fire lines. Someone needs to use it before it rots."

She looked up. He didn't fool her. Maybe there was wood, but he had made this bed out of kindness, and sympathy, perhaps. Again her throat filled.

His face gentled. "This way Marta can see to you easier."

Noelle glanced toward the kitchen, but it was silent. "Where is Marta?"

"Probably fetching something for you. Chicken soup, mustard plaster, cod liver oil . . ."

Again he joked. Rick Spencer with a sense of humor. She studied his half smile as though she'd never seen it. Maybe she hadn't. In their interactions, she'd recognized his authority, respected that. But now she sensed . . . him.

Had he changed? Hadn't he given her haven, seen to her comfort from the start? He charged her only thirteen dollars a night, for heaven's sake. He hadn't changed; she had. Something had opened up that had been blocked, her ability to see beyond herself, her need. Was she ready to?

"Is it all right?" He motioned to the bed, but she knew he meant more. He meant all of it, all of her.

She cleared the emotion from her throat. "It's wonderful. Thank you, Rick."

"You're welcome."

And now that she could talk, "Rick, the hospital said you paid my bill."

"I filed against my liability insurance."

"But I signed a waiver."

He shrugged. "The waiver protects me from lawsuits. The purpose of liability insurance is to cover accidents that occur on the property."

Accidents caused by willful disregard to the rules? He could have argued that one. A sudden thought chilled her. What would he gain by paying her debt? She'd been so swept up in the comfort, the kindness. Now wariness, suspicion rushed in. He wanted something. She saw it in his face.

He sat down on the edge of the table, resting his forearms on his knees. "Noelle, I need to know what's going on."

She stared. "I don't know what you mean." But she did know.

"Why are you here?"

First Morgan, now Rick. And of the two, she'd rather face Morgan. "I just am."

He held her gaze so long she felt she would break, tell him everything. But how could she? *I don't know why I'm here. I ran. I ran and my heart said stop.* She couldn't say it, or he would ask why she ran. And she still had no answer to that.

He dropped his gaze, shaking his head. "Fine." But before she could breathe, his eyes were back, compelling. "I think you should let your family know what's happened."

Her throat constricted. "There's no one who needs to know."

"I'm sure your father would want to." His gaze deepened. "Or Michael . . ."

Her head spun. A vise gripped her chest. She wanted to run, to shield herself from amber eyes. "Michael?" Her voice broke.

He leaned forward. "You talked about him in your delirium. If you're in trouble, Noelle—"

"I'm not in trouble." The blood pounded in her ears. Not unless he found her. Not unless Rick told people where she was. Would he? Had he already? No, he wouldn't have; somehow she knew that. But he might if she couldn't convince him.

"I'm not in trouble. I just don't want to be found right now." His scrutiny sank deeply inside her. She stared at him hard, willing him to believe. It must sound crazy, but was it any crazier than admitting she didn't know why she had run away? He had to simply believe her.

Their wills battled, and she knew what his could do. She'd seen it take the wild heart from Destiny and claim it.

*No. Please.* Then she felt him retreat, and an irrational disappointment vied with her relief.

He rubbed his hand over his face and stood up. "All right, then."

She couldn't meet his eyes. She hadn't been honest. She knew it, and so did he. She wasn't in trouble, not the way he might think. But things were far from right. He stood a long moment, allowing . . . What? A chance to change her mind? How could she?

"Noelle . . ."

"Please don't." She was weary. If he pushed, would she remember? It was there locked in her mind. Maybe if she started talking, if she tried . . . but then where would they be?

He rubbed one palm against the other. He would drive her crazy standing there like that. *Stop it. Leave me alone.*

He hooked his thumbs into his belt. "Morgan called. Marta told him about your fall. He's coming in."

The subject change caught her off guard. "When?"

"Tonight." He watched for a reaction, but what was she supposed to say or do or think?

Releasing a slow breath, he nodded slowly, wiped a hand through his hair, and left. She drew a jagged breath. What if she had said she was in trouble? Would he keep her safe, keep her hidden? What would he require in return? She didn't understand him at all. No one did things for nothing. But she couldn't see what he wanted.

She had resisted his will . . . this time. What if he didn't stop? What if it was like Destiny, a slow, constant battle? She'd thrown him, but she knew he'd get up. Every time. She didn't know how to stop him. She didn't understand him.

She glanced at the Bible lying on the table. What did he find in those pages? What would it tell her? By stretching she could just reach it, though it shot pain through her ribs. The book's binding was soft, worn leather, warm and smooth as a baby's skin.

She thumbed through. The pages were marked and penciled with dates and notes. It opened readily to one section where the top right corner was worn thin. *The Gospel of John.*

She hesitated. She didn't have to believe it any more than the other philosophies she'd studied. She could read for curiosity, for knowledge only. "*In the beginning was the Word, and the Word was with God, and the Word was God . . .*" Its beauty touched her. If nothing else, it was a great literary work.

She settled into the pillow. *"The Word became flesh and made his dwelling among us. We have seen his glory, the glory of the One and Only, who came from the Father, full of grace and truth."* Her heart raced. It wasn't just the words or rhetoric. She was touching power, the same power she had touched on the mountain before the storm.

She shuddered, closed the book, and dropped it to the floor.

---

Rick heaved the hay bale into the truck. Where did his responsibility lie? William St. Claire was among New York's legal who's who. Old money, an estate on Long Island, senior partner of a major law firm, the foundation for youth. The man's reputation was sound. By the articles Rick had read, he was well respected, especially for a defense lawyer. And Noelle was his daughter. Hardly a nobody drifting through as she'd like him to believe.

But something was wrong. She was afraid. It had been palpable, and his instincts kicked in. He wanted to help, to stand in the gap. But how could he when she shut him out so completely? He curled his gloved fingers under the wire of the next bale.

He couldn't force her. At twenty-three, she was competent to make her own decisions. Maybe William St. Claire knew where she was. Maybe he didn't care. But surely the man had a right to know his daughter had been injured.

Rick tossed the bale. It wasn't William that troubled him most. It was Michael. Just mentioning Michael had made the pupils of Noelle's eyes dilate, her lips quiver. He'd heard the sharp intake of her breath. It was Michael she feared. But who was he?

Rick closed the tailgate and spread his hands. *Lord?*

But the Lord kept his own counsel. Rick rubbed his chin with the back of his glove. With no clear direction, he could do no more. He got into the truck. It was fruitless to push her. Besides . . . Morgan was coming back.

# 17

Noelle sighed. Marta fluttered around her, elevating her leg, plumping pillows, darting in with a cup of homemade soup, just as Rick had predicted. So far neither the mustard plaster nor the cod liver oil had appeared, thank goodness. But Marta clicked her tongue like a mother hen; no, like a . . . mother. And nothing could have been more comforting. So why wasn't it?

"Here, in case you get thirsty and I'm not within hollering range." Marta set a pitcher on the table with a glass beside it.

"Thank you." Noelle thought of the pitcher she'd filled with flowers on that one crazy impulse. No one gave her flowers now. Who would be so frivolous?

"And have you finished that soup?" Marta peeked into the bowl on the tray across Noelle's lap. "You need nourishment to set yourself right again."

Noelle stared into the broth. Marta meant well, but nothing would set her right again, not with the gloom inside her from talking to Rick. "I'm not hungry."

Marta shoved a pillow behind Noelle's neck. "Don't give me trouble now. This was a hard thing all around, but you need to accept help as gracefully as poor Aldebaran."

Noelle flicked her eyes up, hoping she wouldn't see exactly the expression she saw on Marta's face.

Marta shook her head. "Oh, if you could have seen Rick leading that horse down . . . wrapping her leg and poulticing."

Noelle's heart sank further. She pictured the willing mare. Aldebaran. How she'd scorned her at the start, then come to appreciate her steady gait, her eager response. Now she'd maybe crippled her, could have caused her death.

"Of course, he was more worried for you than the horse."

Noelle scoffed, "He's afraid I'll sue."

Marta frowned. "No such thing. He has a heart of butter, can't stand to see any injured or broken creature."

"It wasn't his fault."

Marta set a folded fleece blanket at the end of the daybed. "It's not a matter of fault, just compassion. Now, what would you like for dinner?"

Noelle shook her head. "Whatever Morgan likes. Cook for him." She was heartsick. Rick knew too much. Would he tell Morgan? She trembled as though she'd done something wrong, but she hadn't! She dropped her face into her hands.

"What is it, dear? Does it hurt?"

Noelle nodded. Yes, it hurt; it hurt so much. And it was threatening to surface though she'd spent so much effort burying it deeper. Hearing Michael's name . . . What had she said in her delirium? How much did Rick really know?

"Well, look at the clock. You're due your medication." Marta went to the cabinet that held the sewing basket and took out the bottle of Tylenol Codeine prescribed at the hospital.

Noelle held out her hand and took the pills and the glass Marta poured half full of water from the pitcher on the table. "Thank you." She swallowed the medication. Maybe it would help. The pain in her leg throbbed, and her injured ribs kept her from breathing fully.

Mostly, though, it was Rick's questions that drained her. She lay back on the pillows and Marta took the tray. Noelle closed her eyes, her head aching. The hawk came sooner than she expected, hovering even before she was deeply asleep. She struggled to regain consciousness but couldn't fight the drug, couldn't fight the hawk. She moaned, but there was no escape.

The first thing to penetrate was the smell of barbecued chicken, one of Marta's specialties. The next was the warmth of the fleece blanket, the smell and crackle of a fire. She peeled her eyes open, verified that a fire did burn in the fireplace. September in the mountains had a definite chill. She was not allergic to codeine, but it certainly did strange things with her mind. For a moment she'd pictured Rick sitting on the hearth with his guitar, plucking the strings with deft fingers, fingers that had poulticed Aldebaran's leg, had probed her own injuries. But there was nothing there when she raised her head. Only the fire.

The door banged open and she startled, heart rushing. But it was Morgan who entered, cashmere overcoat unbuttoned, paper-wrapped flowers on his arm. "Good grief, Noelle! I leave and you fall apart." Painfully, she pushed herself up to a sitting position as he slid in beside her on the daybed and handed her the collection of pink roses, blue statice, tiny mauve carnations, and baby's breath. "I should know better than to trust you to Rick."

Something seemed wrong in that statement, but her thoughts were still thick. He smelled of Acqua di Gio, the scent she'd given Daddy for his birthday.

Morgan waved a hand in front of her face. "Hello? Are you in there?" He took the bouquet back and laid it on the table.

She wet her lips. "It must be the codeine. I feel very slow."

"Well, you look good enough to eat." He cupped her cheek, his palm cool and dry, his eyes cobalt.

"You'd better settle for Marta's barbequed chicken."

"Aha. Not so slow as you pretend." He leaned close. "But let me see . . . hmm . . ."

"What are you doing?" She pulled away from his hand.

"You made me a promise. I'm not so sure you've kept it."

She looked away, finger-combed her hair, stroking back the fringe of bangs that now reached her cheekbones. She did not need Morgan psychoanalyzing her.

He chucked her chin. "Did you miss me?"

"I've been a little preoccupied."

He took her hand and raised it to his lips. "There wasn't a lonely night I didn't think of you."

"You don't have lonely nights."

"Do I dare believe you're jealous?" He smiled crookedly.

"Probably. You're a master of delusion."

"Ouch." He leaned over the pitcher on the table. "What does Marta have in there, persimmon juice?"

"I'm sorry." She sighed. "That was unkind."

"And untrue; I've no delusions left." He unwrapped the flowers and stood them in the pitcher, to her great amusement. She could hardly wait to see Marta's reaction to that repeat of her own performance. He reached over and knocked on her cast. "Sure wish I could take you dancing."

Undaunted as always. She shook her head. "I'm pretty boring these days."

He reached across her shoulder, slid his fingers into the hair behind her neck and cradled her head. "Never boring, my dear." His eyes engaged, deepened. His lips parted.

She knew what was coming and froze. With Morgan's kiss her muscles tightened. She pressed against his chest, and he backed off.

"What?"

Where was Rick? Marta? Why didn't someone come in?

"You look like a deer in the headlights."

What could she do? Scream, cry, beat him with her fists? Ridiculous, yet it was how she felt. "Why did you do that?" Her voice was tight.

"Because you need kissing." He spoke frankly, as though he'd simply identified a problem and corrected it.

Her jaw clenched. "No, I don't." That was the last thing she needed—not now, not from Morgan, maybe never again.

He toyed with the hair that lay across her shoulder. "You promised you'd quit hiding. I just want you to be free."

"Like you, Morgan?"

He spread his hands. "Exactly. What you see is what you get."

"And everyone gets everything."

"Well, not everyone." He dropped his gaze to her lips.

She turned away. Was she supposed to feel special?

He sank back, shaking his head. "What do you want, Noelle?"

"I don't want anything."

"Everyone wants something. You're just so mixed up, you don't know what it is anymore." He ran a finger over her hand. "You know what I think?"

"Do I want to?"

He snorted. "Probably not, but I'll tell you anyway. I think you don't believe a thing you say."

She bristled, but he went on.

"I think you want to be loved . . . adored, maybe. I think you want some man to lose his head over you."

She brought up her chin. Tears stung her eyes. "What makes you think some man hasn't?"

Morgan studied her a long moment. "Is that it? Did you come here on a broken heart?"

She turned away, angry that once again he had drawn more from her than she intended. But he grasped her shoulders, gently pulled her to his side, and brushed her temple with his lips.

She stiffened. "Don't." She could not face those tender feelings. They triggered something else, something she didn't want to grasp.

"Okay." But he kept her in his arms, fingers loosely interlocked across her collarbone, until some weak comfort seeped in. Morgan meant well. She knew that. On some level she trusted him, but he wouldn't leave it alone. Now he'd pressed a new barrier by kissing her. Why did it bother her so much?

Rick came in, blowing on his reddened hands. He looked as though he'd worked himself raw, and his expression had soured. He was definitely angry. "There's a nasty drizzle out there, Morgan, and it's cold enough to freeze. You'd better give yourself time in the morning."

Morgan saluted, then as Rick went into the office and shut the door, he said, "What's eating him?"

Noelle didn't answer. What could she say? *I won't tell Rick what he wants to know—who Michael is, what happened, and what will happen if . . .* But she couldn't think about that.

Morgan stroked her shoulder with his thumb, and she sensed his concern, his confusion. She hadn't asked him to come, but he had.

She looked up. "You're leaving in the morning?"

"Got to. But we could make tonight worth remembering." He formed his rogue's smile.

His persistence astounded her, though she realized it was partly intended to provoke. He simply would not let her close down. "If you think that, you've wasted your trip."

He squeezed her shoulders. "I have no illusions, even if I do have to leave in the morning." He wore the expression of a naughty boy who knew he was adored. "Will you miss me?"

She sighed, unwilling to lie altogether. "If I say yes?"

"I'll kiss you."

She bit her lip. "Then no."

He kissed her anyway.

She fought the panic that rose up. She wanted it to be all right, but it wasn't. Her heart pounded, and she pushed away again. She had to. She struggled to get up but couldn't.

Morgan caught her hands together. "Don't freak out on me."

She pulled against his grip.

"Stop, Noelle." The sharp words commanded.

She stopped fighting and closed her eyes against the tears. She could almost feel the talons in her flesh. She couldn't stop him. Couldn't . . .

"What is it?" Morgan's voice was soft.

Both Rick and Morgan. Why couldn't they leave her alone? "Nothing."

"Well, excuse me, but I have kissed a few women, and no one's ever acted like I had the plague. Perdition is not contagious."

Tears burned. He was so far from understanding what really— Images suddenly flashed in her mind: a dark closet with louvered doors, a hand. *"Give us a kiss."*

"Hey." He stroked her cheek.

She opened her eyes, caught his hurt before he masked it. For a moment she wondered what Morgan needed. What drove him? But she didn't want to know. "I can't, Morgan."

"Fine." He could leave, spend the night on the town. But he sat with his arm crooked around her shoulders until Marta brought Noelle's meal on a tray and called him to the dining room. One cabin family with teen kids joined him there. Rick emerged from the office and passed by without speaking. She felt invisible.

Picking at the food on her tray, Noelle could hear Morgan engaging them all, the life of the party as always. He talked about the spoiled family who owned the corporation he was trying to reorganize. His anecdotes brought gales of laughter. She might have joined in; it was hard to resist Morgan's humor, but her isolation spared her.

Instead she was left with her thoughts. And that was dangerous. Her head ached and she had no appetite, but Marta would be hurt if she didn't eat something. She looked up at the log ceiling. She had felt so content when Rick first carried her inside. Now . . .

Morgan came and leaned in the doorway, keys in hand. "Let's go to town. If you can't dance, you can still listen."

She smiled. "If I could, I would, Morgan. But there isn't a part of me that doesn't hurt."

He dangled the keys from his finger. "Ever read Flannery O'Connor?"

Noelle tipped her head. "Some." Did he have some instruction for her from that tragic, if genius, author? Would he advise her to look more deeply into life, see its ugliness? She shuddered, but Morgan didn't say anything like that.

He took a paperback from the pocket of his coat that hung by the door. "Someone gave me these stories on the plane." He came and stood over her. "Going to eat that?" He indicated the food on her tray.

She shook her head. No sense pretending.

He set the tray on the table beside the pitcher of flowers, then pulled the blanket up around her and took his place beside her. He couldn't be serious. But he must be. He opened the book. Morgan would stay home and read to her, when he could have the crowd at his feet? It was too much to take in.

———

In the office, Rick ran the numbers four times. The accounts were in order, he just couldn't think straight. He shut down the computer and sat before the blank screen. Morgan was in rare form. Reading by the fireside? It surprised him Morgan could still read. Was there no limit to his efforts? He never worked so hard for so little reward. Didn't he see?

Rick rubbed his eyes. Or was he the one who had it wrong? He pictured Noelle tucked into Morgan's arm. It did seem to be working at last. Morgan was wearing her down, little by little, and maybe she'd meant it that way all along. Maybe she knew the harder Morgan had to fight the more he'd want the prize. Maybe it was her game as much as his. But Rick felt a check in his spirit—or was it his pride? Or something else?

Morgan was hooked, that was certain. To fly out for one night just to see she was all right—or had he other plans? Would Morgan disregard the house rules? Given the chance, Morgan would disregard anything.

Rick pulled the dust cover over the monitor. He was almost glad for Noelle's injuries that kept her in the open where he could watch, listen. He shook his head. Was it only a few days ago he'd carried her off the mountain, limp and trembling in his arms? His fault, yes, but he'd done the best he could to right it, covered her bill, spent hours at her hospital bedside, made a comfortable place for her where he'd know what she needed.

And then he had carried her home, seen her joy and gratitude, felt his heart swell at having her back inside his walls. But it had certainly been downhill from there. First his fruitless attempt to get answers, then Morgan's return to the scene.

He dropped his head to his palms. *God, why did you bring her here? What is your purpose? Don't you know I'm only a man? If you want me to help her I'm willing, but don't make me choose.* He clenched his fists against his forehead. *Morgan is my brother.*

————

When Noelle woke the next morning, her eyes were heavy, but the first thing she saw was Morgan in the corner chair. How long had he been watching her sleep? It couldn't be late; the morning light was dull in the window. But he seemed sharp and professional already.

His overcoat lay across his knees. He really was leaving, and soon. Why had he come? To comfort her? She'd fallen asleep while he read, hardly the response he'd wanted. She gingerly raised up onto her elbow, wincing with the pain in her ribs. "You're going now?"

He nodded.

Rick came to the kitchen door. "Coffee, Morgan?"

"I'll get Starbuck's at the airport." He stood and put on his overcoat against the drizzle outside.

Noelle sensed his disappointment. He'd expected more from this trip, more than she'd given him. Why? She had told him from the start . . .

He crossed the room to her, smiled wryly, and leaned over. "You're a gorgeous morning after." He caught the back of her head and kissed her lips.

She didn't panic this time and that was something, she supposed. "Thanks for a wonderful time." His eyes were amused, yet still hinted of regret. He gave Rick a careless wave and walked out.

She stared after him, unsure what to feel. As his rental car started and left the yard, she glanced at Rick. His expression was inscrutable. There was none of the warmth, the care he had shown in the hospital or when he'd brought her home. No anger either, but his face was as unyielding as the crag she had ridden up to paint.

He straightened in the doorway. "I have guests coming in from

Iowa tonight. I think you'd be more comfortable in your own room with some privacy."

Her heart sank. "All right."

"I'll have Marta get it ready for you."

"I'm sorry for the trouble."

"It's no trouble. Oh . . . Morgan asked me to give you this." He handed her a box, then left.

She opened the box. Inside were two halves of an eggshell held together with a rubber band. Puzzled, she slipped off the band and they fell apart. Inside was a slip of paper. She unfolded it. *To the real Noelle. Anytime.*

She leaned back on the pillows. *Oh, Morgan.* She looked at the shell halves, amazingly thin and fragile. She could crush them with her fingers. But her own wasn't so easy to break through. When did the running end and the healing begin? Or did it ever? She closed her eyes. What Morgan wanted she couldn't give. She didn't love him. Maybe she would never love again. She could live with that; why couldn't he?

Rick didn't stay in for lunch but grabbed a sandwich and took it back outside. Marta brought hers on a tray: grilled cheese and tomato soup, comfort food for both her condition and the weather. Noelle lifted Morgan's book. Why had he stayed reading to an invalid when he could have lit up the Roaring Boar and made his trip worthwhile? Because he hadn't flown out for a night at the Roaring Boar. He'd flown out for her.

*I will not panic.* So Morgan cared. Maybe. Maybe it was all part of his act. And now he was gone with nothing more than a kiss between them. Most women would thrill to his kiss. He hadn't had to say it. She was just . . . what? Paranoid?

She flipped open the Flannery O'Connor book to "A Good Man Is Hard to Find." Dark reading, but it seemed to fit both her and Morgan's state, people making decisions with no idea of the tragic consequences they'd set in motion. She settled in, then realized she had reread the same page again and again. The hours dragged. Rick did not come in. She had no doubt he could find work to keep him out twenty-four-seven if he wanted.

He was angry, and maybe his God was as well. She glanced at the Bible near Rick's chair. He had picked it up from the floor and replaced it on the table. But she didn't touch it. She didn't want to know his

God. Believing didn't help Morgan, and belonging was unthinkable. She covered her face with her hands and sank into the cushions.

"Noelle?" Rick woke her from a doze. "Are you ready to go up now?"

She glanced up the stairs to the open door and imagined how the walls would close in on her. She almost begged to stay down, then swallowed the ache. "Yes." She pushed herself up, ignoring the pain, and reached for the crutches.

His expression softened. "I'll get you." He lifted her into his arms.

She was too aware of his strength as he carried her up, his muscles, his will, his determination. She couldn't fight that. She couldn't even argue. He set her down gently, then went back for the crutches and leaned them on the wall beside her bed. "You'll manage all right in here." He wasn't asking; he was informing.

She nodded. "I'll be fine."

"Marta can bring your meals up."

Her throat tightened. She hoped he couldn't see how trapped she felt.

"All right, then." He left her.

She searched the room with her eyes. It seemed even more Spartan than before. Plain, serviceable, empty. She straightened her shoulders. She needed nothing more.

# 18

"Cats. I can't believe I'm seeing *Cats!*" Jan's eyes actually shone from her sunken sockets. She'd washed her hair and agreed to wear the dress Michael provided. He could overlook the smell of cigarettes on her breath for the pleasure of her excitement. He didn't tell her that if she let him take care of her, she could see shows like this more often. He would let the experience speak for itself—as only *Cats* might.

Jan had loved the soundtrack since she was a little girl, crying when the old cat sang "Memories." But she usually resisted any attempts on his part to lure her into theaters or museums or anything that smacked of culture.

Sometimes Michael wished he hadn't done so well. Then maybe Jan wouldn't have chosen her sad existence for her own identity. But *Cats* was too big a temptation for her to resist, and if she enjoyed it enough, maybe he could lure her with another. Broadway was magic, and some of the new shows would tickle Jan if she just gave it a try. It had to beat getting high with Bud.

He watched her throughout the show, held her hand when she cried through "Memories." She was so fragile—trying too hard and blowing it badly. Why couldn't she see? She was young enough he could make her over like Eliza Doolittle, introduce her to the new members of the firm. He could increase her life expectancy, her quality of life a hundredfold.

But inside she didn't trust him. Oh, he was the one she called when her car broke down or she couldn't make rent, but she had never really forgiven him for taking William's offer and leaving her behind. The difference in their ages would have caused a separation at some point but not so soon as William's position had made it. She'd convinced herself she didn't need him. And what she did now was punish him.

She knew her lifestyle hurt him, and she took adverse pleasure in wiping his nose in it. She did it to embarrass him, as well, and to keep him from forcing her out of it. He could bodily remove her, lock her up, choose her clothes, her companions, follow William St. Claire's example—only Jan wasn't compliant as Noelle had been.

*Noelle.* The evening crashed in on him. It should be Noelle at his side, glittering, drawing all eyes in the theater. He started to sweat, felt it beading on his forehead. It chilled in the air-conditioned auditorium and left him clammy. The show couldn't end soon enough.

Jan glanced over as they stood to applaud. "That was tight, Michael. Made me glad to live in an alley. That's where life really happens."

He wanted to slap her, frustrated at her stupidity. He pushed her out between the seats and gripped her arm through the chandeliered lobby.

"Ouch. Where's the fire?"

He loosened his grip. "Sorry."

"I just can't believe I've seen *Cats*. I've loved it so long."

"I know." He composed his fury. It wasn't really Jan. It was Mother and Noelle and the pressure inside, as if he'd stepped on a mine and one move would blow him to pieces.

"I used to pretend I was a cat. You know that fire escape from our bedroom window?"

"With the broken ladder?"

She nodded. "But I'd climb up to that little ledge over the handrail. I even meowed, thinking another cat might come visit."

It might have been a cute story except the only cats that might have visited in that neighborhood were likely rabid.

"Would you like to see another show?"

She shrugged. "I don't care much for shows. Only *Cats*."

"Want to see it again?"

She hesitated on that one, then shook her head. "Nope." She swung her hips as three black men in tailored suits walked by, then sent them a glance over her shoulder. He didn't tell her they were way out of her league.

They took the taxi first to Jan's so he could see her safely in. There was a light inside. "Did you leave that on?"

She shrugged. "Probably Bud." She reached for the door.

He caught her arm. "You don't know?"

She smiled saucily. "Nice of you to be concerned, big brother. But I live here. It's no big deal."

"Let me get you another place." He hadn't meant to push it tonight, but it was out now. "Nothing fancy." Just safe and clean.

"I like it here. Like I said, it's where life happens."

"Death happens too." To punctuate his words, sirens screamed by with lights skidding across the building walls.

"Death happens everywhere." She pulled open the door and climbed out. "Thanks for the show." She walked away singing "Memories."

———

Four days in her room, and Noelle was climbing the walls—or would be if she had the strength. The doctor said her developed dance musculature would help the healing but not to expect too much. Was it too much to hobble between the bed and the bath? She felt so weak, so trapped, and her mind was her enemy, wearing her down worse than broken bones and torn ligaments. She must get strong again. She must.

She heard voices in the dining room below: Rick's and two others, the guests from Iowa. They were staying in the third cabin, which she couldn't see from her window. She thought maybe Rick knew them. There seemed to be more camaraderie than usual in their discourse. They had nice voices. The woman laughed a lot, and Rick laughed with her. Noelle hadn't heard him laugh so much before. She couldn't catch the words, only the waves of conversation and the laughter.

A soft knock came at the door, and Marta wafted in with pancakes and bacon on a tray. Noelle straightened as Marta laid the tray across her knees. She wasn't nearly as hungry for food as for human contact, even Marta's brusque conversation.

"How are you today?"

"Better. Much better. Thank you, Marta."

Marta cocked her head and studied her. She wasn't easily fooled.

"A little tired of sitting around." Noelle tried a smile. It must have passed.

"Well, you have to take it slowly. Can't force things."

Any slower and she'd stop functioning altogether. "How are the people from Iowa?"

"Nice." Marta tucked in the corner of the bed sheet and straightened. "Friends of Rick's."

So she'd been right. Noelle felt a quirk of pleasure at her detecting skills. A year in this room and she'd have everything figured out. "Old friends?"

"Mmhmm." Marta plumped a pillow up behind her head. "Better?"

"Thank you," Noelle said. "They seem to be enjoying themselves."

"They are." Marta pulled a loose thread from the coverlet. "They're leaving today."

"Oh." Noelle's heart sank. She'd enjoyed imagining them as they conversed over meals. "Are the cabins rented out?"

Marta smoothed the corner of the spread. Noelle had made the bed when she got up to wash, but her efforts were clumsy, and she had climbed atop with the cover askew. Marta would probably love to tug it into place. "I don't think so."

No one to glimpse from the window, to hear through the floor. Noelle sighed. How had she ever thought she liked solitude?

"You're getting lonely?" Marta was perceptive.

Noelle forced a smile. "No, I'm fine."

"Can I bring you anything else? Something to read?"

Noelle shook her head. She looked at the window. What scenes she could paint with the trees changing color. But her paints were lost. The case had been crushed in Aldebaran's fall. "No, I don't need anything. Thank you, Marta."

Marta left her, and Noelle stared at the food on the tray: the thick fluffy pancakes with a pat of butter melting down the center, syrup to the side, two strips of thick-cut bacon, fried crisp but not browned. It was extra work for Marta to fix a tray every meal, and Noelle could tell she made a special effort to coax her appetite. Maybe it was the medication, maybe just the suppressed functioning of her body as it healed, but Noelle barely tasted the food Marta went to such pains to provide. She ate anyway. She had to get strong.

She took the codeine only at night, when the pain of knitting bones and wrenched ligaments was too great for her to sleep. The stupor included dreams and visions, but they had increased again on their own, so what did it matter? These dreams were more fantastic than before, often repeating the same images. No, one image. A window filled with color and wings, long, sweeping wings. And they were more terrifying than the others.

She shuddered, then forced another bite of pancake. When she finished, she set the tray aside and looked around the room. The voices below had stopped. Rick and his guests must have finished eating. Maybe his friends were preparing to leave. Was he with them, saying good-bye? Would he miss them?

Noelle looked out the window. The autumn beauty was at its peak. They must regret having to leave such majesty. She saw the branch sway on a pine just outside as a dark gray squirrel with tufted ears pattered by and disappeared. Noelle chafed. She had been still long enough. She grabbed the crutches and pulled herself to her feet, wincing at the pain in her ribs.

She had more or less only moved between the bed and the bathroom. Now she meant to do more. She worked open the dresser drawer and took out her jeans. None would fit over the cast unless she slit the leg. She shook her head and put them back. Shorts would be cold, but the khaki pair was baggy enough to pull up over the cast. She took them and a sweat shirt.

After dressing, she opened the door and went along the balcony to the top of the stairs. They were wide, broad stairs, but still the sight was intimidating. She'd never used crutches before, and her leg was stiffly casted to midthigh. Not conducive to the bending required by stairs. Clenching her teeth, Noelle balanced the crutches on the first stair down, then with her cast extended, swung her other foot down. She released her breath. Fourteen to go and already she was winded. She was weaker than she thought. Her arms shook as she lowered the crutches again.

But before she could swing her leg down again, Rick bounded up. "What are you doing?" He caught her arm.

"I'm going outside." She gripped the crutches tightly to keep her hands from shaking and met his gaze. She would *not* be dissuaded.

He stood there, barring her way, then suddenly reached around her waist and lifted her. The crutches clattered to the stairs. If he carried her back up, she would drag herself out on her belly! But he went down.

Mouth slightly agape, Marta opened the outside door. Noelle felt the rush of cool air with the keen scent of pine, always the pine. Rick carried her across the yard to a grove of aspens beside the stable. He set her down among the white trunks that seemed to watch her with their black eye-shaped sworls. She looked up. The sun had turned the leaves to paper-thin sheets of gold trembling in the bracing breeze. Overhead the cerulean sky spread cloudless from peak to peak over the valley. It was beautiful . . . so beautiful. Tears sprang to her eyes.

"Did I hurt you?" Rick asked.

It had hurt when he grasped her, but not as much as working her way down with the crutches. And it wasn't pain that brought the tears. She shook her head. "It's just so wonderful."

Rick's own expression had softened and deepened. "Well, sit as long as you like. I'll check back."

As she watched his retreat, Noelle dropped her chin to her hands folded over her knee. She was in his debt, more deeply than she'd ever intended. How had that happened? She had tried so hard to be self-reliant, and here she was more dependent than ever. She was at Rick's mercy.

Her chest tightened and the shakes came with vengeance. She raised trembling hands to her face, fought the image, but it came. Her heart hammered. She threw up her arms to ward off the talons of the hawk, the monstrous gaping beak, the amber eyes boring into her soul.

She cringed. *It's not real!* She was never attacked by a hawk. She dug her fingers into her scalp. Her chest heaved as the image faded and was gone. Her arms dropped. Sweat beaded her forehead. She wiped it away. It was crazy. Maybe she was crazy. Maybe that's why Daddy had run her life, and Michael . . .

She closed her eyes tightly. She would not think of him. It was all behind her. What she needed was a plan. She needed to get strong. She grabbed the cast on her leg, willing the bone to knit, the ligaments to fuse, the muscles not to wither. She would do it. She would heal herself, then somehow pay her debt and go away.

Her stomach lurched and she looked at the ranch house, golden in September light. Maybe she wouldn't have to leave. She sagged against the tree, closed her eyes, and thought of all the days she'd spent there, the things she'd done and learned.

She had grown, and her art reflected it. She'd even learned to cook a little. She had trained Destiny. Even Rick admitted it worked better with her there—though he might just be saying that. He had a way of slipping in kind words when she wasn't expecting it. Like telling his father she was competent. She sighed. He wouldn't be saying that after what she'd done to Aldebaran. That had been stupid, so stupid it humiliated her to think of it.

But she hadn't been thinking. She'd panicked, lost control. And she realized now it could happen again. The fear inside was not healed, was not even controlled. How could it heal when she couldn't even look at it? She startled at the snapping twig and her eyes shot open.

Rick stood over her with a lunch basket. Marta must have sent it, but Rick didn't leave it and go. He sat. "Are you doing all right?"

*No. I'm falling apart, and I don't know how to stop it.* She nodded.

He tipped his head up and the light through the leaves played over his features. "Nothing like aspens in the fall."

She followed his gaze up through the dappled gold to the azure sky. The sight soothed her and she longed to capture the shades on paper, to hold the moment forever, to take back inside with her when it was over. But she thought of the last time she had done that. Maybe it was better to let the moments pass.

"Are you chilly?" Rick's glance touched her goosebumped leg below the hem of the shorts.

She shrugged. "I'm fine. This one's warm." She knocked her knuckles on the cast. "It's the new look, you know."

The corners of his mouth deepened. It sure took a lot to make him smile. He opened the basket and handed her a sandwich. "Turkey, I think."

She took it, feeling the first hint of appetite. It must be the fresh air. "Did you have a nice visit with your friends?"

He glanced at her. "Yeah." If he wondered how she knew, he didn't ask. But he seemed more relaxed than the last time they'd spoken, when he'd carried her to her bedroom and left her there.

She wished she could recapture the ease they'd developed working Destiny. He must be training without her. She could smell the horses on him. "How are Hank's foals?"

"Coming. The bay is quick. She's learning well." He unwrapped his sandwich.

"What did you name her?"

"Jasmine."

"You like exotic names."

Rick shrugged. "I suppose. Mostly a name should fit or mean something." He bit and chewed his sandwich. "Like Noelle."

"Oh, that." She waved her hand. "I was supposed to be Michelle, but when I came the day before Christmas, Daddy chose Noelle instead."

"First your birthday, then the Savior's. Guess Christmas was something in your house."

She laid the sandwich across her knee. "I only remember one. I was six. It was the year before my mother died." She narrowed her eyes. "I can picture the house—every room glittering with candles, lights, fresh holly up the banister. Daddy told me not to run my hand on it, but I cut my palm anyway."

One side of his mouth drew up. She knew what he was thinking. Maybe she *was* willful. There had been other things just like that. She'd be the model child, then some little thing like refusing the red tutu for her recital. She hated red. And red dresses especially. Her thoughts jammed, and she turned them back to Christmas.

"I had my own little tree in my room, all colored lights and dancing bears. . . ." She raised her sandwich. "That was our last Christmas."

"Why?"

"After my mother died, Daddy . . . didn't see the point." She breathed the aroma of fresh bread, peppered turkey, and mayonnaise. "He always made a big deal of my birthday, though."

Rick took a bite of his sandwich and chewed slowly. Noelle did the same. The breeze flicked her hair across her face. She brushed it aside and took another bite.

Rick said, "It must be hard to lose a parent so young."

It must have been, but she could hardly remember. She remembered Daddy's face, hard and gray, and the strict schedule that began and continued every day of her life after. She was too busy to miss her mother, too tired to mourn. But she'd grown used to that. It was something else that she never got used to—the look of fear on Daddy's face as he crept into her room at night and hunched beside her bed.

She hadn't understood his fear, but she absorbed it. Something must be wrong. Something bad would happen. And it had. She realized Rick was watching her with that probing look. The quiet between them grew awkward. She brushed her hair back with her fingers. "What did you name the other horse?"

"Dulcinea."

She smiled. "Of La Mancha."

Rick stretched out on the ground and pulled apart a branch of grapes. He shot her a half smile. "Maybe I got carried away on that one."

She tried to reconcile the romantic names to the practical man. From what unplumbed depths did the names come? "It's nice that you name them something special."

"Dad raises some sweet horses. Aldebaran came from him."

Guilt flushed her face. "How is she?"

"She didn't break anything. Still favors the leg some, but not as much as you do yours."

Noelle stared at her cast. "I'm sorry. I never meant to hurt her."

He looked away. "I don't blame you. I thought you knew that."

He sounded sincere, but Noelle couldn't meet his eyes.

He tossed his napkin in the basket and stood. "Guess I'll get back at it." He scooped up the basket. "Do you want to go in now?"

She shook her head. "Just a little longer?"

He cocked his hip and grinned. "Are you ever satisfied the first time?"

"Never."

"I believe that." He took off his worn leather jacket and hung it over her bare knee. "No sense getting chilled."

She watched him walk away with his purposeful gait. The jacket warmed her leg, but her heart warmed more. Why had she feared him? How could she have thought he would hurt her? Because she'd been fooled before. No one was above doubt.

Rick came back out of the house and returned directly to her. He said, "Ms. Walker's on the phone. Do you want to talk to her?"

She nodded. "I guess I should."

"Hold on around my neck."

She obeyed, and he lifted and carried her to the house. He had left the door ajar and he nudged it with his boot, then set her on the couch. The daybed had been removed, the room put back as it was before. He was obviously not planning her return to the lower level. Rick brought her the phone, then left.

"Hello?" As Noelle leaned back against the pillows and listened, her heart sank. "Oh, I didn't realize it was a seasonal business. Not till June?" She shut her eyes. "Yes, if your friend in Boston will take them. Yes, by money order at this address. Thank you." She turned off the receiver and dropped it to her lap. The shop closed for the winter?

Her source of income gone, her body crippled . . . What more could possibly go wrong?

———

From the couch that evening, Noelle watched the light flicker warmly as Rick bent and poked the fire in the great stone fireplace. When he straightened, she gathered her gumption. "Rick, would it be possible for me to pay the winter's rent next spring, when the gallery opens again?"

He squatted and slid the log deeper in. The fire played across his features, accenting the angles and planes as he finally turned and faced her. "Noelle, you need to be honest with me."

A knot tightened her stomach. "About what?"

"Why you're here."

Her mouth went dry. "Is there a law against privacy?" Morgan would know that tone and back off.

Rick merely stood up. "Why can't you talk to your father?"

"I don't want to." It sounded peevish.

He sat down on the table across from her. "I can't decide anything until you level with me."

It was fair. She was asking him to support her through this time, giving him no reason whatever for doing it. Maybe if she told him something—even that she didn't know, couldn't remember. Of course, then he'd think her nuts and be less inclined than ever to have her in his home.

Her pulse suddenly throbbed in her ears. The shakes started up her spine. She fought the panic, but it was no use. In a moment she would hear the flapping of wings, feel the talons in her flesh. The hawk coming for the kill.

"Tell me the truth, Noelle. I can't keep you here unless I know the truth." Rick's voice compelled like no other. It wasn't only Rick speaking but something else as well. She wanted to respond, to be free of the terror. Her heart rushed, then fear and fury stopped it.

She gripped her moist hands together. "If you want me out, I'll go. There are other places."

"I didn't say I wanted you out. And where would you go with no money for rent?"

Her cheeks flamed. "Do you think I'm begging for charity? Ms. Walker has a place."

"A shack." He stood and paced to the window. "And it doesn't go free."

She raised her chin. "She'll discount it for a higher percentage on my work."

"You have to have sales to earn a percentage." He swung his hand wide. "The shop's closed."

Noelle's throat tightened. "She's sending my stock to a Boston gallery."

Rick cocked his jaw. A brief flash of anger crossed his face, the same anger he'd displayed on the shale slope. "Just tell me what I need to know."

"You don't need to know anything." Her voice shook. She thought he might holler, might—

But the anger faded from his face, replaced by regret. He spread his hands. "Well, Marta's leaving this week for the winter. I don't take guests past September. I guess it's best if you find another place." He stalked to the door and went outside.

Her breath caught jaggedly. What had she done? Why didn't she just tell him? What if she said, yes, I'm in trouble, Rick; I need your help. But she couldn't. She pressed her hands to her face. What would she do?

She tightened her jaw. She should have enough money for the first month on Ms. Walker's shack—the Taj Mahal. Ms. Walker had suggested it more than once as part of their partnership. After that, there'd be sales from Boston. There had to be. She picked up the phone and dialed. "Yes, Ms. Walker? Is your rental property still available?"

When she hung up, she saw Marta standing behind her at the doorway to the kitchen. "Could you please bring my crutches, Marta?"

Marta slowly shook her head but brought the crutches. Noelle didn't want to hear her regrets. She took the crutches and started for the stairs. Up was easier, at least not as intimidating. Still hurt the ribs. That was one good thing; there were no stairs in Ms. Walker's shack.

Marta followed. "I'll help you pack your things."

"I can manage."

"Maybe you can. But I'd like to help." Marta started on the dresser drawers.

Noelle was thankful for the assistance—as long as it didn't include an opinion.

Rick pressed his knees into Destiny's sides. The horse plunged through the creek and up into the forest. Overhead, stars pricked the sky in the deepening dusk. He climbed to the top of the hill where the trees stopped and Destiny's hooves clattered on stone. He looked up to the sky.

*God, I can't break through. I can't see my way.* And now his anger turned to hurt. He dropped his head and pressed his palm to his forehead. He ached at the thought of turning Noelle out. Why had she even come? What was she there for? There had to be a reason. Maybe it was none of his business.

Then why did it feel like he was ripping his own heart out? "God, if you want something from me, say so." He waited in the moonlight until calm returned to his spirit. He would talk to Noelle again. Maybe there was some way to get through. If she would trust him, he could help her. But the Lord was right. It had to come from her. He rode back, semi-hopeful, but he found Noelle in the entry, standing on her crutches with her tote and another bag on the floor beside her. She had obviously made up her mind.

"You're leaving now?" His tone was dry.

"I called Ms. Walker. She'll give me a ride." Noelle wouldn't meet his eyes.

Why was she so stubborn? Couldn't she see he would help? *Lord?* What more could he say? He went to the cupboard under the bookshelf and pulled out the pine box he'd fashioned. He had intended to rub in an oil finish, but there wasn't time for that now. He set it on the table beside her. She looked puzzled.

"Open it," he said.

She did. Inside were her paints, brushes, and the easel he'd repaired. Sudden tears glittered in her eyes.

He cleared his throat. "I picked them up when I went back for Aldebaran. I'm afraid the pictures were ruined in the rain."

She didn't answer for a long moment, then whispered, "Thank you."

His spirit stirred. Maybe now . . . "Noelle . . ."

Tires ground on the gravel outside and she turned away. "There's Ms. Walker. Will you please get the door?"

Rick lifted the wooden case and her bags as she gripped her crutches.

He opened the door and let her out. Ms. Walker sat in her Land Rover, popping her gum. This was wrong. It had to be. *Give me the word, Lord. Just give me the word.*

The night was still and so was his spirit. The rest of him was anything but. He carried the tote and bag and put them into the backseat. He wanted to jerk them back out and carry them and Noelle right back upstairs. But God knew better, and if Rick acted against that belief, it would certainly be worse.

Noelle eased herself into the front seat. "Thank you, Rick. For everything."

He took the crutches and slid them into the back with her bags. He'd done all he could. So he nodded, then watched the Rover turn and the taillights disappear. When the cold penetrated his woolen shirt, he went inside. Marta sent him a hopeful look, but he shook his head.

"I have pie straight from the oven," she said.

He smiled. "Thanks, Marta." If only pie would help.

# 19

S*hack* was a generous term for Ms. Walker's rental. One week there was like solitary confinement in the most dissolute penal system in America. Noelle looked around the cramped area that housed the tattered couch, single lamp, lumpy bed, and kitchen. Well, kitchen stretched the definition: a white gas oven that practically blew up when she lit it, a tiny refrigerator, and a Formica table with one foot missing and two vinyl chairs.

She sat down in the peeling chair, dropped her elbows to the table, and wept. This place was hideous and ugly and dirty and cold. Why hadn't she told Rick what he wanted to know? Her anger flared, and she shoved back from the table. She reached down and threw her shoe at the spider on the wall, then sighed.

Yesterday she had made her way on crutches to every business in town that stayed open through the winter. No one needed extra help when they scaled back for local business only. No one needed a hobbled woman with no work experience.

So where did that leave her? Thanks to Rick's gift, she could paint and hope that the gallery in Boston would sell her watercolors. Ms. Walker had sent off the last of her work, then closed up and left town, leaving a post-office box address at which she would accept any new work.

Noelle reached for the case Rick had made, ran her fingers slowly over the smooth wood. His eyes had been so gentle when he presented it, and regretful. Would she ever understand him? But that didn't matter anymore.

The ranch had been a haven for a time, but she no longer needed it or him. She had a new place and a means to support herself—if the paintings did as well in Boston as in the local gallery. Of course, at Ms. Walker's shop the tourists were looking specifically for local art. In Boston she would be competing with a much higher quality of artists and myriad styles and themes.

What if nothing sold at all? Noelle looked around her. In this depressing place it was easy to imagine complete meltdown.

———

Michael was on fire. He'd won the case. Even at second chair, it was his work, his finesse, his points that turned the jury. William was thorough, but Michael had been brilliant. And William knew it, demonstrated by his nudge when they walked out together with their client to the whirring cameras, the microphones shoved into their faces. William was putting him first.

With his breath turning white in the cold, Michael accepted the spokesperson's position, while William pushed Burton Wells through to the car. Michael raised a hand to quiet the barrage of questions. He wanted to make a fist and punch the air in victory, but he straightened his coat and looked gracious.

The questions came fast, and he answered. "As you know, Mr. Wells was clearly exonerated. We're very pleased. . . . The city will have to look elsewhere to solve its case. . . . Yes, I hope they'll find Ms. Baker's assailant. . . . I have no information on other suspects. . . . Mr. Wells will be spending time with his family where he belongs. Thank you very much."

He stepped down and pressed his way through the crowd respectfully. He loved it. He wanted to smear the grins off every face when they lost, but when they won? The press was his fan club. Whether they meant it or not. He got into his cab. William's limo had already left. But they were meeting in an hour, and Michael anticipated the congratulations.

He wasn't patting himself on the back; he was exulting in overcoming the almost crippling ache he carried inside every day now. William didn't know. No one knew. Michael had re-created himself so thoroughly that not even William suspected he dreamed every night of Noelle. Dreamed of finding her, holding her, and more.

She was out there somewhere, and sooner or later she would contact her father. Michael had to maintain his professional and personal relationship with the man whose esteem he coveted as desperately as Noelle's love. Then he would have both.

———

Inside the limousine, William toasted Burton Wells. Their glasses clinked and William sipped the Dom Perignon he kept for such occasions. He was pleased to represent and vindicate an innocent man. And he was humbled by the depth of gratitude he saw in Burton's eyes. "I guess we'll both sleep tonight."

Burton nodded silently. He'd been a man of few words throughout the ordeal. A class act. Though the circumstantial evidence had shown opportunity, they could prove no motive for Burton to have attacked his young neighbor. There had been racial bias—accusations and innuendos against the only African-American in the gated community.

But not once had they drawn on that for their defense. Burton had not wanted the ACLU or black extremist groups riding this wave. He wanted to be cleared as an individual, not a black man done wrong. He smiled now, an elegant, satisfied smile. "I think we will. Unless, of course, Taniya has other designs."

William smiled, then sobered. "There will be difficulties."

"I'm prepared for that."

"No, you're not. A verdict of not guilty is not the same as innocent."

The lines in Burton's face lengthened and deepened as they passed the guard station and pulled into the circular drive. "A man in my position is used to suspicion. How can that black man afford a house like this? Did he make his money in drugs?" The tendons pulled tight in his neck. "I will sleep tonight, regardless of what my neighbors think."

William nodded. He had done his job well. More than that, Michael had done his. Looking at Burton now, he could well believe this client no longer needed his advice. He held out his hand. "It's been an honor."

Burton gripped it, then grinned. "Right back at you."

William chuckled as Burton climbed from the limo. He glanced at his watch. Nearly an hour before he and Michael were meeting for dinner. He crossed his hands behind his head. "Just drive, John. Tavern on the Green by seven." The only thing that could have made this evening better was to share it with Noelle. He closed his eyes and tried to keep the hurt and worry from spoiling the moment. Myron Robertson had not found her. Yet.

———

Noelle stared out the dingy window. The first of November, and the snow fell in earnest. October's rent and half of September had taken all but twenty-three dollars of her money. She had no phone and would soon have no utilities according to the latest notice. Perhaps it would be a while before they actually disconnected her, but she kept the heat low to limit the debt until she earned something.

Her leg itched in the cast, and she raised it to the table. It was long past time to have it removed, but she had no transportation back to the hospital, nor funds for a follow-up visit, not to mention the physical therapy they'd expect. Enough was enough. She took the serrated knife from the drainer on the sink and hacked at the plaster until the blade snagged in the wrapping beneath. Then she pulled apart the two halves and scrutinized the small scar at the side of her knee, the shin where the bone had knit, and the withered muscles. Then she scratched the skin red.

She put her foot on the floor and tried her weight. It hurt a little, but mostly it was weak. She would exercise it tomorrow. Right now she was too discouraged. She dropped to the chair. How had she come to this? Every choice had been hers. Had she used her freedom so poorly, or did forces conspire against her? Forces? Or God?

Rick's God. If He existed, He was no doubt as grim and unswerving as Rick, as unyielding, uncaring . . . Unbidden she recalled Rick's head bowed in the corner of her hospital room, the warmth and comfort of his grip as he stilled her fears, his payment of her bills—and the look in his face when he gave her back her paints, her livelihood.

Was he uncaring? Hadn't he tried to help? It was her own refusal to trust him that had her where she was. But how could she tell him? How could she give substance to the nightmare? He asked too much. She dropped her chin to her palm. Maybe . . . maybe her paintings would sell in Boston.

———

Rick paced to the window and looked out at the snow. December twelfth. He loved winter's solitude, the physical labor of repairing and building. He liked connecting with neighbors he saw less frequently in the summer when his ranch was in use. In the winter, Bruce and Simon would stop by and they'd play backgammon or brag about their hunting and fishing. In winter he sat by the fire and read, played his guitar.

Rick looked at it now, leaning against the couch, and thought of Noelle, of the night she'd seen him play, of the way he'd wanted to play for her. In twelve days she would have a birthday. Would she celebrate with friends in town? The people he talked to said she kept to herself. Rudy saw her when she needed paper, which meant she was painting, using the materials Rick had gathered from the mountainside and repaired.

Maybe things were going fine and she'd found the independence and control she wanted. Maybe his doubts were groundless. He shook his head. She'd made it very clear that she didn't need his help. So why the nagging concern?

He paced the room again. She wasn't far. He could go down and visit, see how she was getting along, how the leg was healing. In a way it was his responsibility to know. He had accepted medical responsibility, at least.

But then he pictured her wounded face when he tried to get answers. She did not trust him, did not want his help. If he hadn't forced the issue . . . But, no, he'd done what he had to. They couldn't live together on the ranch the way they'd been, not just the two of them, not the way things had developed. If he didn't interfere now, maybe she'd go home and face whatever had made her run. That thought left a sizeable hollow.

He forced himself to sit. What was it? Why was he so stir crazy? He glanced at the Bible on the table. Maybe he should have made a better effort. He rested his head in his palms. Then he dropped to his knees and prayed.

———

Noelle pulled open the cupboard and groaned. Part of a box of oatmeal and a handful of tea bags . . . and on the table Ms. Walker's final notice. Though she had waived the signing of a lease, Ms. Walker did expect to be paid. Both November and December's rents were past due, but Noelle had used all of her cash. If she didn't pay the rent by the end of the week, she was out, and nothing had sold. At least no money had arrived from Boston.

She raised her brows and stared at the table where her paints were spread. Maybe no one liked her work anywhere but here. Her head spun, and she blinked away the dizziness. She limped across the cracked linoleum and sat down at the table. Outside the smudgy window, snow blanketed the ground and fell again, soft and silent.

She lifted the paintbrush that lay beside the jar and stared at the paper. What was the use? A racking cough seized her and shot fire through her chest. She dropped the brush, staggered to the bed, and lay down, grabbing the covers up as her teeth chattered together.

Scarcely aware of time passing, she lay with fever raging. Her trembling was so violent her muscles ached from exhaustion. As the sun sent its last, weak rays over the mountain, she dragged herself across the floor to the sink and drank directly from the faucet, then staggered back. She just . . . needed . . . sleep.

Dreams faded in and out of her consciousness. Professor Jenkins stood at the table in her father's library and drilled her Latin. *"The human spirit and part of the divine." I don't know it, Professor. It doesn't exist. "It exists, Noelle, in the beautiful. You must find it . . . find it . . . find it . . ."*

The real Noelle. Morgan held out the eggshells. *"Come out. Come out and dance. Dance with me." I can't. My leg is broken. I can't dance. I can't.*

*"The Word became flesh and made his dwelling among us. We have seen his glory, the glory of the One and Only, who came from the Father, full of grace and truth."* The light was so bright it hurt her eyes. *"The truth. Tell me the truth, Noelle."* Rick's eyes probed. He held the guitar and sang words she didn't know. She felt her resolve crumbling. No. No. . . .

———

Rick banged again. If she didn't answer that, he'd kick the door down. He had tried yesterday with no luck, but he would bet she wasn't out in today's snow. Maybe she meant to ignore him, and she had the right, but . . .

Noelle opened the door, and he couldn't help but stare. Her eyes and cheeks were hollow, her lips cracked. Her hair hung in strings. The bones of her hand on the door stood out, skeletal through her skin. The flannel nightshirt and leggings hung on her, and her lips and fingernails were blue.

He hid his shock and held out the envelope. "This letter came for—"

"Thank you." She snatched it and shoved it into the pocket of her nightshirt.

That was it. He'd done what he had to, brought her mail, and she was obviously not welcoming him inside. He started to turn, then pushed the door wide, shoved past her, and went inside. His breath formed a cloud. "Noelle, it's cold as a tomb in here!" And the place was a hovel.

"I've had a cold and been in bed." She coughed and held her ribs.

Rick looked hard at her where she stood, shivering and clammy. "Your power's off?"

"I keep it low."

He reached for the light switch and flicked it up. Nothing happened. He crossed the room, pulled open the cabinet, then the refrigerator. He spun. "What's going on?"

Again a cough racked her. She slumped against the wall and sank to the floor. "Just leave." She closed her eyes.

Rick yanked the cover from the bed and wrapped it around her. She didn't fight him, and he wasn't surprised. She was weak and limp as a kitten as he lifted her and carried her out to the truck.

But when he slid her into the seat, she seemed to come to. "What are you doing? I didn't ask for your help." She coughed again as he tucked her legs in.

His anger surged. "No, you didn't." He shut the door and walked around, forcing composure. Even so, he didn't look her way when he climbed in. The sight of her feverish eyes, hollow cheeks, the blue tinge of her lips . . .

"Where are you taking me?"

"Dr. Bennington." He started the engine and headed for the small, gray Victorian house up the hill from the highway on Bragg Street.

"He's retired."

"How do you know?"

She coughed, a deep, hollow hack. "Rudy told me months ago, when I first came."

"He sees almost as many patients now as he did in regular practice.

People just don't bother him with inconsequential stuff." But her condition was hardly inconsequential. Had she no sense at all? He parked in front of the white wrought-iron fence.

He scooped up Noelle and carried her up the porch steps and into the back room of Dr. Bennington's home, sharp with antiseptic air. He was so angry it made him shake, but he set her on the examining table and backed off. *Calm down. This isn't about you. You did what you had to.*

But he kicked himself anyway. And he ought to kick her. Well, not literally. But what did it take? How stubborn could she be?

Dr. Bennington hung the stethoscope on his neck. "How long have you been coughing?"

"I'm not sure." Her voice was weak.

The doctor listened to her breathe. "Umhmm." He examined her leg, feeling the muscle tone with his slightly palsied hand. "This leg isn't looking so good either."

Noelle didn't answer. Her eyes had closed, and she lay wheezing on the table. She looked as though a breeze would blow her away. The doctor clamped Rick's shoulder. "Step out now while I examine her."

He waited outside, the floorboards lamenting his pacing feet until Dr. Bennington joined him. "How is she?"

The doctor kept his gravelly voice low. "Pneumonia. Dehydration. The fever's wasted her, no doubt, but I don't think she's eating well. Is she anorexic?"

Rick shook his head. "I don't know. I'd guess just broke."

Dr. Bennington made a note on his chart. "I injected an antibiotic that should kick in with a bang. You'll have to fill this prescription elsewhere." He handed him the slip. "I'd say take her to the hospital for an IV, but she'd probably pick up a worse infection, and those young scalawags wouldn't know pneumonia from tetanus."

Dr. Bennington's opinion of current medical care was well-known. "I'd say if you can get some fluids in her she's better off up here. With proper care, she'll be all right." He turned briefly to the door. "I wouldn't leave her unattended, though."

Rick hardened his resolve. "I'm taking her to my place."

"Good. Once she's well enough to stand and walk, we'll worry about the leg. I can't imagine what kept her from getting help sooner."

Rick could. But this time he'd do more than imagine.

———

Lying on the table in the doctor's office, Noelle rolled to her side. Something crinkled in her pocket, and she felt the envelope Rick had brought her. Rising to her elbow, she tore it open and read: *Dear Ms. St. Claire, Your talent has been well received. Enclosed please find a money order per your request* . . . Noelle sat up and stared. Her head spun, and after all the other delusions, she was unsure whether she imagined what she read. But it was there on the money order. It must be real.

She clutched the letter to her chest. She had no idea her paintings could sell for so much, far and above what she had earned through Ms. Walker. Maybe Rick had been right—maybe Ms. Walker had kept back more than her share. What did it matter now? With money like this . . .

"Good news?" Rick came in with the doctor.

She handed him the letter, still riding the burst of energy the news had infused in her. "Dr. Bennington, may I pay you when I've cashed this money order?"

"You may. But now I want you in bed directly. You need plenty of rest these next days if you don't want to end up here again." He extended a hand to help her down.

*Rest.* Yes, she needed it. If she was going to continue her success, she must get well. A wave of exhaustion extinguished her false strength. Her head spun, but she kept her feet and allowed Rick to support, but not carry, her to the truck.

She hated to ask anything of him, but right now she was too weak to manage alone. "Rick, can you cash this for me at the bank?"

He turned the key and the engine roared. "I can."

"Now?"

"No." Rick backed the truck. "You heard the doctor."

"I'll rest better with the money in my hand." She may as well have talked to the wall.

He only shook his head and started up the road to his ranch. She noticed his direction but didn't argue. She couldn't bear the thought of setting foot once more into Ms. Walker's rental. Besides, her eviction notice was probably in the mailbox. Eviction. Had she even known that word before?

She glanced at Rick. His jaw was set, his hand firm on the wheel.

She could sense his controlled fury. Why was he angry? How had she offended him? What business was she of his?

He eased her out of the truck, wrapped in the coverlet. In the cold, still air she could smell its rank odor. What must he think? He made no comment but replaced the blanket with a thick green afghan as he settled her onto the couch. Then he went to the kitchen.

She looked around her, dismayed by the comfort she still found in the familiar log walls. Outside the window the evening had deepened, and the moon shone through the icy clouds on the snow-covered spruce. In spite of the room's warmth, she shivered.

Rick handed her a cup of instant chicken broth. "This'll warm you up." His words were gentler than his grim face.

She sipped. It tasted good, and the warmth coursed down her throat. How long had it been? Too long. For the moment she could focus on nothing but the hot, salty broth, and it warmed her from the inside. The steam moistened her face as she blew the surface cool enough for the next swallow and the next. She drained the cup and set it on the table.

Rick tossed another log on the fire, then turned. "Why didn't you tell me you needed help? Or call Morgan?"

"Morgan?" How many months had it been since he'd gone? How would she even know where to find him? And what would he care?

Rick spread his arms. "Is it so bad to admit you need a hand?"

Not when he put it that way, but it hadn't seemed so clear. "I thought . . ." The cough burned her chest.

"Listen to you. That's pneumonia."

"I didn't know."

"Like you didn't know your power was out?" He didn't shout, but each word was stressed.

Her anger flared. "I *didn't*. They must have shut it off when I was in bed." She frowned. "I didn't know the town hibernated all winter. I couldn't find work, and I had no way to get anywhere else."

"Not without asking."

She hadn't the energy to argue. She wanted sleep. She wanted peace. "So what do we do now?"

His expression softened, and he released a slow breath. "I guess you should take a long, hot bath and go to bed."

She smiled weakly. "I don't think anything's ever sounded so good."

Bathing in the tub in the bathroom at the end of the hall, she let the hot water soothe her aches. Her scalp tingled from her scrubbing, and though she felt dozy, it was not the same delirious exhaustion as before.

She closed her eyes and exulted. To soak in a decent tub instead of the chipped and rusting one at Ms. Walker's was ambrosia, but she shouldn't overdo it. Soon she would be too loose to move. She stood and took the towel from the rack. Her head spun, but only for a moment.

She could almost feel her strength returning. It was as though her body knew she'd come home. *Home.* She toweled dry, then wrapped herself in the thick terry robe that hung on the door. It enveloped her in spongy warmth . . . and smelled of Rick.

Well, he hadn't brought her clothes along when he burst in to play rescue ranger, and she would not even consider dressing in the sweat-stained things she'd worn these last days. She tied the robe at her waist and limped painfully down the hall to her room.

Her room. She collapsed on the bed and stared at the log ceiling. She pulled the covers up around her. Her heart rushed with longing. Surely he'd let her stay. Surely . . .

CHAPTER

# 20

Rick jolted up in bed, wakened so suddenly he wasn't sure why. Then he heard Noelle and scrambled from the covers. He pulled on his jeans as he rushed for her room. She didn't answer his knock so he pushed the door open. In her bed, she thrashed, throwing up her arms, fending off some unseen attack.

He hurried over and caught her hand. "Noelle."

She sprang up and fought him, striking with her fists. He took a jab in the jaw before he caught her arms and grabbed her close. "It's all right. It's okay now."

Her chest heaved in sharp wheezing breaths as the fight left her, but she shook uncontrollably, and he stroked her back, willing her peace. "It's all right." He soothed her like a spooked foal, gentling the fight and fear from her. "It's all right now."

She was in his robe. It swallowed her up and she seemed more fragile than ever. Her hair was satiny soft, her cheek warm and damp beneath his palm. His own heart quickened with a powerful warmth, a warmth so real and right it staggered him.

He fought to restrain the rush, to remember everything he'd told himself for months. But when she slowly raised her face, he cupped her cheek and kissed her. He hadn't planned it, hadn't intended it, but there was no denying it. Her lips charged his with sweet desire, but it was not his purpose to seduce her, just to comfort if he could. He cradled her head against his neck, gaining control and clinging to it.

She whimpered. "It was horrible. He was there . . . at the door. And there was nowhere to hide in the dirty little room." Her tears collected in the hollow of his throat. "And it was there, above him, the hawk with the horrible beak and the amber eyes. So big . . . so awful."

She was still in the throes of the dream. He didn't expect it to make sense. He just stroked her back, willed away the fear, and silently prayed. *Lord, help me. I'm over my head, out of my head. Hold me firm.*

She pulled away, and he let her go. Her throat worked, but whether she meant to speak or merely fought her tears, he couldn't tell. He waited, unwilling to force her, though he needed the truth now more than ever. *Oh, God, let her be ready.*

"I need to tell you about Michael. Now, before I make myself forget again."

So he'd been right. This Michael was the problem. He nodded, afraid that anything more would scare her away. "I'm listening." He cupped her hand in his.

"I don't know if you can understand how it was. My father is a very powerful man."

Rick nodded. He knew that already. But her father wasn't Michael. Where was she going with this?

She drew a shallow breath. "So powerful he built, well, a human fortress for me. Everything I did, everywhere I went was planned. You could almost say I was guarded."

"Bodyguards?"

"I suppose. My friends, my teachers, the men I dated, they were all screened and approved . . . or not."

That wasn't necessarily a bad thing, but Rick didn't say so aloud.

"Then there was Michael." Her hand trembled in his cupped palm. "He was Daddy's protégé, handsome, amusing, brilliant. He'd so completely won Daddy, I was tired of hearing about him before I'd ever seen him. Maybe I was jealous or a little threatened . . . I don't know. I resisted all Daddy's attempts to introduce us."

She wheezed and cleared her throat. "I knew what Daddy wanted, but I was no longer a child, and I was not about to let him handpick the man he thought I should marry. What century did he think it was? So I rebelled—until I saw Michael for myself." She shuddered. "We met on my twenty-second birthday. Michael was . . . He had something about him, some energy. It was magnetic, overwhelming." Her hand dropped to her lap.

"Soon I was seeing more of him than anyone else. Eight months past my birthday, we were engaged."

Something traitorously close to jealousy stung his heart.

She turned and stared at the wall. "Then things changed. He changed. First it was just comments. If he'd given me something, he'd ask why I wasn't wearing it. He chose our friends, our entertainment, everything. And he told me how to dress, how to act. It was worse than all the years of Daddy's protection. He controlled . . . no, he owned me."

"And your father allowed it?"

"I allowed it." The despair in her voice tugged his heart. "And it got worse." She was scarcely above whispering now. "If I voiced an opinion or disagreed with him, he got angry."

Rick's hand tightened reflexively. "You didn't tell anyone?"

"In between he'd be so . . . wonderful." She pulled her hand free and swiped the tears. "I know what you think."

"No, you don't." He said it softly. He could lose her here. He saw the signs.

She cleared the thickness from her throat. "I was . . . ceasing to exist. No other friends. Only Daddy and Michael with their mutual adoration."

That explained her refusal to talk to her father. She must feel betrayed. She'd been betrayed. Whether William St. Claire knew it or not. Rick couldn't imagine her hurt. But he sensed it wasn't over. Her sudden gaze hit him like a blow.

"When I broke off the engagement, Michael went crazy. He was sure I had someone else, was obsessed with the idea." She pressed her palms to her eyes. "He swore he would never let me go. He hit me, then . . ." Her breath came short and quick. "I can't see the rest—it fragments." She shuddered.

She didn't have to spell out the rest. He knew what had happened. Rick caught her hand, willing her strength, then as her tears came, he pulled her close and let her cry.

Her voice broke with the sobs. "So I ran."

Fury surged inside him, but he stroked her hair, kept her close to his chest. How had he not suspected? It had been there in her face, her inability to trust. Too many things came clear. "Does Morgan know?" His voice was raw.

"No one knows."

Not true. God knew, and now he knew. All the glimpses he'd had of her struggle came together and made sense. And the Lord would show him what to do with it—if he didn't get in the way. This was no time for the sort of things stirring inside his own soul.

He held her until he sensed her exhaustion, then laid her gently back. When he was certain she slept, he went down and searched God's Word. As he read, he wrestled with the rage. Rage at Michael for hurting her, at Morgan for coming on to her, at himself . . .

*Oh, Lord, I asked you to show me, but I don't know what to do with it. I didn't mean to care the way I do, and that's the last thing she needs. But it's there, deep inside, where I can't root it out.*

He turned back to the Bible. His eyes ached as he read. His body cried for sleep, but he had no peace. Suddenly one line stood out on the page, and he read it again. *"Above all, love each other deeply, because love covers over a multitude of sins."*

He glanced out at the paling sky. *"Love each other deeply."* It wouldn't be hard to get to that, at least on his part. He was already further along than he wanted to think. But what about Noelle?

*"Love covers over a multitude of sins."* Could his love cover the sins against her? Could he love deeply enough to take away her pain? He dropped his forehead to his palm. Not alone, he couldn't. But with Christ loving through him . . .

He closed the Bible, pulled on his coat, and drove to the small house beside the church. Pastor Tom did not rise with the sun. That was evidenced when he shuffled to the door, bleary eyed. His gray hair stood up in peaks. "Rick."

"I'm sorry to wake you."

Pastor Tom pulled the door wide. "Come in. Whoo, it's cold. That'll wake me if nothing else."

Rick followed him into the small kitchen.

"Mind if we sit with a cup of coffee?" The pastor reached for two stained ceramic mugs.

"I could use it."

Rick waited while Pastor Tom ran the water through the coffee maker, then breathed the comforting aroma. He sipped the coffee, letting the heat and caffeine bolster him. "This is confidential."

"I guessed it might be."

Rick told him Noelle's story. When he had finished, Pastor Tom reflected his own concern. His bushy gray eyebrows drew almost together in one line as he cupped his mug in his gnarly hands. "I'm no expert on rape, but I know enough to say her trust won't come easily."

"I don't expect it to be easy. I just want to do the right thing."

Pastor Tom leaned back, crossed his hands against his chest. "What are your feelings for her?"

The pastor had read more into his telling than he intended. "Pretty dangerous."

Pastor Tom smiled. "I thought so. Has she faith?"

Rick shook his head. "Not that I've seen."

"Then that's the starting point. Share your faith with her."

That wasn't what he wanted to hear. He wanted something concrete, practical. Sharing his faith with one as closed as Noelle was like teaching a horse to fly. She lacked the right equipment.

He felt a prick of conscience. Wasn't every human being created with a sense of God, a need and a longing unfulfilled by anything else? Hadn't Satan's attack on the mountain shown as much? Why would the lord of darkness be concerned with someone who had no chance, no hope of salvation?

And how could he think of loving her—He stopped short in that thought. Did he love her? How could he if he couldn't share his faith, his belief, his love for God, and his trust in God's grace? He felt the doubts crowd in.

Feelings were one thing. They were not predictable, not dependable. Love was a commitment, a promise, a joining together as one. How could two from such different worlds as his and Noelle's come together in any way that made sense? But even as he thought it, he realized he wanted it.

"I can try that, Tom. But there's the practical problem also. I can't exactly winter alone with her at the ranch." If last night was any indication, her vulnerability would make quick work of his resolve. He was more likely to fall from grace than she to attain it.

"How about your family?"

"Send her to Iowa?"

"Take her to Iowa."

Rick considered that. They'd be willing, he knew. She already had Dad's affection, and his mother would welcome her. He felt a selfish reluctance that made it all the more clear he couldn't keep her at the ranch.

Pastor Tom leaned forward, his gaze piercingly clear. "Rick, do you realize she may not return your affection? That you may help her in every way—even bring her to faith—and have nothing to gain?"

The words shredded his prideful assurance. Yeah, he knew better than to expect success where even Morgan had failed. But, then, his intentions weren't the same. "I know that."

"Then take her to your family, surround her with warm hearts and faithful spirits. Teach her what it means to belong."

Belong. He felt the quickening in his spirit. *Yes.* He nodded. "Thank you, Tom."

————

Noelle awoke to the familiarity of her own room. She had half expected to find Rick still holding her hand, but the room was empty. Maybe she'd dreamt it. But no, he'd been there. Even in his absence she felt his comfort.

Her heart jumped with the thought, but it scared her. There was more than comfort in his arms last night. She'd wanted his kiss, asked for it. What was wrong with her? How could she even think . . .

She limped to the bath and washed. The burning in her chest was gone except when she coughed, and even that was lessening. The injection must have been a potent one, and she rubbed the aching spot where she'd received it. But if it did the trick, that's all that mattered.

She made her slow descent downstairs. The house was silent. She missed Marta's humming, but Marta was gone for the winter. Rick wasn't in the kitchen. She leaned against the refrigerator to catch her breath, then pulled open the door. Every shelf was stocked. What an incredible sight.

Rick came in and tossed the newspaper on the table, then leaned over her to see into the refrigerator. "Something exciting in there?"

His ease calmed her. "I was reveling in the sight of food." She closed the door and turned.

He smiled. "You must be feeling better."

His smile churned her emotions. She didn't want what he was making her feel. She said, "I'm sorry for last night."

"What part are you sorry for?"

"Waking you." She breathed the scent of woodsmoke in his shirt. Her pulse quickened.

"What about the rest?"

"I'm not sorry I told you. You deserved the truth."

He raised her chin. "And the rest?"

He meant his kiss, his touch. She remembered the first time she'd seen him gentling Destiny with his hands. He'd held hers with the same comforting power. Did he know how healing his touch was?

He released her chin. "Have a seat, and I'll make you breakfast."

"You?"

"Yes, me. And I won't poison you either." He pulled out the carton of eggs and a chunk of ham. "Go on, sit. You shouldn't even be out of bed."

"I feel much better. That injection—"

"Oh." Rick patted his shirt pocket. "This is yours." He set a prescription bottle on the table.

She picked it up and read the antibiotic label. "Thank you." She sat down at the little table and watched him crack the eggs into the bowl, then whisk them together with milk. He set that aside and diced the ham.

"You know what you're doing."

He added the ham to the bowl. "You bach it long enough, you learn."

"Then why do you have Marta?"

He went to the refrigerator and took out half a bell pepper. "Marta's worked summers here since I built the place. She frees me up for other things in the busy months." He diced the pepper and stirred it into the eggs. Then he poured it all into the skillet with a sizzle.

"Toast?"

She shook her head. "No thanks."

He scrambled the eggs with a spatula, then filled their plates and set them on the table. She looked from the eggs to his face when he took her hand in his. He closed his eyes. " 'He who dwells in the shelter of the Most High will rest in the shadow of the Almighty. I will say of the Lord, "He is my refuge and my fortress, my God, in whom I trust." ' Lord, thank you for your bounty and your care, and thank you for bringing Noelle. Please bless this food. Amen."

"Rick . . ."

"Eat first. Then we'll talk."

She took a bite and savored it. "I hate to admit it, but . . ."

"It's great, isn't it?" He cracked a sideways smile.

She returned it. Maybe her hunger enhanced his efforts, but the food was great. She finished it all.

Rick laid down his fork and eyed her. "Noelle, I understand why you couldn't go home. I guess I see why you stayed in that hovel and nearly froze to death. But you could have come to me."

She stared at her plate. Not without telling him. But now that she had . . .

He leaned forward and took her hands between his. "I want to help."

Her chest tightened. "Why did you kiss me?"

"I don't know. It just happened." His eyes held no guile. If Morgan was veneer, Rick was solid hardwood. He was telling her the truth.

She bit her lip, uncertain what to think, what to feel, but he demonstrated no uncertainty. He was in control.

"We need a plan of action."

"What action?"

He ran a hand through his hair. "First, do you want to press charges?"

She searched his face. Charges? Against Michael? "It would devastate Daddy. I don't want him to know."

"Are you sure?"

She imagined the shock and embarrassment, the way the media would jump like wolves to tear him apart. Daddy had made no secret of his pride in Michael. It would be a circus the moment word got out that William St. Claire's protégé had raped his daughter. They would find every ugly angle. Her picture would be plastered on every newscast, her unconventional youth sensationalized and criticized. Part of her cried out that he deserved it. But she knew it wasn't true. He'd been as deceived as she.

"I'm sure."

He replaced his hand atop hers. "Then I want to take you to Iowa."

"Iowa?" What was he doing; what was he saying?

"Come home with me."

She felt the trembling in her spine. "I am home."

He shook his head. "We can't stay here alone. It wouldn't look right. That's partly why I let you go before."

"What was the other part?"

"To get a grip on my feelings for you."

Her heart warmed, and amazingly she felt no fear. "And did you?" She could see his struggle, and that meant more to her than all Morgan's easy claims.

His fingers slid to the nape of her neck as he leaned close and kissed her gently. "Obviously not." He had enough gravel in his voice to convince her.

# 21

Noelle shivered with more than the December cold as Rick bundled the quilt around her in the truck, then closed the door. Actual grief clenched her stomach at the thought of leaving the ranch; grief and anxiety. She watched Rick through the windows.

He walked with confidence and purpose as he once more checked the tarp that enclosed the bed, then climbed in. "Ready?"

*No. Please don't take me away from here.* Especially not back toward the place she'd fled, closer to the danger she had escaped. Michael could find her. She knew it. But she nodded. Rick had made up his mind. A flicker of panic shot up her spine. As they started across the yard, Noelle turned back and stared out the rear window, then gripped his arm. "Do we have to go?"

He touched the brake, then let the truck move on. "We can't stay."

They'd been over it already. His reputation and hers. Appearances. And Rick's feelings for her. She wasn't sure what to do with that. But that wasn't what scared her. She was alone in his truck driving across the country, yet Rick was safe. She had to believe that. If she couldn't trust Rick, she'd rather be dead. What scared her was leaving the ranch.

He reached over and held her hand. "It'll be okay."

But as the ranch disappeared behind the rise, she pressed her other fingertips to her forehead, almost faint with tension. Was she losing her mind? She tried to get her breath. Only the strength of Rick's hand kept her from jumping from the truck and running back. Tears stung her eyes.

"Believe me, Noelle. It's the best choice."

"I don't recall a choice."

He sent her a smile. "Decision, then." His decision.

In the day she'd spent at the ranch, Rick had seen to all her business, paying her bills, canceling her rental agreement, collecting her clothes, not that many of them did her any good in the frigid temperatures. She had filled the gaps with sweaters and two pairs of jeans from the general store.

Rick glanced over, and she sensed his concern. She tried to smile, then bit her lip and looked away. His hand tightened. "God's watching out for us."

She shook her head. "I don't believe that. If there were a God, bad things wouldn't happen."

"Bad things happen because people have free will."

She stared at the road taking them through town and away. She did not buy it. Her whole body tensed as they passed the last of Juniper Falls. "Rick . . ."

"Trust me, Noelle. And trust Jesus. Let Him prove He's real."

"If we stayed you could tell me—"

"There's nothing magical about the ranch, Noelle."

"I just—" Her voice broke. How could she make him understand?

"Lord," Rick said, "Help Noelle. Let her know you're real. Bring her peace. Don't let her be afraid." His voice soothed; his strength convinced. "You have everything under control, and we submit to your wisdom."

He might submit, but the most she could do was try to relax. She fixed her eyes on the rocky walls of the canyon as they descended, recalling her ride up on the bus and Rudy's recommendation that she might try the Spencer place. Rick's ranch had been perfect, exactly what she needed, as though he'd built it just for her. "Why did you come here, Rick?"

"I love the mountains. We vacationed up here a lot when I was a kid, and I pretty much set my mind on having land in Colorado someday. Soon as I had the chance, I took it."

She sighed. "Do you always know what you want?"

"No, but if I think I'm meant to do something, I do it."

She pulled up the quilt around her, though the shivering had stopped. It was going to be all right. Rick knew how to make it all right. If she could simply trust him.

Rick let Noelle doze as he drove. How could he reach her? How could he show her that trusting God was the only way to peace? How could he share his faith when she was so set against it? He'd taken a chance praying. He knew God would answer, even if Noelle didn't recognize it. But he could have antagonized her.

That bothered him. He didn't want to risk their fragile relationship. Rick frowned. But as Pastor Tom said, she might not return his affection. As things stood right now, he could handle that. He had invested little more than his concern and charity. If he concentrated more fervently on his desire for her to know Jesus than to love him, he could keep it that way.

Noelle awoke confused, and he steadied her with a hand. "We're still driving."

Touching her came too naturally, though she didn't resist. He watched her doze off again and wondered what it would be like to fall asleep with her, to wake up to her. He'd experienced the same wonder after fighting the fire and finding her waiting. Coming home to her had felt so right. He'd always believed that if God intended him to marry, He'd provide someone who would be a counterpart to himself.

He hadn't thought too much about it, except on long winter nights when the wind howled off the mountain and the ranch creaked, empty except for him. And of course lately, since Noelle's coming—or more specifically, since she went to Walker's hovel. He hadn't expected to hurt the way he had. Maybe more of himself was invested than he wanted to admit.

She sighed and came fully awake but still looked drained. Though the antibiotics had done wonders for the pneumonia, she was not strong yet. Maybe driving it straight through was not the best plan. He got off on the next exit and found a roadside motel. "Wait here."

He went into the office and put two rooms on his credit card. He signed the receipt, took the keys, and went back outside. Her tension was tangible when he climbed into the truck. He handed her one key card and showed her his different number. "Gotta trust me, Noelle."

He drove around to their doors. Ground level, thankfully. "I'll get you in, then bring the bags."

She said, "I can help."

"Yep. By getting out of this wind." He took her key from the envelope, slid it into the slot and quickly out. The light flashed green, and he turned the knob.

"Rick?"

"Yeah?" He caught the door with his shoulder.

"Have you been with a woman?"

He looked along the row of doors and windows following the sidewalk to the dumpster at the corner of the lot, then back to her. He supposed it was a fair question after all she'd shared. "If you mean intimately, no."

"Why not?"

He rested his hand on the doorknob, holding it slightly ajar. He might have chosen a better time and place for this, but Noelle seemed urgent. "It's not right."

"How do you know? How do you always do what's right?" Her green eyes searched over his face.

He could give her the biblical version but decided to be honest. "I learned from Morgan's mistakes. His senior year of high school, Morgan got his girlfriend pregnant. He wanted to marry her, but her family stepped in. They took her for an abortion and broke off all contact with him." Rick tried not to show it, but even now he resented the pain and disappointment that had rocked his family.

Then he thought of Morgan. "It really tore him up." He looked down into Noelle's eyes. "All of us, actually. But it showed me there's a right order for things." He laid his palm against her cold cheek. "God's way, Noelle." If he could just make her see it.

She closed the door behind her and looked around the room. It was about the same size as her room at Rick's but with a double bed. She listened to the water come on in Rick's room next door. She had no idea what to think. She'd never known anyone like him.

*God's way.* Had God brought her to Rick? Was there some mysterious being who ordered and controlled the universe? It was a terrifying thought that the same God who held Rick back now had unleashed Michael. She wrapped herself in her arms. Maybe God's were the talons. God's the amber eyes.

———

The snow lay thick on the fields as they approached the house sitting long and low in the drifts. Rick drew a long breath. It was still home. Gray shutters flanked the windows hung with white lace. Dark shrubs lined the front, and tall, bare trees stood behind, sweeping the roof with their branches.

Along the drive and across the fields, the white fences marked out his childhood boundaries. But with Noelle beside him he felt anything but boyish. He was twenty-nine years old, and he'd still spent most of the night fighting the emotions that flamed up when his thoughts touched some aspect of Noelle. His bringing her home would definitely raise eyebrows. But he would be careful, very careful.

He glanced at her. "You all right?"

She nodded. "I didn't sleep well last night." And she looked it.

"You can rest when we get in." The tires squeaked on the snowy drive, then ground to a halt.

As Rick helped her down, his dad came outside. "Careful there. It's slick." Dad's smile faded as he looked at Noelle, but he reached out a hand to both of them. "Welcome."

Noelle hung heavily on Rick's arm, her limp more pronounced. Probably the hours in the car. She'd been alert but silent most of the day. What was she thinking?

His mother met them at the door. "Come in, come in. You look half-frozen."

"Heater's acting up in the truck." Which was why he'd kept Noelle bundled in the quilt. His fingers just touched her back. "Mom, this is Noelle. Noelle, my mother, Celia." Mom's hair had gone more gray than brown, he noticed. But she'd lost none of her vigor. She was a ranch wife of the old school, hardy and warm.

She squeezed Noelle's hand. "That's a hard drive in a truck."

"Thank you for letting me come." In contrast, Noelle looked like a fairy princess, the sort that got hidden among peasants from a wicked enemy. Or was that his own mind making the analogy?

Rick brought her in and motioned her toward the couch. "Have a seat while I unload."

"I'll give you a hand out there." Dad clapped his shoulder.

Rick knew what was coming. Dad's tone had been just a little too casual, not that he expected it wouldn't come up, but he didn't have a good explanation yet. He left Noelle to his mother and went outside. He unfastened the tarp, well aware of his father's scrutiny.

"That's not the same young lady I met last summer." His dad pulled out two of the bags.

"She took a fall on Aldebaran, broke her leg and bruised her ribs."

"That accounts for the limp." Dad started for the house.

Rick grabbed the last bags. "She moved into a shabby place in town and caught pneumonia."

His father paused on the stairs. "There's more here than you want to tell?"

Rick nodded. "Not just now, Dad."

His father pursed his lips, considering. "Your mother won't let you off so easy."

He grimaced. "I'm sure you're right."

———

"Rick! Mom, you didn't tell us Rick was coming!"

Noelle startled and sat up on the couch, confused by the unfamiliar place, unfamiliar voices.

"When did you come? Are you staying all the way till Christmas?" Girls' voices.

Rick's came from behind the double doors. "You think I'd miss seeing you open your bags of coal? Ouch! Cut it out or I won't show you what I've brought."

A young voice spoke. "What have you brought?"

"Something sorely lacking in this house."

"What?"

"A lady." He said it in a tone Noelle had not heard him use— teasing, taunting.

"You have a girlfriend, Rick?" This voice was huskier and brusque.

"All I said is she's a lady. Unlike you female brutes."

"Rick . . ." That was his mother. Noelle felt a pang to hear a mother chide her son. Even an adult son. Hers and Daddy's had always been an adult relationship. *How was your lesson, Noelle?* "Fine, Daddy. How were your cases?"

"Where is she?" The little voice again.

"In the living room." He quieted. "I'll let you see her if you can be quiet."

The double doors swung open, and four bright-faced young women poured through, all talking at once. Noelle looked from one face to another.

"I knew it was impossible." Rick frowned. "Now you woke her up. Everybody, this is Noelle. Noelle, my sisters from oldest to noisiest, Therese, Stephanie, Tiffany, and Tara."

"Don't put me next to Tara in noisiness." Tiffany, the black-haired sister, tossed her head.

Therese smiled, very like Rick, especially in the eyes and her tall, slender poise. Brown hair rippled down her back. "It's nice to meet you, Noelle."

Stephanie sat down on the coffee table, elbows to her knees. "I'm curious what *you* can find attractive about Rick."

He yanked the brown braid that hung down her back.

The youngest, Tara, turned eyes as blue as Morgan's to her. "So you're Rick's girlfriend?" That was the little exuberant voice.

"Mind your own business, Tara." Rick turned her about. "And you can all clear out now." He punctuated his words with a shove to Tara's back and waved the others through the double doors. "Go get your milk and cookies."

"Grow up." That from the husky voice, Stephanie.

Rick dropped to Noelle's side. "Sorry they woke you."

She stared. "You never told me you had four sisters!"

"You never asked."

"Well, I'd think if you came from a family of eight, it might come up now and then." It was absurd that it hadn't.

"I'm sure Dad mentioned them when he came out."

"I might have heard the names, but there was no context." Of course, Rick had never been forthcoming about anything, and Morgan had other things on his mind.

"Mostly Morgan and I try to forget they ever happened. We had it so good for nine years."

"Not true." Noelle pushed his arm. "I saw your face when they all piled in here."

He shrugged. "Sorry they put you on the spot. My sisters make broad assumptions. Are you feeling better?"

"Yes. But I'm embarrassed to have fallen asleep on arrival." Rick's mother had left her to check something on the stove, and she must have dozed off on the couch. Not exactly Emily Post.

"Don't be. It's probably the last rest you'll get. I forgot how noisy it is." Rick rubbed his sandpapery jaw.

She smiled.

"What?"

"I can't think of you with four sisters."

He cocked his head. "Why?"

"You're so . . . such a man, I guess."

He eyed her. "Does it bother you?"

She searched his face. It should. His manliness should terrify her. "No."

Rick's sisters came back en masse. He did have a point about the noise.

"Mom said come celebrate Advent." Tara reached for her hand and tugged.

Rick got to his feet. "That's the other thing. Don't expect one free moment." He faced his sisters. "Take Noelle. I'll get my guitar."

Noelle followed them to the table, as large as the one Rick had at the ranch. In the center was a wreath trimmed with greens. It held four candles, though they didn't match. Three were purple, one pink. It should at least be two and two, she thought.

Rick came in with his guitar, squeezed her shoulder, and whispered, "God songs."

Was it a warning? So she'd be prepared—or so she wouldn't embarrass him? She looked around at the glowing, teasing smiles of his sisters. Four sisters. And neither he nor Morgan had mentioned them. That could only be a man thing.

She watched Celia light three of the candles. Noelle almost pointed out the missed taper, then realized there must be a ritual reason for the irregularities. She didn't wonder long, though, because Rick began to play. As before, his music touched her. She watched his fingers pluck and stroke the strings like a true minstrel. Her heart quickened, but she stood silent as the rest of them sang a sweetly haunting melody. *Oh come, oh come, Emmanuel, and ransom captive Israel.*

Here was Rick's God magnified. Morgan alone was absent, and she wondered how it would be if he were there. She could almost imagine the irreverent humor in his eyes and felt better but still nowhere near comfortable as all the eyes seemed honed on her.

Hank picked up the large family Bible and read a story about someone named Zechariah who was struck dumb for questioning the angel messenger sent by God. So questions were not even allowed, and Zechariah's had seemed so reasonable. *By the way, my wife and I are too old to have a kid; how exactly does this work?* She glanced at Rick, but his eyes were closed. Her chest tightened, and she wished she could get away. As one voice after another lifted up prayers, Noelle clenched her hands and endured it.

Supper followed, so clamorous with voices and laughter, she could hardly eat. Even when she and Daddy entertained, it had not been so boisterous. She was thankful that as soon as it was finished, Rick insisted she go to bed.

She went to her room, or rather the room she was sharing with Therese, who followed her in and stretched out on one twin bed. Of all the girls, she seemed the most like Rick in temperament. Noelle sat down on the other bed. It was awkward sharing space with someone she didn't know, someone several years younger but worlds different. She'd never shared a room with anyone before.

Noelle cleared the stiffness from her throat. "May I ask you something?"

"Sure."

"Why do you do that . . ." How did one describe the little ceremony they had?

"The advent prayers?" Therese asked.

Noelle nodded.

"It's preparation."

"For what?"

Therese stared at her. "The birth of Christ."

"That happened two thousand years ago."

Therese nodded. "Historically, yes. But each Christmas we prepare our hearts to receive Him again, new, and . . . deeper, you know."

No, she didn't know. All she knew was that Rick's mealtime ritual suddenly seemed tame. His simple prayers, his silent reading, his music. She'd heard the devotion in his voice, though, the first night she heard him sing. He'd played for his God, with no one to applaud him.

He had stopped when she intruded. But now she was part of it. He wanted her there, wanted her to believe. But what did she want?

―――――

After seeing Noelle and Therese settled in, Rick went to face the inevitable. Mom was in the kitchen waiting for him. She even had a mug of hot chocolate and a plate of coconut macaroons, as though he were a little boy coming home from school. And as always, she wasted no words.

"How serious are you about her?"

He leaned on the counter and bit into the macaroon. May as well sustain himself. "I told you my reasons for bringing her."

"You told me she needed a place, and the ranch wasn't it."

"That's right."

"Because you care for her."

He hadn't told her that. "Yes, I care for her. She's . . . special."

"Even if she doesn't share your faith? You can't have missed her discomfort."

"I expect she will, in time." Or did he hope it only?

"Those are large expectations."

Rick chased the macaroon down with a gulp of chocolate. "Wait till you get to know her. There's a lot more than you can see."

"I see enough. She's very beautiful, very vulnerable."

He warmed. He wanted so much to protect her, to heal her. Had his mother chosen those words to show him his own vulnerability? He knew it already.

"But it takes more than that," she said. "You should know."

"I do. She won't disappoint you, Mom. Just give her a chance." He watched his mother's face settle. She might not approve, but she would be fair. The rest was up to Noelle. If she even wanted to try.

---

Three days with Rick's family felt as though she were landed inside a beehive. Noelle was growing accustomed to the endless voices, laughter, and even the tiffs. She felt more welcome and included than she had thought possible. A house full of sisters! And Rick and Hank . . .

Only Celia seemed reserved, but they were such different women. And they'd had little time together. Rick's sisters had hardly spared her a free moment. Noelle watched now as they pulled on skates, coats, and mufflers from the closet.

"Where's my other glove?" Stephanie looked pointedly at Tara.

"How should I know?" She turned to Noelle. "They think since I'm the youngest they can blame me for everything."

Noelle smiled. "How old are you?"

"Fourteen. We're stairsteps. Fourteen, sixteen, eighteen, and twenty. Then there's the big gap to Rick and Morgan. How old are you?"

Brazen. But Noelle answered. "Twenty-three." Almost twenty-four, but she wasn't about to let anyone know that.

Tara cocked her head. "That's about right."

"Right for what?"

"Rick's twenty-nine. But boys are immature. You need that many years between to have any kind of meaningful relationship."

Tiffany tugged a hat over Tara's braids. "Rick said to mind your own business."

"But she *knows* so *much* about *romance*." Stephanie clasped her hands over her heart.

Rick came in as the girls burst into peals of laughter, then filed out to his truck. He eyed Noelle in one of Therese's coats. "You're going?"

"Why not?" Noelle wrapped a scarf around her neck.

"It's thirty degrees out, they're skating on a pond, and you have pneumonia."

"I'm over that. All I needed was a good, strong antibiotic and a little rest." Though rest had taken on a new meaning. She shrugged. "I'm not planning to skate—just to watch."

He shook his head. "Let me drive them over and come back. They'll understand. They've had most of your time since we got here." He reached out and took her hand.

Her pulse quickened at his touch. What power was there in his hands? She pictured Destiny shying and Rick's hands on his neck. Rick had mastered Destiny. Would he now master her?

Tara rushed back in. "Come on, come on."

Noelle smiled. "I think we should go."

"Okay." He motioned her through the door.

The girls huddled in the back of the truck as he drove them to the lake. Then they made their way to the ice, pulled off their boots, and tied on their skates. Noelle watched them wind the laces around their ankles and step onto the ice, its gray surface laced with white.

Rick stood beside her. "You've made quite an impression on them. The whole family, actually."

"That's because I came with you."

"Why do you say that?"

Noelle tipped her head. "Something Therese told me last night."

He raised her chin with his gloved hand. "I heard you all laughing and hushing each other in your room."

She raised her eyebrows. "Those late-night chats are very informative."

Rick frowned. "If you're discussing me, they can't be very interesting. Not like Morgan."

"You just run deeper."

He released her chin. "So what did she tell you?"

"That every girl in the youth group wanted to date you, but you wouldn't have any of them."

"I was the youth leader," he said. "It would have been highly inappropriate."

"They told me you'd say that."

He raised a hand. "It's the truth."

"And they told me the tricks you played on them, ice cubes in their shoes, switching their school uniforms so they'd put on each other's in the rush to get ready, the garden snake in Stephanie's bed . . ."

"She deserved that." He looked up as Tara and Tiffany collided and fell.

Noelle saw his concern, but they untangled, laughing, and got up again. "They also told me all the scrapes you got them out of. The time you restrained Stephanie's date."

"She's got a dumb streak that gets her in trouble."

Noelle glanced up at him. "I think there's a hint of armor beneath that sheepskin coat."

He turned. "You are imaginative."

She shook her head. "Did I imagine that you saved my life?"

Rick looked away. "I don't know that you'd have died."

"I had given up." She saw that now. Her weakness and depression had so incapacitated her, if he hadn't come to her door, she might never have gotten up from the bed again. She reached out and touched his arm. "You saved me."

He caught her hand and brought it to his chest. "It's not me, Noelle."

"It is." Her heart swelled with emotion when his arms closed her safely in.

# 22

Noelle took up her drawing pad and tucked her feet underneath her in the corner. While Stephanie and Therese stitched tree ornaments, she sketched the two of them. She studied Therese's long, slender features, then transferred the line of her cheek and jaw to the page. Next she drew in the shape of her eyes, well placed beside the straight nose, then added the generous mouth.

The real task was bringing the features to life on the page, portraying Therese's gentle way, her warmth, her quiet strength. Noelle caught the shadow at the edge of her mouth that hinted at a smile, an inner contentment, the same completeness she'd seen in Rick.

Satisfied, she turned to Stephanie. She was thicker, like her mother, her eyes wider set, a harder mouth. She kept her hair in a braid, too busy for vanity. Noelle captured her frank, saucy manner.

Therese came and looked over her shoulder. "That's amazing. It looks just like us."

Stephanie leaned over to look. "Ugh. You got my broad chin."

Noelle held it out. "I haven't done much with people before."

"Why not?"

A shadow passed through her. Why did she avoid human subjects? She shrugged. "I never found them very interesting."

Stephanie flipped her braid. "But we are?"

Noelle smiled. "Yes, you are. I always wanted sisters. You're lucky to have each other."

"Most of the time," Therese said.

"Except for Tara."

Noelle smiled. "I think Tara's adorable."

"You haven't lived with her the last fourteen years." Stephanie rolled her eyes.

Therese knelt beside Noelle. "Have you drawn any others?"

"A few." Noelle flipped through the pages. "Here's one of your father. And here's Tara reading."

"She looks almost tame." Stephanie leaned closer. "Have you done Rick?"

"Yes, but I'm not happy with it." She flipped to the sketch. "He was watching the football game with your father and kept yelling and frowning. It came out harsher than I wanted. But I'll try again."

Therese laughed. "That's Rick's serious-citizen face."

Noelle said, "I'd rather get his smile."

Therese studied the picture. "It's so real. How did you make him look so real?"

"It's mostly in how you see the subject. Then it's just copying it down." But it pleased her to have Therese's acclaim. Though three years younger and still attending the small community college, Therese seemed wise in ways Noelle was not. How was she so content?

"It's the eyes especially." Therese sat back on her haunches. "You're very talented."

"Thank you. Have you studied art?"

"Me?" Therese jabbed a finger to her chest. "I'm terrible."

"I'm sure you're not," Noelle said.

"Oh, yes she is." Stephanie stretched out on Noelle's bed. "Undeniably awful."

"Speak for yourself." Therese tossed a pillow onto her sister's head.

Noelle smiled. Their sisterly banter was totally foreign. But it filled an emptiness that nothing else had. This was family, really family. Rick didn't know how lucky he was.

Tara bounced into the room, all legs and energy, and flopped onto Noelle's bed beside Stephanie. "So what are we doing?"

"Having a private conversation." Stephanie nudged her with a stockinged foot.

"Oooh. Are we talking about Rick?" Tara rubbed her hands.

"None of your business."

Tara pouted. "Why is it private?"

"Because you're not invited."

Tara turned her blue eyes to Noelle. "So is he a good kisser?"

Noelle's heart jumped, but she couldn't tell whether it was fear or something else.

"Get out, Tara." Stephanie stood and dragged Tara out. She closed the door behind her. "Was I that obnoxious at her age?"

Therese smiled. "No, Tara's an original."

Stephanie settled back onto the bed. "Where is Rick, anyway?"

"Getting presents." Therese sent them both a conspiratorial look. "He acts like he wouldn't dream of it, but he's very generous."

"She knows that. She's his girlfriend." Stephanie tossed the pillow back.

Noelle's throat tightened. "I'm not his girlfriend. We've never even gone out."

"Oh." Stephanie clamped her mouth shut. "I thought . . . oh."

The pillow soared and caught her in the face. "Don't be such a goose, Steph."

"I'm not!" This time she flung it past Therese's head. "It's just, you know Rick. I figured it must be serious if . . ."

Therese sent Stephanie a look that Noelle read all too well. With what she'd learned about Rick, it was no wonder they assumed . . . And then there were his own feelings. Hadn't he said as much? Did he hope for something more between them? She waited for the trembling to set in, the true panic to wash over her. But it passed.

Therese retrieved the pillow and tucked it behind her head. "Anyway, Rick's gone Christmas shopping."

"I hadn't thought about gifts." Noelle straightened her leg and rubbed the muscle. "My bills took all the money I had." It was shocking how quickly the money had been spent. And now she was penniless and once again thrown on the mercy of strangers. Only they didn't feel like strangers anymore.

Therese sat up. "Make a picture. We're big on homemade gifts."

"Do a portrait of everyone." Stephanie struck a pose.

Noelle's spirits rose. "You'd all want that?"

"Are you kidding? We'd love it." Therese's face lit.

"I did bring my watercolors. . . ." She bit her lip. "You'd have to act surprised."

Therese laughed. "We're big on that too. I know what both Tiff and Tara have for me already."

"You don't know what I have for you," Stephanie said.

"You don't have anything. You never have your gifts until the last minute."

"You're right. That way you don't know what they are."

Therese wrapped her knees in her arms. "It's hard to keep secrets around here."

Noelle leaned back. "If I make sketches of everyone, I can work from those for the portraits, and then no one will suspect what I'm doing."

"And our lips are sealed. Right, Steph?"

"Right."

"I wish I could frame them." Noelle sighed. "But that takes money."

Therese waved her hand. "Have Rick make them. He's good with wood."

Noelle pictured the daybed he'd fashioned just for her. Of course he could make frames. He might even enjoy it. "Then he'd know what I'm doing."

"Just tell him you need frames. He'll think you're working." Again Therese showed her wisdom.

Noelle felt a warmth spread inside her. "This will be the first Christmas I've celebrated since I was six."

Both mouths dropped open. "No Christmas?"

Noelle shook her head. "Not since my mother died. She loved Christmas. I think it was too hard for Daddy without her."

Therese looked like Rick when he wanted to say something but didn't. Stephanie was not so constrained. "Do you remember her?"

"Not as much as I'd like." There were images, but the face was fuzzy, unclear. And the last ones were frightening. Noelle remembered looking at her mother but not recognizing her. She'd been changed, shrunken, as though her skin used to fit but couldn't anymore.

Rick tapped and opened the door. "Noelle?"

She turned. His cheeks were reddened with cold. He must have just come from outside.

"Telling secrets?" He glanced at his sisters.

"Absolutely," Therese replied.

"Then I'm taking Noelle." He strode in and helped her up.

"There was something I wanted to talk to you about, anyway."

Noelle winked at Therese and Stephanie. She followed Rick into the hall. "Can you make me some frames?"

"Picture frames?"

She nodded.

"Are you going to paint?"

She hoped her smile didn't give her away. "Yes."

He shrugged. "I'll see what wood Dad has."

"Thank you."

"But tonight." He took her hand. "I thought we'd go out."

Noelle hid her surprise. Rick was asking for a date?

He took a box from the table in the hall and held it out. "I didn't think you brought anything dressy, and the restaurant is . . . nice."

Her heart beat fast. What had he done? Didn't he understand how gifts, expectations . . . She stared at the box. She wouldn't take it, wouldn't open it. No, she had nothing to wear to a nice restaurant, had brought only jeans and sweaters and one woolen skirt. But she didn't care.

He opened the lid of the box, and she saw a winter-white angora dress. Synthetic seed pearls lined the scoop neck and the gathered shoulders. Folded in the box, she couldn't tell its cut, but it was lovely, as lovely as anything she'd owned with a designer's name. But she could not take it.

She looked from the dress to Rick, saw the realization dawn in his eyes. He closed the lid. "I didn't think. I was out shopping and saw it and . . ." He shoved the box back onto the table. "I'm sorry."

She hadn't expected that. She thought he would wheedle and coax or simply insist. She glanced at the box. Her face pinched and her voice sounded tight. "It's beautiful."

"You don't have to wear it."

She reached for the box. Slowly she lifted the lid and slipped the dress out. It was as soft as it looked, straight cut tea length. The sleeves tapered from the gathered shoulders. She held it to her throat and closed her eyes. She had to choose.

Rick wasn't Michael. His gift didn't bind her. He wouldn't force her to wear it. She opened her eyes. "I'll try it on."

———

Walking down the hall in the new dress, Noelle caught sight of Rick standing in the living room in a charcoal three-piece suit. She stopped still and stared. That couldn't be Rick. Not the Rick who landed in the dirt and shoveled out fires and built his own ranch log by log. Oh, she knew the clothes didn't make the man, but . . . he was great in a suit.

He turned, and his eyes went down the dress that sheathed her in simple elegance. "It fits."

She smiled. He was still Rick, still putting so much into so few words.

He held out his elbow. "Ready?"

Was she? Until now she could pretend he was nothing but a friend, someone willing to help, to listen and understand. But she knew his nature now, thanks to bits and pieces from his sisters and what she'd seen for herself. He didn't date idly. He was offering her something more than he'd offered before.

Her fingers trembled as she took his arm. "I'll have to call you Richard, tonight." *Richard the Lionhearted.*

His mouth quirked. "Watch it." He led her out front where Therese's compact idled.

She glanced up. "Why not the truck?"

"I'm having the heater repaired. Unless you want to go to dinner in a quilt." He let her into the car. The truck's heater had been acting up on the drive out, but Rick looked ungainly in the car. And instead of woodsmoke and horses, he smelled amazingly of cologne.

As they drove, Noelle tried to reconcile this new Rick. She had defined him differently. "Why haven't you dressed up before?"

"Didn't have a reason to."

"Well, you were made for a suit."

He glanced sidelong. "It'd be real sensible when I'm getting thrown from a horse."

Ah, there he was. Practical, no-nonsense Rick Spencer. He parked outside the restaurant at the edge of town.

She looked at the white stucco walls and arched windows, the pillared garden that lined the walk to the heavy girded door, the red tiled roof. Italian or Mediterranean. She wouldn't have thought such a small town would possess a formal restaurant. It was probably no more than three stars, but something kept her from going in.

Would it recall other occasions, other nights, dining in style while the noose tightened around her neck? The evenings with Morgan had not, but she hadn't remembered it all then. Rick must have sensed her hesitance. He reached for her hand. "There's a McDonald's down the road."

She laughed. He understood without her saying anything. Was that a good thing? "I think this will do."

They were seated at a small side table, and she leaned forward to sniff the single red rose in the vase. The firelight flickered on the white stucco walls of the Mediterranean alcoves, and the candle in the amber globe softly scented the air.

She looked across the table at Rick. She wouldn't have pictured him here. His face still had the strong, straight lines, but it was no longer hard. Maybe he had gentled, or maybe she'd seen only the surface before. Maybe he, like Morgan, had kept his real self from her. Did they all wear masks? She felt hers slipping.

He returned her gaze without flinching, then took her hands in his. "You're beautiful, Noelle."

Her heart skipped. She had heard those words all her life, but coming now from Rick it was different. He didn't use them cheaply. He was saying what he thought, not trying to impress or score. His hands on hers were strong and sure.

She remembered his first firm grip when he'd introduced himself, his hand in the hospital, when she couldn't bear to let go. And again when she told him everything. Now she felt his hands crushing her shell, yet she clung to the fragments. She had to.

He released her when the waiter came. She ordered club soda, and Rick asked for coffee. By now, Morgan would have been well into his first Manhattan. And she'd be fending him off. Glib, suave, outrageous Morgan. But it wasn't Morgan across from her now, and she wasn't sure what to make of that.

She picked up the menu and studied the entrees. "I loved veal until I learned how they treat the poor things."

"Ignorance is bliss." Rick's eyes were on his menu.

He didn't fool her. His remark sounded callous, but she knew he'd never hurt or condone the mistreatment of any animal. Why did he hide his sensitivity? Was that his weak spot? At least in his opinion?

The waiter returned and Noelle ordered. "Scallops in lemon angel hair."

The waiter noted it. "Salad?"

"Endive with balsamic vinaigrette."

"Soup?"

"Minestrone."

Rick ordered steak skillet fried with mushrooms and Kalamata olives. He hadn't ordered for her, hadn't even suggested anything. But when the waiter left, he said, "Fishy marshmallows, hmm?"

"What?"

"Scallops."

She smiled. "Only if they're not fresh."

"This is the finest restaurant in town, but we're not exactly on the coast."

She frowned. He was right about scallops. If they weren't done right, they'd be awful. And no, they weren't on the coast. But when their bowls of spicy minestrone arrived, she breathed the piquant steam with pleasure. She could tell a true minestrone from the steam alone. That boded well for the scallops. She lifted her spoon, but Rick caught her fingers and bowed his head.

" 'Praise the Lord, O my soul; all my inmost being, praise his holy name.' Thank you for your providence. Amen."

She glanced around as he blessed their food. Even in public he wouldn't forego it. "You're the only person I've seen pray."

"In this room or ever?"

She had meant in the room, but if he wanted to include the rest of her life, he could lump that in too. "Why do you do it?"

"Everything I have is God's gift. I'd be nothing without His grace. It's only right to say thanks."

"Everything you have you've built with your own hands. You raise the horses—"

"He created them." He took a spoonful of soup.

"That's so archaic."

He dipped his spoon again. "How do you know?" His eyes came up, serious and challenging. "How do you know that my beliefs are wrong, outdated, stupid?"

She'd never said that, but it could have sounded that way.

"Have you studied Christianity?" He rested his spoon in the bowl.

She clasped her napkin in her lap. "It's all through history. The Inquisition, the Salem witch trials . . ."

"How about Christ? Studied Him?" Rick's voice stayed low, but his eyes deepened.

"No." She met his gaze with her own. She was not about to search out the power she'd glimpsed on his worn pages. *"The Word became flesh and made his dwelling among us. . . ."*

"Are you afraid you'll learn something you'll have to believe?"

"I don't *have* to believe anything. And I'm not afraid." But it had terrified her to sense something bigger, more powerful than anything human. It was ludicrous. Some trick of the mind, a Jungian bogeyman from a collective unconscious . . . The image flashed into her mind. A red-robed figure with sword and wings, giant swooping wings and light blazing through its face . . . Someone grabbing her from behind, someone so big she was swept off her feet and carried, a hand clamped over her mouth. Her lungs seized as though the hand even now stifled her breath.

Rick's face changed. He reached across and took her hand. "I'm sorry." He apologized more than anyone she'd ever known. But she couldn't answer.

"Noelle?"

She fought the panic. Why now? He closed her hand in both of his, and it was like a rope she clung to. She couldn't be carried away while he held on. The shakes started. She wanted to run, but if she let go she'd be lost. Her head pounded. Was she losing her mind?

"Please forgive me." Rick's voice was so gentle it hurt.

"It's not you." Bright, colorful light and someone grabbing from behind . . .

"What, then?" He couldn't understand. How could he?

She shook her head. "I don't know." Tears stung her eyes. "I feel like I should remember, that there's something there, but . . . it can't be real. It's not part of the other—I'm almost sure. It's deeper, more vague. Maybe it's a dream, maybe . . ."

The waiter came with their salads, but Rick didn't let go. Their server sensed enough to leave the plates and go without asking if they were finished with the soup they'd hardly touched. The terror passed and the image faded.

Noelle's breath eased. She looked at her hand in Rick's and, sighing, pressed his fingers. "It's gone." She slipped her hand out and pushed aside the minestrone that had been so promising.

He nudged it back. "Try it."

She looked up into his face. She'd lost her appetite, but he wanted her to try. She dipped her spoon and tasted it. The flavor was rich and spicy, though it had cooled to lukewarm. Her mouth responded and her stomach. She was hungry after all. They ate their soup in silence. Then she reached for her salad.

Rick glanced up. "Are you okay?"

"Yes."

"Want to talk about it?" He wasn't pushing, just offering.

She took a bite. "This salad is good. They used an aged vinegar."

He reached for his own, but she could see food wasn't first in his mind.

She handed him the glass ramekin of crumbled bleu cheese. "It's better with a little of that."

He took it. "I don't like bleu cheese."

"It's an acquired taste. That's what Daddy always said. I guess I acquired it."

"Noelle . . ."

"Have you been here before?" She speared a fringed leaf.

"Twice."

"With a date?" She took the bite.

He drew a slow breath. "I took my mother for Mother's Day, and Therese for her birthday."

"Haven't you ever dated?" She wanted him to say yes, to ease the pressure that was building inside.

"Not like this."

What did he mean? She speared another bite compulsively.

He said, "I don't think it's fair to set up emotional attachments unless there's a possibility of permanence."

Her fork squeaked on the plate like fingernails on a chalkboard. Permanence.

He said, "I haven't dated because I haven't met someone I thought I could spend my life with."

She stared at her plate, glistening with speckled oil and fragments of endive. She waited, but no trembling began.

Rick watched Noelle squirm. He finished his salad and pushed his plate aside. "I didn't mean to make you uncomfortable."

"I'm not."

He half smiled. "I don't have Morgan's flexibility with the truth."

"I don't want you to."

The waiter brought their entrées, and Rick eyed Noelle's scallops dubiously. He'd take his steak any day.

The waiter smoothed the cloth across his arm. "Anything else I can bring you?"

They shook their heads and thanked him. Rick cut into his steak, then glanced up as Noelle tried a scallop.

She chewed it slowly, then smiled. "They must fly them in fresh."

He should not have bought the dress. In it—across from him with that smile—she made his heart rush. He was falling in love. There were no other words for it.

"Would you like one?" She held up a creamy scallop.

He took his bite of steak. "No thanks."

"Chicken?"

"Chicken I would do, but round, squashy fish?" He shook his head.

"This is a night of firsts." Her eyes actually teased.

He laid down his fork. It was a first to be there with her, to have said the things he said. To have meant them. He passed her his side plate, and she laid the scallop in its center, then passed it back. He nudged the scallop with his fork.

"It's dead." She almost giggled.

He speared it and brought it to his mouth. The aroma stopped him, but he made a second pass and got it in. He chewed, swallowed, and took a drink of lemon water from his stemware.

"Well?"

He looked into her green eyes. "Edible. Just."

She smiled down at her plate. "It's an acquired taste."

"Ever tried Rocky Mountain oysters?"

She raised her brows. "How can you have oysters from the mountains?"

"They're not exactly seafood."

She twisted a noodle around her fork. "I don't want to know."

"It's an acquired taste."

She laughed. Their eyes met and held. He remembered the day they'd been caught in the rain. He should have known then. Maybe he did.

Now he wondered how he'd had her under his roof and not marveled at her slender fingers. He watched her dab her mouth with the linen napkin and noted her soft, pink lips. Long curving lashes veiled her eyes when she glanced down, but when he caught the full thrust of their focus, they were mesmerizing.

She daintily savored each bite as he made quick work of his steak and fettuccine. She was as graceful as a swan, fragile as a snowflake, and sitting across from her Rick felt such a powerful need to protect that it crushed out all other senses. Whatever had frightened her before seemed to have passed, but he'd felt her trembling, had seen the panic. He would do anything to keep her safe.

"May I present our dessert tray?" The waiter hovered once again beside the table.

Rick raised his brows, but Noelle shook her head. He said, "Just the check, thanks."

He rested his fingertips on the small of her back as they walked out. The dress was soft, but he could feel the bones of her spine through it. Too thin still. But he couldn't afford Antonio's every night. Mom's cooking would have to do.

He parked Therese's car beside his mother's Taurus station wagon. The thin covering of snow crunched beneath his loafers as he walked around for Noelle. *Loafers.* How far would he go? He helped her out of the car and walked her to the door, then stopped her.

She sparkled in the porch light like the fairy princess she was. "Thank you for a wonderful evening."

He leaned his palm on the wall beside the doorjamb and thought about kissing her. "First date should be special." He hadn't waited all these years to do it poorly.

A strand of hair slipped across her shoulder and she caught it back with her fingers. "It was special."

His heart raced. "I'd really like to kiss you good-night." If she shied at all he'd back off.

She said, "Well, then I'd have an answer for Tara."

"What?"

She gave him an impish smile. "She wants to know if her big brother is a good kisser."

"Oh, great." He pushed off the wall and tried to hook his thumbs in his belt, but the suit coat got in the way. He raised his hands and dropped them at his sides. "And I'm supposed to kiss you after that?"

She started to laugh, and he pulled her into his arms, tipping her back. "Here's what you tell Tara." He pecked her lips. "And here's what you keep to yourself." He kissed her deeply. He couldn't help it.

Noelle kissed him with surprising joy. She felt closer to him than she had since the night she told him about Michael. But, then, he'd kissed her that night too. This time was different, but even now he was not coming on to her, he was sharing himself.

They parted, but he rested his wrists on her shoulders, fingers locked behind her neck. He seemed reluctant to let go, and she almost hoped he wouldn't. But he reached behind her and opened the door. The house was quiet, and he flicked on the light to hang the gray woolen wrap Therese had loaned her. He slipped it from her shoulders and hung it in the closet. Then without warning, he kissed her again, turning out the light with his elbow. He pulled her tightly to his chest and whispered hoarsely, "Good night."

"Good night," she whispered back, but he didn't let her go. They stood a long time holding each other, not moving, not speaking. Then he let go. She made her way down the hall, slipped into Therese's room, and undressed in the dark. She felt for a hanger and hung the dress on the rack, then stroked her fingers over it once more.

Rick had chosen it; Rick had bought it, wanted her to wear it. And he had liked her in it. It had shown in his face all through the evening. She thought of Morgan asking her to wear the wine-colored dress, to lose the blouse that hid its revealing cut, of Michael choosing svelte and expensive gowns made especially to show her off.

Now Rick. Was she a fool? Then she felt his arms again, holding her, just holding her. He gave more than he asked. She slipped into her bed.

———

Noelle screamed, but no sound came. Her heart raced faster than any human heart as she cowered beneath Michael, hovering on wings with the talons of a hawk. She saw every detailed feather, the rings of scaly skin ending in deadly claws. The golden eyes broke her will, claimed her spirit. He screeched and dived, and she threw her arms over her head.

Suddenly Rick was there, standing over her, eyes filled with wrath. Michael's talons tore into his flesh, laying bare the bone of his shoulders. She screamed again, then wrenched her mind to consciousness and opened her eyes to the darkness.

She gripped the bedcovers against her throbbing heart. And she remembered—the picture on his wall, the picture of the hawk. She had stared at it, transfixed, dissociating, the hawk coming in for the kill less terrible than Michael's attack. But this time Rick had been there, standing above her as he had when he guarded her from Destiny's hooves.

She stared into the darkness, forcing away the memory of his torn flesh, his bare bone. He had taken the attack in her place. And now the shakes began. She lay down, but she knew sleep wouldn't come.

# 23

With the aroma of roasting potatoes wafting into the living room from the kitchen, Noelle sat sketching Tara curled like a kitten on the couch, reading. The older daughters were helping their mother, but Celia didn't want Noelle in the kitchen. She'd offered early on and been politely refused.

So she took the opportunity to sketch Tara for her Christmas portrait. Not only did it save her from showing her culinary ineptitude, but also it gave her a chance to be still and quiet. She had told Rick she was healed, but though the antibiotic had cured the pneumonia, she still wasn't strong. The dreams and lack of sleep didn't help.

Noelle looked from the sketch to Tara. The child was a good study, her blossoming beauty, her energy, even contained as it was at this moment. She was a little spoiled, and it showed around the mouth, but she had an exuberance that was hard to resist. It was rare to find her so quiet, and that was another reason Noelle seized the moment.

But at the squeak of tires on the snow outside, Tara sprang up cat-like to her feet. She pushed her face to the window, fingertips resting on the sill. "It's Morgan!" She rushed to the kitchen. "Mom, Morgan's here!"

*Morgan.* As if things weren't crazy enough. Noelle went to the window. Now she'd see him with his family, see them all together. And the energy would rise. It had to if Morgan were there. She felt tired just thinking of it, but Tara urged, "Come on, Noelle," and tugged her along with the rest of them through the door.

Noelle hung back on the porch as Morgan climbed out of a white Lincoln with rental plates, looking as roguishly handsome as ever. She smiled when his surprised eyes met hers over the heads of his swarming sisters. He hugged each one but squeezed Tara until she squealed. Then, as Noelle tensed, he came to her with rakish purpose. "Hello, gorgeous."

She started to answer, but he pulled her into his arms and bent to kiss her. She barely turned her face, and his lips brushed the corner of her mouth and cheek. Her heart hammered, then she felt Rick beside her, his hand on her back. Morgan looked from her to Rick and their eyes locked. Then he turned away and greeted his parents.

Celia had missed none of it, and Noelle sensed her protective anger. She kissed Morgan's cheek and held him a moment longer than she might. "Oh, it's so good to have you."

Morgan shook Hank's hand. His father pulled him into a hug and patted his back. "Hello, son."

Rick spoke in Noelle's ear. "It's cold. Come inside."

But she knew it wasn't the cold he avoided. She went with him, aware, even as she turned, of Morgan's gaze.

"Don't worry about it," Rick said as soon as they were inside the door.

But she looked up into his face and saw his own discomfort. She said, "I didn't know he was coming."

"He doesn't—"

The door pushed open and the family crowded in. Noelle stepped aside, her back pressed against Rick's chest. She might have found comfort in that if Morgan hadn't noticed. She didn't want this. Too much had happened. Too much had changed. Morgan was another life, another Noelle. She was healing now. Couldn't he see?

Celia clicked her tongue. "Don't you ever tell us you're coming? Some things never change." But she patted his chest. "Oh, Morgan, you look fine."

Noelle was amazed by the display. After what Rick had told her, she had imagined Morgan the black sheep. But in the eyes of each person she watched, he now seemed the returning hero. Only Morgan could accomplish that.

"I'm fine, Mom. I spent last week in Paris." He glanced at Noelle. "Strolled the Champs-Élysées."

"Not fair!" Tiffany squealed. "You can't even speak French."

"I know how to ask for the bathroom."

She pinched him.

"Ow. It's not my fault my clients have holdings in Paris—which amazingly seem to have escaped their inept management."

She wailed, "I'm the one who should see Paris. I've studied three years of French!"

Hank put a hand to Morgan's shoulder. "Take your things to your room, Morgan. Mother has dinner ready."

"Which room?"

"Rick's in the study, so you get the den."

Morgan groaned. "Not the old rollaway. I'll get a motel."

"There's a new pullout in there." Celia patted him again on her way to the kitchen. "Hurry, now, before the steaks char."

Morgan lifted his bag and headed down the hall. Noelle wished he would take a motel room. The tension in all the adults was thick as pudding, though thankfully the girls seemed to have missed it. Rick relaxed behind her, but she felt tight and worried now that her presence would spoil the holiday for all of them. Oh, why had Morgan come?

But sitting across from him at the dinner table, she couldn't miss the pleasure his unannounced visit brought his family. She gleaned that he hadn't been there last year, and that made this appearance all the better. Or worse. Though his sisters hung on his stories and jokes, Noelle heard the strain in his voice.

He played his part anyway, raconteur extraordinaire. "I could see the guy understood every word I spoke. Most French have some English at least, but he just ignored me. So I took the woman's hand and kissed it. Suddenly, in perfect English, he gave me the directions."

Morgan looked from his mother to Noelle. She dropped her gaze, suffocating in Rick's tension every time Morgan looked her way. She could have cut it as she did her meat.

"If you spoke French he'd have answered you the first time." Tiffany ripped her roll in two. "I would have asked directions in French."

Morgan chucked Tiffany under the chin. "Next time I'll take you along. My translator."

"Not fair!" Tara dropped her fork and it clattered to the floor.

Noelle was thankful for the distraction, anything that took Morgan's eyes from her. She cut a bite and forced herself to chew.

Hank tossed down his napkin. "You boys want to see the stallion Burt Rawlings has for sale? He's giving me first look if I come tonight."

Noelle turned to Hank. How could he ask something so mundane in the midst of this strain? She was certain Rick would refuse, but he nodded. "I'll have a look."

"You can't bid against me." Hank held up a finger.

"I'm not in the market. Just like to see what's out there."

"Morgan?" Hank raised his eyebrows.

Morgan shook his head. "Don't care what's out there, Dad. Not in horses anyway."

Hank and Rick stood. Was he really leaving? After standing guard all through the meal, he'd just leave her to Morgan? Celia began clearing the dishes, and Noelle stood to help, but Rick's mother waved her off. "We'll get it, Noelle. You relax."

In other words, stay out of the way and don't cause any more trouble than you already have. Noelle got the message, but why did Celia think this was all her fault? It was Morgan who'd pushed things. She had given him no reason to think—

Morgan waited for her in the living room. "Let's take a walk." He held out one of his sister's coats.

Resigned, she slid her arms into the sleeves, and he pulled it over her shoulders with the all too familiar stroke of his hand. She followed him out. Her breath was white in the moonlight as she limped down the stairs and started along the drive beside him. "I can't go too fast."

"Really." He turned. "I'd say you went plenty fast."

"I meant my leg."

He wasn't distracted. "What's between you and Rick? He's sending daggers every time I get near you."

She looked out along the fences. What was between them? She thought of their date, their kiss, her dream. Last night it had all seemed so right. With Morgan she was still broken, but with Rick . . .

Morgan stopped and took her hands in his, stared hard into her face. "Don't tell me you think you're in love with him."

Was she? "Morgan . . ."

"I don't believe it!" He dropped her hands. "Why?"

She shook her head, searching for words. If she loved Rick it was because he never forced it, never . . .

Morgan kicked a piece of ice across the surface of the snow, then stared up at the sky. "What about us?"

Her heart ached. "Morgan, it's been months since I've seen or even heard from you. A lot has happened."

"Obviously."

"You were never serious—"

"How could I be? You freaked out every time I got close. I've never spent so much time and emotion on a woman I didn't even sleep with!"

Noelle trembled. "You wanted what I couldn't give."

"But you could give it to Rick?" Morgan laughed coldly. "I didn't think he had it in him. Mr. Celibate."

She burned. "Rick hasn't touched me. He knows . . ." Her throat constricted.

"What?" He sent her a bitter glance. "I suppose you told him everything you couldn't tell me?"

Noelle shivered. Her chest grew tight. Yes, she had told Rick. And it had cost her every defense she had. Except Rick himself. He'd been there in her dream, but he wasn't there now to stem Morgan's anger. She started to shake, and Morgan gripped her arms.

"Don't you dare panic." He searched her face. "You have no reason to fear me. I never hurt you, Noelle. I never would."

Tears stung her eyes. "I'm sorry, Morgan." She gripped her hands together beneath her chin and drew a jagged breath. "I can't control it."

He shook his head. "That's where you're wrong. It's all in your control. You just have to take it. Don't let this thing get hold of you." He pulled her close until her fists lodged between them. "You're in charge, Noelle. Not Rick. Not even me."

She swallowed. Maybe he was right. She had to take control somehow. That wasn't what Rick believed. But she couldn't do it his way. God's way. She lowered her face wearily. Maybe Morgan was right.

---

Rick paced the study in the dark. Three paces out, three paces back before he might knock his shin into the pullout frame. How many years had it been since Morgan spent Christmas with the family? Two? Three? Why this one? Why now?

Noelle was asleep when he came home. Or at least she was closed into her room with the lights out. It wasn't that late, though Dad had talked extensively with Burt Rawlings. After the initial pleasure of seeing a fine horse, Rick had chafed every minute. But he'd gone along to show Dad everything was under control. He'd suspected the invitation was Dad's way of taking charge of the situation. Only Morgan hadn't kept step. As usual.

Rick turned and paced. His mind churned. How could he help Noelle with Morgan interfering? Help? Rick clenched his fists. It had gone past that, hadn't it? He expelled a sharp breath and closed his eyes. He loved her. He wanted her with him, at the ranch, sharing his life, his love, his faith.

Pastor Tom had said to start with faith, but could he? Shouldn't he first show her human love so she could understand divine? Especially now, with Morgan muddying the waters. Rick turned and paced. No doubt Morgan had cornered Noelle at the first chance. What had she told him?

Rick gripped his hands together. He hadn't made his intentions known. Did she understand that he would never have gotten to this point if he didn't believe the Lord had directed him to love her? And that didn't mean check it out, see if it feels right. It meant commit. He didn't do things half way.

Rick turned. *Lord, you've charged me with her care. You had to know I would love her.* Of course God knew. God had intended it. Rick rubbed a hand over his face. How else could he make sense of her appearance at the ranch, the way things had happened since, the way he felt? He'd lived with Noelle under his roof two months, another three worrying about her in town. Not a lot of time, but long enough to make her part of his life.

Maybe it wasn't the sort of courtship he would have planned. The Lord knew better. He'd laid her on his heart from the moment He directed him to let her stay. Of all the places she could have run, she'd come to him. He was the one she trusted with the truth of her situation. Not Morgan. He checked that thought. He did not want to pit himself against his brother.

*Lord, show me.* Even as he said it, he wasn't sure he wanted to see. What if it wasn't God's plan? Did he imagine his own purpose as God's?

Mom's doubts, Morgan's interference . . . Rick spun and paced too far. He hit his shin and jumped back with a stifled exclamation. Holding his shin, he spun and sat down on the thin mattress over the springs.

He bowed his head and waited for the pain to pass. Then with his head still bowed he whispered, *Lord, take my thoughts captive. Align my will to yours.* But something inside felt treacherous. Human desire. For the first time, he came close to understanding Morgan.

––––––––

Noelle could hardly breathe with the tension so heavy the next morning. Would breakfast never end? Morgan gave halfhearted answers; Rick spoke hardly at all. Celia looked as though she hadn't slept. Even Tara was glum. Noelle would have given anything to hear her chatter and Morgan's bravado and all the other voices at once.

But nothing broke the quiet except a few painfully polite comments. And it was her fault. She'd seen the closeness of this family. She'd been a part of it. Now she felt like a pariah. As soon as Tara stood to clear her plate, Noelle excused herself as well. She went to her room, sat on the edge of the bed, and looked at the wall. What could she do?

Rick tapped the door and came in. "Let's go for a drive."

She looked up bleakly. "Back to the ranch?"

He smiled, and her heart jumped. As he held out his hand, she took it. It didn't seem so bad when she was alone with Rick. Maybe they could go back to the ranch. Morgan's coming had changed things. Rick might see it differently now. He led her into the hall, then dropped hold of her hand when they reached the living room and stepped out.

They took his truck. He was quiet as he took her past the neighboring farms, but the quiet, now, seemed right. She could almost pretend all was right with the world as she watched the stubble of cornfields and fences pass. Cattle lay in clusters, their breath making misty clouds a foot above the ground. A shaggy brown-and-white dog chased the truck, barking, until they outran him.

They came to a small woods, and Rick parked at one end of an old footbridge. He got out and came around for her. When she climbed down, her leg buckled.

He caught her elbow. "You all right?"

She nodded. "It does that."

He closed the truck door. "Needs therapy."

"I know." She walked with him to the arched center of the bridge, brittle shards of ice crunching beneath her feet. The stream below was frozen silent. Stiff, brown grasses poked through the snowy banks beneath the leafless willows. "Morgan spoke to me last night."

Rick nodded. "I figured he would."

"He's hurt." She glanced up.

Rick laid his hand over hers. "He'll get over it. Morgan always does."

"But, Rick . . ."

He took her in his arms, and she breathed the scent of his sheepskin coat. It smelled of horses and mountain air, and she wished they were back in Colorado. "Take me back to the ranch."

"I can't."

"But it's different now."

"That's why I can't." He turned her face up and kissed her. "I love you, Noelle." He held her face between his hands and stared into her eyes, his own deep and soft and penetrating.

She had no defense against his searching gaze. Shards of fear pierced her. The hawk screamed and plunged, wearing a garment the color of blood. Her fingers dug into his arms.

He pulled her tight. "What's the matter?"

"The hawk. Am I crazy?"

"No." He stroked her back.

"There was a picture on Michael's wall. A photograph of a hawk going in for the kill. I see it in my dreams and . . . things trigger it."

He stroked her hair. "Do you see it now?"

She looked into his face, firm and determined, saw the fringe of trees behind him, the pearly sky, the pale wafer sun. One V of tiny black birds, but no hawk. She shook her head. Just as in her dream, Rick had come between her and the terror.

She slid her arms around his waist and laid her cheek against his chest. "In my dream you stood over me, as you did that day with Destiny. Will you help me, Rick?"

"Yes." His arms closed her in.

"I just want to heal."

He kissed the crown of her head. "I'll help you heal."

His embrace stilled her. The terror was physical, no doubt some reaction to the trauma that had not loosed its grip. She knew now what had happened, just not how to make it stop hurting. But Rick would heal it with his touch, just as he did any trembling animal, any creature in need. His touch didn't hurt.

She slid her hands up, rested them on his chest. "What do we do now?"

"I don't know." He drew his brows together.

But she needed him to know. He had said when he believed he was meant to do something he did it. Where was that surety?

"I don't have all the answers, Noelle. I trust God for that."

He could believe that if he needed to. She would only trust him.

As they drove back, Noelle stared through the windshield at the gathering in the yard. All Rick's family was bundled up and waiting when they pulled in, even Morgan, who stared directly at her. Stephanie tugged Rick's arm as he climbed out. "It's about time. We were going to go without you."

Go where? Noelle wished she didn't have to leave the truck. But Rick came around for her, and she climbed out. Her stomach tensed as it did before a dance performance. That irked her. Was she on stage? What did she have to prove?

Hank handed Rick an ax. "I have a bum shoulder."

Rick glanced at Noelle. "You can't walk this far."

"What's happening?"

"Tree cutting." He held up the ax. "We're getting the Christmas tree." He pointed way out over the rise to a grove of evergreens.

"She'll stay with me." Celia unfolded her arms. "Come inside, Noelle. I'll make us some tea." Spoken kindly, it was a command nonetheless.

She looked at Rick, but his face told her nothing. This time he was leaving her to face his mother. Celia started for the house, and Noelle followed. The water was already steaming in the kettle. Celia must have intended this.

"You can hang your coat on the chair. Kitchen's warm as an incubator." Celia steeped the tea, then poured them each a cup. She sat perpendicular to Noelle and spooned sugar into hers. Noelle would have liked cream, but Celia forgot to offer. Her face looked lined and worn, but there was no weakness in it. She looked up. "I suppose you realize both my sons are in love with you."

Noelle startled. She'd expected some preamble.

"When Rick arrived with you, I thought Hank had it wrong last summer when he said Morgan was seeing a lovely young woman at the ranch."

Noelle sipped her tea. "We spent some time together. It wasn't serious."

"It's not always easy to tell. Especially with someone like Morgan."

"*I've never spent so much time and emotion on a woman I didn't even sleep with!*" What if she told his mother Morgan's interest was only physical? But that would be a lie. He had cared, had tried to help in the best way he knew how.

"Morgan is not always as he pretends to be, as though nothing fazes him, nothing matters." Celia dissolved another spoonful of sugar. Did she like it that sweet, or had she forgotten she already did it? "He wants to make things right. That's his genius and his cross."

Genius, she understood. But what did she mean—his cross?

Celia stirred slowly. "He sees what others miss, whether he wants to or not."

"I know. Rick told me what he does."

"Not just in his professional life. His mind is always going, always seeing, always wanting to fix." She laid down the spoon. "He's not afraid to risk, even when it hurts him."

Noelle met Celia's eyes. Here was a mother defending her son. A wave of pain went through her for what she'd missed. What would it be like to have Celia fight for her? To have a mother's love? She wanted to reassure her, to prove she hadn't treated Morgan callously. "I was honest with him. He knew. Morgan's not in love with me."

"Then let's discuss Rick, who most certainly is." Celia sipped her tea. "If I offend you, I'm sorry."

Noelle shook her head. She'd rather hear it all than have Celia's tight-lipped treatment. At least this way she had a chance of showing . . . what? That she didn't mean to cause trouble? That was practically her motto. Don't disappoint. Don't offend. Don't make waves. She had set something terrible in motion when she rejected what Michael and Daddy had intended for her, and she didn't know when it would stop. Why couldn't she handle life like that fire fighter? Face it down and not look back?

"Rick doesn't squander his affection. But once given, his heart is steadfast."

"I know that." She'd heard it from his sisters but also felt it in his embrace, in his reluctance to demonstrate anything before he could no longer restrain it. Had he given her his heart? He said he loved her, but . . .

"It's the same with his devotion to God."

Noelle set down her cup. "I appreciate Rick's faith."

"But you don't share it."

"I'm trying to understand it." And that was not easy. Her experience reading his Bible, her encounter on the mountain . . . How could anyone take that lightly?

"Do you know what it means to be unequally yoked?"

She felt like a dunce, but Celia was speaking a foreign language. Noelle shook her head.

"It's when a believer tries to make a life with someone who doesn't share his faith. Throughout biblical history, it has proved devastating." Celia sat back, her gaze as penetrating as Rick's. "If Rick had to choose between you and his beliefs, which would he choose?"

"His faith."

Celia raised her brows. "Why?"

"It's who he is."

"Because he loves you, he's now at odds with his brother. I don't want him at odds with God. Do you understand that?"

"Yes." Celia obviously believed as Rick did, probably taught him the steps he'd followed. She could have no idea how strange it was for someone looking in. But Noelle did understand her urgency. Without faith, what would sustain Rick?

"Well." Celia's eyes softened. "Thank you for letting me speak frankly. And now I'll tell you something else. I see what he loves in you, and so do my girls. I appreciate your bearing with them."

It was so unexpected, tears stung her eyes. Bearing with them? Celia couldn't know what it meant to be swept into this family, included. "I don't have any sisters. I'm an only child."

"Then this must be especially daunting."

"It took a little getting used to, but it's been really great. My mother died a long time ago. I've only had my father, and he's a very busy man."

Celia squeezed her hand. "Well, you're welcome here. I hope you know that."

Noelle looked down at the brown-speckled hand covering hers. She suddenly remembered her mother's hand, dry and skeletal. She had pulled away because it didn't feel right, then had seen the pain in her mother's face. A deep ache filled her.

Tara burst into the kitchen, her hair standing out like a feather duster over the knitted headband. "Come and see it, Mom. Come on, Noelle."

Celia sent Noelle a quick, indulgent smile and stood. Pushing away her memories, Noelle followed her out and watched Hank and Rick shove the tree, bottom first, through the door. They hauled it to the corner of the living room and stood it in the stand.

Rick stepped back and slipped his arm around her, the first public sign of affection he'd shown. He said, "Tara chose it. The resemblance to her was irresistible. All limbs and no filling."

Tara pummeled him, and he laughed as he fended off her blows. Didn't he even wonder what Celia had said to her? How it had been while he was out choosing that tree? Did he know his mother had seen what was growing between them and that she didn't like it? He must have guessed. Maybe he'd been grilled himself. Had he told his mother he was in love? Or was that something a mother just knew?

Hank stood back and surveyed the tree. "Well, the grove needed thinning."

Therese held up one limp branch. "You can't tell until it's decorated."

Hank rotated his shoulder. "Morgan, you get the lights on. My shoulder's acting up."

Noelle almost smiled. For such a hale man, Hank's shoulder got him out of a lot.

"Hot chocolate in the kitchen." Stephanie took her father's hand. Noelle watched their easy affection. She was close to Daddy, but it was different. He adored her from a distance as though anything up close and personal might break her.

"Oh, sure," Morgan said. "Go enjoy yourselves and leave the work to me." He glanced over. "Give me a hand, Noelle?"

Rick frowned but followed the others to the kitchen. In spite of the tense time she had just spent there herself, she would gladly have returned. Morgan had been less than pleasant the last time they were alone, and she wasn't up for any more explanations, especially when she had none.

But he only handed her the string of lights and then, taking the end, climbed the stepladder and wrapped the top, swagging the string across the sparse branches. The ebullience in the kitchen underscored their own silence, but Noelle didn't know what to say. Letting the wire out little by little, she followed Morgan around and back until the string ended.

"The next one's in the box there."

She looked where he pointed and brought it over.

"Have a nice chat with Mom?"

She did not want to discuss that with Morgan. "Yes."

He half smiled. "You're a pitiful liar."

She bristled. "It's very kind of your family to have me here."

"I forgot the violins."

She didn't answer. He could bait all he liked. Then she thought of Celia's comment. Morgan wasn't baiting; he was hurting. The silence stretched again. She got the next string without direction, and he climbed off the ladder to hang it on the middle branches. Now he was right beside her as she fed it out. A moment ago she had dreaded what he might want to say, but now she couldn't stand the quiet between them. It was so unlike Morgan. She held up the end for him to connect the plugs on the last string. "I'm sorry, Morgan."

He pressed the ends together. "Yeah, I'm sorry too. I'd be less sorry if Rick would keep his hands off you."

Before she could answer, Hank came back in with an enormous box and set it on the floor beside the tree. "Ornaments and doodads. I've done my duty; now Mom and you kids can have at it."

Celia caught his arm. "Oh no, you don't. Put on the carols and perch on the sofa." She nodded to Noelle. "You can help me unwrap. The others like to hang."

Noelle sat beside her on the floor as Celia opened the big box. "These, Noelle, are the family heirlooms." She pulled the tissue from a decoupage block with Rick's school photograph on it. Noelle eyed the gap-toothed grin with amused delight until he snatched it away.

"That doesn't need to be hung."

"Oh yes, it does." Celia pointed him to the tree and unearthed a tin star with TARA painted across it. The R was backward, but Tara took it proudly to the tree.

Rick hung his picture block in the back, then knelt beside Noelle and rummaged through the box. "Here's one I carved in Boy Scouts." He handed her a wooden . . . bear, she guessed. "Morgan's got one in here, too, somewhere. A wolf." He dug through. "Here it is."

Noelle took it. "That's good."

"For a twelve-year-old." Morgan hung it on the tree.

So far the entire box had held homemade ornaments, and one after another the family members claimed their own work and found places on the tree to display anything from yarn and crayon shapes to the cross-stitch designs Therese and Stephanie had completed this year.

With a children's choir singing "The Coventry Carol," the smell of freshly cut pine, and laughter and banter, the box emptied and Noelle's heart swelled. These were not crystal and gilt ornaments such as she'd seen in Tiffany's. There was no champagne, no hors d'oeuvres, no chamber orchestra, designer gowns, or tuxedos.

These were real people, enjoying their memories and each other, and including her. It was unlike even her memory of Christmas before her mother died. There, all had been festive and glittering but not touchable. She unwrapped a Popsicle-stick cross with "I love Jesus" painted down the front.

She was surprised when Morgan took it from her and hung it on the tree. She pictured him making it as a little boy, before he'd rejected the faith it symbolized. Celia, too, watched him hang it. Though it didn't show in her face, Noelle guessed at the disappointment she must feel. Her son was thirty-one years old and so far from the child who had painted those words on a cross. For a moment, Noelle wondered if Morgan was happier now.

Noelle reached in, but the box was empty. Rick helped her up and stepped her back three paces. "What do you think?" He curled his arm around her waist, provoking Morgan, she was sure, but it couldn't be intentional, not by Rick.

She looked at the tree with colored lights twinkling, handmade ornaments filling the gaps, and cheap silver tinsel dangling where Tara had tossed it in her traditional role. "I think it's charming," she said.

Morgan shrugged into his coat and went out. No one discussed his absence at dinner, but Noelle noticed Hank left the front door unlocked when he closed up for the night. He looked resigned. Was Celia?

Recalling their conversation, Noelle guessed not. "*I don't want him at odds with God.*" She'd been talking about Rick, but she must feel the same for Morgan. She pictured Celia on her knees. What would prayers lifted by a mother's love accomplish? Could a divine being be swayed by a fervent plea? And what could God do, anyway, if Morgan was in control?

# 24

Noelle startled awake at Rick's touch on her arm. Only the pale dawning light filtered into the room, and Therese still slept soundly in the other bed. He held a finger to his lips, then whispered, "Dress warmly and meet me on the porch."

He went out and Noelle washed and dressed in jeans and a sweater, then pulled on a coat from the closet and went out. Rick waited in sheepskin coat and Stetson. With the rosy glow of winter sky behind him and the white cloud of his breath as he leaned on the porch post, she stopped just to look. He turned, looped her neck with a scarf, and pulled her close. They kissed, then he wrapped the scarf and handed her some mittens.

"What's all this?" She tugged the red knitted mittens on.

"You'll see." He took her hand and led her down the stairs. "Last night's snow should help."

"Help what?" Her feet crunched on the old snow now covered with a fine powder. The brilliance of the sparkles dazzled her eyes as the dawning sun crested the horizon.

Rick wrapped her in his arm as they walked to the barn. It was so natural a motion, it hardly surprised her anymore. And without Morgan looking on, she indulged in its comfort. Smiling, Rick pulled open the door, then stepped aside.

She caught her breath. "Rick! A sleigh!"

"What would you say to a good old-fashioned sleigh ride?" He looked like a boy with his first set of wheels, and he had obviously not expected an argument. The large black stallion was already hitched and shook its jingle-bell harness. "A little birthday magic."

She turned, startled. It was her birthday. With everything else—all the Christmas activity and then the worry with Morgan—she'd forgotten. But Rick hadn't. She caught his hand. "Don't tell anyone. I don't want them making a fuss."

"Our secret." He lifted her in and pulled the lap quilt over her knees. Noelle smiled as the horse lurched forward, ringing the bells with every prance. As the sleigh glided out of the barn, the wind blew a powdery spray of snow, and she pulled up the scarf Rick had wrapped on her neck.

He nodded. "Don't let the cold get to your lungs."

"I'm fine."

"You'd say that regardless." He reached over and tugged the lap blanket higher.

"No, I wouldn't."

"Yes, you would." The shadow of his hat cut across the bridge of his nose and arced down over his cheeks.

"If I were still sick, I'd say so."

"Okay."

She tossed her hands into her lap. "I hate it when you do that."

"What?"

"Say 'okay' as though you know you're right but you'll concede the point for sheer graciousness."

He chuckled. "I am right. But I'll graciously concede the point."

"You're smug."

"So you've told me." Rick urged the horse through the gate, which led to the pastures, then out across the fields. The harness had the larger jingle bells that made a varied, throaty song as the horse bobbed along to the top of a gentle slope where Rick brought the sleigh around. He stopped, and she looked out at his father's ranch spread below them: broad, rolling hills sparkling in the new snow, the skating pond with the willows that hugged its edges, stoic and bare. A starling called and received a distant reply, then took wing over the pond. The horse snorted, just tinkling the bells.

"It's beautiful," she breathed. "We could be a Currier and Ives print, only you need a top hat."

He grinned. "A suit I'll do, but no top hat."

"It's not much different from your Stetson."

He circled the reins around the hook on the rim of the sleigh.

"Different enough. A Stetson serves a purpose, keeps the sun off when there's work to do."

She flicked the brim with her middle finger. "You just like how you look in it, all western and macho."

"Do you?" His eyes took on that warm molasses look, and her breath quickened.

Of course she did. His looks had not stood out to her when they met, only his persona. Even now she couldn't say he was the handsomest man she knew, but somehow he was. "Yes."

He took off the hat, held it behind her head, and kissed her. Her heart swelled with love, full and uncomplicated. She exulted in his touch, ardent but undemanding. He drew out her response without forcing his own. He gave himself and freed her. He cupped her face in his gloved hands. "You're the only woman I've ever kissed, aside from Mom, and believe me, that wasn't the same."

She believed him.

"I want you to know why."

She looked into his face. Only Rick could look so serious.

"God made the human heart with a huge hole that only He could fill. All my life it's been pretty easy for me to keep that in sight. I know it's hard for you to understand, but it pleases me to worship and obey the Lord."

Did he think that didn't show? That she hadn't seen it in his reverence?

"The other thing I've been pretty sure of is that if the Lord had someone for me to spend my life with, He'd bring me that person."

Noelle glanced to the side. "You didn't make it easy, holed up on the ranch, keeping to yourself."

"You found it."

She tugged the blanket tighter to her waist. "You couldn't have had too many choices. Only a handful of single women came up all summer."

"I didn't want choices. Only the one God had for me from the beginning."

He couldn't be saying what it sounded like. Yes, his love touched the wounded places, but a worm of fear still ate her.

"I wouldn't say any of this lightly. I hope you know that."

"You don't say anything lightly." She threw him a smile, but it didn't break his intensity.

"Not when it's the most important thing I've ever asked anyone."

Her throat constricted painfully.

"Yesterday you asked me what we should do. I didn't have an answer. But now I think I do." He folded her hand into his and pressed it to his chest. "Will you marry me, Noelle?"

The blood pumped in her ears. *This is Rick. Rick.* But fear engulfed her, and she trembled, remembering Michael's proposal. She'd exulted, believing every word he said. And it was lies, all lies. She had sold her soul once; she couldn't do it again. Not even for Rick.

His voice was low. "I want a partner. I want to share my life . . . with you."

*Michael's hands like talons on her arms. "Who is it, Noelle?"*

*"No one. There's no one else." The blow across her face.*

*"You're lying! You couldn't do this unless you had someone else." Another blow.*

She shuddered and closed her eyes. Her words came short and fast. "Rick, please understand. It's not you. You know that."

He dropped his chin. "I know that hurt won't go away until you let it."

"I don't know how."

He pulled her gently into his arms. "Let me love you. Let God do the rest." Raising her chin, he kissed her.

Her emotions warred inside. What if God were as real as the warmth of Rick's arms, the strength of his kiss? What if He could do all Rick believed? Opening her mind to that thought brought an awesome calm. Her trembling stopped. In its absence, she realized how completely fear had permeated her. Without it she felt empty, new. She imagined herself living at the ranch, helping Rick, raising horses and children. Lots of children, just like Celia. Hope sprang up in her heart. Rick's children . . .

He laid his forehead against hers. "Marry me, Noelle."

It was radical, daring, impossibly impetuous. It was facing down the dragon and stabbing with all her might. "Yes," she whispered.

He stared into her eyes, then suddenly he rose to his feet and threw out his arms. "Ye-e-s!" His yell rang over the hills, and she stood up beside him in the sleigh, laughing. He caught her face between his hands and kissed her again.

*Lord, you've put her in my hands. You've given me her love. She's the one you made for me. Thank you, Father.* Rick closed his arms around her. He kissed her eyes, her temple, her hair. "Let's spend the day alone."

Her brows rose. "In the sleigh?"

"It's a little cold for that. We'll go to town, pick out your ring." The symbol that would seal their promise.

A shadow passed over her face, but she nodded. "Okay."

He squeezed her. "Good. I don't want to share you with a single sister." He didn't add "or brother." And he didn't want to think about it. Morgan had had his chance.

Rick tucked her back in, and they rode to the barn, then took the truck into town. Everything was dressed with garland and ribbons. With Noelle under his arm, he strolled the streets toward the jewelry store that might have a ring she would like. But before they reached it, Noelle pointed. "Rick, there's a gallery."

He saw her eager expression. "Want to look?"

She tugged his arm. "Of course I want to look."

Art was important to her. Naturally, she'd want to see what the gallery held. Or was she simply delaying the ring selection? Had he pushed too hard, too fast? He cautioned himself to be patient, as patient as guiding the first awkward steps of a foal. She could have said no, but she had accepted. Give her the chance to get comfortable with the thought. As she scrutinized one painting after another, he walked beside her, unaffected by most of what he saw but willing to participate.

She stopped in front of a watercolor bridge and got that absorbed look in her eyes. "That one's good, don't you think?"

"I like it."

She reached toward it. "Look at the way this line brings the eye up the page, then fades and lets this curve draw it back down."

He watched her fingers stroke the air.

"The way this shadow compliments that shine."

Her nails were narrow ovals with pale crescents at their bases. But her left hand looked bare. He said, "It's nice."

She looked at him, annoyed. He had obviously not shown enough enthusiasm.

"I'm sorry, Noelle. I'm not an art critic. I can tell you if I like it but not much else."

She cocked her head. "What if it were a horse?"

"Then I'd tell you all you need to know." He clasped her in his arms. "I might even buy it."

"Then buy this."

"No."

She pouted. "Why not? Your walls are bare. There's not a picture in the ranch."

"I'll hang your paintings. And you can put flowers in all the water pitchers, and anything else you want."

She dangled her head back. "Plaid throws for the couches in the main room, coordinating window treatments, a floral spray above the mantel . . ."

He kissed her forehead. "Leave me something."

"You can do the barn."

His growl made her laugh. Her laugh touched him deep inside. The Lord was opening her heart whether she knew it or not. It had been impulsive and perhaps precipitous, proposing marriage in so short a time. But he was sure it was right. Her answer only confirmed it.

"Come on." He led her into the jewelry store, to the counter that held wedding sets. "See anything you like?" Probably nothing such as she'd find in Manhattan. Maybe they should wait, find a better store, a better collection. "Don't settle for one if nothing suits you."

"This is nice." She pointed to an elegant square-cut diamond held between the curved prongs of the band. It was simple but unusual.

"That's my best stone." The hovering clerk came closer.

Did he just say that, or had Noelle instinctively chosen quality?

"Would you like to see it?"

Rick nodded. He didn't recognize the man, but he hadn't spent much time in jewelry stores during his time in town. The clerk handed him the ring. Rick studied its elegant line. She could choose the gaudiest cluster ring in the case for all he cared. What mattered is what it meant. But this one was lovely.

He took her hand and slipped it on her finger. A little loose, but beautiful. Their eyes met. "Do you like it?"

She nodded, more tense than she'd been a moment ago.

"Do you want to wait?"

She shook her head.

Rick slid the ring off her finger, handed it to the clerk. "Can you size it?"

"My partner's in the back. He's got a couple orders he's working on for Christmas. Sizing this shouldn't take more than an hour or two."

Rick nodded. "Ring it up." He glanced at Noelle. "Are you all right?"

She nodded.

He circled her in his arm. "Let's make a pact right from the start to always tell the truth."

She dropped her chin. "The truth?" Her liquid eyes came up and filled his senses. "I'm terrified."

He drew her gently to him, kissed the crown of her head, his own heart sinking inside. "You want to reconsider?" Relief flooded as she shook her head under his chin.

"I'm tired of being afraid. I want to make my own decisions."

Not exactly the reason to commit your life to someone. A serious check seized his spirit. Was he supposed to talk her out of it, now that he'd exulted in the promise? "You have to know it's right." That was the best he could do.

"That's your department." She managed a smile.

The weight of what he'd done pressed hard. She trusted him to know. *Lord, I'm walking forward.* He wanted this more than anything he'd ever known, more than his land, his livelihood. Noelle had come to him. A gift. He nodded. "Trust me."

Her smile reached her eyes. "I do."

"Let's get some food."

After eating, they returned to the store and this time the ring fit her finger and stayed there. A surge of pride and exultation filled his chest. It would be all right. It was natural she'd be afraid, but he hadn't forced her decision. She'd made it herself.

"We better get back. Christmas Eve is the big event for the Spencers. And if you're going to be one, you'll have to be initiated." He closed her hand in his. Noelle St. Claire Spencer.

———

If she thought she could downplay the ring, that notion was dispelled immediately. Tara squealed the moment she took off her coat, grabbed her hand, and trumpeted, "What's this?" Thankfully only Therese and Stephanie were within range.

Rick circled his little sister's shoulders. "Don't hyperventilate."

"Is it an engagement ring?"

Noelle was wrong. Celia had obviously heard. She came from the kitchen, her face a study in surprise and concern, neither expression encouraging. Rick glanced at his mother and smiled.

She formed one in return. "Well."

Speechless with joy—not. Noelle hadn't wanted a big deal made

about her birthday. This was far, far bigger. What had she been thinking? If she hadn't chosen a ring, they could have kept it secret, just
between them. Everything seemed better with Rick alone; clearer, more
certain. And this was only *his* family. She trembled, but strangely that
thought strengthened her resolve.

"Another reason to celebrate." Celia's face warmed but didn't
convince.

"Is Dad around?" Rick looked beyond his mother, as though Hank
might be lurking there.

"Outside. Probably the stables."

He nodded, sent Noelle a wink, and went back out. *Wonderful.* A
gentle hand on her shoulder made Noelle turn and Therese hugged
her. "Congratulations."

Stephanie followed suit. "I'm so glad, only . . . I thought you
said . . ."

Therese elbowed her. "Obviously, things changed."

"Oh yeah. They had a date."

Noelle had to laugh. "It's sudden, I know. I . . ." How on earth did
one explain?

"Come have some tea." Celia motioned toward the kitchen.

Those words quickly signaled dread. But this time the girls came
too.

"Have you set a date?" Celia's voice was carefully controlled.

Noelle shook her head. "No. Nothing's definite." That wasn't what
she meant, but the nuance settled on Celia like a cloud. "Rick asked
me this morning and I accepted. We chose a ring, but nothing else."

Celia poured tea all around. Noelle stared into her cup. Would she
ever drink it again without her stomach clenching?

———

Rick found his dad in the stable nursing the back of one of the gelding's forelegs. "How's it looking?" The horse had cut an artery several
days before and bled badly before the vet arrived, but an animal that
size could lose five gallons of blood without serious danger.

"Better. I wish he'd learn not to paw at the door that way."

"No good grasp of cause and effect?" Rick smiled.

Dad patted the horse. "Not that I can see." He looked up. "Did
you need something?"

Rick leaned on the stall door. "Dad, I asked Noelle to marry me."

His dad rested his hand on the gelding's back. "And?"

"She accepted."

Dad cocked his jaw. "I'm sure you've thought it all out."

"I've prayed. I believe it's my direction."

"Has she?"

Rick shook his head. "Mom's already tackled that. I know faith should come first, but there are extenuating circumstances here that make it difficult."

"No one said things should be easy."

"I love her, Dad. She'll learn God's love through mine."

His dad dropped his chin. "That's a tall order, son."

It was. And Rick was less sure than he tried to sound. He knew what Scripture taught: love is patient, love is kind; a man should love his wife as his own body, present her unblemished on the day of judgment. *I'm willing, Lord.* "I think it's right."

Dad cocked his head and nodded. "She's a lovely girl."

More so than he'd ever anticipated. They would work through the difficulties. Faith, hope, and love. And the greatest was love. The others would come.

————

For dinner Celia served Christmas ham and all its trimmings. Tiffany had instructed Noelle to change clothes, saying, "We always dress up for Christmas Eve." So she was once again in the dress Rick had purchased. What if she had refused it? But she stroked the soft sleeve and realized she had accepted much more than an angora dress. And the ring on her finger bore that thought home.

Morgan arrived, impeccable and charming, just before the meal was served. He even interacted, seemingly none the worse for his absence, wherever that had taken him. Maybe getting out had eased his hurt, though the red in his eyes suggested another balm.

After the meal, Noelle followed them all into the den. Rick had said something about initiation. Was this the time?

Tara squeezed her arm. "Tonight this room is dubbed the 'music hall.' "

"Music hall?" Noelle dubiously eyed the old upright piano and mismatched chairs the men were dragging in and setting around the pullout couch that Morgan had been using for a bed but which now was folded in.

Tara giggled. "You'll see."

Noelle sat beside Rick on the couch. He looked wonderful again in charcoal vest and white dress shirt. But if she were truly honest, she preferred him in his denim or flannel or chambray shirts and jeans. Especially when they smelled of smoke and horses and dust. That was the Rick she knew best, the one she fell in love with.

Hank stood behind Celia at the piano. Bowing his head, he folded his hands, and all grew quiet. "Lord, be glorified," he said.

"Amen," voices around her answered. Definitely the shortest prayer yet. Noelle felt Rick's arm come around her as Celia touched the keys and Hank sang "O Holy Night." His wife harmonized in a mellow contralto, their voices blending.

Noelle bit her lip and smiled. Now she knew where Rick and Morgan got their vocal ability. Rick stood when they finished and took up his guitar. He slipped the strap over his head.

Together with Celia on the piano, he accompanied Therese, Stephanie, and Tiffany in a medley of carols. Noelle could tell none were formally trained, but they sang with a freedom and pleasure that professional training might have destroyed. She recalled Professor Jenkins's words, *"Please don't tell me it's because you were instructed . . ."* How much of her own natural inspiration had been lost by the hours and hours of drills?

Tara had taken her place in front with an adorably impish pose and proceeded to dramatize "I Saw Mama Kissing Santa Claus," even shaking her finger in her mother's face.

Noelle leaned close to Therese, who'd filled Rick's place beside her. "She was born for the stage."

"I know," Therese whispered back. "She hasn't a self-conscious bone in her."

"Like Morgan."

Therese nodded. "And they adore each other."

Noelle smiled. "I noticed that."

But when Morgan got up, his manner was nothing like his little sister's silliness. He leaned against the piano with almost a listless stance. Noelle tensed as he rested his eyes on her. *Oh, Morgan, don't spoil it.*

"Play 'Blue Christmas,' Mom," he said, without shifting his gaze.

"I don't know that one, Morgan."

"Then just chord with me." He began to sing the melancholy song with all the pathos of Elvis.

Noelle looked down at her hands, startled by the brilliance of the diamond that announced her acceptance of Rick. She'd seen Morgan's expression when he noticed the ring at dinner. She had hoped he would understand, or at least accept it, but he sang to her alone, and her heart ached.

She glanced at Rick, leaning on the wall. He wore the grim look she remembered so well. Was it Morgan's advances that had caused that same look before, after he'd brought her home from the hospital?

Caught between them, she felt strangled. How did Morgan dare to do this with all his family looking on? His words wrapped around her, and she hurt for the hurt she heard there. She thought of what Rick had told her of Morgan's past. *"It really tore him up."* And Celia's words. *"It's not easy to tell, especially with someone like Morgan."*

Did he care more than she thought? Was he baring his heart in the only way he knew how? Her throat ached with tears. She hadn't realized how vulnerable he was. He'd boasted of his heart of steel.

She hadn't seen, hadn't understood. She had been focused on herself. Rick's love had freed her to feel again. But it was Morgan who first cracked the shell. She closed her eyes. She couldn't love them both.

Tara jumped up. "Now do a fun one. Sing 'Jolly Old St. Nick' with me." Smiling, he pinched her nose and they sang. When they finished, they clasped hands and made a grand bow together, accepting any and all applause. Of course.

"Noelle's turn." Tiffany waved an arm her way.

"That's not fair." Rick came off the wall like the protector he was. "She didn't know the rules."

"But everyone has to." Tara caught her hand and pulled her up.

Noelle stood. "I don't really sing, but I'll play."

Celia moved for her to take her place. Noelle sat a moment, resting her fingers on the keyboard. "I don't know any Christmas songs."

"Play anything." Tara leaned her elbows on the piano top. "Chopsticks."

Noelle drew a long breath, raised her hands, and played, the music of Chopin flowing from her fingers as she'd been taught. It had been so long, but it was still there. Years of practice and study at Julliard did not so easily fade. Closing her eyes, she found the joy in even this clumsy instrument and forgot those seated around her.

She imagined her father in his wing chair, eyes closed, listening, and a pang of remorse seized her. If only she were a little girl again, playing for her daddy with all the promise of her life ahead of her. Her fingers called out the music from the keys. Life was ahead of her still . . . a new life.

There was utter silence when she finished, and she looked up to see Rick smiling in astonishment.

"I'm so *humiliated*," Tara wailed. "To think I practiced in front of you."

Noelle started to stand.

"Don't stop!" Stephanie called.

Tara nudged her back down. "Play something not so serious."

Noelle smiled at the irrepressible girl. She wished she'd had so much fire at that age. Caught up in Tara's mood, she launched into Rimsky-Korsakov's "Flight of the Bumblebee." Her fingers flew over the keys as Tara dragged Morgan to his feet to dance. Noelle finished and raised her hands.

Tara clung to her arm. "I *want* you to teach me."

"Be real," Stephanie scoffed.

Tara collapsed onto the couch, so Noelle joined Rick against the wall.

He leaned close. "I've got to get you a piano."

"Now that we've all had our chance in the spotlight, we'll hear about the true light." Hank opened up his large Bible. "The birth of our Lord according to Saint Luke." He read the story that Noelle had heard in various forms since *A Charlie Brown Christmas*. It wasn't threatening or especially believable—angels telling women they were pregnant, one who had never had relations with a man. How could they believe all that? Couldn't they tell it was a myth like any other? Zeus and the gods of Mount Olympus procreating with mortals to create heroes half god, half man.

It was an interesting twist making Jesus poor and helpless, but many of the other myths included jealous rivals threatening the life of the hero and forcing him to flee. The pattern was recognizable. It even brought astrology into it. How else would the wise men have attributed a star to a human event? Astronomy would have accounted for a stellar anomaly, but only a pseudo-science would ascribe prophetic meaning. Hank stopped reading when the mythical family had fled to Egypt to escape the destruction that all the other babies suffered in place of "God's son." Why hadn't the angel warned the other families, cleared them all out of Bethlehem?

The moment Hank closed the book, Tara jumped up like a music-box clown. "Presents, presents, presents. Come on, everyone, it's time to open presents."

They all gathered around the Christmas tree. Noelle dropped to the floor with the rest of them. She smiled when Hank pulled on the Santa hat and rummaged the gifts out from under the tree. He handed them around in stacks. No one moved until he was finished, then he winked at Tara. "Oldest to youngest, parents excepted."

She wailed.

"She can have my turn." Morgan chucked her chin.

"No way." Stephanie plopped a package in his lap. "We have to follow Santa's orders."

Morgan laughed when he opened the Looney Tunes tie and looped it over his neck.

"That's from me." Tara bobbed up to get her hug.

He squeezed her. "I never would have guessed."

Rick got leather work gloves from Hank. Noelle watched him pull them over his long fingers and try the fit. "Thanks, Dad."

"Noelle's turn." Tara was making sure no one dallied.

Noelle looked down. The small box on the top of her stack had Morgan's name on the tag. She opened it to find a bottle of Parisian perfume.

He smiled wryly. "Just a little something from the Champs-Élysées."

Her chest was tight. "Thank you, Morgan."

"I hope that's what's in mine!" Tara shook the big box that held Morgan's gift to her.

"Oh sure, Tara." Stephanie nudged her shoulder. "Like Morgan's going to bring you French perfume."

"I will next time, Peanut."

Though it was Therese's turn, Tara tore into her package, pulled out the red-and-white-striped footed pajamas, and shrieked. "Oh, I *love* them! I'm going to wear them right now!"

"Wait until you've opened the rest." Celia laughed. "Morgan, how could you?"

He chuckled. "They had her name all over them."

When the family gifts had been exchanged, Noelle handed out the portraits she had done of each of them, finished in the wood frames Rick had fashioned unknowingly. She dropped down next to Morgan.

"Yours isn't framed, Morgan, because I didn't know you were coming." She'd only asked Rick for seven frames. "I painted it from memory." She had certainly not sat and sketched him in the difficult time since he had arrived.

He slipped the paper off and gazed at the likeness of his face. She had painted him as she remembered him best, blue eyes sparkling with fun, mouth drawn into a droll smile. He spoke softly. "You have a pretty remarkable memory."

Last she knelt beside Rick and handed him his portrait. She had used an early sketch of him leaning back against the fence with Destiny behind him. Beyond that were the craggy peaks of the ranch. His pose showed his strength, his mastery, but she had also captured his gentleness.

He laid it across his knees, took her hands, and kissed her. "This one goes in the main room."

"Well." Hank patted his thighs and stood. "Time for Mass."

Noelle glanced up at Rick, and he raised an eyebrow. "Midnight Mass. It's a tradition." He helped her to her feet.

"You can't be serious. You're going to church now?"

"Come with me." He gave her that deep-eyed look.

She knew what it meant to him. She saw Celia watching. Morgan as well. What could it hurt? It was still her choice, her decision.

But when she reached the door of the church, she froze. *God's house.* The phrase leapt to her mind. And it brought a stark terror. Why? Why would God's house scare her so? Again the picture flashed. A tall robed figure with giant wings. Not a bird as she'd first thought. A man. An angel? Why would she be afraid of an angel?

Unaware of her terror, Rick led her through the door with his fingertips to her lower back. The church glittered with candles. Green garlands with red-and-gold ribbon wrapped the pillars. She glanced up fretfully, but there were only small rectangular windows, dark with night sky.

It was a modern, semi-attractive building, unlike the churches in New York. At least the ones she knew of. It didn't seem imposing enough to house Rick's God. Maybe it didn't. That thought relaxed her. She looked toward the altar.

A statue of a man hung in the death throes of suffering on a cross. Not a man to people like Rick; it was Jesus, the Savior, the Christ. "*And the Word became flesh and made His dwelling among us. . . ."* The son of God, the Creator, the one to whom Rick gave complete allegiance.

She wondered, now, how Rick would choose between them. He clasped her hand, but glancing up, she saw his eyes, too, on the cross. His choice would still be for his God.

She looked up at the tortured face of this Jesus. What kind of father allowed his son to suffer like that? Her chest tightened. What kind chose a rapist for his daughter? She trembled. She loved Rick. She couldn't help that. But she wanted no part of his God.

CHAPTER

# 25

Michael left the noise and the lights and the flowing champagne. He closed the door on the madrigal carols, the smell of cider and eggnog sufficiently spiked to assure a Christmas morning hangover. As he passed William's office, he glanced at the dark doorway.

William participated only in the earliest part of the annual Christmas party, where the partners all made their remarks and thanked everyone for diligence and competence, with a few words for those whose efforts had risen above. But he had left directly after as always. This year Michael couldn't stomach the party either. The gag gifts, the hilarity, all those fakes posturing the good life, pontificating bounty and good wishes.

He pulled on his cashmere overcoat and took the elevator down. He walked the streets, festive with lights, music playing from speakers and sung on street corners.

He felt more alone than ever before—and that was saying a lot, since he always felt alone, different. Most of his life he'd been alone, either in actuality or in his own mind, a latchkey child, though his mother was actually home. He'd been small, an easy mark. Then, as a sullen adolescent whose genius had been recognized but who was almost too bitter to grasp the sudden change of fate. Almost. But not quite.

Plucked from his degrading environment by William St. Claire's Foundation for the Gifted and given the highest education, he remade himself into what he should have been. By absorbing every nuance of expression, voice, and carriage, he'd accomplished transformation—made himself in William St. Claire's image.

And he'd been honored tonight by the partners, honored for his accomplishments over the last year, his value to the firm. William had spoken especially warmly. But for once, it didn't suffice. Michael felt like a fake, like the rest of the fakes. Every day he pretended, and tonight, during this season of goodwill to all, he wanted most of all to hurt someone.

He had thought, irrationally, that Noelle would come home. Not that she and William celebrated the holiday—he knew they didn't—but that she would be there anyway. For her birthday, maybe. Or just because this was the time of year families came together. His tension rose. It always did when he thought of family or the idyllic picture the word conjured.

Stopping abruptly, he hailed a cab and climbed in. At Jan's he got out. He didn't ask the driver to wait. He took the concrete stairs down to the "garden" level and knocked. Jan pulled the door open, Bud hanging on her neck like a gorilla. A crowd swarmed behind them in the tiny room. The air was thick with smoke and the smell of booze.

Jan staggered under Bud's weight and giggled. "Hi there, Michael. Join the party." She sloshed her beer at him, and he stepped back sharply.

"Oops." She hunched her shoulders and laughed.

Michael turned on his heel. He took the steps two at a time and pressed through the door into the night. Jan was Mother all over. Well, let her rot.

———

William sat before the portrait of Adelle. The blush in her cheeks was rosy with health, the whisper of a smile full of promise. The photographer had captured the gossamer softness of her hair, hanging in a golden cloud to her slender shoulders, shoulders he could cup in the palms of his hands, bending low to breathe her perfume.

He looked into the blue eyes, blue as the sky above the Seine on whose banks they had met the Christmas Adelle turned twenty. Paris. Though fifteen years her senior, he had married her two months later, and Noelle arrived by their next Christmas together. *Christmas. Noelle* . . . Today was her twenty-fourth birthday.

And she spent it without him. Not so unusual. A woman of twenty-four certainly had better ways to celebrate than with her old stick of a father. Surely there were myriad things she'd rather do. After all, it wasn't only her birthday. It was Christmas Eve.

Christmas Eve. He looked down into the glass he held. The clumped ice cubes stood up over the bourbon like an iceberg and chinked against the side when he raised his glass to Adelle's portrait with a grim smile. "Joyeux Noël, my dear." And he drained it.

———

Christmas seemed unnaturally quiet the next day with Rick's sisters off delivering homemade goodies to their neighbors. Morgan was out somewhere. In the living room Celia knitted on the couch. Beside her Hank conversed with Rick, but Noelle didn't listen. Last night had unsettled her. Something lay beneath the surface, something triggered by Rick's church. But she couldn't grasp it. Didn't want to.

"Good time to build up your line with new blood," Hank droned on. "With Rawlings' stallion, Aldebaran could foal . . ."

Noelle stood up from her place in the corner. Let them talk horses, horses, horses. She threw on a coat and went outside. Fingers of frigid air reached into her collar, and she pulled the coat closer. She hadn't realized it was so cold. But a walk would warm her up.

She should have worn a hat and gloves, but it wasn't worth going back in for them. She shoved her hands into the pockets. Plodding through the snow, she made her way to the corral beside the stable and leaned on the white fence. One of Hank's mares ambled over to snuffle her hands.

Noelle wished she had brought her something. "Hello there." She stroked the soft gray muzzle, ran her hand down the brown neck and the long, coarse mane. "I haven't met you yet."

"Miss T."

Noelle jumped as Morgan reached around her to pat the horse's head.

"Tiffany named her. Kind of a play on Misty but with emphasis on her own initial."

Where had he come from? She glanced toward the house, saw his prints in the new soft snow.

He leaned on the fence beside her. "You were impressive last night."

"Everyone was."

He reached for her hand and examined the ring. "Rick has classier taste than I thought. Or did you choose it?"

"We went together."

"Quick engagement for someone who didn't want a relationship. Or were you just waiting for the right brother to ask?"

It could look that way—probably did to Morgan. But she hadn't wanted a relationship. Rick had made it happen, almost without her. She looked into Morgan's face. "I never meant to hurt you. There are things you don't know. . . ."

He closed her fingers into his. "Why didn't you tell me?"

She turned away. Because he wasn't safe. He was as broken as she, and somehow she'd seen that. Rick was whole. Rick would make her whole.

He brought her hand to his lips. "Come away with me. Let me take you to Paris."

"Morgan, don't."

He threw back his head and laughed. "Are those the only words I'll ever get from you? Can't it once be, 'Morgan, do'?" He pulled her close. "What if I'd been there when the shell came apart?"

Her pulse throbbed in her throat. "I don't know."

He gripped her chin. His kiss was ardent and demanding, but she felt herself respond. How could she?

Morgan lurched away as Rick's fist sent him sprawling to the snow. Noelle gasped at Rick's wrath unleashed, the rage she'd sensed on the mountain. He grabbed Morgan by the collar, but she caught his arm.

"Rick, stop!"

His muscles tensed and rippled. "Don't ever touch her again." He dropped Morgan, grabbed her sleeve, and pulled her toward the house.

Her heart raced. "He didn't mean anything."

"Yeah, right." The vein in Rick's temple pulsed and his face was set.

She began to tremble. "You shouldn't have hit him."

He stopped, turning his full thunderous gaze on her. "No? Were you enjoying yourself? Maybe you wanted it. I've heard Morgan's good."

"Stop it."

"Maybe I should have let him make love to you right there in the snow."

Her hand stung from the slap she delivered as Rick turned away and stalked to the house. From the corner of her eye, she saw Morgan holding his jaw. Shaking with more than the cold, she turned away, limped through the gate and out over the field.

Rick went straight to his room and threw off his coat. His cheek flamed from Noelle's slap, and he shook out the knuckles of his right hand. He'd never been violent before. Never struck someone in anger. He knew it was wrong, but—He spoke through clenched teeth. "Morgan had it coming."

"That doesn't make it right."

Rick spun to face his father. "I'd do it again."

Dad's stance was firm. "If you can't trust Noelle, then you'd better rethink that engagement ring."

"It's not Noelle."

"Isn't it? Would it matter what Morgan did if you knew it meant nothing to her?"

*Would it?* Rick unclenched his hands. "Yes, it would matter. Doesn't it ever matter what Morgan does? We all make excuses for him, but it matters, Dad. You know what Morgan is."

His father flinched. "He's your brother."

"And what am I supposed to do? Stand by and watch? You don't know what she's been through." All the weight of her need crushed in on him.

"You have to let Noelle decide."

"She has decided." He watched the lines draw tight over his dad's face.

"I'll not have you striking your brother. Not here, not ever. Do you understand?"

Rick made one curt nod. When Dad left, he ran his hand over his face. The departing rage left a cold ache. He dropped to his knees. "Jesus . . ." He caught his head in his hands. Noelle needed protecting. Of course she did. Their tenuous relationship, her hard-fought trust. She had asked him to keep her safe. He'd promised.

And Morgan's good looks, his charm, his womanizing . . . Would everyone always excuse him? Did his early mistakes earn him everlasting mercy?

*Yes.* As did all of theirs.

Rick felt the knot in his belly. Maybe his wasn't righteous anger. Maybe part was pure, unredeemed jealousy. Did he doubt Noelle? Did she carry a torch for Morgan? Which of his conquests hadn't? But she'd resisted him.

Not today.

Rick groaned. *Lord, I'm weak. Show me what to do.* He stretched his fingers painfully. He had struck Morgan with all his strength, then turned that same fury on Noelle—if not physically, then with words. He'd deserved the slap. He held his head in his hands and prayed for peace, for wisdom, forgiveness.

When he came out, he found Morgan alone on the porch. "Can we talk?"

Morgan kept his gaze straight ahead.

Rick leaned against the post. "Morgan, I know you had feelings for Noelle. . . ."

"Had?"

Rick faced his brother squarely. "I'm asking you to let it go."

Morgan glanced over. "And if I don't?"

Rick felt the throb in his knuckles. "I don't want to fight you, but I will. It's not just about your wanting her and my wanting her. There are things she's been through."

"So I heard."

"She told you?"

Morgan shook his head. "Only your ears are hallowed enough for the details."

Rick reached a hand to Morgan's shoulder. "I didn't want it this way."

"Well, if you didn't, and she didn't, who did?" He cracked a wry smile.

Rick gathered himself. He needed Morgan to understand. "I love her."

Morgan nodded. "I could have, too, given half a chance."

"You had a chance, Morgan."

"You think I don't know that!" He slapped the post, then dropped his head to his outstretched arm. "She's the only one who came close."

"She's not Jill."

"Yeah . . . I know."

"I'm sorry about the jaw." Rick reached out his hand, hopeful of reconciliation.

"You've got a mean hook." Morgan gripped his hand. "You better go find her. I don't know what you said to make her slap you, but it must have been worse than anything I tried."

Rick guessed it was. He started down the steps.

"West." Morgan pointed.

Rick headed that way. "Noelle!" His voice carried through the deepening dusk. "Noelle!" No answer, but he caught sight of her, sitting, knees wrapped in her arms. Her head was down. She didn't raise it when he approached.

He knelt on the ground before her. Still she wouldn't look, so he cupped her face and made her see him. "I'm sorry."

Her gaze slid from his face. "I need to go home."

It landed like a rock in his belly. "You mean the ranch?"

She shook her head.

"Why?"

"It's where I belong."

Damp cold seeped into his knees from the ground. "You belong with me."

She wouldn't answer.

"Noelle, I'm sorry I lost my temper. I know that frightened you, and God knows I wish I hadn't. But that doesn't mean—"

"You think it's my fault, don't you?"

"What?"

Dewy eyes draped with lashes turned on him. "That I was raped. You think I wanted it, that I made it happen."

He stared at her. Not only was it the first time she'd said right out what had happened to her, but worse by far was how she had twisted his words, taken a meaning he never intended. "Listen to me, Noelle. I never blamed you. I never would."

She burst up from the ground. "You and your God! You're so pure, aren't you! Never dated, never kissed a woman, never—Well, I hate you, and I hate your God!"

Rick froze. *Lord, what have I done? Don't hold this against me. Forgive me. Mend this wrong.* Tears stung his eyes as he stood up. He didn't care that she saw. "Noelle . . ."

"I just want to go home." Her voice broke.

"If you want to go, I'll take you. But you're not going alone."

She screamed, "I am alone! I didn't ask you to love me, and I don't want to love you!" Tears ran down her face.

He pulled her into his arms. "Then don't. I might let you down, Noelle, but God never will. If you can't trust me, trust Him."

"Trust Him? Where was he when Michael beat me, raped me? When I snuck away and ran?"

"He was there. He brought you to the ranch."

"To you?" She said it with such venom, he quailed. Her lip curled. "At least Morgan was honest. He didn't couch what he wanted in pious lies."

Rick held his tongue. She was right. He'd been dishonest with everyone, including himself, pretending he only wanted her well-being, when he wanted her so much he thought his heart might tear in two inside him.

Suddenly she crumpled. "It hurts so much!"

He caught her in his arms, held her. But it wasn't enough. One mistake, one lapse, and he'd torn them apart. He hadn't taught her God's love by proving his own. He had made her fear God's. "The Lord's love is perfect, Noelle. And perfect love drives out fear. Please don't be afraid of that love."

The fight left her, but he kept her in his arms as the twilight deepened around them. It was bone-chilling cold. If they remained any longer they'd both freeze. "Will you come back to the house?" Maybe that was one step she could take.

But she hesitated. "What about Morgan?"

"We made our peace."

She closed her eyes, and he circled her shoulders in his arm. She shivered as he led her back across the field. He hoped she wasn't just coming in from the cold.

————

Noelle sat by the window in the morning light, gazing out at the snowy land. Where before it had seemed beautiful, now it looked bleak. Nothing was as it seemed. Everything had a dark side. Suppressed emotions surged inside her, ready to surface and explode. She jumped when Rick touched her shoulder.

"Morgan wants to say good-bye. He's out front."

Good-bye to Morgan? How many had there been already? But she nodded, then went out alone into the thin sunshine.

Morgan leaned on the white Lincoln rental and pulled a wry smile. "Sure do enjoy Christmas at home. It's so peaceful." He no longer fooled her with his careless, ne'er-do-well veneer. He took her hands. "You all right?"

She nodded. "Are you?"

He patted his chest. "Heart of steel, remember? Jaw too." He worked it side to side as proof.

She didn't believe him on either account. But what use was questioning it? He had his own shell, his persona. Maybe it was better to stay that way. Coming out was too much work and way too painful.

He reached up and rubbed a lock of her hair between his fingers, then bent it under her chin. "I tell you what, if things don't work out, look me up." He leaned forward and kissed her cheek. "But for what it's worth, Rick's a better man."

She blinked back her tears. There were so many things she should say but couldn't.

He chucked her chin. "Hey. No shell."

She sniffed.

"Good-bye, gorgeous."

"Good-bye." She went inside without watching him leave.

Rick stood in the kitchen, hands resting on the counter, staring out the back window at the fields where he'd found her yesterday. She had hurt him out there, but he hadn't defended himself. Just as he'd taken the blame for her fall, he now shouldered all of this. Why? She went and stood beside him.

He said, "Is Morgan gone?"

"I think so."

He turned. "Noelle, I've been thinking. I have to get back to the ranch."

Her heart jumped, then she realized he'd said *I* not *we*.

His tone was carefully neutral. "I've talked to Mom and Dad. You can stay—"

"You're leaving me here?" How could she face his family alone? Or was he trying to be done with it, with her?

He turned and took her hands. "Noelle . . ."

She tugged free, unwilling to hear whatever honorable words he couched it in. "You don't need to say any more." She slipped the ring from her finger and tucked it into his palm.

"What—" He caught her arm as she turned.

She yanked it away. "I can take care of myself. I don't need you or your family."

"Well, in case you hadn't noticed, I need you."

She stood where she was. Rick needed her? Rick, who needed nothing but his land, his work, his God? Why would he say something so blatantly false?

His throat moved. "I was going to say you could stay here if you needed time. We can't go back together the way it is. But I guessed maybe you weren't ready to marry me now." He bounced the ring in his palm, then closed it tightly into his grip. "I'd say my guess was good."

She stood for a moment, staring into his eyes, then dropped her face to her hand and cried. His arms came around her, and she pressed into his chest, need surging inside. "Don't leave me. Please don't leave me."

"I've stayed as long as I can."

"Then marry me." She could hardly believe she'd said it, but if that was all that stood between him taking her back with him . . .

It was a long time before he spoke. "I want you to be sure."

She was sure. What more did she need than Rick and the ranch? She longed to see the crags in the snow, the golden log walls warmed by the fire crackling in the stone fireplace. She wished they'd never left. She wrapped his waist with her arms. "I'm sure."

Rick held her close. He was less than confident. Especially with the ring still in his hand. Did she know he meant the vows to last? He stroked her hair, caught it in his fingers, and turned her face up. "It's forever, Noelle. No going back. No running away."

Her throat worked. "I know." She looked so vulnerable. Did she understand? Maybe her father had taken charge of her life for a reason. What sort of woman nearly died from inertia, as she had in Walker's shack? Again he sensed a brittle spirit. Could she make a decision? One as critical as marriage?

His heart twisted. If she couldn't, he'd make it for her. Otherwise he'd lose her. He knew it. "There's usually a process, preparation classes, mentoring. But if we go back together I can twist Pastor Tom's arm."

Her whole face changed, lit from within. "Will he marry us at the ranch?"

He rested his forearms on her shoulders. "Let's marry in the church and live at the ranch." He saw her resistance, but that was not negotiable. "If we take our vows in God's sight, He'll make our union strong.

A threefold cord can't be broken." He might as well be talking to stone.

She showed no understanding and little inclination, but she said, "If that's what you want."

Well, it was enough that she was willing. They would start out right, and he'd do better this time. With God's help.

# 26

William St. Claire stomped down the stairs in his dressing gown and slippers. Who would disturb him this late on a Saturday night? He pulled open the door. "Myron. What do you have?" He ushered him in.

Myron took off his hat. "First, let me say it's obvious your daughter does not want to be found. There's been no record of employment, no phone, no credit cards, no lease or mortgage agreements—nothing. I thought, until tonight, I'd be telling you it was pointless to retain me further."

William's chest tightened. "Until tonight?"

"I have something. A hospital in Boulder, Colorado."

William made a fist. His worst fears . . .

Myron raised a hand. "They treated a Noelle St. Claire for injuries sustained in a horse riding accident. Noelle rides horses?"

William held his voice steady. "It used to be a passion of hers."

"She was released in September, the claim filed against liability insurance held in the name of Richard Spencer."

William released his breath. "Richard Spencer?" He searched his memory. The name meant nothing to him.

Myron shrugged. "I'm booked to fly out tomorrow. I'll be in contact the moment I have anything."

"Thank you for coming in person. I want to keep this between us for now."

Myron nodded. "I'll be in touch."

William closed the door. Richard Spencer. Had Noelle run off with a man? It was possible, though unlikely. He went to the study and poured a bourbon. But it would explain her lack of communication. If she was embroiled in some romantic affair . . .

He looked up at the portrait of Adelle, the only picture of her in the house. She looked terribly young. She had been young. Their own whirlwind romance swept them both into a life full of gaiety and . . . His throat tightened painfully. Wasted at twenty-seven by the ravaging cancer, she'd gone from the beautiful woman in the portrait to a morphine-dependent husk. In months. It had killed him—the best part of him, anyway—to watch her die.

Then he'd been afraid. Watching Noelle grow so like Adelle, the same sensitivity, the fragile beauty. He'd done everything humanly possible to keep her safe, but inside he knew there were things he couldn't control, and it ate at him. He dropped his face into his hand.

What had gone wrong? Why had she left? Should he call Myron off and leave her alone? Hospital injuries from a horse riding accident. He'd always worried about that, but she'd loved the horses so much. He clenched his jaw. He was entitled to answers, at least.

―――――

Noelle breathed deeply as Rick pulled open the door and let her in. Pine and woodsmoke. The familiar shadows of the main room vanished with the click of the lamp switch, and she looked up into the lofted strength of the house. No place had ever touched her as this ranch did.

Rick rubbed his palm over her back. "Nice to be home?"

*Home.* She'd felt it the first time she looked out at the ranch spread before her, felt its solid beauty. After the hospital, after Walker's shack . . . *Oh yes.*

"Wonder if Simon's up still." Rick glanced up the dark stairs. "Not from the looks of it. We'll let him sleep." He went back out for the bags.

She wandered to the kitchen and turned on the light. A hot cup of tea would chase the chill from their bones. Whoever had fixed Rick's truck heater hadn't done the job right. She filled the kettle with hot water and put it on to boil, then took down Marta's tea tin.

She glanced at Rick's mail piled on the table. Maybe she'd have another money order waiting. As she flipped through the envelopes, a business card slid from the stack. Her heart flipped inside her. *Myron Robertson, Private Investigator.* She jerked a glance over her shoulder.

"What's the matter?" Rick came in behind her, setting the bags down on either side of him.

She handed him the card with numb fingers.

"You know him?"

She nodded. "He's the investigator Daddy uses."

Rick set the card down. "We're calling your father in the morning, anyway."

She stared at him with a mixture of betrayal and disbelief. How could he say that so dispassionately? "What do you mean?"

"Noelle, I'm not a thief. I'll ask his permission—"

"He won't give it."

At the whistle, Rick turned and took the steaming kettle from the stove. "If I can't have his blessing, at least I'll have his knowledge."

She sank to the chair. What did she expect? Rick's sense of honor was overdeveloped. She should have known. Here they were, back in his hallowed halls, and he was once again the dictator. "What does it matter?"

He poured the steaming water over the tea bag in her cup. "It matters."

"Why?"

He laid a teaspoon beside the saucer. "Because you can't keep blaming him for what Michael did."

She tensed, expecting the flap of wings, the amber eyes. They didn't come, but just hearing Michael's name and thinking of Daddy's part in it . . .

Rick took down a box of saltine crackers, slid out one tube, and poured them onto a plate. "He couldn't have known, Noelle. How could he?"

How could he not? He had governed and guarded her, but still he'd hand chosen Michael. She shuddered.

Rick sat down and took her hands in his. Even at odds, his touch brought comfort. What power he had in his hands. She watched the muscles of his forearms ripple as he tightened his grip. She didn't want to listen, didn't want to think of Daddy and Michael. That was another life. She leaned close and kissed Rick.

He hadn't expected it. In his surprise she sensed her own power.

Without knowing, she'd taken an important step, another jab at the dragon. She didn't have to wait to be kissed. As Morgan said, it was her choice. She kissed him again, the pulse in his neck throbbing under her palm.

He took her shoulders and shifted her back from him, saying thickly, "You're not making this easy."

She smiled. He didn't like his control threatened, and for the first time she experienced the thrill of affecting someone else. Intentionally putting forth her will.

"We'll call your father in the morning."

Back to that subject? Not as easily distracted as she'd thought. She frowned.

"Someone's got to walk you down the aisle."

"I can walk myself."

He stroked her cheek. "I'm an old-fashioned guy."

Hadn't Morgan told her as much? Another century, he'd said. "Then let it be Hank." She lowered her lashes and parted her lips.

Rick broke eye contact, fighting her lure. "If it comes to that, Dad would be willing. But your father gets first chance."

Power draining, she closed her eyes. "You don't know what you're saying."

"Oh yes, I do."

————

Michael Fallon stood in the marble entry of the weekend house of Ms. Clarice Overton. He took in the imposing foyer and the massive, crystal chandelier suspended from the towering ceiling. To his right, a sweeping staircase curved up, and at its base stood a life-size marble nude. Resting his gaze there, he thought how much he deserved tonight's entertainment.

Five months of hell warranted a respite, no matter how unsatisfying the replacement might be. After all, hadn't Saturday's *Post* listed him among the most eligible bachelors in New York's most powerful circles? He had clipped the article from the society page to keep it for Noelle when he found her.

He frowned. Yes, *when* he found her. Even though Sebastian had proved ineffective, he would find her. He handed his coat and scarf to the butler, then turned as Clarice caught sight of him.

"Michael." She stepped away from her companions and swept into the entry.

Michael eyed her, an arresting face with too aristocratic a nose, but a figure that drew his attention immediately. She knew how to accent her best features to minimize her worst.

"How nice of you to come. I was trapped in a murderously dull conversation. You're my salvation."

Michael laughed. "Somehow I've never pictured you needing redemption."

"Nevertheless, your appearance here is the pinnacle of my success."

"And why is that?"

"You, my dear Michael, are the prize sought at every event this season. And I am the first to acquire you."

"How very mercenary."

She laughed low, a manly laugh that shook her bosom—intentionally, he was sure.

With her on his arm, he walked into the ballroom—it couldn't be called anything less. Clarice soaked up the glances like a sponge, tipsy with her successful acquisition and the fine champagne carried on trays. Many of the faces were familiar either by acquaintance or reputation, and Michael was greeted with nods as they passed. Clarice was well connected. He might improve more than his personal life this weekend. But how the tongues would wag.

They circled the room, tittering here, tittering there. He didn't mind the attention, but Clarice had a way of wheezing up into her nose before she laughed that made him want to pinch it shut. Maybe he would. He stopped in front of a vibrant eight-foot oil abstract. It was ugly even to his eye. "Tell me, Clarice, what do you see in this?"

She slid her fingers inside the back of his tux and looked up at the work. "I see passion, vigor, obsession."

"Amazing."

"What do you see?" Her nails scratched up the back of his shirt.

*Tacky, Clarice, and way too obvious.* "I see an artist with very little skill. I'm a realist. I want to see things as they are, not someone's warped representation."

She pressed close. "Then how do you paint passion?"

He looked into her eyes, then let his gaze rove downward. "Passion is an experience, not a focal point. Art should reflect what causes passion and leave the experience to the beholder."

"I have something passionate in the library." Clarice wheezed into her nose. "Would you like a private viewing?"

Michael allowed her to lead him away from the crowd, knowing every eye followed them. William would hear of it, think Michael had at last recovered from the blow. Noelle would hear, somehow she would hear. And she'd come back. She would think he'd turned his sights elsewhere. But she would be wrong.

"Is this what you meant?" Clarice motioned upward to another massive work of terrible art.

He eyed the crude painting of a groping pair, grotesque really, with thick lines of green shadow that looked more like slime. He turned away, bored, and glimpsed a decorative easel holding a small, delicate work, so out of place amid Clarice's other choices, he asked, "What's that?"

"Oh, that. No passion at all."

Michael crossed over and stopped before it. Something so subtle would be totally lost on Clarice. The glow of the craggy mountain, the cool growth beneath. The detail both portrayed and hinted. Michael almost felt he was there. "This, Clarice, is art." Then his throat went dry. "Where did you get this?"

"It was a gift, but I can find out. Personally, I don't think much of it—"

Michael gripped the frame and wrenched it from the easel.

"Michael, what is it?"

He stared at the bottom corner. *Noelle St. Claire.* At last.

---

Noelle stood still just inside her bedroom door, hand on the knob. Last night Rick had shown her to the room with a wry smile, whispered, "good night," and kissed her gently, then gone quietly to his own room. She heard him downstairs now with another male voice. Simon? Rick's friend had watched the ranch in their absence and was probably leaving now. She cracked open the door and saw them in the entry.

Simon shrugged. "Didn't seem threatening or anything. Just said her father was worried, wanted to know where she was."

"What did you tell him?" Rick spoke low, obviously trying not to disturb her.

"I told him you were somewhere in Iowa and I didn't know when you'd be back, which was true since you hadn't told me a thing." Simon put on his coat. "I couldn't exactly claim I didn't know her when I'd already recognized the picture."

Rick forked his fingers into his hair. "It's not a big deal. We're taking care of it this morning anyway."

Simon handed the card back to Rick. "Not every day a P. I. comes looking for you, though, is it?"

Rick shook his head. "She had her reasons." He slid the card into his shirt pocket. "Thanks for keeping the place."

"Any time. Gets me away from Bruce and Rob. Nice to have a house to myself sometimes. Those guys . . . well, you know how they are."

Rick smiled. He didn't seem overly worried, but Noelle's heart thrummed. Maybe she could make him see. When Simon went out, she started down. Rick closed the door behind his friend and turned. If she could just—

But he had the phone on the table beside the door. He held it up the moment she joined him.

She frowned. "No good morning?"

He wrapped his arm around her back and kissed her. "Good morning." Then he sat her on the couch and handed her the phone.

She sighed loudly but dialed. The sooner this was done . . .

"Yes?" Daddy's tone was gruff. He must be busy already, but then, it was later there.

"Daddy?"

"Noelle! Where are you?"

But she didn't want to say that yet.

"What on earth are you doing? Why did it take so long for you to call? Do you realize what I've been through?"

Did he realize what *she'd* been through? She started to shake.

"Noelle? Talk to me!"

Fear became anger. "What do you want me to say?"

Her tone must have warned him. She could hear his collecting breath, as he called it. She imagined his eyes closed, his hand rubbing his face. "Tell me you're all right."

The anger faded. "I am all right, Daddy. And I have someone for you to meet."

Silence. She waited.

"What have you done?" His voice sounded old.

"I haven't done anything." She glanced up at Rick and shook her head. He smiled.

"Come home, and we'll discuss it."

"I'd like it if you came here, Daddy." No, she wouldn't, but Rick had forced the issue.

Again silence, then he forced a calm, reasonable tone. "Where are you?"

This time she had to answer, but before she did she said, "I'll tell you, but I don't want Michael to know."

He didn't ask why. Had Michael given some warped version already? "All right. I have a pen."

She made arrangements and hung up before he could press her further, then took a deep shaky breath and looked up.

Rick kissed her. "Feel better?"

"I don't know." In some ways she did. He was her father. But she knew from experience he would not embrace her decision. In fact, he would exert superhuman effort to bring her back . . . without Rick. If they had married before he knew—even then Daddy would find some way.

There was a knock at the door, and Rick opened it.

Noelle looked out past him. "Hello, Myron."

"Hello, Noelle."

She held up the phone. "I was just talking to Daddy. He'll be here this afternoon."

Myron chuckled. "Always a step ahead."

"Myron, this is my fiancé, Rick Spencer. Would you join us for some coffee?"

He rubbed the back of his neck. "Oh, I think I'll get home to the wife. You and William can take things from here."

"I'm sorry you had the trouble of this trip."

Myron shrugged. "I'm glad you and your father are talking. He's been awfully worried."

Noelle only nodded.

"Well, then I guess I'll go." He glanced at Rick, then raised his hand in farewell.

Rick closed the door and turned. "I expected more than that."

Noelle smiled. "He saw all he needed to. But his wife won't have him yet. He'll perch out there somewhere and make sure I don't sneak away."

Rick looked out the window at the car turning in the apron and starting for the drive. "Pretty cold for perching."

"Daddy pays him well." She felt the cage closing in.

Rick studied Noelle as she sat back down on the couch. Something was different, something in her motion, the angle of her head. He recalled his impressions of her the first evening she'd come. It was that same brittle poise. She'd been cool, almost smug, with Myron, a wealthy woman with a lesser. He'd never seen that side of her.

"I suppose he's phoning Daddy with all the details just about now." She looked out the window. "Nice place. Nothing like the estate, of course. No, the man seemed all right, but she called him her fiancé. Not that Daddy hasn't guessed already by what I told him."

Rick sat down beside her, a painful check in his spirit. Why was she doing this? Acting so cold, so above it all. And then there was last night, when she'd been almost seductive. Where was the woman he knew? Or did he know her at all? "What's the matter, Noelle?"

She looked at him. "You have no idea."

He waited.

"You think you can handle anything, that nothing will change what you want."

He covered her hand with his. "Don't worry."

"Don't?" She raised her brows sharply, then looked up and around the room. "I came here to escape."

"You don't need to escape anymore. You're safe."

Her laugh was glass shattering on stone. "You haven't met Daddy. You have no clue what you've put in motion."

Rick tightened his hold. "Whatever it is, we'll meet it."

She sighed, the first crack in her poised indifference. "He'll try to take me home."

"What, he's bringing the militia?"

Her eyes pinned him. "It's not a joke, Rick. If anyone *could* mobilize the militia for personal reasons, it's Daddy."

"I'm looking forward to meeting him."

"I doubt he shares your sentiment."

He raised her hand and kissed her fingers. "You're twenty-four years old. I'm no babe in the woods. We'll deal with your father when he comes." He smiled. "Now, why don't you make us some breakfast?"

"You've got to be kidding." She wore such a superior look he wanted to shake her.

Instead, he grabbed her into his arms, growling, "Have woman. Want food."

"Stop it!" She wiggled free. "I don't see why you're so cheerful. This could be the worst day of your life."

He laughed, but it was wearing thin. "It'll be fine. I promise."

"That's not a promise you can make. No one stands in Daddy's way."

"Noelle." Rick gripped her shoulders. "God brought you to me. Do you really think your father can stand in His way?"

She stared up into his face. "I'd guess they're pretty well matched."

# 27

William St. Claire spied Noelle through the crowd, and immediately his gaze went to the tall young man beside her. He closed the briefcase on his lap and studied the man with an eye trained by years in trial law. He saw strength—both physical and mental—determination, and unmistakable possession of Noelle.

Noelle clung to his arm, limping slightly, no doubt the injury Myron mentioned. And, by her expression, this would not be easy. She was no longer a child, and she'd set her heart on Richard Spencer. That much was clear.

He rose to meet them, gathered Noelle into his arms, and felt his resolve momentarily shaken. What right had he to change her course? He'd done his best to safeguard her future. But wasn't that future hers to choose?

No. Not yet. Not until she'd heard him out. And certainly not until her escort had. He held her out from him and turned to the young man.

Noelle said, "Daddy, this is Rick Spencer."

"The someone you wanted me to meet."

Rick held out his hand. "It's a pleasure, sir."

The handshake was firm and confident, as he'd expected. Eye contact, direct but non-confrontational. William could be equally direct. "I'd like to know the nature of your relationship with my daughter."

"With your permission, I intend to marry her."

Honest, yet diffident. "And without it?"

He straightened. "I'd prefer it with."

William almost smiled. That was as polite an "in your face" as he had received in a long time. He turned to Noelle. "It seems you have a lot to explain."

"Do I?" She'd never been so blatantly defiant. There was something undefinable in her eyes. Anger? Hurt? Blame? For what?

Rick said, "Do you have luggage, Mr. St. Claire?"

"No. I'll be flying back tonight." With Noelle if he had his way.

"Tonight?" She seemed surprised. She must know his purpose.

"Yes, tonight. Unlike my gypsy daughter, I'm not at leisure to go traipsing about the country. I came at your request alone."

"Then come and see the ranch." She took his arm.

William allowed her to lead him to the tan-colored Dodge Ram, not new by any stretch. Rick stayed silent as he drove, but William wasn't fooled. He was a determined young man.

Noelle pointed. "Around this bend is the town, Juniper Falls."

William scanned the little town, then the snow-packed road up the mountainside. Rick's truck handled it, and they stopped in the yard. William climbed out. The ranch spread out around them, spacious, well maintained. He looked at Rick. "You own it?"

"Free and clear."

"He built it all." Noelle took his hand.

William turned to Rick. "I'd like to speak with my daughter alone."

He expected a fight, but Rick said, "Go on inside. I have to see to the stock."

William watched him walk away. Confident young buck. He must believe there was nothing William could say to change Noelle's mind. He followed his daughter inside and looked around. Whatever else, Rick Spencer was no sluggard. The place was well built, if he really had done it himself.

Noelle took his coat and hung it.

He waited until she turned back. "When are you going to tell me what this is all about?"

She started toward the doorway at the end of the room. "I'll get us some coffee."

He caught her arm. "I don't want coffee. I want to know what you're doing here in the middle of nowhere with that man. I have a right to know."

She spun. "Do you, Daddy? Do you have a right to control my life?" Her eyes burned with accusation.

They had never fought. Not once had he seen the defiance he saw now. Oh, she'd been stubborn sometimes, even willful. And on those occasions he'd succumbed. Small things. The instance with the red dress. But this was not small. What he saw in her face cut him. "Haven't I given you everything? Have I denied you anything? Ever?"

Tears brightened her eyes. "Only a life of my own."

He didn't understand. This woman was his daughter, yet he didn't know her. "How was your life not your own? Everything you wanted—horses, music, dance . . ." He spread his hands.

She turned away. "I don't want to fight with you. That's not why I asked you to come."

"Why did you, then? Why call at all?"

"Because Rick insisted." She turned back.

William realized with a shock that, yes, Myron had found her, but what now? If she wanted to sever their relationship she could. But what on earth initiated this rebellion? How had he hurt her?

He calmed himself. His purpose was not to fight either but to bring her to her senses. "So you've had your mutiny. Fine. Now be sensible, Noelle. Come home."

"I am home." She spoke with such depth of emotion he couldn't answer immediately. Why was she rejecting everything she had?

He said simply, "What about Michael? He's been sick with worry since you left. Almost lost his position with the firm." He saw her jaw tighten, but she said nothing. "You left without a word. Couldn't you end your relationship fairly instead of disappearing like some petulant child?"

She turned, her eyes flaming. "You don't understand. And it doesn't matter. Because I'm staying here."

He released a slow breath. "With this cowboy?"

"Yes."

He looked around the bare walls, then back to her. "You'll be wasted here."

"It's my choice."

Rick came in the door, glanced at them, and pulled off his coat. This was his turf and he knew it. William had taken a chance agreeing to come. But what choice did he have? Rick motioned toward the couch and William sat at one end. Rick took the corner chair, and Noelle sat on its arm instead of on the couch with William.

That message was clear. "So." William fixed Rick Spencer in his gaze. "How did you come to know my daughter?"

Rick sat forward, hands between his knees. "She needed a place to live; I had a room to rent."

William was unmoved by his humble position. "You never saw her before she came out here?"

"No."

William looked at Noelle, who avoided his glance. "And the fact that she has a substantial inheritance has nothing to do with this?"

"I knew nothing about you until her accident." He sent Noelle a glance. "I did check things out then, your Web site, mainly."

New information to Noelle, but she didn't seem disturbed. It was understandable for the young man to gain what information he could about Noelle after the accident that put her in the hospital—and allowed Myron to find her. Understandable, yet he'd taken financial responsibility. Why?

William stood, walked to the window, and turned. "You paid the hospital bill?"

"My liability insurance."

"You filed after you learned her financial status?"

"Yes."

William crossed to the fireplace, leaned his elbow on the split log that formed the mantel. "You must have realized she was hardly destitute. Why not let her pay the bill?"

He hesitated just long enough for William to doubt what came next. "She fell riding one of my animals. That's why I carry liability."

"No waivers?" William lowered his arm to his side.

Rick said, "She signed a waiver."

"But you paid her bill." William saw Noelle tense and pressed harder. "Were you buying my daughter's favor?"

To his annoyance, Rick grinned. "No, sir."

Certainly not the reaction he'd hoped to provoke. Did nothing perturb this scoundrel? William jutted his chin toward Noelle. "The accident caused your limp?"

"I broke my leg, but it's healing."

William walked to the center of the room. "Was he responsible for your fall?" He waved his hand toward Rick.

She licked her lips. Did she see the trap he'd laid? "Yes" made Rick culpable for damages. "No" gave him ulterior motive for paying the debt.

"This isn't a court, Daddy."

He felt a flicker of pride. Her best choice, and she'd seized it. He returned his attention to Rick. "You didn't wonder what she was doing out here alone with next to nothing and no contact with anyone?"

"I wondered."

William tired of Rick's succinct and non-informative answers. "You never asked?"

Rick said, "She didn't want to tell." A flicker in the eyes. Not quite the truth. Maybe he'd asked, but she hadn't answered.

With the way she'd acted toward him today, William could believe that. Something wasn't right. She wasn't right. Was it from her past? She'd been high-strung ever since the kidnapping. If she were damaged by that childhood incident, wouldn't someone have seen? Told him? Wouldn't he have known?

He sat back down on the couch. "Are you aware that Noelle is already engaged?"

"Was."

Ah, a touch of hardness in his tone. Rick didn't seem eager to curry favor, nor was he cowed or uncomfortable. Under other circumstances, that might have impressed him. But Rick was not Michael.

"Her fiancé is someone I deeply respect. My foundation sponsored him in a program for underprivileged youth of outstanding ability. Michael Fallon exceeded every expectation. When he completed his education, I took him into the firm as junior partner."

If Rick was impressed, he didn't show it.

William scowled. "I've invested quite a lot in his future, and Noelle's."

Rick slid his arm around Noelle's waist. "Mr. St. Claire, I love your daughter. I intend to care for her to the best of my means."

"Your means?" They may as well both speak frankly.

Rick sat taller. "I have no illusions of equality. But I know what she wants."

William threw up his hands. "She doesn't even know what she wants!"

Noelle stiffened. "I do know. I want to marry Rick and live here at the ranch."

William waved her off, annoyed that he'd been the first to break. "Love affairs are one thing. Think of the rest. Think of Michael."

Neither one of them answered. His frustration mounted. His daughter was a woman. He had no say in her decisions, but he'd hoped she would listen. Of the two, he seemed to be communicating better with Rick. "You'll sign a prenuptial agreement releasing all claims to her inheritance in the event of divorce?"

"Divorce is not an option."

William formed a ghost of a smile. Youth and idealism. "Then you won't mind signing."

"Mr. St. Claire, everything I have is Noelle's. What you do with your money is up to you." He made William's concerns sound cheap and demeaning.

That was a first. With all the work of the foundation, all his other philanthropic pursuits, no one had ever suggested pettiness. Nor had Rick. He'd merely expressed no designs on Noelle's fortune. Well, there was something in that, he supposed.

William released a long breath, looked at his daughter. "This is what you want?"

She nodded. Had he ever been able to refuse those eyes, so like Adelle's? Maybe he had spoiled her, led her to expect every desire to be fulfilled. Maybe he had overcompensated for the long hours, his own escape.

"Very well, I give you my permission. And more than that, I wish you happiness."

It was as though the stick that held her spine erect was suddenly cut. She moved up from the chair and flowed to him, wrapped her arms around his neck. "Thank you, Daddy." At least she gave him the illusion of obsequience.

He set her back. "But I want you to talk to Michael. Explain why you left. You owe him that much." He saw the muscles in Rick's jaw tighten. Rick knew something.

Noelle brought up her chin, but she looked more brittle than defiant. "Michael knows why I left."

And now William wondered. Had his early misgivings been well-founded? Was Michael working him, as he worked a jury? Time enough to find out when he returned. He rubbed his neck. "So . . . how does one hail a cab around here?"

Noelle caught his hand. "You don't have to go yet."

"I do. I'm engrossed in a case we try tomorrow." How many times had he said that over the years? Had he been a negligent father? Would he know her better, understand her better, if he hadn't worked so many hours, so many days? It wasn't as though he'd scraped for a living.

Rick stood up. "I'll drive you down."

Noelle let go. "You'll come next week for the wedding?"

"I'm paying for it, aren't I?" William got up.

Rick dug into his pocket for keys. "Actually, there's not much expense. We're having a small ceremony, with a reception here at the ranch."

William raised his brows. "Not exactly what I had envisioned for you, Noelle."

"It's what I want."

There it was again. What she wanted, though nothing near what he wanted for her. Where had he lost touch? "I'll be back in a week for this . . . simple ceremony."

He kissed Noelle and followed Rick outside. William had intended to solidify the prenuptial agreement on the drive to the airport, but something in Rick's demeanor held him back. Noelle trusted this man, loved him. So he kept his own thoughts down the mountain.

United Airlines had one first-class ticket available to JFK. His chauffer, John, picked him up at the airport and drove him home. He spent the night replaying the previous day's conversation. Was there anything he could have said and didn't, anything that would have changed the outcome? When he slept he dreamed of Noelle as the winsome child she'd been.

The next morning, William went in early and stopped before Michael Fallon's secretary. "Please send Michael in."

"I'm sorry, Mr. St. Claire, Michael flew to Boston this morning on personal business."

William paused with his coat half removed. "He's second chair on the Witherston case."

She shook her head. "He turned it over to Malcolm. He's cleared his calendar for the next three days."

William removed his coat and hung it on the rack inside his office door. The personal business Michael had in Boston would only postpone the personal business he had with him. There had been too much left unspoken in Colorado. Even if Noelle had what she wanted, he deserved answers.

———

Michael stood in the gallery and smiled, the first true joy he'd felt in months. Another painting and across from that another, both bearing Noelle's signature. He had found the place that would lead him to her, but first, he allowed himself the pleasure of viewing her work. What he had told Clarice was true. He appreciated Noelle's subtle, exquisite detail. It so exemplified her.

He remembered her long, delicate fingers on the brush. Her technique had improved and certainly her productivity. When had she begun to paint like that? Oh, he knew she'd studied art, had watched her work, but these landscapes had depth and emotion. She should continue painting as a creative outlet, even market the work if she desired, make a name for herself in the art world. He would support her efforts completely.

But now it was time to act. He glanced at the woman behind the counter, and on cue, she approached. Her wool suit was classic, but she wore a crystal mounted in a silver dragon claw around her neck, a curious complement to the extreme lines of her jacket and skirt.

She smiled. "I see you have an eye for quality. Noelle St. Claire is new in the market but very promising."

Promising was a good word. He would buy the painting, present it to her as a symbol. But he needed to be careful, not too eager. If he'd read this woman right, he could play off her own signals. "Yes, there's something about it, as though . . . I'm meant to have it."

The creases deepened at the corners of her eyes. "Some of the pieces speak to me too. Maybe the artist leaves an aura to which sensitive minds respond."

Michael gave that idea respectful consideration. Of course, he would respond to anything Noelle had done. How could he not? "Very possible. And in this case even more so. I grew up with a Noelle St. Claire." It was almost true. William St. Claire was his spiritual father, if you wanted to look at it that way. "And she was an artist. What do you think the chance is it's the same person?"

"It's an uncommon name." The woman's gaze deepened as though trying to sense the connection. "I read once where a man recognized his father by the vibrations in the old man's sculptures. Maybe her paintings sent vibes that brought you in today."

"If that's true, I must take this one." Let her think she'd sold him. This was a partnership after all; she had information he needed.

"Very good." She took the painting from the easel and started toward the counter. "Not many people listen to their centers, but I think it's important to surround yourself with things that resonate."

"Oh, certainly." Michael joined her at the counter. "You wouldn't have an address or phone number where I could reach Noelle. . . ." He straightened his cuffs and pulled the wallet from his coat.

"I'm afraid not." She wrapped the painting in paper and taped it. "Her work is sent here from Colorado through an agent out there."

Colorado? Michael let his face fall. "Too bad. I had such a strong sense of . . . purpose." He met the woman's eyes, established contact, then showed the force of his disappointment. "What if the vibes were a call or signal?"

She fingered the crystal hanging at her sternum. "Do you think so?" She studied the wrapped painting, obviously missing its power but believing nonetheless. "Well, I do actually have an address where I send her money orders—no checks. Probably doesn't trust the government." She gave him a pensive look, then pulled out a large notebook, flipping to the back. "Yes, here it is. Have you something to write this down?"

Michael was ready with pen and personal organizer. He wrote the address with reverence. "Thank you very much." He flashed his smile as he took the painting in his arms. "You've been invaluable."

"I listen to my center too." The woman rested her hands on the counter.

He sensed her satisfied gaze as he went out. He had read her perfectly. And now—he clasped the address tightly and drew a jagged breath—he had Noelle.

# 28

Noelle read the thermometer through the kitchen window, an unseasonable forty-seven degrees. The January sunshine was brilliant on the snow, illuminating her world. The weight of the last few months no longer pressed her down, though she still could not believe Daddy had approved her decision. Facing him had not been the trial she anticipated, but it had stirred the shadows.

Maybe that was something she would live with. Maybe it would fade. The important thing was she had taken control. She pulled on the kid-leather gloves and western hat Rick had bought her in town, then turned as he came in.

"How do I look?"

He straddled her with his arms against the counter. "Like my bride. Almost." He tipped her hat back and kissed her. "You're all saddled up and ready to go."

"I hope my leg is strong enough . . . and Aldebaran's."

His mouth twitched. "You have to try sooner or later."

She went out and stopped short. Destiny stood tethered to the porch, nodding his head as she came close. She turned to Rick, brows raised.

He smiled. "He's ready for you now."

Her heart skipped a beat. She should be ecstatic, but body memories of the crushing pain, of Aldebaran thrashing, of Destiny's own power and his hooves . . .

Rick led her around to Destiny's side. "It'll be fine."

Why did he always say that? How did he know? But she slipped the toe of her boot in and swung up. "Are you coming?"

"I have work to do." He unwound the reins and handed them up.

"Rick, I'm not sure."

"After all that pestering?" He put on a falsetto. "I can take him myself, Rick. He wants me to ride him."

She slapped his hand for poking fun, but he was right. She had fought for just this moment. "Well, he does and I can—so there." She pulled up Destiny's head and brought him around. He responded to her gentlest touch as she nudged him with her heels. She remembered his gait, smooth and even, and matched her motion to it.

Past the apron, she smiled back at Rick, then urged the horse to a trot without posting. Her leg would not bear the strain, and besides, Rick preferred she ride the trot. She broke into a canter, then let him run up along the frozen stream. Rick knew she had to do this on her own, and she could.

She threw away her caution as Destiny ran over the snowy ground, his mane flying like red flames, like the flames Rick had fought and beaten. Not even nature could stand in his way. As they charged up the meadow, she exulted in the horse's power and speed, then slowed him and slipped into the shadow of the woods.

At the base of the shale slope, she looked up. Snow covered the gray mountainside completely, but she shivered with the memory of her rash behavior. Destiny carried her past without wavering, his young, spirited stride strong and sure. Coming back out, she found Rick at the high pasture and brought Destiny up beside him.

With the same hand that held the hammer, he pulled the U-shaped nail from his mouth and stood up. "How is it?"

"Wonderful. But you already knew that." She leaned down and kissed him. "What happened to the fence?"

He bounced the nail in his palm. "Mountain lion spooked the stallions last night and they kicked it up."

"Mountain lion! How do you know?"

"I saw the prints."

She looked across the pasture. "Will it come back?"

"Probably. But it's after easy prey. You're way too much work."

She stuck out her tongue.

He laughed. "What I wouldn't give for your society friends to see that."

She raised her chin. "Well, too bad. I haven't any."

He cupped her knee in his palm. "I'll see to it you know everyone on this mountain. All one hundred twenty-three of them." He rubbed the place where her thigh muscle joined her knee and the scar was just starting to heal. Then he felt from her knee to the top of her boot, checking her musculature. "Had enough?"

"My leg says yes." Of course, he'd already discovered that. Even in the stirrup it was shaking.

"It'll get stronger the more you work it. Do you want me to drive down, get you unsaddled?"

"No, I can manage."

He nodded. "Put him in the back end stall. I'll pick his hooves and curry him when I finish here."

Noelle nodded and rode down gently, reluctant to let the ride end but aware of the strain in her leg. She would be in pain tonight. She led Destiny into the dim stable and uncinched the saddle. "You are wonderful." She pulled the bit from his mouth and hung it on the wall. He nuzzled her as she ran her hands over his neck and side. "Thank you for carrying me so well." She walked down the row of stalls to Aldebaran.

The mare nickered, and Noelle reached a hand to her muzzle. "I'm glad you're all right now too." The sound of tires on the gravel. Rick must have finished. She went out, blinking in the glare of the sun on the snow, then froze.

"Hello, Noelle."

An apparition. A nightmare. A trick of her mind. It would vanish. But her heart pounded as her eyes adjusted, giving it substance. Michael.

Her throat went dry, and her breath came shallow. She tried to think. Would her leg be swift if she ran? It still shook from the exertion of riding Destiny. Would Rick hear if she screamed?

Michael took hold of her hands. She cried out at his touch.

"I'm not going to hurt you!" But his grip was tight.

Her eyes jerked to the meadow. Would Rick hear?

"Noelle." Michael's voice was calm. "I just want to talk to you."

Think. She had to think. "Daddy told you where I was?"

His brows raised. "I found you through the gallery . . . in Boston. Beautiful work, Noelle. I'm very impressed."

A weight settled in her stomach. Betrayed by her own work, her quest, the success she'd wanted. Her search for beauty and the divine.

"It's been so long." He stroked her hands with his fingers, a tremor in his voice.

She jerked away, calling, "Rick!" and lurched toward the house.

Michael grabbed her around the waist. "Stop it! What are you doing?" He trapped her against the side of the car.

She screamed, then thrashed as he clamped her mouth with his hand, slamming her head against the doorframe.

"Why are you acting like this?" He jerked open the car door.

She writhed and kicked. He smashed his fist to her head, and she fell to her knees in the snow. She screamed, but he kicked her side, kicked her stomach. She couldn't breathe. He gripped and shoved her into the car. From the glove box, he pulled a snub-nosed sidearm and pointed. "I'll use it, Noelle." The look in his eyes convinced her.

He held the revolver on her all the way around to the driver's side, then climbed in and jerked the car into reverse. Dazed and trembling, she gripped the armrest and gasped for breath.

———

Rick looked up from the fence. He stood and stared down the meadow, just able to make out a gray sedan between the house and barn, backing and pulling away. His heart started pounding in his chest. Had he heard a scream?

He lunged for the truck, shoved it into gear and flew down the meadow, skidding to a stop before the stable. "Noelle!" No answer. He rushed into the house. "Noelle!"

He grabbed the rifle from the closet and ran back to the truck. Fishtailing into the intersection in town, he stared around him. There was no sign of the sedan, and there were tracks both ways.

Left would take him down from the mountain, right, up the canyon into the national park. His hands were shaking. "God, help me," he groaned through clenched teeth, then wheeled the truck to the right and grabbed for his cell phone. He barked the nature of his emergency to the dispatcher as he headed up the canyon.

It had to be Michael; he would take her away, out of the mountains.

That was Rick's first thought, but his heart said go up, so he did. If he was wrong, if they'd gone down, he prayed the state police would stop them in time.

———

Michael rammed the car to a lower gear and skidded around the turn. He gunned the accelerator and sped up the winding highway. Noelle whimpered beside him. Why had she panicked? He wouldn't have hurt her. Didn't she know that? All he had wanted was to find her.

And what had she meant by "Daddy told you?" William knew where she was? He hadn't said a word about finding her. Could he have known all along? Had William turned on him too? Pressing the accelerator, he rounded the bend, then jammed the brake and swerved.

The deer thudded against the hood as the car veered and slammed into a snow-filled ravine. Michael landed hard against Noelle, and she made a sound like air through the pinched neck of a balloon. He smelled her fear. His adrenaline surged. They couldn't stay there. He pulled himself up by the steering wheel, then gripped her arm. "Come on."

She struggled, but the gun convinced her to stop. He pulled her out his door, sucking an acrid breath of burnt rubber. His hand shook as he held the gun to her temple. He'd wondered before what his limit was. Could he put a bullet through her head? Never. But he couldn't show her that. "Don't fight me, Noelle."

She went still, believing he could kill her, thinking him capable of shooting the one woman he loved more than anything in the world. What was wrong with her?

He scrambled up the slope, half dragging her behind. "I only wanted to talk to you. But you had to panic. You think I want to hurt you? Why would I hurt you? Why?" His hand hurt from hitting her. Why had she made him hit her? A flash of his father's fists on his mother's drunken face. He'd caught her with someone again.

Fury like acid in his veins. Who did Noelle have? Who had she called for? His throat closed in like a fist. All the same. They were all the same, even his beloved Noelle.

He forced her on until her breath rasped and she collapsed in the snow. "Get up."

"I can't," she gasped, holding her side.

He yanked her up, shoved her on, upward into the forest toward the peaks. He saw a trail marker and turned sharply. He must avoid public areas. He pulled Noelle the other way. She'd lost weight, so thin now he could feel the bones of her arm through her coat, but even so, she dragged on him. He let go and she collapsed. This time he let her lie there as he caught his own breath and searched the area.

The trees were dense, the snow a thin covering where the slope steepened, thick with pine needles and black nubby branches. It was quiet, no sound but the drip of sun-melted snow from the branches and an occasional flutter of a bird taking wing. His urgency lessened, but he gripped Noelle's shoulder again and pulled her up. "We can stop on level ground."

He moved off to the right, climbing toward a ridge with a huge boulder outcropping. That would do. He pressed them both up toward it, then let go of Noelle. She crumpled and lay on the frozen ground. Had he hurt her so badly? He'd only hit her once . . . or twice. It wasn't clear. He dropped to his knees beside her, stroked her head. This wasn't how he'd wanted it. "I didn't mean to hurt you."

She pressed her face to the ground.

"I had to get you away from . . . who was it you called?"

She didn't answer.

He jerked her up. "Who!"

"My fiancé!" She spoke through her teeth and angry tears streamed down her cheeks.

A cold spear pierced him. "So. There was someone else." Again the acid fury burning through his skin.

Her breath came sharp and jagged. "There wasn't then, but there is now."

He slapped her. "Liar!"

Her eyes dilated, and she breathed strangely, the way she had the last time, when it scared him so badly he'd left her alone. And she had run away. Was it an act?

He shook her. "Stop it." Could she even see him? "Noelle!"

A flicker of fight back in her eyes. "What are you going to do? Rape me again?"

"What are you talking about?" He gripped her jaw, pressing his fingers until she flinched. "Rape you?"

"They said I wouldn't remember, but I do."

"You're crazy." What delusion was this? Yes, he'd hit her, lost his temper and struck, but rape?

" 'Spoiled little rich girls need a lesson.' " Her voice was cold, threatening.

Michael started to shake. She *was* delusional. He gripped her shoulders and jerked her close. "Is that what you told William? Are you trying to destroy me?" He had feared that William would learn he'd struck his daughter, but this—this was insanity. "Listen to me, Noelle. I never raped you."

She suddenly spat and clawed. "Don't touch me, God. I'll tell Daddy." Her voice sounded infantile.

God? Had she called him God? He must have hit her too hard, must have . . . What had he done? She was . . . crazy. Searing anguish flooded him. He'd destroyed her. Somehow he'd destroyed the one perfect thing in his life.

One look at her, and everyone would know. It didn't matter that her claims were false. Who would believe him? William? The very thought of facing him—everything he'd fought for, everything he'd gained. His entire transformation meant nothing against a charge like rape. Rape meant prison, and he knew well enough what chance he'd have in there.

Tremors passed through in waves. He scoured his mind. Was it possible? Had he done worse than he thought in his blind rage? He staggered to his feet and stared down at her bruised face, bleeding lip. Was he the monster she believed him?

She pulled her knees to her chest, shaking violently. "I'll tell. I'll tell."

———

Rick scoured the highway, the slopes, the vales. His hands on the wheel were white-knuckled and his temple throbbed with terror coursing through him. Any one of the side roads could be the way, but he stayed to the main highway. *God. Jesus. Please.* He couldn't articulate more. But God knew his need.

There—off to the right—the gray sedan sunken sideways into the ravine beside the road. He jammed the brakes and slid to a stop, lurched out of the truck and ran. The car was empty.

But there were tracks heading up the mountainside. He pulled the rifle out of the cab and started up. Some two hundred yards above the road, he heard noise below and looked back. The sheriff and a female deputy had found the vehicle. One spoke into their radio, then they were climbing the slope behind him. Michael Fallon had better hope they found him first.

———

Pain throbbed in her head and ribs. Noelle's leg burned and when she tried to breathe something wheezed in her lungs. Her stomach churned. She imagined she heard voices, but only dully. Her mind was shutting down and she welcomed the stupor. She was in a room no larger than a closet. Maybe it was a closet, though it was empty of everything but her. If she didn't move, didn't make a sound, the bad man wouldn't come back. *"Are you God?" "Yeah, kid. I'm God."*

She slid down the hard surface behind her and curled into a ball. If she could just hide where God wouldn't find her. She tried to make herself smaller, to fit into the very corner. She pressed her eyes shut, hoping never, never to see God again.

———

Bounding up the slope, Rick saw her. His chest seized. Noelle lay curled up on the ground as Michael scrambled over the boulders above, sprinting up and away. Rage burning, he raised the rifle and sighted Michael. Something tackled him from the side, and he landed hard. Rick fought back, but the deputy restrained him. Michael was getting away. Rick hollered, "Go! I won't follow."

The man yanked the rifle from his hands, then leapt up and ran. Rick crept to Noelle, took her into his arms, and pressed her face to his chest. "Are you okay?"

She didn't respond, just clenched the collar of her coat and drew her knees up to her chest.

"Noelle?" Did she even hear him? It must be shock or . . .

Two state troopers made their way up the mountain. One stopped beside them. Rick looked up, and the man motioned. They had to get Noelle out. This wasn't over yet. Gently, Rick raised her to her feet. She could hardly support herself, and he guessed her leg was damaged again. He would have carried her, but the terrain was too steep and slick, so he bore as much of her weight beside him as he could.

*God, help me.* His fury had chilled to cold rage, worse than anything he'd known before. If he met Michael Fallon now, he would crush him with his own hands. The potency of the thought terrified him.

———

*"Where do I dump her?"* God speaking, then another. *"Leave her at the lions."* Her heart raced. Lions would eat her! Something was wrong with her leg, but they kept making her walk. She didn't want to be alone with God. God did bad things. God was bad.

"We can call for an ambulance."

"I'll take her in my truck."

She knew that second voice but didn't look. Someone urged her into the cab. She smelled hay. Did they feed the lions hay? Shards of pain shot along the side of her knee, but she held herself still, silent until she climbed out of the truck and limped toward the hospital. Recognition flickered. She'd been there before.

Because of her police escort, her companion took her through the emergency room directly into a curtained cubicle. He helped her onto the paper-covered bed. His arms were strong, his hands calloused and long-fingered.

"Sir, would you wait outside?"

The man beside her hesitated. Noelle looked up. Rick.

"Sir?"

He was waiting for her to speak, but what was she supposed to say?

"I'll be right outside." He squeezed her hand and left.

The woman who spoke was huge, not obese, but of Amazon proportions. "I'm Sharon." She pulled the curtain shut. "I know you've been through a lot, but we have procedures we need to follow. This is all to help you out, to get the man who abducted you. Do you understand?"

Noelle nodded mutely.

"I need you to remove your clothes so I can record injuries. Here's a smock. I'll be right back."

Trembling, Noelle took her clothing off, then slipped into the thin cotton smock. She slid down to the floor between the wall and a heavy drawer unit on wheels, then dropped her face to her knees. She jolted when the curtain opened, but it was the same large woman, Sharon, who stopped, then tugged the curtain closed behind her.

"All right, honey, stand up now."

Noelle didn't move. The woman reached down and helped her up. She photographed the bruises on her face, the cut at the side of her mouth, the swelling on her temple. Then she photographed the bruising on her ribs and abdomen.

The lions were stone. They wouldn't eat her. But they were so big! She huddled into the hollow of one animal's side. *"Don't tell,"* God said. *"If you tattle these lions turn real and tear you to pieces."*

Noelle grabbed her stomach and retched. Sharon scrambled for a plastic, kidney-shaped dish. The hand on her shoulder was heavy and warm, and the palm had a soft, spongy feel. The spasms stopped. As the woman leaned over, the gold cross at her neck dangled. Noelle fixed her eyes on it, remembering the cross in Rick's church.

Sharon handed her a paper towel for her mouth. "Just bear with me one more minute." She cleaned the cut beside her mouth, then stepped back. "Are there other injuries I need to know about, honey?"

Noelle knew what she was asking. She shook her head. Not this time.

*"Honey?"* The woman seemed small, calling to her from the steps between the lions. *"What are you doing there, honey? Are you lost?"* Don't tell—don't tell—don't tell.

Sharon gave her a packet of pills and a glass of water. "Just a little painkiller for the cuts and bruises. And you can get dressed."

She swallowed them, amazed they didn't come right back up.

"They'll finish the report outside." Sharon paused, touched Noelle's shoulder with her warm hand. "I'll pray for you." It was almost a whisper.

Noelle looked into her eyes. "Don't." She didn't want anyone talking to God about her.

She waited for the woman to leave, then got dressed. With all the injuries the photographs documented, she should hurt, feel something. She opened the door, and a different woman took her to a tiny room. A desk wrapped the walls, with computer equipment and stacking files. A man stood when she entered. "Ms. St. Claire, I'm Detective Spaulding. I need to get a statement from you."

Someone came in behind her, and Noelle turned. It was Rick. She turned back to the detective. "All right."

He motioned her to a molded plastic chair. "What you say will be recorded. Please be as specific as you can. I know it may be difficult, but the more you tell us now, the better case we have against your assailant. Do you understand?"

She nodded.

He pushed the button on a handheld tape recorder. "Please begin by stating your name."

"Noelle St. Claire."

"Please describe the events of this day, January 4, 2002, from the beginning."

Noelle began hoarsely, then cleared her throat. "I went into the stable . . ."

"At your home?"

"Yes . . . well, no . . . at Rick's ranch." She glanced at Rick, who stood against the wall just inside the door.

"Rick?" Detective Spaulding prompted.

"Rick Spencer. I've been living there . . . boarding there since last July."

He nodded. "Please continue."

"I went into the stable and unsaddled Destiny, the horse I had been riding, and when I came out . . ." Her voice shook. "He was there."

"Who was there, Ms. St. Claire?"

"God." No, that wasn't right. She saw the glance Rick and the detective shared.

Detective Spaulding straightened. "I'm sorry, could you repeat that?"

Bile rose in her throat. "It was Michael. Michael Fallon."

"Are you acquainted with Michael Fallon?"

She nodded.

"Please answer aloud." Detective Spaulding held the recorder a little closer.

"Yes."

"Did you speak with him?"

Noelle pictured the glaring sunlight, Michael standing there like a nightmare. "I asked him if my father had told him where I was."

"Where you were?"

"I ran from him the last time."

The detective leaned forward. "The last time? Has he assaulted you before?"

Noelle closed her eyes, starting to shake. "Yes."

"Did you press charges?"

*"God is everywhere, kid. And he knows everything. If you tell, I'll find you again. You know I will."*

"No. I ran away."

He considered her with a flat, opaque gaze, then said, "Please describe what happened after you saw him at the stable."

She swallowed. Her voice sounded distant, a stranger's voice. It didn't have to be hers. "He grabbed me and hit me and forced me into the car. He had a gun."

The detective made a note on his paper. "And then?"

"He drove into the park. We hit a deer and crashed, then he made me get out and climb the mountain."

"He had the gun with him?"

She nodded, then remembered the tape. "Yes."

Rick put a hand on her shoulder. She scarcely felt it. Sharon came in and handed Detective Spaulding a note. He glanced, then set it down and returned his attention.

"What was your previous relationship with Michael Fallon?"

"We were engaged to be married."

Detective Spaulding leaned back in his chair, tapping his fingers on his mouth. "Was that before the previous assault?"

"Yes. No. I left when he grew violent."

"Did he sexually assault you?"

*"Can you show me where he touched you? Here's a picture. Just touch the places on the picture."*

Michael's face in the woods. *"What are you talking about? I never raped you."*

She glanced at Rick, then stared at the tape recorder. "I don't know."

Detective Spaulding waited. "Take a minute to think about it."

"I'm confused."

He pressed the button on the recorder. "It's very important that you describe as accurately as possible everything that happened, this time and the last." He turned the machine back on.

Rick said, "Tell him what you told me, Noelle. Tell him about the hawk."

He probably hoped to trigger her memory, but she shook her head. "It doesn't make sense. There are pieces I can't see and things I don't remember." And the lines between real and unreal had blurred unrecognizably.

"How long ago was the first assault?"

She pictured the closet walls towering over her. She felt so small. But . . . had Michael locked her in a closet? The picture of the hawk.

That was real, but she didn't know what had happened while she stared at the hawk. The other images didn't fit.

"July. It was the beginning of July, just before I came to the ranch."

"Do you recall the date?"

She shook her head. "I don't know how many days I traveled." It was sounding crazy. She could tell by the cop's face, he was frustrated. "I left a message on Daddy's voicemail."

"Okay. We'll check that out. Is there anything else you can tell us?"

She shook her head.

Detective Spaulding turned off the machine. "Thank you very much, Ms. St. Claire. I promise you, we'll see this through."

She stood up. "May I go now?"

"Yes."

She took a step and winced. Funny she would feel her leg, with everything else so numb. Rick took her arm, led her out. Now she recognized the truck; Rick's, of course. She felt drained of words, and Rick didn't speak. Maybe he sensed there was nothing left to say. She was so numb it didn't matter. Her head felt like fuzz. Maybe the pills they'd given her for pain.

The ranch was dark when they got back. Rick flicked on a light. "Do you want something? Tea?"

She shook her head. "I'm just tired."

With his hand on her elbow, he walked her up the stairs and into her room.

She sat down on the bed. "Have they found him?"

He sat down beside her. "Not that I've heard. But there are two officers outside. There's no way he can get to you again." Rick curled his arm around her shoulders, drew her to his side. He rested his cheek on the top of her head. "Noelle." His breath warmed her hair. "Is there anything I can do?"

He must feel helpless. Rick who always had the answer. Rick the doer. "No." She pulled away and lay down, curled on her side.

He stood up to give her legs room. "I'll let you rest, then. I'll be close. Call me if you need anything."

She had screamed his name, and he hadn't heard, hadn't come. But the rest of it, the rest was becoming a blur. Her eyelids scratched like sandpaper, but she couldn't sleep. Images crowded in, images she could not reference. *"I'm just not sure, Mr. St. Claire. Sometimes with severe*

*trauma the victim forgets. It gets locked away. A protection mechanism.
Then again . . ."* And here the woman looked at her. *"She may have
nothing to tell us. We assume abuse with child abductions. But as you've
pointed out, this was not a typical case with your extenuating circumstances.
There was a different methodology and purpose."*

Noelle stared at the log wall. Her eyes changed focus and made a
double image, superimposed. *"Why won't she talk? How long will it be
before she speaks?"*

*"I'm sorry, Mr. St. Claire. I just don't know."*

*"Well, what do you know!"* And her mama's hand on Daddy's arm.
*"I want to take her home now. I want to take my baby home."*

Noelle closed her eyes. What were these thoughts? Where did they
come from? Why now?

---

Rick dropped to a chair in the kitchen, rubbed his face, then rested
his head in his hand. The night stretched, but he was too shaken to
think, too angry to pray, too spent to feel. He just sat. With the dawn
tempering the darkness he dropped his head to his arm. *Lord. . . .* But
he couldn't get any further.

The phone jarred him, and he grabbed it. "Yes?"

Detective Spaulding's voice. Rick released a slow breath. "Yes, I'll
tell her. Thank you." He hung up the phone and went upstairs, listened
at Noelle's door, but the room was silent, so he went to his own room,
showered, dressed, and came back out.

He cracked Noelle's door. She still slept. He didn't want to wake
her. The news could wait. He went back downstairs, pulled on his
coat, and went to feed the stock. Through the motions of his routine
he found some comfort. When he returned to the house he heard
the shower running upstairs, and went to the kitchen to make coffee.
Twenty minutes later the water still ran upstairs, so he leaned on the
counter, watching another ten minutes click by on the clock.

---

Noelle stood in the shower, the water running hot, tepid, then cool
down her back. Her bruised body ached. Her mind did not. Shutting
off the water, she dried herself and pulled on a sweater and jeans and
went downstairs.

Rick leaned on the counter in the kitchen, a mug of coffee cupped in his hands. His face was drawn, and she felt a ripple of emotion. He set the cup down and reached for her, but she didn't take his hand. His arm dropped to his side. "Detective Spaulding called. They found Michael shortly after we left the mountain. He . . . shot himself before they could take him."

Another ripple. "He's dead?"

"Yes."

Dead. She folded her hands together. There was no sense of victory, no sweeping relief, no sorrow. Michael was dead. She closed her eyes. "It's over, then." And that was how she felt. Like a closed book put back on the shelf.

He started toward her. "Noelle . . ."

"Rick, I need to go home."

He stopped, then drew a deep breath. "Okay. I'll get us—"

"Alone." She hoped he wouldn't argue and make it harder than it was.

He leaned back into the counter. "Noelle . . ."

She looked away. "Will you call my father?" If he cared at all, he'd let her leave without a fight.

He waited too long to answer.

"I'd appreciate it if you called. He'll arrange a jet."

"Fine." His voice was flat. "How long will you stay?"

"I don't know." She unfolded her hands and went upstairs to pack. All her clothes fit inside the tote she'd brought from New York and the duffel Rick had provided for their trip to Iowa. She slid the pine box that held her paints onto the dresser top. She wouldn't need them. Then she went down, set the two bags by the front door, and stood at the great room window. Three hours later, they arrived at the airport.

"You can leave me at the curb."

But he parked and got out of the truck. He carried her bags to the counter, then walked her to the security checkpoint. When she set her purse on the X-ray conveyor belt, she turned. Rick stood, wanting, she knew, to embrace her before she left. But his arms remained at his sides. She kept them there by her will.

"Good-bye." She passed through the metal detector and left him behind.

# 29

William climbed out of the limousine, which had been cleared to the tarmac where the firm's jet had taxied to a stop. Waiting there, he felt more shaken than he could remember, worse than when Adelle had died.

That, he could not have prevented. This . . . from Michael. Knowing what William had told him of her earlier abduction, how could he do it again? How could he strike and injure and molest her? And how could he have fooled him so completely?

He watched the door of the jet, thankful it did not open immediately. He needed to prepare. How could he prepare? Then she was there, looking like glass, and there was nothing he could do to hide what he felt.

John had come up beside him and took her bags to the trunk. William opened the car door for Noelle himself. They were silent all the way to the estate. He walked her inside the house, then asked, "Do you want to rest?"

"No. I want to talk."

They went together into the library, and Noelle sat down in the leather wing chair. She stared at the portrait of Adelle. Did she remember her mother? William sat on the matched chair angled to the right of hers.

Eyes still fixed on the portrait, she asked, "What did Rick tell you?"

"All he knew." William's hand shook on the armrest. He put it in his lap. How could Michael have deceived him? Or had he deceived himself, believed he'd taken an angry, damaged youth and made him . . . what? The perfect mate for his daughter, the ascendant to his throne?

The anger he'd felt since Rick Spencer's phone call drained when he saw Noelle. He felt impotent, bare. "Why didn't you tell me? The first time?"

"He was your protégé, Daddy. Your perfect specimen."

"And you are my daughter." Didn't she know how he loved her? "Your best interest has always been my first concern." He gripped the curved wooden ends of the chair arms.

She turned her eyes on him, lashes drooping. "I know you did your best. Anyway, it doesn't matter now. I just want this put behind me." She stroked her hair back from her face, let it fall over her shoulder. So like Adelle. "May I have the bungalow?"

"Of course." He had ordered it readied for her. Then he realized what she was saying. "What about Rick?"

Noelle looked again at her mother's portrait. Make the eyes blue, and Noelle could be the woman he'd fallen so crazy in love with all those years ago in Paris. She could be Adelle. He'd felt so helpless when she died, so utterly useless. He felt it now with his daughter. Was she giving up all she'd fought for days ago, as Adelle had lost the fight for her very life?

Still gazing at her mother's face, she said, "I don't know."

————

As soon as Noelle walked into the bungalow, she knew it wouldn't work. Michael was too present there. She imagined she smelled his cologne. She walked into the bedroom and looked into the closet filled with her designer wardrobe—mostly Michael's choices.

Michael had shot himself. Why? Yes, it would have been a nightmare for all of them, but he was the brilliant schemer, the dazzling protégé. He had fooled Daddy, fooled them all. He could have pulled it off so no jury believed such a charming, successful man could do the things her fragmented memory suggested he had.

But he was dead. They were flying his body home for burial. Was she glad? She didn't feel that. Sorry? She didn't feel that either. But as Noelle looked over the gowns and outfits he had given her, reaching out to stroke one silk sleeve, she shuddered. She would never wear it again, none of them. She would donate them somewhere.

She went back out to the great room, an open, flowing space that made the remainder of the bungalow seem larger than it was. Again she sensed him. They'd spent too many evenings by the gas fire after dinner with Daddy. And she felt a hovering of wings. Only a shadow, but enough to drive her back to the main house with a bag on each shoulder.

Daddy pulled open the door himself. "Noelle?"

"May I stay here instead?"

"Of course." He took the duffel and tote and turned to Donita. "Make up Noelle's bed."

Noelle followed him to the bar in the study. He poured them each a glass of sherry. As she took the first sweet-fire sip, she thought of Morgan, then that, too, sank into the cotton of her mind. She walked around the room, studying the shelves and shelves of books. Daddy's world. She breathed their scent, not musty but more of a glue-and-leather smell.

A tap on the door and Donita ducked in. "Your room's ready, Ms. Noelle."

"Thank you." Noelle turned. "I'd like the closet of the bungalow cleaned out tomorrow. Donate the clothes." Or keep them. Though Donita was at least ten years older, they were similar in size, and she guessed the woman would help herself. She didn't care as long as she never saw them again.

"Yes, ma'am."

Her father cleared his throat. "Will you move over there after that?"

She shrugged. "We'll see. For now my room will be fine." She thought of the small log room at Rick's, where she'd felt so safe and protected. Then a fresh image entered, a new flash of an old memory. *"Noelle, come out of your room. Come see what Daddy and I have for you." "I don't want to, Mama."* And her mother's hand on her head. *"It's over, Noelle."* But it wasn't.

She went up to the room she'd occupied as a child. For a moment she thought she smelled her mother's fragrance. She must be losing her mind. First Michael's, now . . . but it was gone. She looked at the white steel bed, the Chippendale dresser. She crossed to it, ran her finger over the inlaid wood of her old jewelry box. She opened it, and the little ballerina stood up and turned to the tinkling notes of the "Music Box Dancer."

"*Thank you, Mama. Thank you, Daddy.*" *The little dancer could hide, just like she wanted to. She clutched the box to her chest.* "*Now will you come out of your room?*" Noelle touched the dancer's head, felt it turn beneath her finger. She stretched out her hand. Slowly, she slipped Rick's diamond from her finger, set it inside, then closed the lid.

There was a tap on the door, and Daddy spoke through the wood. "Noelle, Rick's on the phone."

"Thank you." She sat on the edge of the bed and picked up the receiver. "Hello?"

"Hi. I wanted to make sure you made it in all right, that your flight was okay."

"It was fine. Thank you."

She heard his breath. "I miss you."

She swallowed. "I'm sorry. Thank you for calling." She replaced the receiver, amazed to feel nothing at all.

---

Rick hung up and slammed his fist into the wall. He split the knuckles, but he hardly realized it. He went out and stabled the horses for the night. He slept, rose early, and worked hard, pushing himself.

He called again two days later, the day they would have married. Her voice was soft on the line. "I'm sorry, Rick. I know it's not your fault, but it's a mistake to think we can continue."

"I love you. That's not going to change." *Please, God, let her know how much.*

She said nothing.

"I want to do something, Noelle. There must be something."

Still she wouldn't answer.

"Do you want me to come see you?"

"No. I'm sorry, Rick."

He held the receiver long after she'd hung up. Then he sat, going over and over in his mind the memories of her. He saw her perched on the stallion like a wild thing. He felt her, limp and broken, as he'd carried her after the fall. He closed his eyes and tasted their first kiss, salty with her tears, the night she told him about Michael . . . and trusted him.

Some of the memories brought a ghost of a smile, some hurt so bad he could barely stand it, but he played them again and again like a junkie who couldn't get enough. Had Morgan felt that way? Shaking his head, he ran his hand over his face. *Oh, God . . .* What would he do without her?

When morning came he went outside. The air was cold, caught in the stubble of beard on his chin and upper lip. He cared for the horses in the stable, then drove up to check the stallions. He was building them a shelter, so he pulled his tools from the truck and set to work. He took three days to finish it.

He didn't hear from Noelle, so he started on the work he'd intended to do after the wedding. He ripped out all but the support walls in the upper level of the house. He had drawn plans to restructure it in a design more conducive to raising a family. He would modify it to suit Noelle if she had other ideas. Joseph Gregg, his neighbor to the south, offered to help, but Rick declined. With pulleys and levers he could do it alone. And right now he didn't trust himself with anyone.

The master suite took up the back quadrant, with four smaller bedrooms along the landing. One for Noelle's studio. At least until they needed it for kids. Rick wiped his sleeve across his forehead and chugged a soda. He placed a new board and nailed it into place. Maybe he should call again.

He told himself that every day, even sometimes picked up the phone to dial. Then he'd hang it up and give her one more day. Maybe tomorrow she'd call or today if it was still early. Then he wouldn't be forcing her. He'd told her how he felt. Told her he wouldn't change. She could count on that.

He strained to drag a log into position for the next wall. He was losing the daylight, and he had yet to eat. He ought to stop and fix food, but he aligned the log with the chalk line on the floor and took out a spike. He raised the sledge and drove it, then moved down three feet and did it again.

That evening, exhausted after five weeks of labor, he lay in bed in the dark. It was worst then. Who was he kidding? Noelle hadn't called, wouldn't call. She wanted no part of him. But he missed her so much. *Lord, where did I fail? Why did you allow this? Why, Lord?* His whole body ached with fatigue and longing. His spirit trembled with rage. Hands clenched, he pictured her crumpled on the mountain. Death was too good for Michael Fallon, too easy. He'd destroyed everything.

*Why didn't you keep her safe, Lord? Or help me to?* He thrashed to his side. He should never have left her alone. He should have heard, should have known. But how could he? He was only a man. But God had known . . . and kept silent. That's what he couldn't reconcile. Had everything he'd done, believed, trusted, been wrong?

———

William watched his daughter across the table as she conversed with the guests he had asked to dinner.

"Yes, Julliard is a fine school. I enjoyed my studies there." The turn of her shoulder, the direction of her gaze completely excluded the young man he had invited. She acted as though the Palmers were the only guests present.

Adam Palmer nodded. "I understand you're quite talented."

"You've been talking to Daddy." She delivered that with just the right tone, and the Palmers laughed. Young Martin Sternham joined in, for all the good it would do him.

"Would you play for us?" Celeste Palmer fingered the silk scarf she wore to hide the wrinkles at her neck, and her four-carat diamond shimmered.

Noelle folded her napkin beside her plate. "All right." She stood, and they followed her into the drawing room. As she played, her fingers danced lightly one minute and rose in crescendo to snapping power the next.

William's chest swelled with pride. She played with precision, striking each note without error. Of course, she practiced hour after hour to perfect her skill. Every day he came home from the office to hear her working at the keyboard, and it reminded him of her lessons when she was a child. He'd procured the finest instructor, a woman trained at the Rimsky-Korsakov Conservatory in St. Petersburg.

Noelle finished and Celeste clapped her fingertips together. "Oh, darling, that was marvelous. You could play professionally."

"But why would she?" Adam tapped his wife's knee. "That's a grueling schedule."

No more grueling than Noelle pushed herself, William thought. He wished Martin would find his tongue. Though an associate at the firm—Harvard graduate no less—he was reduced to idiocy by Noelle. She stood up and excused herself, leaving him to his guests. William hoped they wouldn't linger.

Noelle closed herself into the library and picked up Anne Tyler's *Patchwork Planet*. Right now she could identify with the protagonist's rejection of his wealthy heritage. *Yes, Mr. Palmer. No, Mrs. Palmer. Of course, Daddy.* She flounced onto the couch and opened the book.

Her father found her there. "You were enchanting tonight."

"Was I?" She didn't look up from her book. The son had just set fire to the dining room curtains.

"What did you think of Martin Sternham?" He took the book from her hands and set it on the table.

"I thought nothing of him." Noelle rubbed a spot on her index fingernail.

"You were cruel, and I think you enjoyed it."

She sat up. "Daddy, I want you to stop inviting every eligible bachelor to dinner and disguising them with old people."

He laughed but it was forced. "Then, what am I to do?"

She stood up and walked to the diamond-paned window. "Let me lead my life the way I want to."

"Noelle . . ."

She looked back over her shoulder. "I'm considering an apartment. Something in Manhattan." She said it to jerk his cord. She could hardly leave the house these days. But Daddy wouldn't know that. He'd resumed his normal hours, and they saw little of each other, except on these evenings where he tried to auction her off.

"An apartment would only seclude you more."

Maybe Daddy was more aware than she thought.

"I think you should see a psychiatrist."

She smiled. "To learn what's wrong with me?"

He sat down on the end of the conversation couch, crossed his leg over his knee, no doubt hoping she'd complete the semicircle so they could chat. "Not what's wrong, Noelle, but how to make it right."

She picked up the Venetian-glass paperweight from the windowsill. It always amazed her how heavy glass could be when it broke so easily. "We've discussed this already. I don't need a shrink."

"Shrink." He snorted. "A counselor, Noelle. A therapist . . . a priest!"

She slammed down the glass dome. "A priest, Daddy?" She started toward him. "What priest? Perhaps you'd have one to recommend?"

He squirmed. "Maybe I would if I thought it would do any good."

"Who, for instance?" She waved her hand. "In your vast experience?"

"You could start with your mother's priest, who baptized you, Father Matthis at the cathedral."

Her mouth dropped open. She couldn't hide her surprise. "What?"

He waved a hand. "It was your mother's foolishness." He looked as though he regretted his words.

But it struck a chord. "She took me to church?" "We're going to God's house, Noelle."

Daddy dropped his hands to his knees. "Your mother was pious. We had a ceremony. Dribbled water on your head. So what?"

"And that's the only time I went?"

"She took you on Sundays. You were too little to remember."

But she did remember. The windows . . . bright, colorful stained-glass windows. Noelle started to shake. Why? Michael was gone. There was nothing to fear.

"But after—" He caught himself and cleared his throat.

"After what?"

He gripped his hands together. "Sit down, Noelle."

"I don't want to sit. I want to know what else you haven't told me."

He removed his dinner coat and hung it over the back of the couch. "It's not what I haven't told you. It's what you don't remember."

She felt her throat closing in. What didn't she remember? A red-robed man, giant wings, someone grabbing her from behind. A hand clamped to her mouth. "Mama!"

"There was an incident."

She wanted to slap him. Stop talking jargon! "What happened to me, Daddy?"

"You were abducted when you were five years old. From the church while your mother was distracted."

Her legs felt like gauze. "Why?" She dropped to the end of the half-circle couch. "Why did they take me?" He waited so long to answer, she turned to him. "Daddy?"

"They wanted me off a case."

It felt like a knife inside her. She'd been taken, terrified, and—A door slammed in her mind. "What case?"

"It doesn't matter."

"Doesn't matter? They took me because of you, and it doesn't matter?" Her words pierced his control, brought pain to his eyes.

"It was a federal case I was prosecuting. We had broken a ring of Russian-Mafia drug smugglers. Our man had deep connections."

The strange accent. She shuddered. No wonder she hated anything close to a Russian accent. Frustration welled up. How much of her life—her likes and dislikes, her fears and aversions—were based on this "incident"?

She stood up, arms shaking at her sides. "What did you do?"

His eyes came up, met hers. "I removed myself." He folded and unfolded his hands.

"Compromised your principles?"

"They—had—my—daughter." His voice shook.

Images flashed. Stone walls, towering pillars. She tried to focus on what Daddy had said. It was his fault she'd been taken. She forked her fingers into her hair, walked to the window. Her mother's portrait was reflected in the cold glass, black with night. *Whisper in God's house, Noelle.* Mama's hand holding hers as they knelt one knee, then stood. Mama told her to wait in the seat, but Noelle wandered over to see the window.

She pressed her eyes shut. It was Michael the Archangel fighting the devil. The devil was black and looked like a lizard with a man's head and bat wings. But the angel was all in red, with a thick muscular leg showing through the cut in his robe. His foot was pressed to the devil's neck and he held a sword upraised. *Michael the Archangel. Michael.*

She'd been standing under the window while Mama talked to someone behind a curtain. The angel was supposed to be good. But he looked so fierce. And then someone had grabbed her. But the hand was so tight on her mouth she couldn't breathe. She kicked, but he was too big. He lifted her, carried her. He was bigger than Daddy, bigger than anyone she knew. *"Are you God?"* He shoved her into the car. *"Yeah, kid. I'm God."*

His accent. Her whole being shuddered as she glimpsed the face in her memory. Not Michael's, another. She put a hand over her mouth and fought waves of nausea.

Daddy stood and came to her. "They said you had blocked it out, a protective amnesia. You seemed . . . after a while you seemed all right. You smiled, you played, you . . . Only your sessions with the psychiatrist upset you. What point was there in continuing? What point in making you remember?"

Her mind slammed shut again. "You were right, Daddy. What point was there?"

CHAPTER

# 30

Rick walked to the upstairs landing, stopped, and looked around him. It was amazing what reconfiguring shape and dimension could do. Instead of independent rooms along a hall, it was a gathering of interconnected spaces. Instead of the linear motel feel, his house now felt like a home. He had built the house practically but now altered it for beauty, imagining it as Noelle would see it with her artist's eye.

Except none of it mattered. He stood there as if he'd woken up in someone else's house by accident. He'd never felt that way before, as though he didn't belong in the very house he'd built log by log. Standing there, he felt like a stranger. He'd never minded being alone, hadn't really felt alone when he was. He'd felt complete and satisfied, and time didn't come at him like some enemy he had to battle off.

He knew his place, his routine. Knew what he needed to do, and he did it. He'd made his ranch a place folks could relax and enjoy themselves in the beauty of nature. He'd protected it from fire and storm, giving both the land and the animals the care required. Now, looking around, he felt as though it had all been a dream. This was reality, this aching loneliness.

He tugged on the jeans that had slipped down his hips, then realized he needed to tighten the belt. It had slid into its well-worn notch when he dressed. Now he moved it one hole tighter. Then Rick rubbed the back of his neck, working out the crick that had formed, and started down the staircase he had widened and curved into the main room.

He slid his hand down over the maple banister he'd built, stained, and oiled to replace the straight pine railing. It deposited him into the one room that had hardly changed.

Bright summer sunlight spilled through the front window in a golden splash over the coffee table. Dust motes rode the beam to his Bible and collected on its cover. Rick crossed the room and picked it up, then wiped the dust with the roll of his sleeve. He flipped the Bible open and felt the urging. He could read it, he could study it, he could even believe it. He just couldn't understand it. And besides, there was a bigger issue. Whatever else, he was no hypocrite. With his heart so hard, how could he seek God's presence?

He laid the book down, went to the kitchen and swigged a cup of reheated coffee, then headed outside. He saddled Destiny and rode up to the high corral where he had started installing the metal gate before he ran out of daylight the night before. He tethered the horse to graze and set to work.

Sweat dampened his brow. He raised his hat and wiped his forehead with the back of his gloved hand. He tightened the bolt one final tug, then stood and swung the gate. It moved smoothly, and he stuck the wrench into the saddlebag, then turned and saw Pastor Tom puffing up the meadow on his stocky, rheumatic legs.

Rick considered meeting him halfway to save him the climb but remained where he was. It was the pastor's idea to come. Rick hadn't asked him. Tom waved, too breathless to greet him, and swiped a handkerchief over his forehead. The July sun was hot. He ran a hand through his thinning gray thatch and looked around. "Sure is beautiful up here so close to God."

Rick didn't respond.

Pastor Tom knew better than to hedge this issue. "I guess you know why I've come."

Rick jerked one side of his mouth. "You're drumming up business?"

The pastor smiled, but it was halfhearted. "It's been months, Rick."

Rick gathered the hammer and lever and slid those into the saddlebag as well. Months. He tried not to think of time in chunks, measured amounts.

"What's keeping you away?"

Rick cinched the bag.

Pastor Tom wiped the back of his neck, then shoved the handkerchief into his pocket. "Now is when you need your faith."

Rick leaned on the corral and looked up the slope. "It's not faith, Tom. It's forgiveness."

"Of whom?"

Rick frowned. "You need to ask?"

"There are several possibilities. God? Noelle? Her assailant, yourself . . ."

"Myself?" Rick turned.

The pastor sat down on an upturned stump. "Ah, Rick. Nothing's as simple as it seems. When the fabric of life frays, not just one thread is affected, but many. When Noelle was hurt, you were all hurt. Perhaps her attacker most of all."

Rick gripped the board. "Michael Fallon?"

"You have no window to his soul."

"I don't care."

The pastor gripped his knees. "Judgment is a dangerous thing. Brings out our own darkness."

Rick slammed the top board of the corral. "Are you suggesting I'd hurt Noelle as he did?"

Tom stood up. "I'm suggesting that sin is sin, and unless you are sinless, you'd do well to forgive."

It was true. No arguing that. Just humanly impossible. The main thing Rick felt these days was anger. He'd given Noelle his heart and soul. . . . And maybe that was it. Had he given her what should have been God's? Or worse, become to her what God should have been? If he'd shared his faith instead of his love, could she have stood against the blow instead of shrinking into the voice that apologized but had nothing else to say?

Rick turned away. "I'm sorry, Tom. I'm just not there."

"Then let me be there for you. All of us. Come to church tomorrow."

Rick shook his head. It would be false.

"Then I'll keep praying."

Rick took a shovel from the rifle case on Destiny's saddle, unfolded the handle, and scooped a pile of manure onto the heap outside the corral. He kept shoveling while the pastor made his way back down. There was a time when Rick would have appreciated the prayers. Now it seemed so futile. When he finished mucking the corral, he rode Destiny down.

Nearing the house, he was surprised to see Morgan leaning against his Corvette parked in the yard. Rick swung down from the stallion's back and shook Morgan's hand.

"I see you tamed him." Morgan nodded toward the horse.

"Yeah." But it was Noelle who had tamed them both.

Morgan smiled. "How's life?"

"Ask Pastor Tom; he's got all the answers."

Morgan sobered. "I'm sorry about Noelle."

Rick slapped the dust from his jeans. "So . . . what are you doing here?"

"Just passing by." Morgan tossed his car keys in his palm.

"Mom sent you."

Morgan laughed. "No, I swear. Just thought I'd drop in for a while. You don't have any beautiful guests we can fight over, do you?"

"I don't take guests anymore."

"Mmm." Morgan nodded.

"Well, I'm busy." Rick tugged Destiny's rein.

"What's with the beard?"

Rick rubbed his jaw and shrugged.

Morgan said, "Stable the horse and have a beer with me."

"I don't have any beer."

Morgan reached behind his seat. "I do."

Rick studied his brother. What was his point? Was this some conciliatory gesture? But then, he shrugged, why not? He put Destiny into the small corral and followed Morgan inside.

Morgan set the twelve-pack on the table beside the door and looked around him. "I guess you *have* been busy." He climbed the stairs. "Wow. Done some major remodeling." He walked across the landing and into the master suite. "Fireplace, Jacuzzi, deck." He whistled softly. "Your room?"

"No." Rick's throat tightened. He felt like grabbing Morgan and removing him bodily. "I sleep down the hall."

Morgan turned. "You're worse than I thought." He gripped his shoulder. "But I know what you need." He went back out to his car, opened the trunk, and returned with two bottles. "Cuervo Gold and my old friend Beam. Got any limes?"

Rick shook his head.

"Then we'll have to drink it straight."

———

Rick woke with a head like a volcano and a mouth full of soot. He rolled over and groaned. His jaw was on something hard, and he squinted open his eyes. Tile. Half his body was wedged under the table, and his face lay on the tiles before the fireplace. He felt like he'd been thrown and trampled. Slowly he slid out from under the table and rose to one elbow.

Morgan sat on the couch, fingers folded behind his head. "Now that you've done it my way, what do you think?"

Rick scowled. His head throbbed, and his stomach felt like something had died there.

Morgan reached for a glass on the table. "Here. This might help."

Rick looked at the glass. "What is it?"

"Bitters and soda."

Rick took it. It couldn't be worse than what he'd downed last night. What had Morgan given him? He took a drink and slouched against the hearth. "How'd I end up here?"

"You just lay where you fell."

Rick rubbed a hand over his face. He couldn't remember. Morgan had poured, and they'd talked broken hearts. Rick had probably spilled more than he wanted to know. But he couldn't remember ending up on the floor. "Is there a point?"

Morgan leaned forward, elbows to his knees. "Thought you should see how bad it could get."

As if he didn't know already. Rick hung his head into his hands. "Real considerate of you."

"The question is, what are you going to do now?"

"About what?"

"No-elle." Morgan drew out her name in two long syllables.

Rick stared at him. "What's there to do? She wants no part of me."

"Yeah. Her shell's probably Faberge by now."

Whatever that meant. Rick swigged the rest of the fizzy brown drink. It did settle his stomach. He stretched his arms. They seemed functional. He was less sure of his legs. "Did you do this on purpose?"

"Absolutely."

"Why?" Did Morgan hope to destroy whatever fiber he had left?

Morgan sat back and crossed his ankles. "Wanted you to see where self-pity could land you."

"You're a good one to talk."

"I'm speaking from experience." Morgan looked down at his hands. "If I'd had the guts thirteen years ago, I might have Jill with me now. My kid wouldn't be dead. And I sure wouldn't greet each morning with that." He nodded toward the empty bitters glass.

Rick looked at his brother. He'd never heard Morgan mention his baby. Not since it all happened. He had no proof that incident still ate him. He must be seriously concerned to bring it up now.

Morgan leaned forward. "First it's pride. You think she ought to come to you, only she doesn't. And then you think you can do without her. And you can, but there's a hole growing inside. Pretty soon it takes all your energy just filling that hole."

Rick swallowed hard. He was waking up now, or maybe Morgan's morning-after draft was working. He rested his forearms on his knees. "I don't know, Morgan. I've thought it through so many times, so many ways. But the first and only thing she wanted was away from me. She never wavered." He shook his head. "I couldn't reach her, couldn't touch her. She was . . . stone."

"Have you tried since?"

"No."

"Then take it from me." Morgan stood up. "Don't wait too long." He reached down.

Rick gripped Morgan's wrist and got to his feet. Blood pounded to his head. Morgan might have chosen a less painful object lesson. But this one was pretty effective. He scrunched his eyes, then stretched his face. By the slant of the sunlight, the horses were probably frantic. They never waited so long for food and freedom. But the thought of his daily routine depressed him. "You hanging around?"

Morgan pulled his keys from his pocket. "Like to, but I've got other problems to solve."

Rick looked at his brother again. He hadn't thought about that lately, how Morgan made a living cleaning up other people's messes. Maybe it was that hole inside he kept trying to fill. "I'll walk you out. The stock probably thinks I died."

Morgan laughed. "I wondered for a while myself."

"No thanks to you."

"You will." Morgan slapped his back. It sent a jolt straight to Rick's head.

They shook hands at the car and Rick watched Morgan drive away. Even the sound of the car made his head throb. One thing was certain.

He would not turn to the bottle. But he knew Morgan's message had been more symbolic. Maybe he was sinking into self-pity. So far it had just felt like preservation.

He let the horses out to pasture. He'd been keeping them in at night with the mountain lions repopulating. *Should I call Noelle?* He closed the stable door and went to the barn. The roof leak was molding the hay. That was first on his agenda. *But before I call Noelle?*

Rick leaned his arm on the post. *Lord?* Nothing. Naturally. You had to listen to hear. And he just wasn't ready. He turned and strode to the house. Maybe Morgan was right. He paused with his hand over the receiver, then took the phone and punched the number. He'd dialed it so many times in his mind he knew it from memory.

"St. Claire."

"Mr. St. Claire, this is Rick Spencer. I'm calling for Noelle."

The pause was expected. But he said, "One moment, Rick. I'll get her."

Rick waited, anticipated the sound of her voice, steeled himself for its impact. No matter what she said, he would have the sound of her voice.

"Rick?" It wasn't Noelle. William cleared his throat. "I'm sorry. She's not available."

*Why? How is she? Make her talk to me.* Rick didn't say any of it, just thanked William St. Claire and hung up. He went out, pulled on his gloves, and hung his tool belt over his hips. The ladder reached the lower end of the barn roof.

Before he climbed, he tied a rope around his waist. When he reached the top of the ladder, he tossed and tightened the rope to the cupola, then pulled himself up. The sun came off the steel like an oven. It was going to be hot work. Rick tugged the hat lower on his forehead and prepared to roast.

———

Noelle looked at her father. He'd hung up the phone and stood there behind his desk, staring as though he couldn't quite place her. What did he expect? What did he want from her? She started to turn.

"Noelle."

She waited.

"I want you to see a counselor."

She turned back. "Because I didn't take Rick's call?"

"You won't take anyone's. You won't go out. You're a recluse."

That wasn't true. She'd gone to the library, stood on the steps, and looked at the lions. *"What are you doing up there, honey? Are you lost?"* And she'd gone shopping, bought clothes to replace her others.

"I've gone out, Daddy. Ask John."

"Not socially. You've refused every invitation. It's not healthy." She looked away.

"I know you've been hurt." He walked around his desk where he'd been working. Even at home he worked. That's how Rick had reached him on the phone. If Donita had picked up, or any of the other staff, Noelle's refusal would hardly be noted. But Daddy had answered personally.

"There are professionals who can help you through this."

"Like the last time?" She raised her eyebrow.

Daddy yelling, *"What do you know?"* The woman knew nothing. Noelle drew a line with her crayon, drew another, harder. *"Draw what God looks like."* A line of red off the edge of the page onto the table. Her back pressed to the wall. Red crayon on the table harder, harder until it broke.

"I'll find you the best—"

"I'm going to a show tonight. Will that make you happy?"

He looked down at his desk. "Why won't you talk to Rick?"

"*Les Mis.* Paige and Sybil invited me, and believe it or not, I didn't turn them down. So you see, your concerns are needless."

"You could at least have taken his call."

She raised her chin. "I thought you didn't want me with that cowboy."

He slammed his fist on the stack of books. "I don't want you like this!" He waved his arm. "This automaton—Get help, Noelle!"

"There is no help, Daddy."

He dropped his face to his hand. "I watched your mother die. I don't want to watch you."

She stood very still. "I'm sorry. I'm already dead."

———

Noelle walked with her companions out of the theater. She should not have gone. It was a poor portrayal of one of her favorite works, and Paige's chatter was getting on her nerves. "I'm just so glad you came with us, Noelle. Jerry couldn't believe it when I told him you were coming.

The whole firm has this idea that you're . . . not the same. I told him of course you're not, not after Michael Fallon. I never liked him; he was so above it all—made Jerry feel like a peon when everyone knows it's the associates who do all the work. But Michael Fallon thought he was God."

Noelle's breath seized. *"Are you God?"* Why did the images keep overlapping? She knew now they were two separate incidents. Two nightmares she'd rather forget once and for all.

"Does it bother you to talk about it? I'm mean, you're so lucky to be through with all that. Jerry has a friend who'd really like to meet you." She waved her hand. "Don't worry. He's not with the firm."

Noelle shook her head. "No thanks."

Sybil said, "I didn't think much of Jean Valjean. He wasn't as sexy as Javert."

Paige snorted. "That one? He had a turned-up nose."

"Great thighs, though. In those tight pants?"

Paige asked, "What did you think, Noelle?"

Noelle shrugged. "I wasn't impressed with any of it. It's a shame to ruin *Les Mis*."

Paige waved her hand. "Jerry thinks *Les Mis* is depressing. And he won't see anything off Broadway. He says co-op theater is like one-ply toilet paper. Only Broadway will do. Jerry proposed after *Cats*. But we haven't been to a show in months. He's too busy. I shouldn't say it, Noelle, but your father works my husband like a slave. I'm afraid he'll have a heart attack and I'll be a widow at twenty-five."

"The music was good," Sybil said. "It's so haunting. Especially Fantine's song to her daughter when she knows she's dying. It breaks my heart."

Noelle felt a tremor. The first time she'd seen the musical, she'd wept when Fantine sang, feeling the mother's pain but also her own loss. Tonight, well, Daddy was right. She was an automaton. She didn't want to feel anything.

They reached the street. Noelle glanced at a young woman standing on the corner. Between her knee-high boots and miniskirt her thighs were whipped pink by the wind and her midriff was bare between her hips and the black vinyl jacket. There was something familiar . . .

Noelle stopped when the woman looked her way. "Jan?"

The stare hardened.

Noelle trembled. Michael's sister. Her platinum hair and burgundy lips made her face spectral, and there was a sheen to her skin.

Paige elbowed her. "Let's go."

Jan thrust out her chin and lit a cigarette. What was she doing there? Working the streets? Again the tremor. Had Michael's death . . .

"Come on, Noelle. Jerry's here with the car."

Noelle left her friends, walked over to Michael's sister. "Hello, Jan."

Jan only glared.

"What are you doing?"

"What's it look like?"

Sadness. She actually felt sadness. Michael had been so afraid Jan would come to that. He'd tried . . . Noelle's hand shook as she stroked it through her hair. She'd had it trimmed that afternoon. Jan's looked like someone's dog had chewed it at the ends.

"Do you want to go somewhere for coffee?"

"Yeah, right."

"There's an espresso bar just around the corner. It would feel good to get out of the wind." A light rain had started as well and blew into her face like spray.

"I'm working."

Noelle looked back at Sybil and Paige. They stood on the curb with the car doors open, waiting for her. Jerry was saying something, probably that he didn't want his leather seats getting wet. Noelle shook herself. What was she doing, talking to Michael's sister? To Jan, who couldn't weigh more than ninety pounds—dressed—who sucked her cigarette and French-exhaled with a withering sneer. She started to turn away.

"So I guess you hate Michael real bad."

Noelle felt her throat constrict. Did she? She was so far from any emotion, she couldn't say yes or no.

"Well, I wish he'd never met you."

Noelle looked into eyes as bitter as hers had ever been. "Jan . . ."

"He'd be alive now if it weren't for you."

Blood rushed in her ears. She wanted to turn and run.

Jan leaned forward. "I wish you'd been there when they buried him."

"Stop it, Jan."

"He loved you."

Loved her? Enough to beat and bruise and . . . If that was love she wanted no part of it. But tears stung her eyes. What right did Jan have to attack her? "How long have you been selling yourself?"

"Since I was born. One way or another." She took a drag and sent smoke out her nostrils. "How long have you?"

Noelle stepped back. She turned, walked to the car, and slid into the backseat with Sybil. As Jerry pulled away from the curb, she saw Jan staring.

# 31

Rick gave the connector one final twist and climbed out from under the sink. "That should hold it, Mary." He stood up and wiped his hands on a paper towel that tore with the first rub. Mary Slague was frugal. Generic towels cost less. He dropped the shreds into her wastebasket. "But if it leaks again, we'll replace the pipes."

"The squeak was the faucet, not the pipes?"

He leaned into her ear. "Leaks, Mary. If it leaks."

"Oh yes. I can't have any leaks." She hobbled into her living room, one nylon stocking bunched around her ankle beneath the hem of her paisley dress. She picked up her pocketbook. "What do I owe you?"

"Not a thing."

She turned, her lips gathered into a circle. "Nothing?"

He headed for her front door. "Just call me if it doesn't hold."

"No, I don't want mold. Not in a cabinet. But you're too nice." She hobbled to the door. A linen calendar from 1987 swung toward him as he opened it. She put a hand on his arm. "I liked you better without the beard."

Rick rubbed the shaggy growth. He'd thought of taking it off all summer, but it was too much trouble. Now that fall was coming, he guessed he'd leave it. He didn't care how he looked.

He patted Mary's fingers. "You take care."

As he walked to the truck he noticed the aspens were starting to turn. It was that day or so of succotash before the whole trees burst yellow. He'd carried Noelle outside and seated her underneath such golden splendor. He got into the truck. Did everything have to remind him?

He thought about what Morgan had said. The hole seemed to grow every day. He'd run out of chores at the ranch beyond the daily maintenance. Now he was reduced to doing everyone else's chores. But since he hadn't taken guests that summer, he was available and willing. The more work, the better.

He drove up to the house and went inside. It hit him when he walked in the door, a feeling so bleak he almost staggered. He sagged against the doorframe, then sank down and sat on the floor. He dropped his face into his hands. It was time to stop running. No amount of kind deeds was going to change the fact that he was in rebellion.

He folded his fingers and pressed his hands to the bridge of his nose. *Lord, forgive me.* He thought of what Pastor Tom had said. *"Unless you are sinless, you'd do well to forgive."* Could he? Was it even possible?

Rick sighed. Tom had been right about the rest too. It wasn't just Michael he blamed. More than anything, he blamed himself. He had tried to be enough, when he knew what Noelle needed was God's own love and healing and salvation. He'd captured her heart for himself when he should have won her soul for Christ. And now he'd lost it all.

His brows drew together and he pinched the bunched skin. *Jesus, I failed. And I don't know how to make it right.* He had willingly stepped outside God's plan, let his own desires lead him away. He'd wanted her so much. He dropped his head back against the doorframe.

There was only one way to fill the hole, one lasting way. Faith. Belief that God still had a plan. Rick stood up and got his Bible from the table. He opened to the book of Jeremiah and found the passage he wanted. " *'For I know the plans I have for you,' declares the Lord, 'plans to prosper you and not to harm you, plans to give you hope and a future. Then you will call upon me and come and pray to me, and I will listen to you. You will seek me and find me when you seek me with all your heart.'* "

He pressed the Bible to his chest, then closed it carefully and set it down. He went to the closet, took out his guitar, and tuned it. Then he sat on the hearth, played, and sang as he hadn't for too long. His fingers stopped. He dropped his face to his hand and wept.

God's mercy would be sufficient. *Please, God . . .* And then he prayed for Noelle. Prayer was the only thing he could give her.

Noelle couldn't stop thinking about Jan. She hadn't ventured out for two months since seeing Michael's sister. Paige had tried three times to set her up with Jerry's friend, though Daddy seemed to have given up matchmaking. She was twenty-four, living at home, and doing nothing with her life. No, that wasn't true. She practiced the piano every day and read voraciously—she'd even read a French cookery book from cover to cover. She was sure if she tried, she could prepare . . . something. But what was the use?

She sat up on the bed and threw her book across the room. Why had she seen Jan? Why hadn't she looked away, walked away? "He'd be alive if it weren't for you." She didn't want to think of Michael in any way except as her attacker, didn't want to consider Jan's loss, his mother's . . . How was she living now? Michael had been her sole support. Insurance didn't pay for suicide.

Noelle pressed her palms to her temples. Why should she care about them? He deserved to be dead. "He'd be alive if it weren't for you. He loved you." Had he? She felt his fist crashing into her skull, his kick in her stomach, his slap across her face.

That triggered the other memories, hands in the dark where no hands should be, her back against the wall. But was it Michael? Or the other face—the face of God? And then there was the window, Michael the Archangel crushing the devil's throat. Why? Because he'd angered God. She stiffened her arms at her sides, clenched her fists. *I never told!*

That thought stopped her short. Never told what? "Give us a kiss." Memory rushed in. She had scratched and kicked until he stunned her with his slapping. Her whole body shuddered. "Spoiled little rich girls need a lesson." And all she could picture was the window, God's angel stomping the devil. Her mind shut the man out and filled with the picture instead. Had the same thing happened with the hawk?

Had Michael's blows triggered the same separation, disassociation? And did she really know what happened while she fixated on the picture on his wall? "You're crazy! I never raped you." And then she remembered that too. Michael staggering back, as stunned as she that he'd hit her, and scared. "Stop it, Noelle! What's wrong with you?" And all she could do was stare.

Michael hadn't raped her. It was the other man's hands. She bit her upper lip until she tasted blood. Michael's fists had triggered the terror, the terror that had made her run. But he hadn't instigated it. That had come much earlier, been buried far deeper. And it carried more horror than Michael's violence ever could have.

She stood up and staggered to her door, lingered there, then went back to the bed. Her mind had overlapped the memories. Maybe the trauma of Michael's violence had triggered the old terror. Staring at the hawk, her body remembered the violation of her innocence. And she had attributed all of it to Michael.

*"Are you trying to destroy me?"* Had he killed himself because of her accusation? *"He'd be alive if it weren't for you."* Assault and battery was not rape. He could have gotten off with probation and mandatory anger management. But she'd accused him of worse. Had she pushed him over an edge because she didn't know, couldn't put together the pieces that were tearing her mind apart?

Overwhelming dismay seized her. Had she caused Michael's death? She groaned as the shakes seized her. Not fear now, but . . . guilt? Her teeth chattered. Maybe she did need help. But she didn't trust anyone to give it.

———

Noelle ran her fingers over the piano keys, stopped, and fingered the passage again. The phrase was difficult, but she could master it. She caught motion from the corner of her eye and looked up.

Her father said, "There's a man here to see you."

She frowned. "Tell him I'm not interested." Daddy should know that. Whomever he'd put up to it this time . . .

"Noelle, I am not your personal secretary. Tell him yourself."

She slammed the cover down over the keyboard and saw him wince. Then she rose from the piano and stalked out to the entry. She stopped. Her heart skipped a beat. "Morgan!"

His smile was rascally as ever, and it caught something inside her and tugged. The curt dismissal she'd intended died on her lips. Instead her voice rushed on. "Daddy, this is Morgan Spencer. Morgan, my father, William St. Claire."

Morgan shook his hand. "It's a pleasure." Then he turned and brushed her up and down with his eyes.

She spread her hands. "What are you doing here?"

"Business. But in between, I thought I'd have dinner with a beautiful woman."

She found the familiarity of his words strangely comforting.

Her father nudged her. "How can you refuse?"

"Thank you, Daddy. I can accept my own invitations." She turned back to Morgan. "I'll need a moment to get ready."

"Make it count. We'll go somewhere nice."

Naturally. She felt his eyes all the way up the stairs. Morgan. What on earth had brought him? And why did it matter? In her room, she changed into a teal rayon dress, elegant but not overstated. Then she brushed out her hair. She started to work it into a braid but stopped and shook it loose.

What was she doing? Why had she said yes? Because she wanted to go. Could it be that simple? Something had awakened in her with Morgan's visit, and she wanted it to stay awake. The times they had spent ran together in her mind and mattered.

Walking down, she heard Morgan talking about his latest project. No doubt Daddy was interested in more than Morgan's profession. She joined them and recognized Morgan's admiration as she pulled on her silver fox fur. Fur might not be politically correct, but there was nothing like it against your neck on a cold night, and she could tell he agreed.

She kissed her father's cheek, then took Morgan's extended arm. He wasn't sweeping her off to some mountain hole-in-the-wall; he had entered her world, and he fit remarkably well. His cab waited outside on the circular drive and started off as soon as he had tucked her in beside him.

She said, "I suppose you know where we're going?"

"I do."

Did he ever not? She stared out at the city lights. Morgan stared at her. Familiarity again.

She moistened her lips. "How did you know where I lived?"

"Give me credit for half a brain."

She smiled. "I'm not listed in the phone book."

He only smiled back.

She looked back out the window. It didn't matter how he knew. The fact that he did meant a lot. It had been nearly a year since she'd last seen him, lounging against his white Lincoln rental car outside his parents' house. Funny she should remember that so clearly. She didn't say anything else while they drove, and surprisingly, he stayed quiet as well.

He led her into La Belle Maison, waited while the maître d' seated her and laid her napkin across her lap, then after the familiar stroke of his hand across her shoulders, Morgan took his own seat. "So." He crossed his leg and studied her. "How are you?"

Did he really expect her to say? "I'm fine. How are you?"

Their waiter approached, and Morgan said, "Dom Perignon. Nothing younger than 1990."

"We have a fine vintage, 1987."

Morgan nodded, and when the man left, he said, "I'm not drinking it alone."

"It's never concerned you before." She smoothed the napkin in her lap.

"Killing a bottle of champagne by yourself is depressing."

Was it possible his eyes were bluer? The fine lines at their edges etched a little deeper? A hint of a shadow showed along his chin and upper lip, and his cheek creased when he half-smiled. What was he thinking?

The waiter brought their champagne, allowed Morgan to approve the label, then opened the bottle and poured half an inch into two flutes. Noelle raised hers and sipped, now that protocol included women in the approval process. He'd made a good choice. Dom Perignon was Daddy's favorite as well. Since neither of them protested, the waiter filled their glasses, tucked the bottle into the ice bucket, and left.

Morgan raised his glass. "To my muse."

The flutes clinked, and Noelle raised her eyebrows. "Your muse?"

"Inspiration."

"For what?"

"This evening." As though he needed inspiration to enjoy himself.

She sipped, then opened the leather-cased menu and studied the selection. For some reason she thought of the Italian restaurant Rick had taken her to. The only restaurant he'd taken her to. *First date should be special.* Her thoughts shied. It was easier with Morgan, though her first date with him had left her walking up the mountain in the dark. She closed the menu and set it at the edge of the table. He closed his as well.

A moment later, the waiter came and stood at his elbow. Morgan motioned for her to order and she named her choices, then Morgan his, in barely discernable French. Noelle covered her smile with her fingers.

Unabashed, he smiled back. "Atrocious, isn't it? You're fluent?"

"More or less."

"Been to Paris?"

She looked at the crystal vase holding a single stem of yellow orchids. "Once. After my coming out, Daddy and I went."

"What did you think of it?"

She leaned back. "Very old, deep, and sad."

"Sad? *Gay Paree?*"

"My mother was from Paris. It's where she and Daddy met. It was painful for him to go back there without her." She laid her hands in her lap as the waiter set the shallow bowl of carrot bisque before her.

"Why did he take you?"

"I wanted to see my mother's home. In true adolescent oblivion, I didn't think how hard it would be for him." She spooned the creamy carrot puree garnished with a dab of yogurt and carrot curl. She knew how it was made. There'd been a recipe for carrot bisque in the French cookery book.

"Was the rest of Europe more pleasant?"

She raised her brows. "How do you know there was more?"

"Just a hunch."

She dabbed her mouth. "If we hadn't gone to Paris first, it would have been better. But all through the trip, I'd catch Daddy looking at me as though I were . . . someone else. As though I should have been my mother."

"You look like her."

"How do you know?"

Morgan spooned the last of his consommé. "I waited in the library while you dressed."

"Oh. You saw her portrait. It's the only picture of her in the house."

Morgan cocked a brow. "Why?"

She set her finished bowl aside. "Daddy has the others stowed away somewhere. He goes to the library when he wants to think of her. Otherwise he doesn't want to be reminded."

Morgan's eyes deepened, as though what she'd said struck a nerve. "Does it work? Out of sight; out of mind?"

Noelle shook her head. "I don't know. Daddy's singularly focused. Maybe it does."

The waiter brought her *fricassee de poulet au Chablis* and Morgan's lobster *Parisienne*. She raised a bite to her mouth and thought of Rick blessing the food at Antonio's. *"Everything I have is a gift."* She took a tender forkful, but it was less savory than she'd expected.

"Tell me about you, Morgan. Still saving people's fortunes?"

It was safer to turn the conversation over to him. Morgan talked. He poked fun at the sort of people Noelle knew all too well. She laughed. "What if they don't follow your recommendations?"

He shrugged. "Then I move on. I don't waste my time with unteachables."

"And you're always right?"

He shrugged. "It's not a matter of right so much as a feel for what needs to be done. No two solutions are exactly the same, but I tend to find the right one for the situation."

Noelle toyed with her chicken, recalling the conversation with Celia. *"He wants to make things right. That's his genius and his cross. He sees what others miss, whether he wants to or not."*

What was he seeing now? Did he think because he fixed struggling corporations, he could fix her? She shook her head. Morgan expected too much. Besides, everyone she trusted had hurt her. But then, she'd never trusted Morgan.

"Hello . . ."

She looked up.

"Where'd you go?"

She set her fork down and used her napkin. "You're on a project now?"

"You could say that."

"Someone in New York needs saving?" No, that didn't come out right. She could see his mind turning.

"That's one way to put it." His eyes deepened.

She poked the cherry-tomato rosette with her fork but didn't eat it. "So is it a family corporation or publicly held?"

"Oh, definitely family." He sipped his champagne.

Except for the first sip, she hadn't drunk hers. "And you walk in and tell them how to reconstruct their lives."

"Something like that."

She wished he wouldn't look at her that way. What did he want?

What he always wanted—to break through, find the real Noelle . . . or force *her* to. But she'd found her now, and it was darker and more depressing than she'd imagined. Still, she appreciated his effort.

"Penny for your thoughts."

She sighed. "This is nice, Morgan. I haven't been out much."

"Whose fault is that?"

She laid down her fork. "No one's. Just . . . the way it is."

"So why did you come tonight?" He finished the champagne in his flute. "I'd like to think it's my charm and charisma."

She smiled. "Of course."

"Oh, you can be patronizing."

She pushed her plate aside. "Why do you think I don't mean it?"

"Do you?" He'd caught her.

She bought time with her napkin, dabbing her lips and carefully folding it alongside her hardly touched plate. What did he want from her? She couldn't . . . But she did feel something. She cared for him— not his flair and charisma, but . . . She looked up into his eyes. "You are charming, Morgan."

"And you are beautiful." His gaze liquefied. "I thought so the first time I saw you. Do you remember that day?"

"Yes."

He reached out and took her hands. His warmth penetrated, sent a quiver up her arms. Same old Morgan, making her feel what she didn't want to feel. "Dresden china on Rick's front porch, like a rare shipment to the wrong address. But even here, you're too fine. Everything else looks plain."

The blush burned her cheeks, startling yet another response she'd thought dead.

"Rick, now, he looks like hell, all bearded and skeletal."

Heart lurching, she yanked, but he didn't let go.

"Sorry." He sighed. "I had to see if you still loved him."

Something tore inside her. "What I feel for Rick is none of your business."

"What do you feel?" Again he resisted her attempt to free her hands without making a scene.

"Nothing! Stop it! Why are you doing this?"

He stroked her fingers with his thumb. "Because I'm fool enough to want you and Rick reconciled."

Her pulse throbbed. Morgan wanted them reconciled? "Then why are you holding my hands?"

"Just wretch enough to enjoy the process."

It wasn't true. She saw his hurt. If she had reacted differently . . . but then, maybe not. Morgan had given her up before . . . to Rick. She didn't want to think about Rick, picture him hurting. She had enough guilt over Michael. Rick was better off without her. But bearded and skeletal? "Does he really look bad?"

"A regular desert hermit. Except he's lost his faith."

"He can't have. It was more to him than anything."

Morgan didn't answer. She wanted him to tell her it wasn't true. She pictured Celia's frank face. *"Because of you, Rick is at odds with his brother. I don't want him at odds with God."* Because of her. What if she'd accepted his faith, shared it? But what did it matter now?

She closed her eyes. "It's no use, Morgan."

"Why? You love him."

No. Yes. How could Morgan tell?

"And he loves you. This is tearing him apart."

Tears stung behind her lids. "Do you think I want to hurt him?"

"No. But that doesn't change the fact. And for what? You both want to be together. You have something special."

"That's not the issue."

"What is it, then? Sex?"

Her eyes flew open. No one had laid it bare like that. But how could she marry Rick when the very thought of intimacy terrified her? And then there was what she'd done to Michael, the images, the dissociation. How would it come out next?

She forced a level tone. "Why would you think that?"

His mouth pulled to the side. "Partly my ego. How else could you resist me?"

Where it should have annoyed, instead it broke her tension. "And partly?"

"I know what rape does. Rick told me about Michael once I loosened his tongue with enough cheap whiskey."

Whiskey? Rick? But he could only have told what he thought they knew, not the truth she now lived with.

"It wasn't Michael." She rolled her lips in, fighting the nausea from just the thought of speaking the rest aloud.

"What do you mean?"

"It was and it wasn't. He was violent. But Michael didn't rape me. His battering triggered something else." She couldn't do it. She'd kept it in too long.

Morgan folded both her hands together in his and leaned close. "Tell me."

She whispered, "I can't." *Please don't let him push.* She didn't want to shatter. "It happened a long time ago. I didn't remember until Michael hit me. Pieces kept breaking through, but I thought they were about him." She drew a jagged breath. "He died because of that."

"You can't really think that."

She pressed a hand over her eyes. "I accused him, and he killed himself."

Morgan slowly shook his head. "He made his own mistakes. But you have the chance to stop making yours."

She shook her head. "I can't—"

"Noelle, Rick loves you. He'd live celibate if that's what it took."

Tears started in her eyes. She blinked them back furiously.

"Let them come, Noelle," Morgan murmured. "It's been long enough."

But she fought to maintain control. She couldn't face the grief. It would wash her away.

Morgan stood and tossed cash on the table, though their bill had not been delivered. Probably the waiter had hesitated to interrupt. She felt transparent. Morgan wrapped her in her fur and led her out to one of the cabs waiting at the door. He gave the driver directions, then climbed in beside her, slid his arm around her shoulders.

He was breaking her, crushing her defenses, and it would hurt too much. She sat stiffly against him, looked out the black, light-spattered window, and saw with relief he'd brought her home.

"This the place?" The cabby stopped outside the gate.

"Yes. Keep the meter running." Morgan climbed out and drew her out with him, keeping his hand on her elbow as he walked her to the gate.

Noelle pressed the combination to admit them. She wanted to go in, to forget this night had happened. But then she didn't. She was torn in two.

Morgan walked her halfway up the drive, then stopped and took her in his arms. "I'm going to kiss you, Noelle. And then you're going to tell me again how much you love Rick."

She shook her head to protest, but he stilled her motion with his hands on her cheeks. His lips were tender, and she felt no revulsion, no panic, and no flapping of wings. Yet also none of what she had felt once with Rick. There was no sense of belonging, no sharing her innermost self.

"Now." Morgan drew back without releasing her. "Break my heart again."

She smiled through the tears spilling down her cheeks. "Oh, Morgan . . ."

He held her close. "I'm not leaving until you say it . . . but you can take as long as you like." He stroked her back.

She laughed, sniffed the tears, and swiped the back of her hand over her eyes. Then she gathered her voice. "I love Rick. And I love you, too, Morgan, only not the same way."

"Story of my life." He chuckled. "What are you going to do about it?"

She shook her head. "I don't know. But I'll think about it."

"Well, that's a start."

"Thank you, Morgan."

He cradled her head a long moment, then sighed. "If I hold you any longer I'll forget everything I said about Rick. Come on." He walked her the rest of the way to the house, kissed her lightly on the cheek, and left.

She climbed the stairs to her room and went straight to her dresser. She opened the lid of the jewelry box and lifted out the ring. She stared at it a long moment, then clasping it tightly in her hand, she held it against her heart and wept deep, painful, aching tears. When she had no more left in her, she replaced the ring in the box and closed the lid.

The house was silent. It was late and she needed to sleep, but she couldn't. She felt empty. It wasn't the absence of feeling she had grown accustomed to, it was a void that wanted filling. She crept down to the library and lit the recessed spotlight over her mother's portrait.

She'd done that with increasing regularity, trying to understand. How had Mama let her be taken? And so shortly after, she'd left her forever. It wasn't rational. Her mother had had no control of either, certainly not her own death. Noelle looked at her now, her mother's eyes so happy, so filled with love. It contrasted with her foggy memories of a dying woman wasted by disease.

Daddy had kept them apart at the end. He'd filled her days with magic, and like the selfish creature she was, she had run off to enjoy herself. How could she know what death was? How could she know it would be too late?

Noelle stooped down and searched the cabinets for the wooden box carved in Oberammergau. Her mother's treasures. She worked the box free and sat on the floor with it as she had when she was small. With both hands she opened the lid and let her eyes trail over the contents, the bundle of letters and cards from Daddy, some of her own first drawings, the jar of antique jewelry.

The jewelry had been the big attraction when she was little. She lifted the jar and held it to the light. Then she took out the packet of letters. She'd never read them. They were tied in a blue ribbon, her father's words of love. Had he any? He must have once, though he'd lost them along the way.

As she put them back, her fingers touched a book. She brushed aside the photographs. A Bible. She remembered the feel of Rick's worn leather binding. She closed her eyes and pictured him sitting in the corner, reading.

"He's lost his faith." Morgan's words gave her a pang. What had it been now? Four months since Rick called? She should have taken his call. It was unkind to refuse it. But how could she stand hearing his voice? What could she say?

She took out her mother's Bible. The pages were gold-edged. She had a flash of memory, light glinting off the golden pages. She was on the floor playing with the buttons and the sunlight danced off the book in Mama's hands. Where did that memory come from?

Her fingers trembled as she opened the Bible. A lavender ribbon marked a page, and she slid it open there. The top of the page said Psalms, and there was a note and a date in the margin beside number 121. She held it up to read. *For Noelle, November 12, 1984.* Four days before Mama died.

The underlined section read, *"I will lift up mine eyes unto the hills . . ."* She pictured Rick's meadow, the slope up the craggy mountain. " *. . . from whence cometh my help. My help cometh from the Lord, which made heaven and earth."* Noelle closed her eyes. Oh, Mama. Tears blurred her eyes, and she blinked them away to read the other underlined verses.

*"He will not suffer thy foot to be moved: he that keepeth thee will not slumber. . . . The Lord shall preserve thee from all evil: he shall preserve*

*thy soul. The Lord shall preserve thy going out and thy coming in from this time forth, and even for evermore."*

How could that be? If God preserved her, why had she been hurt? She had run to the hills. Rick said God had brought her to the ranch. Then why let Michael find her there? It didn't make sense. It couldn't be true. But when Mama was dying, she had marked these words. Did she believe them even as God was taking away her life?

Noelle pictured Rick in the airport, wanting to hold her, wanting to help—but she wouldn't let him. Had she refused God's protection as well? If she had trusted Him when Rick tried to show her, would it all have been different? God hadn't stopped Mama dying. Noelle looked up at her mother's face. Why did He take a woman so young? A mother from her child? Yet in her last days, Mama had marked these pages for her.

Noelle trembled. Shards of fear pricked her spine. *"Perfect love drives out fear."* Rick had said it, but it wasn't his love he'd meant. It was deeper, more encompassing. Perfect love. God's love?

CHAPTER

# 32

The next morning John drove her to the cathedral. Noelle asked him to wait. It might be minutes if she couldn't do it. She climbed the steps, looking up at the round, gothic stained-glass window between the towering lacy spires. She pulled the heavy arched door, but it didn't open. Nor the one beside it.

She was almost glad. But then she saw another, over to the side. She walked across and tried it. It opened. Holding her breath, she walked inside the silence that smelled of candle wax and age. A wide aisle went down the center, but she didn't take it. Her eyes had gone immediately to the window, the one nearest the back on the left.

She started to shake, but her legs drew her nearer until she stood beneath it. Overcast sunlight came through the red robe, not brilliant as it had been the last time, but dull. The face, though, was just as fierce, the leg crushing Satan as heavily muscled, the sword upraised. The wings . . . She shuddered.

"I sometimes get that feeling too."

She screamed, spun into the wall, and pressed her hand to her mouth.

"I'm sorry!" The young man in black shirt sleeves and white collar looked truly alarmed. "I'm awfully sorry. I didn't mean to scare you."

Her heart retreated from her throat, but her legs would not function. She gripped the edge of a pew and sat down.

"Gosh, I feel terrible." He looked like it, his face drawn together in the center. "It's these shoes. The air soles are so quiet."

She looked down at his Nikes and cleared her throat. "It's not your fault." She drew two long breaths and stilled her shaking. "I'm . . . I have . . . actually, something happened to me under that window."

He sank into the next pew forward. "Oh boy. And then I . . ." He suddenly grinned. "This is one of those awful situations I often find myself in."

Noelle looked at him. His eyes were deep set beneath black brows, and his nose had a large bump and was bent to one side. It seemed only fitting his chin would also be cleft. "Are you a priest?"

"Ordained this year."

She said, "I was looking for Father Matthis."

He shook his head. "Retired. He still says mass, but he's not attached to the cathedral anymore."

Noelle expelled her breath, glanced up at the window.

"Could I help you?" he said. "I'm Father Mike."

She startled, stared back at him. "Mike?"

He nodded. "That's why that window sometimes gets to me. My namesake is intimidating."

Noelle looked at the angel's face. "He's scarier than the devil."

"Well, when they make it look like a poor lizard in agony. If I'd painted it . . ."

"Do you paint?"

"As a hobby. Religious themes." He waved his hand toward the window. "I'd have made Michael's face more noble and Satan's much, much uglier."

She smiled.

He rested his arm across the pew back between them. "Do you want to tell me about it?"

When Daddy had suggested a priest, she'd certainly not pictured Father Mike. He was probably not much older than herself, with a boyish frankness that brought down her walls. "Yes. I would."

He listened well, dismayed when she told him she had believed her abductor was God. He shook his head. "I can see it. Of course it makes sense, but how awful."

"It was more awful by far." In staggering words she described the closet and what happened there. Strange that in this place where it started she could speak it for the first time. "I didn't remember any of it until my boyfriend—Michael—" she glanced up at the window—"got violent. When he hit me, my mind started coming apart."

She described the images, dreams of the hawk and also symbolically the window. "I accused him . . ."

He waited, then softly said, "Nothing you tell me will leave these walls."

"I accused him of rape, and he shot himself when they tried to arrest him. Now I have this terrible ache, the fear that he's dead because of me, and I feel so guilty."

He pulled his brows into a perplexed furrow. "He beat you up, and you feel guilty?"

His terse reply caught her by surprise.

"I'm sorry." Father Mike's face reddened. "My father's an alcoholic. I can't remember a time he didn't beat my mother. That's where I got this." He rubbed his nose. "Trying to protect her." It helped somehow to know he shared the pain. His face sank. "But that's not your story. What happened to your kidnapper? The first one?"

"I don't know. I only learned of it a short while ago, but I don't think he was ever apprehended." Then she told him how her mother died, how Daddy guarded her, how she ran to Colorado and met Rick and Morgan. How she left Rick and damaged his faith.

Hours passed, but no one came in. Father Mike admitted the side door had only been opened because he had run in on an errand. He laughingly said that was a God thing. They talked until she couldn't think of anything else to say. She shrugged. "And now I don't know what to do."

"But God does." He looked up into the vaulted ceiling. "Somehow, someway, He has a purpose in it all." It might have sounded trite, until he added, "My father's in prison for killing my mom."

Noelle felt it in her chest, a pain as deep as her own. No wonder he had responded as he did. And there it was again—God allowing atrocity. Yet this man not only believed but also dedicated his life to that Being. "If it's His purpose . . ."

"How can He be good? How can He be God?" Father Mike jumped into her thought.

"Why does He allow it?"

"Sin. God doesn't make evil happen. It comes from the heart of man and the Prince of Darkness." He pointed up at the window. "That's why I would have made Satan uglier."

"But can't God stop it?"

He looked at her intently. "In this world you will have trouble. But be of good cheer, for Jesus has overcome the world."

"I don't understand."

He opened his hands wide. "Through Jesus we have eternal salvation. But while we're in the world, there's still darkness."

"But . . ." Noelle took her mother's Bible from her coat. She pulled it open with the ribbon. "Here. 'He will not suffer thy foot to be moved: he that keepeth thee will not slumber. . . . The Lord shall preserve thee from all evil: he shall preserve thy soul. The Lord shall preserve thy going out and thy coming in from this time forth, and even for evermore.' " She looked up.

Father Mike folded his hands atop the pew. "Nothing can happen to a child of God outside His perfect will. Whatever happens here is for a purpose."

"So you accept what happened to your mother?" Noelle dropped the Bible to her lap.

"I embrace it. It was the worst thing in my life, but it happened for God's glory."

"How?"

He smiled. "It brought me here. To help you." His eyes reminded her of Rick's. "Let me tell you about Jesus. And how He set me free."

It was as though crusted layers crumbled and fell. Rick had tried to tell her, but nothing could get through. Now, for the first time, she listened without animosity or fear. Just listened, drinking it in. Jesus on the cross was not a victim of his Father's cruelty. He was the greatest gift his Father gave. If only she could receive it.

---

Snow flurried along the highway as Rick drove. He squinted through the windshield, wondering why he'd agreed to go home for Christmas. It was Mom's voice, her need to see he was all right, that made him agree.

But he wasn't all right. At the ranch he'd managed some form of sameness. But now, driving, he imagined Noelle beside him as she'd been the last time, so fragile. He could almost feel her head against his shoulder, see her eyes turned up to him. He remembered her amazement when she'd met his sisters. He remembered her sitting in the sleigh, saying she'd be his wife.

Maybe he should have called again, tried again. But if she couldn't trust him, if she blamed him, feared him . . . His knuckles tightened on the wheel. Pastor Tom had asked if he was willing to help her even if she never returned his affection, and he was. He didn't regret trying. But he hadn't realized how much it would hurt.

The house was quiet when he arrived. His sisters must be out, and he wondered if his folks had arranged that to gauge his condition before exposing the girls. He drew a deep breath and went inside. His father's embrace showed more clearly than words how concerned he was. Rick hugged his mother, trying not to see the ache in her eyes. It was hard enough without knowing that his family hurt with him.

Rick passed into the kitchen and lifted the lid to the cookie jar. May as well face the inquiry. But the jar was empty.

His mother said, "I haven't baked yet. You'll have some tonight." Her laugh was strained, so she reverted to plain speech. "How are you?"

"I've been better."

"How are you with God?"

"Better than I was." He slid the jar back to the corner.

"Meaning?"

Of course she wouldn't accept his abbreviated version. "Meaning I'm trusting and waiting and praying. That's the best I can do right now."

She nodded, then brushed her hand over his shaggy chin. "Morgan told us you'd grown a beard."

Rick leaned against the counter. "He told you he came out?"

His mother nodded. "And no, I didn't send him. But I thought about it."

Rick wondered how much Morgan had reported. He would bet there'd been no mention of his old friend Jim Beam and the Cuervo Gold. Rick was glad. That had definitely been a low point. "I'm all right, Mom."

Dad said, "Have you talked to her?"

Rick looked at his father seated sideways at the table. He had hoped, foolishly, that they could skip those questions. But of course Dad would want to know. He was fond of Noelle himself. Rick shook his head. "No."

"Have you tried?"

"Not for a while." Rick drew a deep breath, then slowly exhaled. "It has to come from Noelle." He ran his hand over his beard. He'd trimmed it before coming, but it was still full and soft. He hadn't set out to grow it, just let nature take its course. That's how he was these days. "I guess I'll unpack."

Morgan had not come, but the rest of them gathered around the table, lit the Advent candles, and prayed. Rick hadn't brought his guitar, not a conscious act, just an oversight. They sang a cappella, then went to praise and petitions. The prayers were playful and energetic, full of the contentment in his sisters' lives, and it was healing to hear it. But he closed his eyes and his throat tightened when Tara prayed, "Please help Noelle to come back."

If only it was as easy as that. The faith of a child. Though he tried, his prayers had limped at best. An honest attempt, nothing more. Because while he asked for God's will, his heart still prayed to have her back. Wasn't that just what Tara had done? But she didn't have ulterior motives, and he most certainly did.

After an improvised version of "Whose Line Is It Anyway?" and a round of hearts in which Stephanie stuck him twice with the queen of spades, he was ready to call it a night, though not to sleep. Alone in the dark of his room he dropped to his knees. "Lord, God . . ." He gripped his hands together. "Oh, Jesus . . ." He dropped his head to his hands. He had maintained a good humor all through the evening for his family's sake, but now the grief overwhelmed him. He knew what he had to do, but it was too hard.

Forgiveness had been one thing. He'd worn himself out hating Michael. It had almost been a relief to forgive. This was different. It was releasing his will, surrendering his hope. He groaned deep inside, but there was no denying it.

*Lord, your ways are not my ways. I lean not on my own understanding.* There must be a reason, something bigger than himself, something he couldn't see, couldn't fathom. Rick pressed his folded hands to his throat. He had to accept life without her, be sold out to God's purpose, embracing His will. Embracing. Not grudging. There in that house where he'd first dreamed of their life together, he had to let go of that dream. With a hoarse voice he said, "Your will be done." And in his heart, he meant it.

———

Noelle had not planned anything special for her twenty-fifth birthday. Daddy had honored her request for a quiet dinner together, then presented her a lovely emerald necklace. "It was your mother's, Noelle."

But she had already recognized it from the portrait. "Thank you, Daddy."

He fastened it around her neck. "You're so like her."

And more so each day as she delved into her mother's faith, finding there the peace she hadn't believed possible. But she couldn't tell Daddy that. She knew too well the animosity he bore anything religious. Though in his frustration he had ordered her to see a priest, his disdain had been palpable. As her own had been, though with more personal justification—another thing Daddy didn't know: the details of her ordeal with the man who claimed to be God.

Maybe someday she would tell him. Maybe then she could tell him that studying the nature of God, learning to know the person of Jesus, was giving her the only possibility of happiness she could find. He might understand it as an intellectual pursuit, but could she ever explain the sort of surrender Father Mike encouraged in their discussions? If she took that step, would Daddy shudder at her weakness?

She had spent most of her life making him proud, soaking up the moments he showed it, performing in all the areas he approved. He would not approve her dedicating her life to Christ, calling Jesus her Lord, joining the rank and file of the "religious non-thinkers" who blindly followed "God's will." But more and more, she believed that was the only way she could face the solitary life laid out before her.

Daddy had gone to bed by ten, but she had John bring the car and drive her to Manhattan through the crowds to the cathedral for midnight Mass. She sat in the back, packed in with all the twice-a-year churchgoers. The archbishop said the Mass, but Father Mike assisted.

Last year it had taken all her resistance not to run screaming from the reality of God. Now the last of her resistance melted and she surrendered to the incredible love. The sadness was still deep inside her and the knowledge that she might never recover what she'd lost as a five-year-old child. But she no longer faced it alone. Rick had told her Jesus would never abandon her; she had to trust Him. Tears came, as they had every time she thought of Rick since Morgan's visit. *Please don't let him hurt, Lord.* But that, too, was in God's hands.

———

Rick was outside when Morgan arrived two days past Christmas. Probably he had his own reasons for not repeating last year's scenario. Rick watched from the doorway of Dad's stable as his brother drove up in a rental car, then went into the house. The girls would no doubt mob him, so Rick didn't go in.

Though he had considered leaving tomorrow, Morgan's arrival meant he'd have to stay another day at least, and it would be good to be all together without the tension they'd had last year. Rick almost smiled at the first silver lining he'd found. At least he was at peace with his brother, and Dad would have no need for lectures.

Sooner than he expected, Morgan joined him in the stable. "Just can't keep away from the horse scene, can you?"

Rick grinned. "Checking out the yearlings Dad got." He peeled open the lips and examined the horse's teeth.

"Do you have to do that?"

Rick petted the tawny muzzle. "It's only teeth, Morgan." He'd forgotten his brother's squeamishness where large animals were concerned. That had given him one of his only advantages growing up. If he couldn't beat Morgan any other way, he could always gross him out.

Morgan tucked his hands into the pockets of his black cashmere overcoat. "You'll never guess who I had dinner with."

Rick ran a hand over the horse's withers and spine. "Then save me the trouble."

"It would be worth your effort."

Rick bent low and stroked his hand under the horse's belly. Dad had offered him his pick of the three, and so far he was liking this animal.

"No guess?"

"I've played enough games the last few days. Just tell me."

Morgan said, "Noelle."

Rick jerked his head up. "What?"

Morgan shrugged. "I was in New York on business, so I looked her up."

Anger surged through him. Would God be so . . . Then he checked his thoughts. He should have expected an attack. He'd made a serious step forward, and that always wreaked havoc. Telling his heart that was another story.

"Aren't you going to ask how she was?"

His insides constricted. "How was she?"

"Gorgeous."

It hit him low. Rick spun and grabbed Morgan by the collar, nearly lifting him from the floor. "What are you trying to do?"

"Take it easy, Rick! I'm telling you to get out there and fight for her—before I do it myself."

Rick slowly released his grasp. His heart thumped in his chest. Fight for her? He had only just relinquished her. If Morgan wanted to make a play, it wasn't his place to stop him. So why was Morgan telling him this? Some sense of brotherly honor? Or was he just the snake in the garden, stealing the victory?

Rick shook his head. "I can't."

"Why not?"

How could he make Morgan understand? "I stepped outside God's will before. I won't do it again."

Morgan spread his hands. "Rick . . ."

Rick pulled his coat closed. "I don't expect you to understand."

"How do you know it isn't God's will?"

"It's the Lord she needs. I only get in His way." Rick shoved his hands into the sheepskin pockets, knowing the truth of it. They would still be unequally yoked, coming at life from two different worlds. He had thought he could bridge it with love, lead her to faith over time, but now he wasn't sure. His prayer last night had felt sure. "I have to be willing to live without her."

Morgan pushed the horse aside and walked around. "Maybe you just had to be willing."

"Morgan . . ." But Rick stopped. Was it possible? Had God only wanted his surrender? That would be a good kick in the pants after taking so long to get there.

"What are you afraid of?" Morgan asked.

"It's not that." Rick leaned his shoulder to the wall. "She's been pursued enough. I won't go after her like Michael."

"Michael didn't rape her."

"What?"

Morgan rested his elbow on the stall. "It was some other incident, breaking through her subconscious. I'm guessing a child molestation when she was really small."

Rick's stomach twisted. It had been hard enough to face the first. But to think of Noelle as a child . . . "How do you know?"

"She told me. Sort of." Morgan slid his fingers into his hair. "She actually feels guilty for Michael's death."

That hurt somewhere low in his stomach. "Why?"

"Because she accused him wrongly, thinks she pushed him over the edge."

Typical Noelle, twisting things in her mind. He wished he could set her straight.

Morgan shook his head. "She loves you, Rick. I don't think she'll run."

Rick met his eyes, then looked away. *Lord?* He'd meant his prayer; as hard as it was, he'd truly meant it. *Jesus, show me.* Was God speaking through Morgan? Unlikely—no, he had to stop thinking that way. Morgan's lifestyle may not reveal it, but he'd been almost . . . noble through it all. God could surely use him if He chose to. *I'm the one who's been pigheaded and rebellious. Show me, Lord.*

First peace, then hope; Rick's heart swelled to accept them. Just as swiftly fear tried to choke it out. What if he was wrong? He couldn't go through it again. Neither of them could. He wouldn't do that to her.

He banished that fear with a sharp, silent command. The risk was worth it, as long as he stayed in God's will.

Morgan squeezed his shoulder. It had been a long time since Rick had felt that close to his brother, longer still since he'd trusted him in a spiritual matter. *If I'm wrong, Lord, stop me now.* His hope increased. Rick clasped Morgan's hand, then headed for the house.

"And Rick," Morgan called, "lose the beard."

Rick rubbed his hand over his whiskers and grinned.

With a patchwork combination of airline tickets he could arrive at JFK by late afternoon. On each of the flights that jockeyed him indirectly to Noelle, Rick prayed, *Let me know your will, Lord.* His Bible lay open across his lap. He scrutinized the Scriptures. He had to do it right this time, but he kept coming back to the same verse from the first letter of Peter. "*Above all, love each other deeply, because love covers over a multitude of sins.*"

Why would God give him the same words, when he'd gotten it wrong before? If he wasn't supposed to love her, but to share his faith, then . . . He searched other passages, but he was sure he had the one he needed. Had something changed? Something besides him? Was a door open now that had been shut before? Was his heart ready in a way it hadn't been? Or was Noelle's?

He turned to the Psalms, found the verse that had come to his mind. *"See, I have refined you, though not as silver, tested you in the furnace of affliction."* Rick looked up at the seat back in front of him. The furnace of affliction. He closed his eyes, and the new verse that came to mind brought an ache so poignant, he paused before turning to the page. He knew it without looking, but he read it anyway. First Corinthians 13: *"Love does not delight in evil but rejoices with the truth. It always protects, always trusts, always hopes, always perseveres. Love never fails."*

Rick leaned his head back and closed his eyes. *I'll take the chance, Lord. I just pray I've heard you right.*

CHAPTER

# 33

William pressed the intercom. "Yes, Margaret?"

"Rick Spencer to see you. No appointment."

*Rick.* William strode quickly and pulled open the door. From the look of him, young Spencer had grown up some this last year. It was in his carriage and in his eyes. Not quite as cocky, but definitely as determined. "Come in." He offered him a chair.

Rick followed him inside but didn't sit. "I won't stay long, Mr. St. Claire."

"William."

Rick nodded. "I wasn't sure I'd catch you here between Christmas and New Year's."

"I have work to do these days the same as any others."

Margaret slipped in with two cups of coffee on a small enamel tray. She set them on the desk and went out.

"My secretary shows up to play Cratchit to my Scrooge." That won a smile from Rick, but that wasn't why he was there. "What can I do for you?"

"I've come to take Noelle home."

William raised his brows. "Has she agreed?"

"I haven't seen her yet. I came here first in case your mind had changed."

"I see." William was amused. "You're removing obstacles."

Rick ducked his head sideways.

No, he wouldn't be so bold as to say it. But that was it, nonetheless. Don't get in my way, William St. Claire. But he had no intention of doing so. William sat on the edge of his spacious desk. "Your brother was here."

"I know."

"Did you send him?"

"No."

William hadn't really thought so. Morgan's visit had been a surprise, and even more Noelle's reaction. He'd thought Morgan might hang around. But he had only come once. And she'd been more pensive and mysterious since, though also less irascible. Still, it wasn't a promising picture for Rick Spencer. "Noelle is . . . slow to heal. I don't know how she'll respond to you."

"I have to try."

Hearing the depth in his voice, William nodded, thankful and . . . hopeful. He stood up and gripped his prospective son's hand. "I hope you succeed." He walked him to the door. "Oh, by the way, I'll be working late tonight. Tell Noelle I won't be home for dinner, will you?"

Rick smiled, then left with slightly more spring to his step.

William looked down at Margaret at her desk. "Do you pray, Margaret?"

"Why?"

"That man was Noelle's fiancé."

————

Noelle crossed the entry and opened the door. She froze as her eyes met the ones she had tried so hard to forget. And Morgan was wrong. Rick didn't look bad at all. Thinner, but then, so was she. Food had become so incidental. But he had strength, the strength she remembered; the line of his jaw, the hollow beneath his cheekbones more pronounced than before. His Rocky Mountain face. No beard.

He said, "Can I come in?"

Her heart leapt at the sound of his voice. How could he do that? She moved aside, and he stepped in. Suddenly her home seemed like the set of a movie, an illusion. Rick didn't belong there.

"Do you mind if I take off my coat?"

She released her breath and closed the door. "I'm sorry. Yes. I'll hang it for you."

He gazed around him. "This is nice."

She nodded. He would appreciate the workmanship, the quality of the house's design and construction. It was four generations old, and the carpentry was excellent. She tried to think of a response. Why was it so much harder than with Morgan? Then, the words had been released; now each one seemed torn from her lips. "Would you like something to eat or drink?"

"No thanks." He turned. "Can we talk, Noelle?"

Direct. To the point. She remembered that look. Her lungs constricted. "We can sit in there." She led him into the scarlet-walled living room and sat stiffly on an ecru wing chair. Instead of taking the matching chair or the striped divan across the room, Rick perched on the large square table directly before her, a position all too familiar. She sent her gaze around the room, on anything but him.

His was fixed on her. "I hear you had dinner with Morgan."

She hadn't expected that opening. She shrugged one shoulder. "Morgan and I both eat."

He nodded slowly. "But why have dinner with Morgan, when you wouldn't even take my call?"

Was it jealousy that had brought him? Yet she sensed no anger. She waved her hand. "He came here, and . . . I was glad to see him. That's all."

He leaned forward. "Are you glad to see me?" There was an edge to his voice, a shadow of pain, but also hope. And it was the hope that scared her most.

"I don't know." She didn't want to hurt him. Why would he risk it again? If it had been as bad as Morgan said, threatened even his faith in God . . . She knew now how destructive she could be.

He reached out and wrapped her hands in his. "I love you."

"I know that, Rick." It was so evident it hurt.

"I told you that wouldn't change, no matter what you think you're responsible for."

What she knew she was responsible for. "Morgan told you?"

He nodded. "You were right to fear Michael. He was violent and unstable."

"But not what I thought."

"That wasn't your fault either."

She started to shake. "I've put together the pieces. All those fragments I didn't understand." But understood now too well. "I had buried it so deeply, what happened when I was little. But it affects me; my need for safety and control, the panic attacks and delusions. It made me see Michael as a monster." Unspoken was that she had seen Rick that way as well, if only for those moments on the shale. Didn't he understand? Her voice broke. "I'm not sure it'll ever be gone."

"I believe Jesus will restore you." He held her face and made her look. "In this world there's trouble, but Christ has overcome it."

Father Mike's words.

"We just have to trust. Sometimes you get thrown so many times there's no part of you that doesn't hurt. But you have to get up and try again." He raised her to her feet. "I want to take you back with me, help you find faith, help you heal."

Was that all he wanted? She couldn't expect more after hurting him the way she had. But she could give him something now. "You don't have to help me find faith."

A shadow passed over his face. "Oh, Noelle. It's the most important part."

"I know." She smiled.

He stared at her. "You do?"

"I should have listened before. Surrendering to Jesus gave me the only hope I have." His face was such a mixture of surprise and joy, tears sprang to her eyes. "How else could I face the rest of my life without you?"

He caught her hand and pressed it to his heart. "You're not wearing my ring anymore. But I gave it to you with a promise. I don't break my promises."

"I don't know that I can—"

"If we never share physical love between us, I still want you for my wife." He drew her close. "I love you."

She sank into his arms, felt them close around her. *Oh, Lord . . .* Was it possible? Heart racing, she looked up, caught his face with her hands, and stared into the brown depths of his eyes. She pulled his face down and kissed him.

He kissed her deeper and whispered, "Marry me."

Where was the fear, the fury? *Oh, Lord my God.* She had felt the peace of her surrender, known her soul was safe, but she hadn't guessed until now there could be healing. Rick placed her face between his hands and turned it up, waiting for her answer.

She smiled, a little shaky, then said, "Okay."

His breath expelled sharply, and he pressed his jaw to her forehead.

"We'll have to fly back to Iowa for the truck, but I can have Pastor Tom waiting . . ."

"Or . . ." she said, "We could see Father Mike, right here in New York."

Tears filled Rick's eyes, and he crushed her to his chest. They held each other so long, exulting. She could feel his emotion but guessed he couldn't find words. He didn't need them.

At last she loosened her arms. "Daddy will be home soon."

"No, he won't."

She looked up.

Rick laughed. "He's making sure I have plenty of time."

"You saw him?"

Rick nodded. "I'm doing it right, Noelle. Love the Lord your God with all your heart, mind, and strength. Honor your parents . . ." He smiled. "And love one another as Christ has loved you. Christ gave His life, Noelle." He held her again, and her heart swelled. That was the love he had for her. She could hardly take it in.

———

Though he had anticipated it, the phone call still sent a jolt to his system. William gripped the receiver. "Yes, Rick?" It was too soon. Did he want to hear that Rick had failed to bring Noelle back from the brink? He could only imagine the depths her grief would take this time.

"William, could you meet us at the cathedral?"

He sat silent a long moment. "Are you saying what I think?"

"Someone's got to walk her down the aisle. And if Ms. Cratchit's there, we could use another witness."

"We'll be there." He hung up, giddy as a schoolboy in true Scrooge fashion. Had he missed something all these years? He whisked his coat from the rack and stopped at Margaret's desk. "Margaret, grab your coat. We're going to a wedding."

———

Rick stood with Father Mike at the altar in a side chapel of the massive cathedral as William walked Noelle in, radiant in the soft white dress he had bought her last Christmas. Her eyes glittered as William placed her hand in Rick's, and he fought tears of his own.

He could see her love, and now she shared his faith. He would help it grow. They'd grow together, linked by more than their hearts. Yes,

God had chosen Noelle for him, but not the way Rick had tried to make it. God had a bigger plan, a better plan. He turned her to the altar.

There were no guests, no music, no flowers; only the two of them and Noelle's father, his secretary, and the priest. In the suit he'd packed for midnight Mass with his family, Rick said his vows. His heart swelled with Noelle's response. They exchanged wedding bands purchased on the way to the church. Rick slid the gold band next to the diamond on her finger and listened to the priest pronounce them man and wife. Then he kissed her, catching her up into his arms.

He let her down when William approached and put a key into his hand. "What's this?"

"The key to the cottage on the shore for your wedding night. And if I make it yours, maybe you'll come visit now and then."

Rick looked from the key to Noelle, felt her smile deep inside him.

William stepped back. "Noelle knows the way."

"Thank you, William."

"It's Dad." William smiled.

They took a taxi to the shore. Rick unlocked the cottage door, lifted Noelle, and carried her in. The place was well appointed. He stood with her balanced in his arms, remembering the first time he'd held her that way, then gazed around. "Not exactly your backwoods cabin, is it?"

She tipped her head. "Do you mind?"

He set her on her feet and took her hands in his. "No, I don't mind, Noelle." It was a generous gift, but he supposed that came with the territory. There'd been no talk of prenuptial agreements this time. Hand in hand they walked through the cottage, then stopped at the floor-to-ceiling windows to watch the breakers on the shore. "If it weren't December, I'd say let's have a swim."

"We could sit on the porch and watch the moon rise." Her voice was soft with no tremor.

"Yes, we could." He wrapped her silver fox fur around her, and she nestled against him on the wooden bench. His wife. The breakers surged and ebbed, and she was warm and real beside him. *Lord!*

"Morgan said you had a beard."

"I did."

She ran her finger over his jaw. "Why did you take it off?"

"I didn't know how you'd like it." He'd needed every detail in his favor.

Her finger traced his lips with a light, electric touch. "I've never kissed a man with a beard."

Smiling, he controlled the surge. "I'll grow it again, and you can have at it." If that was all it took for her to want to kiss him, the Lord was good indeed.

She threaded her fingers through his. "He also said you lost your faith."

"It was pretty black until I stopped fighting." Had his stubborn resentment kept them apart longer than God intended? That was a lesson learned. Trust—no matter the circumstances, the bleak appearances. He stroked her fingers.

"Father Mike said nothing can happen to a child of God that isn't in His perfect will."

Rick nodded. "It's all for a reason." Though he might never conceive why Noelle had suffered what she did. To think his intellect could grasp God's wisdom was pride at its worst.

"Rick . . ."

He turned.

She wrapped her arms around his neck and kissed him. "It's really cold out here."

His heart hammered his chest. "You want to go inside?"

She nodded. "I liked the way we did the front door." Her lips traveled to his earlobe, sending a message he could hardly ignore.

"Noelle . . ."

Her lips came back to his. "You could build a fire in the fireplace."

Breathing grew difficult. "Do you know what you're doing?"

The length of her kiss was answer enough. He lifted her into his arms and carried her inside.

———

Noelle fretted as Rick banged on the door. How would they receive her? They must blame her for the pain she'd caused Rick, caused them all. Would she be excluded, judged? A knot tightened in her stomach.

Rick hollered through the wind, "Hope they're not gone somewhere for New Year's Eve." He pulled her into the shelter of his arm, but in a moment the door opened. Hank's surprised mouth spread into a broad smile as he looked from her to his son.

"Let us in, Dad; it's cold out here."

The rest of the family swarmed as Hank admitted them. Though Morgan stood back, she caught his wry smile. What would he say or think? He must know he'd been part of it.

"Mom, Dad, everybody . . . my wife, Noelle St. Claire Spencer."

"Your wife!" Tara shrieked. "And we *missed* the wedding?"

Rick pinched her nose, then jutted his chin at Morgan. "I wasn't sure you'd still be here."

Morgan reached through and took Noelle's hand. "And miss kissing the bride?" He pulled her close and kissed her squarely on the mouth.

"And that's the last time you'll do that." Rick tugged her back, but his eyes met Morgan's without rancor.

She looked at the two of them, one daring to love her, the other to not. They had been part of her healing from the start, each in his own way. Her heart welled up, then overflowed as she was mobbed with hugs and kisses from the rest. Even Celia's eyes held a warmth she had not seen before.

"Welcome back, Noelle."

----

Two days later, they drove home. The sky hung pregnant with snow over the frozen summits and rocky crags of the canyon. Once again, Noelle went to the mountains, not seeking obscurity this time, but promise. She looked up at the towering crags, stretching their jagged edges to the sky, the pink granite walls beneath the white snow.

Overhead a hawk soared, wings outstretched, floating on the air. Its shadow passed over the ground below. She watched it, circling, circling . . . It meant nothing more than it was. Her gaze left it and rested on the summits. " 'I will lift up mine eyes to the hills, from whence cometh my help.' "

Smiling, Rick squeezed her hand. "Yep."

# ACKNOWLEDGMENTS

Special thanks to Terri Urban, who invited me to share a room at the Colorado Christian Writer's conference and read the very first copy of this story. Thanks to all those who read and offered critique, who listened to thousands of ideas from small tweaks to major twists.

Special thanks to Sarah Long, Dave Horton, and Carol Johnson, and all the others at Bethany House Publishers who partner with me.

My love and thanks to my family for their support, enthusiasm, and patience, and especially to Jim and Jessie for their invaluable input.

My deepest gratitude to my Savior in whose vineyard I labor.